Praise for Tom Toner's Amaranthine Spectrum

'A sprawling space opera likely to remind readers of complex works such as Gene Wolfe's *Book of the New Sun* ... Readers who enjoy a challenge will appreciate both the book's complexities and its beautiful language'

Publishers Weekly

'The final book in Toner's ridiculously ambitious trilogy will force you to redefine what space opera can do ... To put it simply, this is bold, challenging science fiction ... those who have challenged themselves to absorb the breadth of Toner's vision of the future will find themselves satisfied by its striking conclusion'   *Barnes & Noble*

'(An) unceasing display of wonders ... Toner has a knack for maximum suspense and variation. His dialogue is precise, witty and revelatory. His neologisms and general nomenclature rivals that of Jack Vance. And his staging of action scenes, both small and large, is laudable. This third novel honours the accomplishments of and promises of the first two, and serves as a fitting capstone to a unique creation ... tempering the challenging abstruseness of Ada Palmer's novels with the anything-goes action swerves of A.E. Van Vogt and with the poetry of Le Guin, Tom Toner's Amaranthine Spectrum delivers a new flavour of space opera that is bound to dazzle and delight'

Paul Di Filippo, *Locus*

'To call *The Promise of the Child* one of the most accomplished debuts of 2015 so far is to understate its weight – instead, let me moot that it is among the most significant works of science fiction released in recent years'

Tor.com

'One of the most ambitious and epic-scale pieces of worldbuilding I've read. Reading *The Promise of the Child*, you feel you're in the presence of an author at the height of his powers. If this is what Toner is like when he's just getting started, I think we can expect great things from him. Utterly absorbing; a tremendous adventure'

Karl Schroeder, author of *Lockstep and Sun of Suns*

'Bold and intense from start to finish, *The Promise of the Child* is a master-class in innovative, evocative worldbuilding. The entire book buzzes with imagination'

Michael J. Martinez, author of *The Daedalus Incident*

'An amazing debut – a colourful space opera in the post-human tradition of Iain M. Banks, combined with the razor-sharp plotting of Alastair Reynolds. It left me feverish with delight'

Loren Rhoads, author of *The Dangerous Type*

'Humming with energy, this is space opera like you've never seen it before. Absolutely brilliant'

Adam Roberts, author of *Salt* and *Jack Glass*

'A gorgeously written, wildly imaginative book. It's like no space opera I've ever read – compelling and addictive'

Will McIntosh, Hugo-award winning author of *Soft Apocalypse* and *Defenders*

'An amazing debut. Intriguing, disorientating. Like Hannu Rajaniemi's *The Quantum Thief* or Moorcock's *Dancers At The End Of Time*, it's told with the heightened vibrancy of a fable, and the melancholic sense of age and decadence so prevalent in Jack Vance's *Emphyrio*'

Gareth Powell, BSFA Award-winning author of *Ack-Ack Macaque*

'A series to savour and enjoy... The amazing thing about *The Tropic of Eternity* is its sheer ambition. This is a massive, sprawling epic that crosses timelines, galaxies and viewpoints as easily as crossing the road. Toner's lyrical prose is massively engaging... It's an almost Terry Pratchett-esque approach to worldbuilding, where you wonder how some things were even thought of, let alone put to paper. It's engaging, it's pretty bloody brilliant, and it's the kind of worldbuilding that will leave you wanting to dive into the world and explore for yourself... Vast, exotic and mind boggling' The Roaring Bookworm

'Fans of George R. R. Martin's works will appreciate Toner's similar ability to draw distinctive and compelling personalities out of such a vast cast... it will throw you in at the deep end, but richly reward your patience'

Horror Hothouse

'Extraordinary, beautiful and original... there are moments, places and characters here that are described with such gorgeousness, as well as not a little horror, that the book bewitches... I'm in awe of Tom Toner's genius in creating this extraordinarily rich, warm, frightening, loving and rewarding future universe. There is so much to wonder at, puzzle over, be scared of and enjoy... glorious'

ForWinterNights

Also by Tom Toner from Gollancz:

THE TROPIC OF ETERNITY

Volume Three of the Amaranthine Spectrum

TOM TONER

This edition first published in Great Britain in 2019 by Gollancz

First published in Great Britain in 2018 by Gollancz
an imprint of the Orion Publishing Group Ltd
Carmelite House, 50 Victoria Embankment
London EC4Y ODZ

An Hachette UK Company

1 3 5 7 9 10 8 6 4 2

Copyright © Tom Toner 2018

The moral right of Tom Toner to be identified as
the author of this work has been asserted in accordance
with the Copyright, Designs and Patents Act of 1988.

A CIP catalogue record for this book is
available from the British Library.

ISBN 978 1 473 21143 8

Typeset at The Spartan Press Ltd,
Lymington, Hants

Printed and bound in Great Britain by Clays Ltd, Elcograf S.p.A.

MIX
Paper from
responsible sources
FSC® C104740

www.orionbooks.co.uk
www.gollancz.co.uk

For Andy

'We must imagine "Primitive" language as consisting (chiefly at least) of very long words, full of difficult sounds, and sung rather than spoken ... early words must have been to present ones what the plesiosaurus and gigantosaurus are to present-day reptiles.'

Otto Jespersen
Language: Its Nature, Development and Origin

AUTHOR'S NOTE

There are a few odd formats used throughout this odd book.

Whole chapters are occasionally written in italics, and these take place in the past. Anything written in the present tense can be assumed to be a dream, or taking place in a dreamlike state.

PREVIOUSLY

The Tropic of Eternity is the third volume of the Amaranthine Spectrum.

The first, *The Promise of the Child*, began in the year AD 14,647.

Earth, now known as the Old World, has changed beyond recognition and become the forgotten haunt of talking beasts and the twisted, giant-like remnants of humankind known as the Melius. The lifeless, apparently sterile local stars – discovered, much to everyone's surprise, to have been visited and subsequently abandoned seventy-nine million years earlier by an intelligent species of dinosaur known as the Epir – are now in the possession of the Amaranthine, a branch of immortal humans left over from a golden age.

Their empire, known as the Firmament, extends outwards from the Old World for twenty-three solar systems to the edges of the Prism Investiture, a ring of grindingly poor planets and moons occupied by the Prism, a cluster of dwarfish primate descendants of humanity.

In the Vaulted Lands of the Amaranthine Firmament, the Perennial Parliaments are jostling for power, with one sect challenging the Emperor himself for the Firmamental Throne. Their nominated ruler is Aaron the Long-Life, a recently discovered man of incredible age who they hope has the power to heal the Firmament and push back the ever-encroaching Prism.

On the Old World, in a remote estate near the former

Mediterranean Sea, lives Lycaste, a shy giant Melius man and legendary beauty. Pining for a girl who does not love him in return, Lycaste's life changes when a census-taker arrives from the distant ruling Provinces. Lycaste and the man find themselves immediately at odds, and one night, when the dispute becomes physical, Lycaste mistakenly believes that he has committed murder. Terrified, he flees his homeland for the first time in his life, making his way through the war-torn Old World Provinces. The Melius eventually falls into the hands of Sotiris, an Amaranthine mourning the death of his sister, who realises that Lycaste is far more important to the fate of the Firmament than ever could have been anticipated.

Sotiris has been tempted by the mysterious Aaron the Long-Life with the possibility of seeing his sister again. He eventually accepts the devil's bargain, agreeing to rule the Firmament on Aaron's behalf, but not before turning Lycaste over to his old friend, Hugo Maneker, a one-time confidant of Aaron's who he knows will keep him safe.

In the lawless worlds of the Prism Investiture, Ghaldezuel, Lacaille Knight of the Stars, is contracted to steal a miraculous invention: the Shell, a device apparently capable of capturing and preserving one's soul. He delivers it to the Old World and its new owner, Aaron the Long-Life, along with the mummified remains of one of the star-faring dinosaurs. Aaron is revealed to be the spirit of a dead Artificial Intelligence created by the creatures in the distant past. He has lain dormant in projected form for seventy-nine million years, whispering into the ears of the powerful until he could be reunited with a body. Aaron uses the Shell to conjoin his soul with the dinosaur's corpse and takes physical form. He tells Ghaldezuel that together they must travel to Gliese, the capital of the Firmament, before his ancient plan can be fulfilled.

On a lonely, windswept planet, the true Emperor of the Firmament speaks to the voices in his head. Although everyone thinks him half-mad, the voices are in fact real: they are the souls of other long-dead AI substrates, relatives of Aaron the Long-Life, bound to the world where they died just as he once was. Panicked, they tell the Emperor that Aaron has freed himself and embarked upon a course of revenge, pursuing those who wronged him so long ago. The Emperor tells them not to worry, for many thousands of years ago the Firmament also created an artificial soul called Perception. Somewhere Perception's spirit still resides, and it might just be able to help them.

The second volume, *The Weight of the World*, follows on at the turning of the Amaranthine new year, AD 14,648.

Vaulted Proximo, closest Satrapy to the Old World: in a lonely, storm-swept tower, we encounter the Spirit of Perception, forgotten now for four thousand years.

Lycaste, accidentally Bilocated from the Old World by the fleeing Maneker, awakens to find himself inside the same great Vaulted Land. For company, he has with him the Vulgar soldier Huerepo, also Bilocated from the Old World. Proximo is under siege, fought over by millions of risen Melius slaves and the hordes of arriving Prism, and Maneker has no time to spare; he must get to the home of Perception, hoping that the Spirit will join their cause.

On the water moon of AntiZelio-Coriopil, Captain Wilemo Maril and his crew find themselves stranded on a lonely island without hope of rescue. They discover that they are sharing their island with the *Bie*, a species descended from the Epir and watched over by an enigmatic elder, whom Maril and his crew have nicknamed Gramps. But others have heard of their arrival, and a party of Zelioceti slavers land upon the beach in search of the shipwrecked crew.

Eranthis and Jatropha, her immortal guide, have made their way to the greatest port in the Tenth, in the hope of securing passage to the West. Secretly journeying with them are her sister, Pentas, and the baby Arabis – Pentas's child with the Plenipotentiary Callistemon, now half a year dead. The child, heir to the Secondling bloodline and inheritor of the throne of the First, must be hidden at all times from the Jalan that occupy the region. Jatropha buys a Wheelhouse – the *Corbita* – and vows to take them in secrecy past the fringes of the annexed Provinces to meet with Callistemon's old family, and thence to the First. But the stalled invasion has changed the land, leaving entire Provinces unpassable, and Jatropha must plot a new route through the Westerly country of Pan, an enigmatic land owned by a very different people.

Rumours of their precious cargo pursue them along the roads, and it is on the borders of the West that they realise they are being hunted. A vagrant Awger catches up with them and steals the child, making off with her into the dark.

Sotiris, returned from his dreams of his missing sister Iro, travels to the Firstling Court to meet Aaron the Long-Life in his dinosaur body at last, there to discuss the prospect of a deal: Sotiris will serve the spectral being, and his dead sister will be returned to him.

Lycaste, Huerepo and Maneker cross Proximo's sea during a storm and are boarded by hostile Melius. Before they can jump overboard, Maneker is attacked, his powerful eyes cut from his head. Lycaste grabs him, and together they swim for the lonely tower on the sea's far shore: the home of Perception.

Following Sotiris's rushed coronation as Firmamental Emperor, he is put to sleep by Aaron, as promised, so that he can find and bring back his sister. Sotiris awakens in the time of the Epir, the world of Aaron's birth, aware that he is wandering in Aaron's memory. He finds Iro imprisoned, but she is unable to see or hear him, and remains always beyond his reach. It is here that we discover Corphuso, also lost in Aaron's world.

Captain Maril and his crew are taken by the Zelioceti to the neighbouring moon of AntiZelio-Glumatis, a volcanic world ruled by the barbarous Quetterel monks. There they find that their Bult pursuers have also been imprisoned. While Maril and his Vulgar are waiting to be flayed for the crime of trespassing, one of the Bult escapes, opening his companions' cages and slaying every Quetterel in the monastery.

Maneker comes face to face with Perception, promising the Spirit that he will release it on the condition that it hears his terms. Perception, furious with all the Amaranthine for their duplicity, finally submits after taking a shine to Lycaste and Huerepo. Together they leave the tower, only to be attacked by an Oxel ship, the *Epsilon India*. During a heated firefight, Huerepo realises that one of the enemy soldiers is his cousin, and fighting ceases. They are invited aboard, making a deal with the Oxel to set sail for Gliese, capital of the Firmament.

Ghaldezuel, Knight of the Stars, embarks upon the Colossus battleship the *Grand-Tile* accompanying Aaron and the remaining Devout Amaranthine for the long voyage to Gliese. On the way, however, he is tasked with journeying to the moon of Port Maelstrom, there to free the infamous Melius bandit Cunctus – beloved across the Investiture for his daring crimes against the Firmament – in the hope that he and his gang will assist Aaron's cause. Ghaldezuel knows that once Aaron has got what he wants he will leave the Firmament for ever, abandoning it to the chaotic demise that he has brought about, and resolves to betray him.

Upon arrival, Ghaldezuel opens the treasure trove of Maelstrom beneath the prison, gifting Cunctus and his gang the Amaranthine ships and weapons Aaron knows they will need, but asking them sincerely if they will join his own cause instead – that of the Lacaille – to bring about a new order and stability to the galaxy: a New Investiture. Cunctus accepts the bounty gratefully and, together with his witch and Spirit Oracle Nazithra – who winkles from Ghaldezuel the fact that he acts as he does for his true love, a Bult woman – they make their way to the Vulgar capital, Filgurbirund.

Lycaste, Perception, Maneker and the crew of the *Epsilon*

India arrive within the *Grand-Tile*'s enormous wake, where they encounter the Feeders, the motley groupings of Prism ships that follow every Colossus battleship, where Maneker plans to hire as many Prism battalions and mercenaries as he can to aid them in the struggle against Aaron.

On the volcanic world of Glumatis, Maril and his crew have been freed from their cells by Gramps and are on the run from the Bult cannibals. With every Quetterel dead, they head deep into the forest, only to discover with Gramps' help the Threshold, one of many ancient portals into the next galaxy. They climb in and are transported instantly to the Hedron Stars – artificial snowflake-shaped worlds – at the Milky Way's edge.

Their mercenaries hired, Maneker, Perception and Lycaste at last catch up to the *Grand-Tile* as it speeds to Gliese, every soul aboard preparing for the greatest battle Mammalian kind has ever faced.

PROLOGUE

GULPMOUTH

There were stories of the lagoon dating back nine thousand years, from the time of Drolgins' first visitors; tales passed down through the generations, lingering in people's collective memories until, like the folk who told them, they had twisted into something else entirely.

Impio was a vast body of chalky water, possessing near its southern tip a murky blue hole lying visible on the sandy bed. The first travellers to reach the place called the hole Saint Anthony's Mouth, after the soft, glottal sounds that filtered up from its depths. It was thought to be nearly bottomless, a fissure reaching down all the way through the moon's sulphurous crust – home, the oldest of them said, to giant fish with glowing illicium lures – and into whatever realms lay beneath. It was a place of odd currents and indeterminable effects: those who swam over the hole would suddenly sink like a pebble, and anyone venturing down after them never returned.

As the ages passed, the hole acquired a new name, having eaten so many hundreds in its time: the Gulp. The voices that bubbled to its surface were spoken to and parroted, the way someone might talk to a pet, but no longer studied. Soon even they were ignored, and the great, venerable moon of Drolgins moved on.

*

A small, leaky Vulgar fishing boat bobbed on the tide, dredging for sluppocks and crablings with a ripped net, its occupants dozing off in the midday heat and batting lazily at the flies. Their boat, its anchor rope snapped, had drifted over the course of the morning from the rocks of Milkland and into the cloudy, pale waters surrounding the Gulp. By mid-afternoon they were almost directly over the hole, rocking and creaking in the warm wind, the flies dispersing. In place of the insects' drone, the dreams of the Vulgar on board were filled with strange voices and faces. The faces asked the crew questions about their lives, and, in their dreams, they answered.

The boat remained in place, its shadow falling over the small blue mouth until something stirred in the depths, rising in a cloud of sand to investigate the hull. It passed beneath, a blue shadow rocking the little vessel and tinkling its bells, and made its slow, sinuous way towards the harbour.

Muerto Hichie, Muerto,
Omer, muerto . . .

The Vulgar Ogarch Berphio of Gulpmouth sang a little more of the sweet song, a lamentation for dear, young Hichie, as he cracked the top of his giant breakfast egg and dug into it with a spoon.

'Muerto Hichie, oh, how I loved you!' he breathed, dribbling yolk into his beard and grubbing for his napkin. 'Taken away, so soon, too soon. Taken away from meeeee . . .'

The mayor stopped to listen as he ate, scooping busily around inside the egg. *Bells.*

He laid down his spoon and looked sharply out of the window.

'Berf!' It was his brother-in-law, Kippo, calling from down by the estuary.

Berphio swung open the window and leaned out. '*What?*'

'Get down here!'

2

He moved through his keep at a fast walk, knotting his cravat, and sat by the door to tie up his boots. One of the Gurlish soldiers at the gate offered to help and he submitted, leaning back and listening to the growing commotion outside.

'Follow me,' he said to the soldier when he was done. 'And get Jem and Lamlo.'

Outside, the grey drizzle wet his face, carried on a crisp, stench-laden wind that snapped at the ribbons of his cape. Berphio adjusted the chinstrap of his large hat and strode down the steps to the black sand of the estuary's edge.

Kippo came running for him along the sand, his clothes billowing about him. A carriage dragged by four excited hounds stood waiting.

'So?' Berphio asked, wiping drying yolk from his beard.

'Cethegrande. Beached himself this morning.'

They climbed into the carriage, the mayor looking out along the milky water's edge to where the lagoon broadened beyond the harbour. 'Who?'

Kippo sucked his flask, the bark of the hounds adding to the frenzy as they bounced along the sand. 'Dunno. Don't recognise him.'

Berphio leaned out of the window and bellowed at the houndriders. 'Faster!'

They came rattling around the gloomy headland, the hounds barking. Filgurbirund, a stately ball of faded dirty blues and pinks, sat brooding on the horizon.

Berphio scanned the black beach, spotting stragglers following the large crowd that had already gathered. They seethed like flies at a point near the Lunatic's castle, obscuring whatever had come ashore.

'Clear them out of the way,' he instructed, opening the door of the carriage before it had fully stopped and jumping awkwardly out onto the sand. The two soldiers leapt after him and strode ahead, firing their spring pistols into the air.

The crowd dithered, apparently unimpressed, only moving a little when Berphio himself waddled up and shoved his way through, eyes widening at the sight.

'Anyone know this fellow?' Kippo asked, breathing hard as he joined Berphio and staring into the ring of Vulgar.

'It's not ... it's not *him*, is it?' the mayor whispered.

'Howlos has a couple of broken incisors,' Kippo said.

'Howlos was never chained,' replied one of the soldiers, keeping his distance.

Berphio thought for a bit, placing a hand on his hat to stop it blowing away. 'Get on the wire, call up one of Andolp's men...' He exhaled, running his eyes over the apparition that had beached itself on his land. 'And send for a Champion, before the good sir wakes himself up.'

Drolgins, Filgurbirund's largest moon, was the size of the Old World, home to eleven billion Vulgar and counting. It clung to its vast parent planet like a meaty, half-grown child, dragging seasonal storms across its mother with each languid rotation and blotting out the daylight over some countries for a week at a time. It was a wild world, possessed of a Firmament-renowned sea of horrors: the Lagoon of Impio.

The six-wheeled vehicle motored along the hill road, smoke rolling from its chimney. Its lights came on as it grumbled down onto the sand, illuminating the black beach with a harsh yellow glare that lit the faces of the watching Vulgar.

Champion Tomothus climbed out as the Vulgar ran across the shore to him, locking the roller and pocketing the key before leaping down. He stumbled on the sand, unable to decide whether he was still drunk, aware of a fermented stink seeping from his breath and clothes. He hitched up his loose pants, singling out the mayor in his ribbons and hat, and pushed his way through the crowd to him.

4

'Where is it?' Tomothus asked without preamble, having not sighted anything on this stretch of the beach during his winding trip through the hills. Across the bay, where the water churned milky against the black rocks, a ramshackle castle brooded. Dark, scrawny trees poked from the waters, their branches thick with squeaking birds.

The mayor bowed. 'This way, Champion.'

They trudged across the sands, the chill wind whipping sharp little grains into his eyes. Most Drolgins beaches were populated with gaunt shanty dwellers that scraped a living digging worms and salvage out of the shallows, but here the sands were empty. Rounding the rocks, Tomothus saw them all, milling and drinking and gawking. A fleet of unsound wooden boats bobbed in the grey-blue waves, clustering around the new arrival.

He studied the markings on the half-submerged tail, waiting for the crowd to part.

Over the heads of the Vulgar, he could see, running along the crest of the thing's mottled back, a fringe of wet auburn hair – so wiry that it was often used for rope – and, visible between the crowd, a vestigial clawed hand. Tomothus watched a clump of hair stir in the wind, accompanied by a reflexive ripple of muscle beneath the skin.

He walked closer. This fellow wasn't particularly large so he couldn't be very old, and yet his skin was pocked and criss-crossed with scars, which Tomothus had taken for spots a few moments before. Thick orange links of sea-denuded chain dangled from the mammal's flanks, crusted with barnacles where they fastened into his skin. Colonies of glistening, finger-sized sluppocks dangled from the puncture holes, and some of the braver gawkers were already scraping them off with poles improvised from the morning's driftwood.

'Stop them doing that, would you, Berphio?'

The mayor sent his men, who grabbed the scavengers' sticks.

He stepped closer. The Cethegrandes of Drolgins, as these beasts were known, were a relatively disparate, long-lived bunch. A great interest was taken in who sired whom, and, as a Champion of Milkland, Tomothus had seen the rolls. He studied the shape and colours of the thing, still unable to see its head, tucked away somewhere as it slept.

'It might be Scallywag,' he said.

The mayor planted his hands on his hips, his hat, now unsupported, in serious danger of blowing away. 'A pup, is it?'

Scaleag: sired of Jumjagh and Nerephanie, grandson of the Formidable Marjumo.

Tomothus shrugged. The Cethegrande wasn't old: barely past his first century. His bastardised name was the result of a rather spirited companionship he once maintained with an Investiture-renowned criminal.

Tomothus looked at Berphio. 'Count Andolp holds the land deeds here, does he not?'

The mayor looked flummoxed for a moment. 'He does, but—'

'You'll have to send him word. This doesn't bode well.'

As the Champion spoke, a pack of tawny hounds approached along the beach, dragging a massive wooden trough on wheels.

Tomothus pointed at it. 'What's this about?'

Three great piles were being offloaded from the trough, their smell already reaching the onlookers.

'Sugar, lard and salt,' Berphio said, gesturing at each in turn. 'A breakfast for the good sir when he wakes.'

'You cannot befriend the Cethegrandes,' Tomothus said. 'If he wants to smash your port to smithereens, he shall.' They regarded each other, then the new arrival. 'Let me put the boot in him for you.'

The mayor looked uneasy.

Tomothus rubbed his gauntlets together and made for the beast's flank, the Vulgar moving back.

'Wakey-wakey!' Tomothus shouted, aiming a kick at a

soft-looking part. His boot bounced as if connecting with a wall of rubber. He kicked harder, gratified after a few moments to see he'd left a mark. The crowd made an *ooh* sound.

'Up you get now, Scallywag!'

The entire beach fell silent, waiting. Children that had been running and screaming and fighting stopped, punches half-thrown, eyes expectant.

String music from along the beach drifted merrily through the grey air. The wall of scarred blubber grumbled, rippling.

'Up now!' Tomothus repeated. 'Have your breakfast!'

Muscles stirred beneath the skin, tensing, contracting.

'Come on! Have your treats and be off now!'

The crowd on the far side of the creature stepped back as one, some scampering away along the beach. Tomothus hesitated, his boot raised.

The beast rose a little on its hands, digging gouges into the black sand, and untucked its meaty head. It yawned, spraying spittle into the wind and revealing man-like incisors, then turned its eyes on him.

Tomothus gazed back, holding his ground. He could see once again why the Amaranthine called them the cousins of wolves.

Scallywag's shrunken ears were those of a hound, tufted with the same gingery hair at their tips and beaded with seawater. Its snout, which it licked as it woke up, was slitted with coiled, expressive nostrils. It swallowed as it regarded him and ran its huge grey tongue across its nostrils again.

'Breakfast,' he said loudly, gesturing at the piles.

The Cethegrande swung its saggy head and snorted, eyeing the treats, then looked back at him, its mouth hanging open. A spark of uncertainty hovered in its gaze. Tomothus smiled a little.

'Berphio,' he called to the distant mayor. 'Show him your food's as good as your word.'

'What?' the mayor called. A light rain had begun to sweep in off the sea, dampening his voice.

'Show him you're not trying to poison him.'

The mayor made his nervous way to the mounds, adjusting his hat and casting quick glances at the Cethegrande. Its greedy blue eyes followed him, the sheet of increasingly heavy drizzle dampening the beast's colour so that it was as if a pale apparition watched him through the rain.

He arrived at the mountain of salt and buried his finger in it.

'See?' he called, tasting it and grimacing. 'Salt.'

Scallywag remained motionless, though its eyes flicked to Tomothus, then back again.

Berphio went and dug his hand into the next offering, the sugar. He smiled as he licked his fingers. 'Best sweet sugar, from Filgurbirund. Very expensive, this.'

This time, the Cethegrande's eyes didn't leave his.

The mayor swallowed and went to the last pile, a creamy, peaked lump, shiny in the rain. The stink of putrefaction hung around it. Berphio slid a finger into the cold jelly and examined what came out. 'Fat,' he called out through the drizzle. 'Best fat.'

He licked his finger and swallowed with difficulty.

'There now,' Champion Tomothus said, spreading his arms and looking at Scallywag. 'What do you think of that?'

The crowd on the beach held its collective breath while Scallywag considered the offer. The Cethegrandes were technically beholden to the Vulgar kings, vassals bound by ancient agreement, and every now and then they'd even been commanded in war. That said, boats on their long crossings of the lagoon were never entirely safe from being swallowed, and Tomothus sensed in this one an especially anarchistic streak, something that would make his job here difficult.

8

Scallywag's muscles rippled, and with a heave of effort the Cethegrande slithered forwards on its belly, pushing towards the offerings. Berphio scampered back, yanking his hat down. Tomothus held his ground as best he could, allowing the beast to pass him by in a blast of pungent air. The crowd began to whistle and he took a trembling bow.

Five minutes later, it had laid waste to the piles, rolling to sun its belly as the weather cleared and smacking its lips. The mayor sidled up to Tomothus, clutching his hat.

'Now he's on his back, shouldn't we—?'

Berphio gestured over at the Cethegrande's great swollen belly. A tendon of pinkish flesh ran between its vestigial legs, crested with another ridge of ginger hair. 'They buy it by the bucket in Napp now – for breeding, for the war.'

Tomothus looked. Scallywag's pendulous white testicles must have weighed half a ton each.

'How much?'

Berphio pursed his lips. 'Eight, nine hundred a barrel.'

Tomothus glanced back. The Cethegrande's penis was invisible, likely shrunk up inside the scrotum in this cold wind, though it wasn't impossible that some rival had bitten it off during a fight. Nevertheless, you didn't get chances like these every day.

He turned to Berphio. 'Better get to work, then, while he's sleepy.'

Tomothus returned from his roller, having completed the semi-successful task of radioing the fortress at Blackburrow. Millennia of accumulated orbital debris around Filgurbirund and its moon had made communications perpetually choppy, and it had been impossible to determine whether the squeaky person he'd spoken to would pass on the message, but he'd done his best.

The bravest of the beachcombers were almost done.

They crouched, sleeves rolled up, crowded around the Cethegrande's swollen member. Tomothus took a moment to savour the absurdity of the situation while his hangover abated. Finally Scallywag bucked, squirming, and gave them what they wanted, hurling off all but the bucket man, who had clung onto the creature's sparse mane. The bucket itself nearly toppled over when he made his way down, and Tomothus breathed a sigh of relief when the precious load was laid before him on the sand.

'Right then,' he said, knotting his scarves against the wind and approaching Scallywag from the side, so that its lethargic blue eye could roll over and see him. The beachcombers beat a hasty retreat to the edge of the waves.

'You've had a nice time, Scallywag; you've had your breakfast, filled our bucket. The lord of these lands wants you gone now.'

Silence but for the patter of rain, the shuddering moan of the wind in his eardrums.

Berphio would later say that he saw it coming, but in truth the Cethegrande gave no sign. Scallywag rolled onto his side and turned back to the rainy sea, great belly jiggling as he ploughed through the sand. Even Tomothus looked surprised.

But then Scallywag paused, and everyone on the beach knew that he'd changed his mind.

Everyone but Tomothus. The fool stood his ground. Berphio had smelled the drink on him; saw how it had given him courage. By the time the Champion realised, Scallywag had already begun to lunge.

With a snap, he had Tomothus's leg between his teeth, hauling him into the air. There were gasps and even whistles from the crowd on the beach, the Champion's pleading screams lost to their roar. Once he had Tomothus in his jaws, however, Scallywag didn't appear to know what to do with him. Berphio stared, transfixed, as Scallywag let him dangle there, wriggling like a worm from a cat's mouth. The Cethegrande surveyed the crowd for a moment, Tomothus's screams growing hoarse, and turned again for the water, stubby feet pushing off against the sand until it had launched itself with a massive surge of spray back into the sea.

Tomothus came to some miles out in the lagoon, the hot sun beating down. He floated blearily, a blot of red surrounding him in the still water, the pain rising as if seeping out of the sea. The monster must have found him unpalatable, he thought, paddling to turn himself. He looked down into the water, breathing hard.

He saw the hole was almost beneath him. It was like a blue-black, diffracted eye, watching him from the seabed.

He gargled a yelp and began to paddle in the water, knowing what happened to any who swam over it; but something was dragging him there. In a minute he was directly over the Gulp.

What felt like invisible fingers grasped the remains of his legs, worming their way into the shredded muscle, and pulled, dragging him quickly beneath the calm waters.

THAT BELOW

She trails her fingers along white stucco walls, waiting.

'Who was she, Aaron?'

He looks at her with those colourless eyes, the kindest eyes she's ever seen.

'Who was who, Iro?'

'The woman you loved more than me.'

They met again in the evening. The sculpted trees looked pink in the light.

Her hands trembled and she tucked them into her armpits, not wanting the man to see how she'd missed him. He sat across from her in the grass, his eyes filled with gentle apprehension. She hated that look, loving it more every time they met.

'Whom do you love more?' she asked, glancing away. 'Tell me.'

When he answered, it was as if an age had passed. 'She's dead, Iro. Love can be shared.'

'No it can't.' She shook her head, rocking in the grass. A lover would try to reach out and touch her now, but he never did.

'You blame me for meeting her first?'

She looked at him. His eyes, though they possessed no colour of their own, could reflect it sometimes, and this evening they were rose-gold, like the light. 'When did you meet?'

'Before you were born.'

'What did she die of?'

He hesitated. 'Bad things, done to her in my absence.'

She took this in. 'And did you think you could ever love again?'

'No,' he replied quickly. Though the answer was clearly intended as a compliment, it hurt Iro all the same.

'Why won't you tell me her name?'

He sighed, the pink glow in his eyes apparently searching for an answer. 'It's not that simple. You wouldn't understand.'

A silence fell, intensified by the woodland birds, in which she could contemplate his words. Those were the worst parts, those silences, in which everything said had a chance to settle, unchallenged, and become real. At that moment, she didn't want to look at him any more, but worried that if she turned away he'd disappear, as he had so many times before.

Iro blinked away tears, her eyes closing, squeezing the drops between her lashes. In the warm, hot darkness she forgot for a moment why she cried, and felt an absurd freedom.

She opened her eyes. The heat of tears hung on their lashes.

'Come into the water, Iro,' said his voice from behind her.

She turned. On the lake's surface, like an inverted reflection, stood her old friend, her old love. 'Aaron.'

He beckoned. 'Come into the water with me.'

She stood, aware that she was coolly naked in the evening air, her skin marked with the pink impressions of grass, and went down to the lake's silted edge where the birds strutted, oblivious. On the far bank, a man watched her, and she felt vague irritation.

Aaron extended a hand, waiting. She grinned and stepped in, swallowed by dark water. Leaves floated still on the surface, and yet Aaron seemed even lighter, his bare, beautiful feet planted just over the meniscus, like a dayfly's.

'Closer,' he said, smiling, and yet somehow sad. She paused as she saw his face, then continued on into cold blackness.

'Deeper.'

TWENTY-ONE FIFTY-NINE

He cupped the piece of light, carved shell in his hands, rubbing a thumb across its engraved message. The object was an invitation, delivered in an aureate golden box the previous morning. Sweat popped out across his skin as he contemplated the trip he'd been planning to take that day: an image of the liveried courier waiting on his step and turning away, the message returning unopened.

Trang Hui Neng stared vacantly from the window of his carriage, his fingers trembling in his lap, the scrimshaw placed carefully on the seat beside him. The city was a place of coils – affluence nestled inside poverty, ugliness ringed again by wealth – each loop invisibly cordoned by some higher, spiral geometry. Hui Neng passed, deep in thought, through boroughs of darkness and light, registering nothing.

He was unable to resist, as was his nature, contemplating how it would feel when it was all over; that it would almost suit him better were it not to happen at all. He'd turned down plenty in his life, reasoning after forty-four years of disappointment that ups seldom merited their downs. But this invitation wasn't like the others. There was no end to this, if all was to be believed.

The carriage rolled into a side street and slowed to a crawl. Hui Neng's heart raced, urging the vehicle backwards. He might make a fool of himself – or worse, be made a fool of; what if they'd summoned him here simply to refuse him? He smoothed a hand over the lapels of his jet-grey suit, a compulsive gesture that only served to wrinkle the fabric further, and so he repeated the gesture again, and again, and again.

Black gates of wrought iron swung open. The carriage passed through and into a marbled courtyard that appeared larger than any he'd seen in the city. Pale Corinthian pillars enclosed the space like a forest of petrified classical trees, grey strips of shade looming among their trunks. No sounds of the city drifted into the square. A pigeon or two, unaware of the significance of the place, strutted, bobbing.

Steps extended down and he shuffled out, heart squirming, glancing at the vast open doors to the interior of the palace.

'Welcome to Carlton House,' the footman said, taking his hand and helping him down. 'They're waiting for you.'

Hui Neng nodded and stepped into the winter breeze, the cold sinking into his cropped hair. The doors stood like monoliths, darkly impatient. He attempted a leisurely pace; there would be others, recently arrived as he was, standing before the Panel, but to scamper was beneath him. Nobody invited to this great marble courtyard had ever scampered, he was certain of it.

He ascended the steps and into darkness, making out dim candelabra in the gloom above. The ceilings were painted with cracked frescos of frolicking putti, a yellowed cloudscape advancing into false perspective over their tousled heads. He glanced up, aware that he could hear the burble of a host of people further inside, and experienced the usual panic of tardiness. Why hadn't he scampered? Perhaps everyone scampered, after all.

Silence fell, the proceedings quite obviously begun, and he found himself quickening his step up the winding stair, aware of how *foolish history would regard him were he to slip and fall mere moments from Immortality.*

Doors twice his height confronted him at the top of the stairs, their tarnished gold knobs waiting. He grasped them and pushed into the room.

Twenty pairs of eyes flicked up at the sound, examining him. Hui Neng bowed, pathetically glad to see that some of the eyes were paired with smiles, and moved to stand among the watching figures at the side of the room.

The only person that hadn't turned to regard him was in the process of receiving the Communion. She knelt, tongue extended, before a stooped senior member of the Panel, a man whose twisted, deformed face signified that he was among the first to have partaken of the Imperfect Communion. Hui Neng had arrived just in time to see the wafer pass from the old man's slender white hand and into her mouth.

The woman became very still, waiting for the momentous little thing to dissolve, her eyes closed. When her mouth began to move, inaudibly answering a question from the panel, Hui Neng knew the wafer was fully gone.

He looked at her, foolishly expecting to detect a difference in her, however subtle. Already, mere seconds after delivery, the mitochondria in every one of her cells had wound down into a contented sort of hibernation, their tickings slowed almost to nothing, their walls hardened, gates slammed and welded shut. Energy would come instead from her own motions, her slowed respiration still generating heat in smaller, more economic quantities. He tried to see what he could of her lightly flushed face, still turned away, conscious that age would never trouble her again. No known disease could ravage her, instead passing flummoxed through her systems without finding purchase and issuing back into the wide world. Water, should she choose to drink, would trickle uselessly through her innards and drizzle out again; solid food, they were told, would suddenly hold no appeal, churning in nothing but its mashed original form, unaffected by the barren tubes inside which it had spent the night.

15

Her hair and nails would cease to grow, any last ova within her would pause their gradual drip and ossify, and the flora of her gut would perish and disappear, scoured away as if by a hundred thousand years of blustery weather.

Now she glanced around the room, nodding at the soft congratulations of her peers, and Hui Neng saw that it was someone moderately famous, someone whose face he knew well without recalling her name.

His eyes strayed to the pieces of wafer arranged upon the linen-covered table, a burnished little nameplate set beneath each one. Whatever those small wafers contained was a mighty force indeed, he reflected from the safety of the shadows; a potent, dangerous concoction like medical cytotoxins of old, its destructive power now harnessed to sterilise. Only the Panel held the secret of the wafer's ingredients, refined over thirty-five years into its present form. He looked at the wizened figures standing sentinel at the end of the room, with their dour, burn-victim faces. These were the first to pay the price of experimentation, and they would be venerated in the age to come.

It was his turn approximately ten minutes later, after two more had been inducted into the ranks of the newly ageless. Hui Neng stepped forward, feeling all eyes on him, and paced across the black and white tiled floor to where the Venerable Wylde stood, his pale hands extended.

'Do you come with the Panel's blessing?' Wylde asked softly when Hui Neng had knelt before him.

He nodded, eyes flicking briefly to the man's melted face. 'I do.'

The bony hand hovered into his field of view, palm open.

There it was: a square tab of moulded protein, stamped like a miniature waffle with exquisite designs. He stretched his neck forward, scenting something acrid, and let it be placed upon the tip of his tongue.

A second passed, then five. Hui Neng did as the previous people had, keeping his eyes closed, attempting to savour any sensation.

After a moment of panic at the idea that it might have somehow fallen from his mouth, he closed his lips and tasted. There: a lingering flavour fainter than a belch, leaching immediately away.

'Congratulations, Trang,' the Venerable Wylde whispered, patting him weakly on the shoulder. He rose, bewildered at the lack of sensation, shuffling back only when he saw the next person waiting on the tiles behind him, a young man he knew, dark-skinned and wiry – Harald something.

Drinks were served in the wintry gardens, and the newly honoured guests mingled among the skeletal conker trees without much enthusiasm, each person struck dumb and mute with a kind of melancholy that Hui Neng felt just as keenly. That was it. Their dearest wish had been granted. He found himself staring at steps and irregular ground with an intense mistrust; far from feeling more secure now that he had achieved Immortality, he actually felt more vulnerable. Any little external thing could still kill him, and in just as many violent ways as before. A great and terrible depression hung over him, growing darker and more livid as he spoke to people and swallowed his useless mulled wine. He examined the red scum in the bottom of the glass – a base of city water that must have passed at one time or other through a thousand plague victims – and went to find a bench as far from the crowd as possible. He noticed the occasional blank-eyed member walking back into the palace, perhaps with the intention of leaving early, and sat with his glowering thoughts.

'Trang.' It was Wylde, stooped and unwholesome in the white winter light. 'There's someone I'd like you to meet.'

Hui Neng thought he'd seen the man accompanying Wylde at the ceremony, standing among the watchers at the side. He had a soft, pleasant face, like a parish priest's, the fatness in it conveying a genteel innocence that Hui Neng found immediately soothing. The man's eyes were at first one colour, then another, the depths of a lake under moving cloud.

'The Viscount Hereford,' Wylde said, inclining his head. 'This is his home.'

17

PART I

TERMINAL

Out beyond the shoals of the Amaranthine Satrapies, in the deep, cold pockets, something moved. It was visible in most spectra as a cloud of thrown motion, like a vehicle dashing along a dusty road, revealed only by the havoc it wrought. From a distance, the streak of its comet tail was ponderous, widening to a smudge of purple that encompassed thousands of following ships, all lagging now, spreading in a haze as they fought to keep up with the thing as it ploughed through the Void at seventy-eight times the speed of light. The tiny follicle at the head of this contrail was the *Grand-Tile*, the three-mile-wide Colossus flagship of the Lacaille navy. As it flew it listened, wave antennas concentrating on the silence behind it, never once thinking of looking up.

In the rushing silver light hundreds of thousands of miles above, a trajectory of colour whipped silently overhead, outpacing the *Grand-Tile* and curving slowly down to meet it. This second cloud was made up of six hundred and four individual ships, their motions only detectable by the small cone of turbulence they left in their wakes. These ships – unlike the Colossus they chased, which ripped untidily through space like a cruciform bullet – hardly made a mark.

Ships in the Void travelled like someone falling. Most Prism craft attained a terminal velocity of forty or fifty billion miles an hour after a week or so, thrusting radiation and matter into a bulging teardrop around them and crossing the Investiture in what was known as a Silver Month.

Some ships, of course – many millions of hotchpotch things built from wood and plastic and plated with the thinnest, cheapest tin – flew immensely slower, juddering and dancing along like feathers caught in a gale, their interiors often without gravity and possessed of such limited stocks of air that they stopped every few days for resupply. The feral occupants of these ramshackle craft spent their lives hopping around the great celestial island chains of the Firmament and the Investiture, paddling from moon to moon just to catch their breath, asphyxiating, starving, driven half-mad from subsistence and whittled to weaklings by the absence of gravity. Some ships even fuelled the fires of their engines with the very materials they were built from, the crew taking their vessel apart piece by piece and shoving it into the furnaces, until all that was left on arrival was a small, tumbling chamber stuffed with drooling, emaciated creatures ready to set about devouring whatever unfortunate place they happened upon.

It was just these desperate folk that the Amaranthine Hugo Maneker had set his sights on, spending a portion of his own huge wealth on hiring the very best of a wild but enthusiastic bunch, and together – their ships improved and refitted by a mysterious and powerful voice that lingered in everyone's heads – they fell in a glowing, thrumming convoy, the largest seen anywhere in the Firmament in sixty years, past the diminishing speck of the *Grand-Tile* and towards the growing black sphere of the Vaulted Land of Gliese.

Perception trailed wispily from the tailfins of the *Epsilon India* like a veil of spider silk spooled and stretched fine in the wind. The onrushing silver of the Void caressed its strands, bathing and warming them with gentle friction, and yet the Spirit was the furthest it had ever been from relaxed. There, lagging hundreds of thousands of miles below to port, it could see the thunderous signature of the *Grand-Tile* churning colours in its wake. Having silently overshot the battleship that morning, they were now within range for Perception to extend itself through the frequencies and speak to its quarry, if it so chose – but of course that would spoil the game. It imagined the ancient, anxious mind of the Long-Life aboard that ship, sweating metaphorical buckets as he glanced behind, unaware that his enemies circled in the Void.

Perception grinned an invisible grin and stilled itself, willing away the phantom adrenalin. Sounds, amplified by the great cathedral caverns of the galaxy, screamed by. They weren't too different from those a falling person would experience, Perception supposed: the tumultuous muffled battering of wind in your ears, a slapping cacophony that hid within it a deep and deadly silence.

The one difference out here was that this silence contained a faint, eerie chorus: the electromagnetic signatures of the stars, all competing to make their song heard. They warbled and whistled and squealed like a jungle at dawn, an ecosystem of unique, high voices that Perception had by now grown attuned to. As they swirled distantly by, their songs shifted into a lamentation, and once more the Spirit held still, savouring. It could hear the deeper tones of other galaxies, great yawning belches of conglomerated sound, and lying nearer, the turgid, chattering nebulae of unexplored stars. Closer still lay the distinguishable voices: the wailing of Sirius long passed (home of the Pifoon honey world where they'd made repairs); and the gibbering of its neighbour, Vaulted Ectries, and her many satellite worlds. Passing between their Satrapy borders, Perception had heard a hollow, sighing breath, like wind blowing through empty window frames and haunting an abandoned house: the ruined shell of the Vaulted Land of Virginis, destroyed the year before by a skycharge implanted in its sun.

And there ahead, the whining snarl that almost drowned out every other sound: Gliese, growling as if baring her teeth, as if she knew the chaos that was coming.

The *Epsilon* and its hundreds of followers had already risen in a wide arc above their quarry, outpacing it while still concealed in the onrushing dark. The circumvented light shooting past their fins burned glowing emerald against the silver in rippled fans of colour, but wouldn't give them away to something moving more slowly. To the *Grand-Tile* they were invisible, moving too fast to reflect anything but the Overlight, the silver gloss that showed through the mass of stars whenever a craft went superluminal.

But they would not be intercepting the *Grand-Tile* in the Void. Not yet. Perception's weapons weren't ready. The Spirit peered back down into the depths, training its view on the twinkling rush of the Colossus's following comets and debris. They would meet, when they finally *did* meet, in atmosphere, where things could go as planned.

Spread out before them lay the many blotches of the Gliese Satrapy, a handful of estate planets, Tethered and Free moons, all held in thrall to the system's single Vaulted Land. Perception sighted on what it believed to be the moon of Great Solob, a delicate little world currently lying partway inside Gliese's long shadow. It extended a tendril of itself and reached into the cockpit, exciting the comms.

Satrap Alfieri.

'*Aha. Perception, I take it?*'

Nail on the head. We're making our approach.

The voice of Perception drifted through the hangar, growing in volume. Lycaste jumped as it swept past him, having been engaged in the useless process of polishing his new boots and helmet. During times of intense activity, he'd found that taking a cloth and vigorously wiping something made him wonderfully invisible, and people tended to leave him alone. So far, Lycaste had successfully employed the tactic every time Perception called the crew to action.

He felt the Spirit hovering near him.

Please stop trying to look busy, Lycaste, not now. Get some practice in.

Lycaste cleared his throat and nodded, putting aside his helmet and other birthday gifts – a new bandolier containing a rather solid-looking spring pistol and plenty of sparker-tipped bolts, a fine red Amaranthine cape of fur-trimmed silk and a silver wine flask engraved by all the crew – and glancing fondly at them.

You'll make nothing but a pretty target down there, Perception said, evidently studying Lycaste's things, *unless you learn to use that stuff.*

Lycaste snorted, picking up his glossy Amaranthine pistol and checking it over for Perception's benefit. As he did so, he noticed the smudge of fingerprints ruining its patina; Poltor had borrowed it that morning.

'What do you think he wanted with it?' he asked the invisible presence of the Spirit at his side, rubbing away the grubby prints.

Brainless creatures like shiny things.

Lycaste wrinkled his nose, making sure he'd got every last mark.

Perception had swiftly become their captain in all but name, and had spent the few days since their departure from the Bunk Barge reordering almost every system and practice on the *Epsilon India* and its accompanying ships, riding fired shells between the convoy to issue orders and strategies, inspect their crews and soldiers, and examining every minute piece of equipment. Huerepo and Poltor, as Perception's twenty fingers, had been engaged in manufacture for the last three Quarters straight, with Huerepo even devising a shorthand so that he could note down all of Perception's myriad orders as swiftly as possible. The Oxel ran the *Epsilon's* other functions and sequestered parts, and Lycaste supposed the twenty-five thousand other troops and pilots and mechanics on the six hundred following ships were the manual labour.

Lycaste took his stance in front of the charred wooden board set up against the bulkhead, before which a selection of objects – pans, bottles, candlesticks and the dirty partial skeleton of a Filgurbear, to name but a few – had been arranged. He fiddled with his pistol, only realising after some experimentation in their makeshift firing range that he could narrow the weapon's field of fire by turning the jewel set in its stock, a little ruby blob he'd thought purely ornamental. He did this now, thinning the range to the slimness of a blade, and aimed at Filgurbear's skull.

A small square section of bone punched silently out of existence, to a thickness of about an inch. A bored Oxel with a piece of tin sheeting scuttled behind the wooden panel, checking for damage to the bulkhead, before returning to his stool. Lycaste aimed again, twiddling the jewel, and zapped away four of its teeth, wondering for the hundredth time where in the galaxy they might have ended up. Once again, the Oxel climbed off the stool to check, giving him the thumbs-up.

Lycaste turned and glanced at the sleekly red three-man jet sitting bolted into gantries near the hangar's large doors. Perception had shown a passing interest in it, and had dictated a long list of improvements for Huerepo to make to the thing. Sometimes, in the depths of the ship's false night, Lycaste would climb out of bed and come to sit at the jet's controls amid the pungent scent of rubber, running his fingers over the knobs and dials without touching anything, always fearful that someone might spot him and give him a telling-off. Soldered to its dented snout was a bolt rifle, operated by crude wires running inside the cockpit, and accompanied at the rear by a meaty-looking lumen turret pilfered from a Lacaille corsair. Lycaste watched Poltor unscrewing the nose and inspecting the insides, his whole body disappearing as he climbed inside, and found himself – despite the sheer terror flying must surely entail – envying the Oxel that would get to pilot it.

*

Maneker observed Lycaste's movements around the hangar, turning his head carefully lest his fancy trinket fell from its socket. He saw the ship's interior now, shabby and cluttered and almost unbearably cramped – a quality in a vessel that had served him well as a blind man, needing only to stretch out his fingers and trace the sticky passages to and from his chamber – but above all dark. Most of it was lit with half-busted strips of lightwire that ran along the ceilings and floors, fizzling and snapping on and off.

But he could *see*. Anchored inside his eye socket was a little marble of Perception's devising, a simple light-gathering pellet designed to collect the monochrome signal and feed it into his optic nerve. As usual, however, the Spirit had done its job too well. Maneker had screwed it in to see, for the first time, the crew he'd travelled with for so long, recognising only the grotesque but somehow welcome faces of Lycaste and Huerepo as they swam out of the murk towards him.

What he hadn't been prepared for was the extra shadow each person trailed behind them, his skin crawling at the sight of a dozen creeping ghosts.

'Are you happy with it?' Lycaste asked, clumping sweatily past.

Maneker studied the Melius's new shadow.

He should be, the voice said at their side. But this time Maneker didn't just hear it. A writhing, snake-like smudge fell across his lap as the voice had spoken, forcing Maneker to recoil. All around the hangar he could see it, spread like a giant amphibious serpent waiting in a swamp for its prey. Perception's tendrils lay everywhere, snaking and worming their way into the very matter of everything.

Maneker glanced down and flinched, noticing how the dull shadows had made their way across his lap and up his belly.

You see me.

'I do,' he breathed.

Lycaste had stopped beside them, wide-eyed.

I had a choice of spectra; thought I'd combine a few.

Lycaste glanced up, habitually, at the sound of the Spirit's voice. 'But you can't see yourself, can you, Percy?'

I cannot.

Maneker smiled, turning his wicked-looking prosthetic on Lycaste. The thing had been made by Poltor from a couple of cracked lenses (which Maneker remembered belonged to one of the defunct optisockets in the flight deck) and contained a dark blob of something mechanical, like a pupil, deep beneath the glass, which stared perpetually.

'Can you see mine?' Lycaste asked.

Maneker nodded with pleasure, observing the oil slick drift and settle as Lycaste moved a little, like something greasy dribbled into deep water. The Spirit's shadow swam close, almost protectively, around Lycaste, and Maneker saw something he hadn't anticipated: Lycaste's smoky, scummy shadow was reaching out towards Perception's, sucked as if by a gust of wind, and had become intermingled a little in its depths. Maneker sat back, understanding that he was watching the Spirit's own powerful gravity at work before him, drawing other souls towards it.

He looked down and observed his own shadow drifting inexorably closer, coiling, blending.

Huerepo struggled over the riveted doorframe into the hangar, hauling the wheeled cart behind him. It juddered as it mounted the step, bouncing back down and almost rolling away before he could catch it. It was a good thing he had, for it contained almost every dangerous invention Perception had so far come up with on their voyage: an agglomeration of horrors designed for maximum carnage. He glanced around as he dragged the thing in, noting with satisfaction the looks on Maneker's and Lycaste's faces. Here was the fruition of his six days' labour, more important by half than whatever they'd both been up to.

'Is all this what I think it is?' Maneker asked, striding up and focusing that unpleasantly beady new eye of his.

Huerepo doffed his little cloth cap that doubled as a rag and gave the Amaranthine a flamboyant bow. 'Perception's latest crop of inventiveness, Sire, for your consideration.'

'Please,' Maneker said, the excitement in his features clearly visible. 'Show me.'

Huerepo took the edge of the cloth and flapped it aside, exposing the jumbled contents of the little wooden cart.

'Perception has striven for ruthlessness,' Huerepo said, poring through the goods. Under the hangar's lighting strips, the collection looked more than a little home-made, built as it was from anything they had to spare aboard the *Epsilon*.

'Splendid,' Maneker whispered, shouldering his way past Lycaste and gazing into the trolley.

Huerepo climbed in and sorted through the weaponry. He hefted out a rifle with a funnel-shaped barrel that could fire bolts around corners and passed it to the Amaranthine. 'Same principle as those winged bullets we took from the Lacaille ship, Sire. Repelled by hard stuff, attracted to soft.'

My first stab at the problem, Perception said, as if from within the trolley. *Useful, but nothing groundbreaking. Indeed, I lifted the entire concept from your own Decadence technology.*

'Now, let's not be modest, Perception,' Maneker said, eyeing the haul greedily. 'Show me what else you have.'

'Sunbombs,' Huerepo said, holding out a handful of little misshapen lumps of solder, like factory offcuts. 'Throw these into a room and they detonate with a little flicker of sunlight.'

'Sunlight?' Maneker asked, taking one dubiously.

Fusion, on a tiny scale. Will probably burn a hole through the floor and disappear, blinding everyone in the process. To be used sparingly, I think.

Maneker put it back.

'Now then,' Huerepo muttered, searching. 'This should please you.' He opened a chest and handed the Amaranthine a needle-fine filament possessed of a tiny bulb of blown glass at one end. Inside the bulb, a small amount of waxy white paste had stuck to the inner curve.

'What's this?' the Amaranthine asked, handling it carefully.

Only my life's work, Perception said beside them.

'Spider venom,' Huerepo supplied. 'Cultivated over the centuries by Perception in its tower.' Carefully, he took it back and returned it to the chest with the others. Perception had designed a bespoke high-velocity needle rifle to fire the things, capable of piercing the thickest armour. Having tested the venom on the various stowaway vermin aboard the ship, Huerepo could reliably state that anything the size of a Lacaille would probably go down after a second or so and be dead within a minute. Huerepo had the first rifle made, displaying it proudly above his bunk.

'How did you get the poison out?' Lycaste asked, peering carefully into the chest, as if the very act of going near the needles might be dangerous.

'That was a bad business,' he responded, closing the lid of the chest and latching it shut. 'Catching the buggers and milking them. I had the Oxel do it. They stamped on a few, so I had to do a lot of scooping with Smallbone's desert spoon.' He looked thoughtfully at Lycaste, hoping what he said next wouldn't be taken badly. 'There *might* be one or two still ... on the loose. Poltor said he saw one in his bunk, but it must have sloped off to one of the warmer places on the ship.' Lycaste looked a little pale all of a sudden, and Huerepo remembered that the Melius occupied one of the hottest chambers above the battery.

I searched through the ship and synthesised some of my own poisons, too, Perception said. *From rust and mould and whatnot. They're in little canisters inside the nail bombs. Be sure to get out of the way if someone throws one.*

Huerepo nodded vigorously. Perception had thought up

some truly indiscriminate weaponry, capable of maiming enemy and friends alike if it wasn't lobbed far enough.

That said, I have some armour replacements for you. Huerepo – if you'd do the honours.

Huerepo nodded, opening up another crate and lifting out the heavy garment at the top. It was a simple Voidsuit reinforced with steel-plate armour: nothing a billion Prism didn't have stashed away in their ships' cupboards. He adjusted something at the shoulders, fastening twin pauldrons of dazzling coppery chain mail and connecting them via a wire to the suit's backpack generator.

Do you see the chain?

Maneker agreed that he did, fingering the links. Huerepo thought he'd done a damn fine job.

Magnetic fields, strong enough to taste, the Oxel tell me. Should repel any metal ordnance fired your way, or at least soften the blow enough for your plate armour to take the shock. Lumens, of course, they cannot deflect. It paused. *Lycaste – are you listening?*

'Hmmm?' Lycaste looked up, flummoxed.

Lumens. Get out of the way if they're firing bolts of light.

'Ah, yes. Just the metal stuff.'

Good.

Huerepo couldn't help but smile. The Spirit cared very dearly for poor old Lycaste, and he was glad. They'd have lost the Melius a handful of times now at least if it hadn't been for their invisible friend.

'You've shared all this with the allied ships?' Maneker asked. 'And the Satrap Alfieri?'

Perception hesitated. *Was I supposed to?*

Maneker scowled.

The laugh that rebounded through their heads was rich and throaty. *Of course I did.*

'The Jurlumticular have their own arsenal, too, of course,' Huerepo added, swinging down from the trolley and checking nothing had fallen out. I believe they've got an Amaranthine skycharge sitting around on one of their ships—'

'The *Diaphene*, yes,' Maneker said. 'It was stolen while I was still Satrap of Cancri, a hundred years ago. At the time, of course, I was livid.'

'They've a haul of Lacaille fizzbombs,' Huerepo continued, 'good vintage ones with the seals still intact. Should make a big old mess when we drop them.'

'*Good*,' Maneker said, as if to himself. 'If we're to fight them inside the world as Perception wishes, that'll be what we need.' He looked in the direction Perception's last words had come from, no doubt seeing the Spirit properly as the others could not. 'A big old *mess*.'

Huerepo looked doubtfully at him, then at Lycaste. Both he and the Melius had been there when Perception roundly defeated Maneker in the making of their grand strategy, humiliating the Amaranthine enough to send him scuttling off to his chamber. Only the gift of the artificial eye had drawn him sulkily from his room.

Maneker's plan, carefully worked out during his blind nights alone, had consisted of isolating and attacking the *Grand-Tile* while it was still hurrying through the Void; mobbing the Colossus and pummelling it with everything they had before it could reach its destination and release its legions from its single great hangar. Hearing this, Perception had swiftly and loftily interjected, delivering a step-by-step strategy to replace Maneker's own and relegating him awkwardly to the sidelines of the conversation. The Spirit had a better plan, one guaranteed to bring down the *Grand-Tile* almost instantaneously, but it could only be achieved inside Gliese's atmosphere, where there was a greater risk of it releasing its thousands of bombers, jets and troops – let alone awakening all the dormant Decadence weaponry that might be buried, waiting – before it could be destroyed.

Huerepo, for his part, was inclined to trust Perception, but still he was frightened.

A grand mess is a fine idea, Huerepo, Perception continued. *One can reliably ruin any fool's plan with a show of smoke and mirrors, I think.*

'You consider the Long-Life a fool, do you?' Maneker smirked, staring directly at the space above Huerepo's head. 'You think he doesn't have some reinforcement on its way from the Investiture? He would never risk so much, his entire force, his whole ancient plan, without such backup.'

I believe he tried, *of course, but things did not go quite to plan. He's out there on his own now.*

'How can you tell?' Maneker blustered, his rage building again. 'You proclaim all these things with such damn confidence, but really you know nothing! It's all guesswork!'

Estimation, Hugo.

Huerepo could only admire the Spirit's patience. He hoped it was right.

GREAT SOLOB

Great Solob, the smallest of the multifarious moons hiding in Gliese's looming shadow, was a desertified wasteland, a world composed of cracked escarpments of salt and wild groves of scrawny black trees. It was a brittle, dead place, inhabited only by algae and pollen spores and crawling pink shrimp, for it had been mined and panned to extinction by ancient Amaranthine engineering to fuel the industrial successes of Gliese over thousands of years. The moon and its sister, Opolie, were now seldom visited, despite their proximity to the greatest Vaulted Land in the Firmament, and for that reason it was here that Perception had arranged their meeting with the Satrap of Virginis and his forces.

Lycaste alone had been given permission to conduct the ceremonies, and his helmet, slippery with sweat from his fingers, lay heavy in his arms. Perception itself stayed aboard the *Epsilon*, high in orbit, conscious that the gravity of the unhollowed moon would imprison it immediately if it ventured too close. It spoke instead through a radio channel: a thin, crackly voice that belied the power on the other end.

Across the salt flat, Lycaste could see the first ships arriving out of the haze. They churned smog across the sky, wavering in the heat of the horizon; a collection of huge, weapon-shaped craft – to Lycaste's eyes they were like giant rifles, and in fact he later learned that they were indeed nothing but great big guns welded onto engine blocks.

'He lost everything,' Maneker said, squinting beside Lycaste at the arriving ships. 'His fortune, his ships, all of it.'

'When they destroyed his Vaulted Land?' Lycaste asked, recalling what they'd told him about Virginis.

'And all of his assets,' Maneker replied, 'requisitioned from the vaults of Gliese when they proclaimed him a traitor.'

Lycaste thought about that, choosing his words carefully. 'But you managed to hide yours.'

Maneker did something he'd never done before. He reached up and patted Lycaste on the shoulder. 'I forget, sometimes, that we are both from the same Old World.'

Lycaste looked at him, sure that he must have said something wrong. Maneker's hand remained on his shoulder, a small weight, squeezing gently.

'Don't ever mention my money again, Lycaste.'

He kept it hidden, Perception crackled from the helmet when Maneker was gone, having presumably listened silently to their conversation through the comms. *And, if I understand correctly, the Long-Life never truly lost faith in him. He locked Maneker away to think about what he'd done, always expecting him to change his mind.*

Lycaste watched the approaching party. Salt and grit chased them on the wind, forcing him to narrow his eyes.

Sire Fridrik Alfieri has pledged his life, and all the loyal Melius and Prism he still commands, to Maneker. But I hope it won't come to that. I shall use his thousand ships as a final blow, if necessary.

'If your plan doesn't work?' Lycaste asked.

Don't be ridiculous. Perception sounded a little affronted. *Of course it'll work.*

The Satrap strode up to Maneker, thrusting out his hand, but their greeting was brief. Alfieri turned instead and singled out Lycaste, marching over and staring up at him.

'Am I speaking to you, or to the helmet?' he asked in First. Lycaste noted that his greyish skin was quite a different colour from Maneker's coppery tone. He had managed to keep his beard – Lycaste had heard that among the Amaranthine they tended to fall out – and was handsomely featured, with small, delicate hands. Alfieri wore the furs and gems and frilled collars of all self-respecting Immortals, but his looked a little dusty and threadbare, as if he'd left his changes of wardrobe behind and been unable to retrieve them. There were even stones missing, Lycaste noticed, wondering incredulously whether the man might have pawned them.

Lycaste gestured at the helmet, tipping the open end towards him. 'The Spirit would like to talk through this.'

Alfieri gazed at the helmet with trepidation, then leaned forwards. 'Perception?' he asked, tapping the faceplate. 'Are you in there?'

Good morning, Fridrik. Are you well?

'Well?' Alfieri winked at Lycaste. 'I'm much better now you're all here, thank you very much. We'll have that scoundrel the Long-Life strung up before the day is out, I think!'

Let's hope. Though I'd venture that stringing him up wouldn't do much good.

The Satrap looked a little crestfallen. 'Yes, well, the *Grand-Tile* destroyed, then, and all our problems over.'

35

Pretty much.

'And just how do you intend to bring it down?' Alfieri asked, bending closer to speak into the helmet as he eyed Lycaste. 'You must have a plan?'

Oh, I do, Satrap. But you won't be needed for that. Just keep them busy.

He scowled at the helmet, mouth working, clearly frustrated at having to talk to an inanimate object.

My thanks.

The Satrap glared up at Lycaste, as if it were him doing the talking, and turned to stare at his men. 'Well then. That's me put in my place. Shall we ascend?'

Yes, please.

Lycaste cradled the helmet, aware that it was still connected via its corkscrew antenna to the *Epsilon*, high above. He glanced up at the sky, foolishly expecting to see the ship.

As he was staring into the blue, he became aware of a whispering in his ear.

'Pardon me, Percy?' he asked, rummaging for his water bottle as he clasped the helmet in one hand.

But Perception was only whistling, clearly half-busy somewhere else while it waited for their return to the ship. Lycaste smiled.

He took a drink of water and looked out across the salt marsh to a stand of spindly trees, dawdling until Maneker had finished speaking to the Satrap. Something, a shadow, was sitting among the copse of black, arm-like trees. Perhaps one of the Satrap's soldiers.

Lycaste stared at it, eyes watering in the glare of the white flats, trying to work out what he was seeing.

YOU.

The sound reached him from across the flats as if it were screamed. Lycaste started, dropping the helmet with a crunch in the salt.

Lycaste, get your act together, said the helmet from its new resting place. *We're good to go.*

The sweat cooled on his skin. He picked up the helmet.

And fetch Maneker.

Lycaste hugged the helmet to him, staring into the trees.

It was time. Perception disconnected from the frequencies and wormed itself into every system on the *Epsilon*, readying the motors, examining its handiwork.

It curled like steam through the riveted iron ceiling of the flight deck and into the newly cleared storage space inside the ship's nose, inspecting an assemblage of frantically twisted piping and trumpets, pieced slowly together by Poltor and his team of Oxel under Perception's direct supervision. Lycaste's Amaranthine-made pistol, studiously analysed, had been the life study upon which Perception had based this, his greatest work so far. Untested, the device carried a risk of calamity, Perception supposed; but wasn't everything wonderful balanced on a knife-edge? Wasn't each living thing also a powder keg of phosphorus and iron, set to blow with just the right fuse?

The Spirit examined the great mass of equipment critically, running metaphorical hands across its oily surfaces, and with a palpable, surging excitement rose back into the flight deck to look out at the world of Gliese, hanging massively to starboard.

INSIDE

A bloom of dusty light, illuminated in Gliese's reflected glow, circled the Vaulted Land's pole. Ahead lay the tiny blue-black dot of the polar orifice sea.

The speck of the *Grand-Tile* slowed, floating down to join with the sea. The silence around it waited, watching.

Hui Neng looked across at Eoziel, oleaginous ruler of the Lacaille, eyes straying to the stumps of the king's missing fingers. They sat in blue-tinged sunlight at last as the Colossus passed through the sea to the interior. Samuel Downfield, Satrap of the small Vaulted Land of Wise, was also present, his skin smeared with fragrant Rubante honey. Two Lacaille dithered at his side with sponges clutched in their hands, ready to wipe him down.

'We don't know for certain that De Rivarol betrayed us,' Hui Neng said, looking to the honey-coated Downfield for support. 'Cunctus was always unpredictable – he could have kept our friend there, perhaps taken the ship for himself.'

The criminals Aaron had meant to be liberated from the Thrasm had made no contact, their haul of Amaranthine ships and treasure nowhere to be seen. The arranged date of meeting, in orbit over Gliese, had come and gone, and now the forces of Aaron's Devout Amaranthine found themselves somewhat short, should anyone be waiting for them inside.

They looked to the Long-Life, whose black lips trembled silently. His *Caudipteryx* body had begun to fail, visibly: a stroke of some kind had befallen him during the last night of their voyage, and now half of his features hung slack and disconcertingly immobile on one side, his wet, pink gums exposed, yellow teeth poking between the lips. But passing within the cool blue of the orifice sea had cast a visible serenity across his hideous face, the hectic pulse that popped in the cords of his neck slowing, the sweat drying. He only needed this body a little longer – a day, perhaps less – and he would surely be on his way. Hui Neng looked at the half-paralysed monster, remembering all the Amaranthines' hopes and dreams for humanity, and felt a furious sadness.

'It was my knight who betrayed us,' Aaron said slushily, a runnel of blood-flecked saliva leaking from between his teeth. 'Ghaldezuel.'

Hui Neng noticed how King Eoziel retreated into himself a little then, knowing where they would point the blame. 'If you'd sent me,' the king said in a reedy voice, 'this might have been very different.'

The Long-Life's crimson eyes latched on to Eoziel's. 'It was a job for the *brave*.' He slouched and turned with difficulty to Downfield. 'Hurry the pilots. We are not safe until the seas are closed behind us.'

Downfield smirked, licking the honey from his lips. 'You needn't worry, Sire. No one could outpace us—'

'*Hurry* them.'

Hui Neng could see then that nothing and nobody else mattered to the Long-Life now. More than once he'd contemplated simply Bilocating off the ship and letting the magnetic winds take him where they pleased. But fear had won, and here he had stayed, hoping against hope that the Long-Life would honour his promise and take Hui Neng with him, leaving Eoziel and Sotiris in joint charge of the doomed, broken mess that was the Firmament. Aaron had dispersed his promises like sweets, but had he honoured a single one? Hui Neng almost didn't want to know.

King Eoziel had regained his smile, perhaps remembering that he was to take command of the *Grand-Tile* again upon their departure, pleased to be of such galactic importance. Hui Neng pitied him. The Lacaille might rule smugly over the Vulgar for a year or two, he conceded, stripping their old enemy of her territories and beginning their reshaping of the Investiture. But by then some enterprising soul would surely have uncovered the Amaranthine weapons in the Vaulted Lands' crusts, and the Prism would obliterate one another for good.

'Sire Long-Life,' Eoziel ventured, his smile broadening. 'Permit me to explain how I intend to govern in your absence.'

Aaron turned, his black tongue probing at a wobbling incisor.

Hui Neng's gaze lingered on Eoziel's toothy smile as he spoke. The Firmament and Investiture were a closed ecosystem, a sealed plastic bag, all the squirming life inside fucking and killing and eating itself, polluting its biome until there was nothing left. There would be no hope of escape, not for the Prism, or anyone else that stayed behind. Once more, Hui Neng reflected on the sphere of glass said to have been discovered around the Old World, in the gone-before times, in the times of the Epir. Aaron alone had possessed the bravery to make that hole, and his makers had flourished. Now, pursuing them into the present, he would make another.

'By now you must know that Berzelius has tried to close the seas of Cancri, declaring himself Luminary?' Eoziel was saying. 'We won't allow that, for a start. My troops stationed on the surface shall tunnel their way in, taking it back for the Lacaille. And then it will only be a small matter of turning the Amaranthine guns in the world's crust' – at this point, he offered Hui Neng a simpering smile – 'for which we are *very* grateful, on any who oppose us.' He spread his scrawny white hands, clearly warming to his subject. 'You have assisted us in the formation of a truly galactic kingdom, and I'm sure, when we meet again, I shall take great pleasure in describing the new worlds that we will have named in your honour.'

Hui Neng waited, watching. The Long-Life's gaze dropped to the floor, his mouth loosing another runnel of drool. What happened then nobody could have expected. The *Caudipteryx*'s face crumpled into a sob, and he began silently to weep.

He rose awkwardly, almost falling, until Hui Neng reached out and steadied his arm, and lurched shambolically off towards his chambers. Hui Neng lingered for a moment, glaring at Eoziel, and followed.

Muttering pursued them into the sparse area beneath the *Grand-Tile*'s cooling funnel; Eoziel was clearly losing his composure. Hui Neng paused to listen, a small smile forming on his lips, before continuing after the Long-Life.

He found him squatting in the orlop deck, one of the places Hui Neng had heard he liked to rest but hadn't yet seen. He walked slowly in, the smell of the bilges infusing the place, gazing at the detritus lining the room – objects and trinkets that must have been the closest Aaron came to possessing belongings of any kind.

'Why do you weep?' he asked the Long-Life after much hesitation, careful to keep his distance. 'We're so close.'

Aaron turned and stared at him, his red eyes sparkling, face hanging. It was a sad sight. 'That... *person* ... is everything I hate, everything that was ever done wrong, in all the worlds that ever were.'

Hui Neng waited, but he would apparently say no more. The Amaranthine's gaze moved past him to the collection of low tables and boxes and chests, and what he assumed were the being's collection of most private treasures. The Long-Life, watching stealthily from the corner, made no move to stop him.

There were little models, made from wood and metal and string, arranged all over the room. Hui Neng had noticed how wooden things in the ship had been scraped and chiselled at whilst he was onboard, always assuming it was the work of some hungry Ringum stowaway busying itself, wasp-like, in the dark, but understanding now that it had been Aaron himself all along.

His eyes went back to the little figurines. A cast of hundreds stood upon the tables, each about the dimensions of a finger and sculpted so exquisitely that he could even make out a likeness of himself at the back. Among the assortment of people – some Amaranthine he recognised, some he didn't, others who must have been folk Aaron had known long ago – there were creatures, things he'd never seen before. Hui Neng stepped closer, transfixed, mindful of Aaron's presence behind him.

'There were all these ... *flashes*, in the sky,' Aaron muttered, as if his thoughts were very far away. 'Before we made the chip in the glass that surrounded the world. None of us knew what they were, what we were going to find out there.'

Hui Neng was so absorbed by the models that he hardly glanced up. Some of them must have represented the Long-Life's makers – the Epir, he had called them, known to the Amaranthine as the *Caudipteryx* – though they were all quite distinct from one another: fat and scrawny, young and old, the heads of the eldest protruding from wrinkled red snoods. Hui Neng's eyes moved along the table, past dozens of grotesques, to the forms he had never seen before: a zoo of curiosities and machine peoples.

'You've been busy,' he whispered.

A trio of peculiar serpents, their bulbous heads jagged with teeth, coiled around a wooden throne, upon which sat a particularly large and detailed member of the same unrecognisable species, its many arms open, as if awaiting an embrace. The creature was so lifelike that Hui Neng could imagine it blinking and slithering off, like the juddery stop-motion puppets of ancient film. He stared into its large, slanted eyes, noticing how Aaron had used little discs of glass to make the irises.

He returned his attention to the modelmaker. Something in the Long-Life's gaze had grown predatory, and Hui Neng realised that in his fascination he had picked up the peculiar figure and was cradling it in his hands. He put it swiftly down, backing out of the chamber with a bow.

Then he felt it. A rumble as the Colossus accelerated. Distant pops and bangs – what Hui Neng thought at first might have been the impacts of tiny comets, until he remembered they were deep inside Gliese already – pinging off the bulkhead. They were under fire.

He lingered a moment longer, still transfixed by the menagerie of beings on the tables, noticing something else. Standing just behind, smaller by an inch or two, was the unmistakable figure of Sotiris.

BILLYUP AND BABBO

Billyup the Awger journeyed parallel with the mountain peaks, forcing his push-gig through meadows of tall flowers, their stems wrapping and tearing in the spokes, frequently grinding him to a halt. The Babbo – carried high on his shoulders, trussed and bound and apt to shit down his back each Quarter – cried at every jolt, and oh how he wanted to *thump* her sometimes. But on smoother pathways they rode like a dream, the push-gig's wheels spinning a wooden sigh, the wind calming the Babbo as if it were night. Sometimes they waded the waterways, the Awger up to his chin, and she would giggle, entranced.

He stopped for a break in the flowers, the bloody light of sunset staining his clothes and hands. The crags and caves of the mountains loomed over them, blowing a seeping chill of night. They had passed into the West just now; he could feel it. Pan, the great wide Province, lay beyond the valley.

Babbo began to bawl, announcing their presence for a Crule in every direction. He struggled with her, clamping a hand to her mouth until she was breathless with tears, and pushed his woollen hood over her head. Sufficiently muffled, he stood over her, panting, wishing he could just toss her away.

The sun sank quickly below the flowers, the colours of the land and sky burning lushly pink and fading to dark. Billyup flattened a clearing for himself and leaned the push-gig over, rummaging in his bags for the old pack of phosphorettes and sticking one in his mouth. He lit up and moved to the edge of the clearing, pulling down his britches. When he was done, he took a handful of excrement and went to work spreading it around his sleeping place, smearing some at each point of the compass and wiping his hands on his clothes.

He took a drag of his phosphorette and surveyed his dirty work, winking at Babbo, who had stopped her bawling to watch in wonder.

Dinner tonight was a few plums found on the Artery, holed where the wasps had got to them. Billyup munched the fruit stones and all, then spat some into his grimy hand and fingered it into the Babbo's mouth. She didn't seem to mind the sight of him – lidless yellow eyes, mangy, balding fur and missing teeth – as most cultivated peoples did, and he watched her try to chew, examining her plump little hands and glistening cheeks. She was supposed to be more valuable than a Province of silk, but he couldn't see why. If they got there and she wasn't wanted, he supposed he'd gobble her up straight away, bones and all. He'd never tasted anything but old dead Melius meat before, two summers ago when he'd found a man murdered in the palm forest. Of course, by then Gheals and Lummeys and all the whatnot of the woods had eaten their fill of the soft parts, so he'd not sampled the best of it. The Babbo was something like a Secondling, though the people he'd stolen it from didn't look Secondish. He remembered the woman, giving him her dinner. Nice-looking, fuckable. Billyup stiffened at the thought. He'd fuck anything, though; fucked a barrel with a hole in it once, fucked a week-old dolfish caught in the harbour. He'd done the Awger these clothes had belonged to, back in the isles; it was how he'd heard about the contract, how he'd discovered the bounty on this little Babbo here.

'Com'ere,' he muttered, bringing the Babbo to him and licking his lips. She wriggled and grumbled as his tongue slid over her, lathering her in saliva. He sat her back down, thinking he might quite like the taste of a fresh one, but promising himself he'd wait, just to see what they'd pay.

Billyup made no fire that night, watching the Greenmoon rise over the meadow and drift away to the south. Stars churned in the gibbering darkness. He peered at the Babbo for a while as it slumbered, thinking about the country beyond the meadow: great hot paddy fields belonging to the Westerly Prince Amure, places he hadn't seen in a decade. He was wanted in Amure's lands, for theft and various other crimes he couldn't much remember, but as long as he stayed off the Arteries, the West was a wild enough place to pass through unobserved. He licked his lips, realising that he might just make it, after all.

SNOWFLAKE

A Hedron Star, floating motionless in the black, like an ice crystal left over from the first galactic frost. Flat slivers of porcelain extended outwards, each a hundred miles long, tarnished with age and stained dark within their fissures – what Maril now knew were vast belts of ancient black forest. Its five points were like flat, geometrically perfect mountains extending in each direction, their white summits capped with exquisite pointed structures like miniature stars. All across the bulk of its forested body, patterns of gold and russet appeared to drift with the world's strange winds, an odd oceanic silt that muddied the spars of white before moving on, bound by unnatural gravity to the gently curved, leaf-like form.

These Snowflake worlds, Maril was told, had not been made by the Osseresis – the ancient, Old World mammals that now inhabited them – but by an unknown, vanished species; people born beneath an older generation of suns. The notion made sense to him now, as he looked out at the towering crown of the Snowflake's far edge. There was a foreign feel to the design of the world, as if it had been built by minds quite alien from his own.

Gramps hurried them along with his herd of excited *Bie*, explaining the necessaries as they scampered across the black branches of the canopy, his sinuous grey-green tail flicking out behind him. Maril and his crew did their best to keep up, following as fast as they dared, conscious of the enormous drop to either side. The huge, suede-black beast that had met them upon arrival – Sussh, he seemed to remember, was its name – waited ahead, its burnished eyes surveying them.

'There were once hundreds of Thresholds into the next galaxy,' Gramps explained, counting the following Vulgar under his breath. 'Now only the Quetterel appear to have any real idea where they are.'

'The Quetterel come here?' Maril asked, breathless at the pace.

'The oldest monks sneak across sometimes, to die. They assume they have the Snowflake all to themselves; it would take a Prism ship over fifty years to get here after all.'

'*Wilemo*,' Jospor hissed, a little further back. 'How much longer?'

'Here,' the *Bie* said, abruptly stopping short and working his way across a notched section of trunk. Maril could see that the grooves led down to a wider, sawn-off section of branch that appeared to have been capped with metal. The great wide trunk of the tree was notched with a spiral of them, winding all the way up. The black creature tensed on its haunches and leapt into the air, opening its great wings in a gust of flotsam-filled breeze and sweeping up through the branches. 'See those steps?' Gramps said, indicating the rickety, winding stair chiselled into the trunk. 'It's just up there.'

They scrabbled up the gluey steps, boots sticking on thick sap, gloves and fingers stained brown with the climb. The *Bie* outpaced them swiftly, their claws perfectly suited to the ascent, and were soon lost up among the higher branches. Maril motioned for his men to pause, exhausted, while they took their bearings. Each Vulgar claimed a step for himself, little legs dangling over the drop.

Maril counted them all once again, convinced the number

had shrunk. There was plump, wall-eyed Jospor, his second, sitting just below. Then Furto, the scrawny, long-armed youth – his arms really were longer than his body, Maril noticed, mind already fogged by the count. Drazlo, sitting below, a loyal half-Lacaille with more brains in his head than the lot of them put together. Little Veril and squat Slupe, packed together on the same step, Veril already leaning fast asleep on his friend's shoulder, and Guirm bringing up the rear, the good lumen rifle perched on his lap, green eyes wide and watching.

The dim light of the place drenched them all, dulling the pallor of their skin and casting a hazy penumbra of shadows beneath the leaves. Maril saw how they might appear to the mammals here: ugly, shrunken and pointy-eared, the runtish off-casts of the family line, left to stagnate back in the small collection of worlds from which they'd once come. Going by what he'd seen of Sussh, the creatures here were huge and elegant, great black bats that rode the flotsam-dense thermals, distant relatives of the Vulgar in name only.

From his vantage point, Maril could see down into the dark, twisted limbs of the neighbouring tree, the view blurred by the seething populations of zipping flotsam creatures. The hanging soup of tiny beasts had thinned a little now they were higher up, tickling his lungs only when he took a particularly deep breath. A charcoal-grey leaf the size of a Vulgar drifted languidly past, and Maril watched it fall the hundreds of feet into the shadows of the forest floor. Looking back the way they'd come, he saw that the scarlet vault of sky was stippled with faint white objects, like stars hewn from blocks of marble. More Snowflakes, each quite different from the last, aligned in a string like a dozen stepping stones.

A tingling giddiness overcame him as a flotsam-filled burp slid up his throat; earlier that day, they were all being held prisoner, realistically expecting to be flayed alive by the Quetterel, and now here they were, catapulted – if Gramps was to be believed – twenty thousand light-years from the Investiture and onto this ancient collection of monuments at the galaxy's edge. Maril felt the grin spreading on his face, the exhaustion turning into a strange inebriation. He rummaged through his pockets, his gaze taking in the parched and sallow faces of his crew, their ears and noses crawling with the minuscule flotsam, the Glumatis ash still lodged in the creases of their ragged Voidsuits. They fiddled with some tin containers of spare parts, replacing batteries and checking their suit collars for hissing, useless radio channels, what was left of the ship's cache of cheap weapons poking out of their waistbands and bandoliers. Furto took out his broken pipe stem and sucked on it, little yellow fangs clamped tight.

Maril found the surgery tin and opened it, his trembling fingers locating the dainty bottle of limewine, packed snug between some wads of pus-stained cloth. He unscrewed the lid and drank, his shaking hand steadying, then spat a few times before he spoke, clearing his mouth of the flitting little beasts.

'You know, there might be some money to be made here.'

Jospor and Furto glanced up at him, their eyes straying to the limewine in his hand. 'You think so?' Jospor asked.

Maril took another swig and passed the bottle down. 'Well, we're not seeing that Amaranthine contract again, are we? And from what we were hearing on the way to Coriopil, the Lacaille were already winning the war.'

'All Filgurbirund could be aflame by now,' Drazlo said from three steps down, the bottle arriving in his hand.

'Either way,' Maril said, wishing Jospor hadn't passed the bottle on, 'keep those eyes open.' He glanced down the cut steps at his men, stomach turning once again at the sight of the drop below them. 'Who's got the pouch?'

'Here,' Slupe said weakly, hoisting an elasticated rubber sack and waking a grumbling Veril in the process.

He nodded. 'Well, start collecting things. Things they wouldn't miss.'

'Hello down there?' It was Gramps, scrambling backwards as best he could down the steps. He dug his claws into the step above Maril and gazed at them, his broad, scaly face concerned. 'Rest is ahead. You cannot wait here.'

Maril exhaled, blowing out a turbulent cloud of glinting gold flotsam, the others cursing and muttering under their breath, whatever brief high the limewine had provided turning quickly to drowsiness. Everyone had the sniffles. They clambered up amid much snorting and coughing. Tin clattered, boots shuffled and clumped. The sour stink of their sweat rose in the warm air around them. Maril kept his back to the step, inching around until he could get a foothold, catching another brief glimpse of the dizzying drop.

Gramps, it transpired, hadn't exaggerated, and Maril felt a certain embarrassment as he came to the dwelling – one of the hollowed-out, bulbous nuts – at the top of the stair after only another few minutes' climb.

The house had been built in a rambling, eccentric sort of way and secured firmly to the branch with globs of dried tree resin. As Maril approached it, the entire branch wobbled and began to rise, working its way ponderously skywards. He staggered, gazing up. A long-limbed mammal, black as Sussh, was climbing the tree, hauling the branch after it on strings tied to its enormous fingers and tying it off at every higher branch it reached. Maril's eyes followed the thing's many-jointed digits, observing that they wrapped almost halfway around the great trunk.

'You can stay here for now, Maril,' said Gramps, smiling at him from an aperture in the dwelling. 'The woodsmen have food and drink.'

At the mention of food, Furto dashed forward, followed by the others. Maril could see in their posture and mutterings that they were close to mutinous: hunted and imprisoned without sustenance, without sleep. One of his eyelids spasmed as he yawned, an incessant fluttering he experienced more frequently as the day wore on. They all needed rest, at the very least, and some kind of liquid other than wine. Maril gazed back the way they'd come, wary of losing sight of the steps.

The hollow dwelling appeared to be used for little save the storage of large loaves of fungus – apparently their dinner that evening. Only the pink light from a small, funnel-shaped window illuminated them as they squatted down together and took their various bits and pieces from their stores.

At that moment, the branch began to move again, rising jerkily and tilting after the long-fingered beast as it continued its climb. Maril peered through the window, watching Gramps rounding up his *Bie*. The sky was darkening, great branches sliding past. Tiny things swirled in, filling the space for a moment and clogging their mouths and noses as they ate, then exhaled away into the evening. It was the smell, especially, that impressed on him how far from home they were. He'd never smelled anything like it, in all his years in the Void, and it triggered something in him, a revulsion like vertigo, as if his body knew innately how far it had strayed from safety and comfort. He closed his eyes and slumped in his corner, gently aware that they were trying to speak to him, from some other place and time.

THE FINER INTERIOR

The lightwire in the hangar fizzled out before Lycaste had a chance to cram his legs in. He struggled inside the wobbling body of the jet's bucket-shaped gun seat, thumping his funny bone.

He almost hadn't come, despite being told they needed his

superior Melius eyes; he'd turned back at the hangar doors, spun around again, hesitated, shuffled his feet, the noises of the *Epsilon* preparing its descent drilling a shrill note of panic through his earholes. Then Maneker had swept by and grabbed his sleeve, just like that, dragging him towards the jet. It was the story of his life.

The darkness inside the hangar was complete. He could hear Huerepo's harsh muttering just in front of him, and Maneker's hiss from somewhere deeper inside, cranking the little motor. Lycaste's breathing sounded very loud as he pulled down the faceplate of his helmet, its rubber flanges sucking tight, and yet he felt absurdly safe for once, crammed into the back seat of this ramshackle little thing: just the three of them together again. He wished Perception could have joined them, too, but it had a greater role here than any of them.

Maneker's voice grew less muffled as he struggled out of the footwell and took Huerepo's place, the Vulgar clambering across to the nose-gun. Lycaste checked his pockets and gripped the open sides of the jet, his heart thumping abruptly into life just as Maneker started the thing up.

The rear of the jet exploded into spluttering, popping percussions, vibrating Lycaste's bones through his thick metal suit and casting a dim furnace light around the hangar. The noise was colossal, almost too painful to bear, so he cut his feed by thumbing a switch over his ear. Inside his helmet, the sounds of Maneker's and Huerepo's fast breathing suddenly drowned out the roar. Huerepo gave a loud cough. Lycaste's skin chafed inside his vibrating suit, beginning to itch all over. His teeth clattered together, slamming shut on his tongue. Blood filled his mouth; the taste of grave mistakes.

You.

His heart thumped harder. He angled his head, trying to hear through the pumping hiss of blood in his ears, but it was gone.

The darkness shifted, his stomach heaving along with some

51

change in direction, and Lycaste understood that the *Epsilon* was beginning its descent through the thunderheads, moving fast inside the world, twisting. He'd never had much of an imagination and was glad he couldn't see out of the hangar door.

But then pale light flew into the space and the doors were folding open, some rubbish and an old broken chair sliding across the hangar and tumbling away. Mist and water droplets drenched his faceplate, accompanied by the vibration of thunder. The *Epsilon* banked until Lycaste felt that the open hangar doors were now directly beneath them. The suggestions of shapes darted in the fog, but Lycaste kept his soundfeed closed.

'Now, push!' squealed Huerepo through the comms. Lycaste spat blood into his helmet and reached out to the sliding gantry, only his arms being long enough for the task. The jet shook, unconstrained and juddery, as he yanked the pulley. They thumped out of the supports, still half-wedged in the bracket.

'Push, push, push!'

All three hammered against the frame until it squealed, something popping and throwing them loose. Lycaste blinked in surprise, his stomach rising into his throat as they dropped from the hangar and into the vastness of Gliese. The tiny three-man jet fell twisting through the clouds. Thunder ripped and boomed around them. Lycaste managed to keep his eyes open, his gauntleted hands gripping the wet stock of the gun, straps strangling his waist. Rain lashed them, soaking his faceplate in a glittering haze of droplets, rushing and whirling from the slick body and wings of the jet in streaming trails. Lycaste could see Maneker's fingers frantically working at the jet's controls, struggling with the stick. The hot *pop pop* of the motor at Lycaste's back stuttered in and out of life. Huerepo's screams drowned his helmet's soundfeed.

And then they were through the clouds, trailing mist and

levelling out. Gloom bathed the wet body of the jet, rain drizzling in runnels along its sides and flowing back towards Lycaste as the vehicle accelerated. He relaxed his shoulders, hearing the cries of relief in his ears, patting Maneker happily on the back. To Lycaste's amusement, the Amaranthine hoisted his fist in a gesture of celebration, using his other hand to steer them deeper beneath the clouds. Lycaste gazed up and around, taking in the fat, torn grey thunderheads they'd fallen through. Their violent landscape obscured the interior sun and the Vaulted Land's other side, as if they were really on the top of the world, not within it. He leaned into the rushing wind and peered over the wing, its riveted flaps working away, loosing little trembling, flying streams of rain. Far beneath them, a wide blanket of dark, mossy jungle swept by, its valleys and hollows shrouded in ragged pools of mist. A white, rushing river wound through the mountains. Lycaste's eyes traced it, the waters leading him to their destination.

'There,' Maneker said over the channel, his voice almost drowned by the thump of wind and the pops of the motor.

Lycaste stared. It was as Maneker had said it would be: a wide, star-shaped crater in the jungle, illuminated with dazzling strips of white light at each of its twenty-four points; the subterranean access tunnel of something monolithic dug into the crust.

'The Foundry once built Firmamental ships of the line,' Maneker yelled over the wind, 'dreadnoughts twelve miles long from nose to tail.'

They banked and swung towards it. Relics of huge pieces of machinery stuck here and there out of the jungle, mossed and forested themselves so that they looked like the twisted roots of mountains pulled out of the earth. As they flew by one of the great spiked relics, Lycaste stared at the trees rising from its summit, their canopies blurred by mist. Huerepo, still manning the nose-cannon, glanced around at him, a little pale face in the oncoming rain, and gave Lycaste a smile. Lycaste returned his clapped Vulgar salute, suddenly immensely proud, his slowly resurfacing fear tamped back down. Maneker, his lank hair glossy and wet, hunched over his instruments. Lycaste could see the Amaranthine had begun to shiver. He glanced at his own moisture-beaded blue armour, the new pauldrons of copper mail rather spoiling the look. In the bucket seat around him he spotted various empty bolt casings, bones and other assorted rubbish that hadn't been thrown loose. His Amaranthine pistol nestled snugly against his side, his Prism spring pistol clipped into the holster next to it. If only they could see him now, his friends back in the Tenth.

Lycaste felt a shiver crawl through him, the distant memory of the shark hunt reflected perfectly in the unfolding scene. Here he was, manning the weapon aboard a small, juddery craft, his two companions gazing anxiously upwards, rather than down, for some beast to descend from the heavens. It was as if life were nothing but a series of mirrors and sets, constantly recycled and reupholstered; a spinning drum of kaleidoscopic chambers, everyone falling from one to the next, cursed to repeat and repeat and repeat.

Lycaste blinked the sweat from his eyelashes, his view misted over. Mirror or no, his old life was gone. He could never revisit it.

The Foundry itself was still some miles distant, and Lycaste swung his gun to look around him. Some suggestion of movement crowded the clouds beyond, and up in the thunderheads flashes of light were almost penetrating the mists.

'Look!' Maneker yelped, excitement yanking his voice into a higher register.

A vast bulge had begun to push through the thunderclouds ahead, parting them in ragged strips like something ripping through grey silk, a shadow making its stately way across the storm, also heading for the great open star of the Foundry entrance.

'Is that—?'

'That's it. The *Grand-Tile*.' Maneker's feverish breathing grew faster in Lycaste's ears.

The clouds swelled, rolling over the battleship's hidden bulk. The flurry of rain turned on them suddenly, slapping hard across the tiny jet and rattling them in their seats. White iron towers shone through the cloud ahead: a ramshackle city disgorged from the storm.

The Colossus burned through its wrapping of mist directly over the Foundry. It was both vaster and more dilapidated than Lycaste had imagined. He narrowed his eyes at the seething lightning storm, realising with a start that the flashes contained within them the discharges of thousands of weapons: Maneker's hired forces were swarming the *Grand-Tile* leaving trails of flashing vapour, vortices of rain catching the light of their munitions. Dark smoke suddenly peeled across the sky as something scored a hit on the one of the *Grand-Tile*'s outer towers, and hundreds of cannons all along its parapets returned fire in florets of smoke, deluging the jungle with a rolling slap of sound that penetrated Lycaste's closed comms and thundered through his bones. The jet stuttered as the force of the sound hit them, juddering up and down like a boat in a gale.

Huerepo squealed amid the din, almost falling out of his seat. The jet puttered and screamed in response, dropping quickly, Maneker slamming his fist against the controls. The dark moss world below rose to meet them.

'The river!' yelled Huerepo over the roar of rushing air and cannonade. Lycaste's stomach and heart swapped places as Maneker swerved the jet violently, directing its wild fall towards the white smear of the water. The river swelled until Lycaste could see the shards of black rock among its rapids. He pressed his body back, as if doing so would somehow break their fall, and tensed, eyes squeezing shut. Just then, he felt their forward momentum increase as the jet accelerated with a scream. Lycaste opened his eyes to see Maneker pumping the motor and leaning back almost into Lycaste's seat, both hands on the stick. They swerved, skimming the water in a rush of spray and barrelling into the bank.

They hit, jarring every bone in Lycaste's body. The jet's left wing instantly tore off, rolling them over and spinning them through the edge of the jungle. Branches raked across the fuselage, squealing. The jet bounced through and back down onto the bank, spinning again, sliding across the mud and diving into the water to lodge with a crippling crunch against a shard of rock.

Lycaste rolled sorely in his seat. Maneker appeared from the footwell, where he'd cleverly wedged himself. Lycaste glanced to the nose of the jet; it was almost entirely missing. Water frothed around it, and yet they appeared to remain buoyant. Before Lycaste could think clearly, their metal hull was grabbed and bobbed by the onrush of water from behind, tearing it away from its mooring against the rock and barrelling them downstream.

Lycaste glared at the crumpled remains of the nose, unable to register what he was seeing. Cream froth surged over the front, shoving them from side to side, tumbling the broken jet almost side-on through the rapids. A jutting rock intercepted them with a bang and bounced the jet further down the river towards another. Each impact almost rolled the jet before it bobbed back up again, unsteerable. Twisted pieces of wreckage from the battle in the sky rained down across the jungle and splashed into the river. A scorched-looking Lacaille ship barrelled in, streaming smoke from its stubby wings, clearly aiming for the river as they had. It dived past, skimming the water, and exploded across the bank.

'*Bugger it!*' screamed a bubbling little voice from behind. Lycaste wrenched around in his seat and with bleary relief saw Huerepo swept along in their wake. He reached and pulled the Vulgar in by the scruff of his collar, dumping him between his legs and pushing quickly off another rock that scraped past. The black water boiled white around them, hurrying the little jet downstream and beneath the looming spectre of the Colossus.

Maneker wrenched the stick with all his weight and ruddered them quickly between some viciously sharp rocks. Lycaste saw their jewel-studded surfaces skim by before his gaze was distracted by flashes from the bank: some scrofulous-looking Lacaille emerging from the jungle. Lycaste patted Huerepo on the head and gripped the gun stock, hauling it around in the direction of the bank. Bolts whizzed by, one or two ricocheting from the fuselage and skimming back into the water.

'What the hell are you waiting for, Lycaste?' Maneker raged, ducking down.

He sighted as best he could while they barrelled along, taking aim over the water and squeezing the triggers. The far side of the river erupted with exploding silt as Lycaste's lumen bolts whizzed into the jungle and raked the bank. Huerepo climbed past him and back towards the nose, which was steadily taking water. Lycaste shot a glance at Maneker, who was still pressing all his power into the stick to try and steer them to safety.

'Give it to me!' Lycaste cried, raking the far bank with a final line of fire before releasing the triggers. He scrabbled out of his bucket seat, tipping them dangerously in the rapids, and clambered across until he and Maneker found themselves occupying the same footwell.

Maneker cursed, trying to swap places and falling against the inside of the jet. A collection of rocks squealed by, spinning the jet as they clambered over one another. Lycaste fell onto the stick, forcing it down with both hands and splintering it. The bank drew closer. The jet tumbled, dragged through the water. Lycaste flattened his ears as a new hail of bolts fizzed into the rapids around them, one or

57

two pinging from the jet. At last, the fuselage crunched into silt. He reached out and grabbed at a rock, steadying them, and climbed quickly from the craft, dragging the wreckage of the jet after him.

Maneker and Huerepo hopped out, collecting what they could. The river roared beside them as Lycaste stared fearfully along the bank and into the dark fringes of the jungle. He glanced back, feeling bruised to his bones, knowing he would miss the battered little jet. Huerepo was limping and bleeding from one earhole; Maneker wiped his bloody mouth: he'd lost a tooth.

The Immortal spat a glob of blood onto the bank and swept past them, his mechanical eye crackling. 'No time, no *time*.'

The *Epsilon India* dropped through a tunnel of flashing cloud, rain tearing at its fins and swirling in a glittering vortex. A strand of Perception sat atop its cockpit like a rider at the reins, pummelled by the storm, the rest of its form twined throughout the ship and controlling its every function. The Spirit's features, had anyone been able to see them, were set in a permanent, gleeful grin as it manipulated the ailerons and aimed the guns, cycling their massive shells into newly cast chambers, ready to fire.

It soared deeper, bursting through the sound barrier. The *Hasziom*, with Poltor once again at the helm, chattered over the shared frequency, some miles away at the head of the Satrap Alfieri's division and closing the distance fast. Perception gazed through the cloud and singled out the massed ranks of the Jurlumticular vessels, a motley swarm of patchwork ships arranged at the Spirit's say-so in a precise and unfathomable formation, each vessel graded on its speed and the power of its artillery. Perception sorted them in its mind swiftly, pleased, then angled the *Epsilon*'s body and soared right, staring up at the slowly arriving mass of the *Grand-Tile*, messily displacing the cloud like bathwater. Perception saw that the Colossus battleship had already opened its single great hangar in a glow of magnesium light and was busily deploying its first ships, their exhausts fuming as they were batted around by the battleship's turbulence.

Nothing it couldn't handle. Perception steered the *Epsilon* away and dived through the cloud, spiralling down to spy friendly ground forces massing in the jungle around the Foundry's huge entrance. The *Grand-Tile* was trying to get as close to the hole as possible, to land, perhaps, and settle into a defensible position. Its underbelly, a sagging collection of irregular exhaust tunnels, was pumping thick black smog as the battleship steadied, a haze of fly-like ships drifting around it. The six hundred Jurlumticular vessels rose in a glittering swarm, soaring up into the open hangar and engaging the first defending ships in puffs of smoke and flame. Something detonated with a flash in the mix, showering slow, bright firework trails among the conflict. Perception watched for a moment more, recognising each individual Jurlumticular ship, then looked away as the Colossus's forty-foot guns opened up, observing through the dashing rain as the Satrap's rifleships came barrelling in and opened fire on the turreted upper towers. Lumens flashed, scoring the rain. Ships detonated, showering the battleship with wreckage and smearing soot across the clouds. Perception swerved away, its fingers poised on the trigger, waiting, watching, dodging the odd lumen zap as it scorched past. A white Lacaille carrier hove into view, dogging Perception's tail with a smattering of fire. The Spirit growled and darted into a spin, popping off a single shell and blowing it to smithereens.

The *Grand-Tile*'s every vibration shivered through King Eoziel as he stood upon the flight deck in the battleship's highest tower, his bony hands clasped and clammy, heart fluttering. It felt as if the Colossus was rattling itself to pieces around them. He looked at his handful of Lacaille knights, the Op-Zlan, as they stood and sat around him, and attempted once more to lower the pitch of his voice while somehow raising its volume as he spoke.

'If it comes to a boarding,' he continued, 'they'll lose.'

'You think that's their aim?' asked the indolent-looking knight Fiernel as he put out a hand to steady himself. 'To get inside?'

'Why not?' retorted Jhozua. 'The *Grand-Tile* cannot be destroyed; to capture it would be a superb feat.'

'If they can get it, they deserve it,' grunted Scarred Pitur, the oldest of Eoziel's knights, close enough for Eoziel to get a whiff of his reeking breath. 'And I for one shall be the first to congratulate our foes when they come to take us prisoner.'

'You shall do nothing of the sort,' snapped Eoziel, his little voice momentarily squeaking. Pitur smiled condescendingly at him.

Eoziel cleared his throat, riding out a judder of the Colossus. The knight Pitur, the wealthiest of them all, would have become king if not for a deft bit of manoeuvring on Eoziel's part. Eoziel looked at him. 'The legions I garrisoned near Cancri should be here any minute.'

Pitur stepped closer, straightening from his stoop. He was a big Lacaille, more than half the height of an Amaranthine. 'If they were coming,' he sneered, 'we'd have received word.' He turned to the others. 'Look at us. We could be in Filgurbirund by now, striking the final blow against the Vulgar. Instead, my *king*, you've dragged us here on your vanity quest while others reap the spoils.' A rumble of assent echoed from the other knights.

Eoziel stared between them, feeling his delicate grip slipping. 'I pledged allegiance—'

'Yes, of course,' growled Pitur, 'for the fortunes of all the Lacaille. But we know what you *really* wanted, don't we?' He reached out and poked Eoziel in the belly with his clawed finger, prompting gasps from the others.

'Imm-or-*tality*.'

The ground forces must have reached the Foundry's entrance: drifts of smoke were coiling from the jungle at the lip of the great star-shaped hole. Perception circled, darting among falling wreckage, soaring into the air again to take in the land below, clean, cool rain pummelling the *Epsilon*.

All right then. Perception cracked unseen knuckles. *Enough now*.

The Spirit went through a final checklist, readying the twisted heap of tubes in the Epsilon's snout and angling towards the chaos of the *Grand-Tile*.

A thought struck it, and it was suddenly afraid.

Perception disentangled its fingers from the equipment, taking the *Epsilon* on a wildly looping course as it banked and swerved through a hail of shells and darting, flaming ships.

Where was the jet? It searched hard, picking through individual trees and scouring the mossy, shadowy undergrowth. Where was Lycaste?

'*Percy!*' Poltor bellowed over the comms. '*Have you done it yet? We're not causing enough damage.*'

Where's Lycaste? Perception replied, twisting in the air. *Has he checked in?*

'*Nothing!*'

Shit. The Spirit glanced back in the direction of the sinking *Grand-Tile*, spotting a ponderous-looking Lacaille ship making its way down through the scrum and darting straight for the Foundry's entrance.

Perception was out of time. It unlocked the mechanism again, invisible fingers caressing the trigger.

Eoziel backed away from Pitur's out-thrust finger, the muttering of the other knights drowned by the surge of detonations and falling shrapnel striking the tower. Fiernel had already made his way out, and Eoziel felt a flash of hideous anger. *Nothing but greedy, useless—*

'There never was a more disappointing king,' Scarred Pitur said, leaning close, his fermented breath steaming into Eoziel's face. Eoziel felt himself unable to move, to speak, his indignation frozen with fear and humiliation. Pitur looked him up and down one last time, and turned to follow the others.

But the turn had broken the spell. Eoziel unsheathed his sword, wavering only a moment before he jammed it as deep as he could into Pitur's pale neck.

Remember that signal I was blathering on about? Perception said to every last friendly ship and helmet channel. *This is it. Get out of here.*

It waited, watching the thousands of craft booming swiftly up and away from the *Grand-Tile*, heading deep into the clouds. A clear and very visible mystification overcame the defending ships as they eddied and banked, droning after them.

Too late for that. Perception's invisible smile widened with a pyromaniac's glee.

It squeezed the trigger.

At first, nothing. Time enough for its racing mind to half-consider the possibility of failure. Then a hail of black grit like buckshot appeared, Bilocated from the battleship's long tail out in the Void and sent straight to the interior pole, where it had hung, caught and held by the magnetic spin, until the Spirit's command.

The mass of comet shards fell straight down like a dark rain, tearing into the *Grand-Tile*. Larger bodies, dropped after them, pummelled the Colossus in waves, a noise like rifle cracks slicing through the air. Wider, denser comets followed, ripping shreds out of the battleship's flanks until it was pocked with smoking holes, the ruins of towers gouting fire.

The *Grand-Tile* faltered in the sky, the Spirit saw, and began to drop. A tongue of flame curled out from the enormous hangar, fed by internal conflagrations.

Perception twisted to watch.

At first, the Colossus appeared to stall in mid-air, towers bent and crumbling. A sudden detonation ripped through its lower decks as an ammunition store caught fire and the battleship angled, tipping away from the gulf of the Foundry and towards the jungle. It tilted almost horizontal, engines screaming as they blared smoke and heat across the land.

Eoziel levered himself up until he could see, his furs sticky and scarlet. Pitur's body slumped beside him, skewered like a fish.

The shadows tipped around him, light spilling into the chamber. The jungle swelled, rising, the king's stomach joining it.

Far below him, the outermost exhausts struck the jungle, a silent quiver running through the battleship's length and whitening the plastic of his window. Eoziel dropped to his knees, entranced, hands trembling against the bulkhead as he watched the *Grand-Tile*'s body deform, crumpling as it drove itself into the ground, the crackling rumble rising. Then something burst in the lower reaches, the flash searing his eyes.

Perception gawped. The Colossus hit the jungle with a slap, a bellow of enraged metal peeling apart, towers crumpling, shearing away. Its great white body bent and popped, throwing shrapnel into the air, until something detonated inside its hangars with a dazzling flash. Perception drank in the sight: an erupted glitter of stupendous, rolling flame, flinging every atom of itself for miles around in streaming, sparkling trails.

They watched its screaming fall. Lycaste covered his ears. The blast was like something consuming the world. The gloom of the jungle brightened instantly, revealing every strand of branch and wet clump of moss, before darkening almost to night as smoke rolled overhead and choked the air.

They stumbled through the smoke-dim jungle, pausing as great waves of the stuff churned through the trees, washing over them.

'It's gone,' Maneker gasped, his false eye wonky in its socket. Lycaste wondered why he didn't just close his helmet. 'Perception did it ... It worked.'

'Do you think we got them all?' Lycaste asked, his eyes still searching the murk.

Maneker looked at him. 'There's only one way to know for sure.'

Eventually the wind appeared to change, blowing the shroud of smoke away across the gully, and the view drifted from grey to green.

The ancient trees, coated so thickly with moss that they practically dripped the stuff, were gnarled with jewel-studded cankers. Glossy red beetles fluttered from the mulch that squelched beneath their boots, the moss exhaling a succulent mist that shrouded the dense carpet of greenery. What sounded like the gabble of hundreds of thousands of birds echoed across the canopy.

Lycaste peered through the stands of trees, searching for movement. They were heading back towards the bank where they'd been fired upon, trying to curve past it. He kept his faceplate locked, vision steamed with moisture and sweat. Huerepo rode once more on his shoulders, and the drumming of the little Vulgar's heart seeped through their various fabrics and metals until it seemed to mix with Lycaste's own.

'Look,' Huerepo said tiredly over the comms.

Lycaste glanced up, following the Vulgar's gloved finger. Clusters of glinting, gem-laden fruit dangled just above his head.

'You Amaranthine are a bunch of bloody hoarders,' Huerepo said after a moment's silence, looking at Maneker. He reached from Lycaste's shoulders and plucked one of the fruits, pulling it apart to get at the sapphires inside. 'All these riches, just *lying* around.'

Lycaste glanced at Maneker, who appeared not to be listening as he studied the jungle ahead. His eye had worked loose now, dangling, though he didn't appear to have noticed.

'But the Prism come to the Firmament, to your house of embarrassing riches, in desperate need of compassion.' He chewed, counting through the blue stones in his palm. 'But you never have anything to give.'

Maneker shook his head, cupping the eye and replacing it before closing his helmet. Lycaste heard the grating sound as he screwed the collar shut, the muffled thump and swearing as his eye fell out again.

They were descending, their footing unsure on the slippery moss. Lycaste braced himself against trees as he moved downwards, working his way into the misted hollow of an unguessably large space.

'Will the lights even be on?' Lycaste asked. 'I thought the Foundry was never used these days.'

'There shouldn't be a problem,' Maneker said. 'The Firmament has run on perpetual motion for six thousand years. These Vaulted Lands will work perfectly until the day they collapse in upon themselves.'

Lycaste glanced up through the trees. 'When do you think that'll happen?'

'Oh, we've got a while yet.'

He looked in Maneker's direction. Only the glimmer of

his single wonky eye shone through the polarised plastic of the eyeholes.

The Amaranthine slowed, Lycaste following suit and staring into the trees. Sounds were filtering out of the jungle ahead.

Single thumps, some seconds apart, were falling across the jungle like the striking of a huge hammer. They rose in volume as the three crept nearer.

'*Someone*'s made it,' Maneker said. 'They've started up the machines.'

They followed a winding valley between green hills of stashed junk so thick with moss that only their sharp angles gave their foundations away. Thick, elderly-looking trees shot through with twisted metal barbs sprouted from them, suggesting to Lycaste that the waste pile they wandered through had been here for a very long time.

He stumbled, his footing abruptly disappearing from under him, sinking up to his waist in the moss. Huerepo grabbed Lycaste's ears to keep from falling, cursing.

Maneker took his elbow, levering him slowly out. Lycaste checked his legs and examined the hole he'd almost fallen through. For a moment, his head swam.

'Old ship parts, stacked high,' Maneker said, hurrying on.

Lycaste nodded, following more carefully. He'd not been able to see the floor of that underground world through the hole that nearly claimed him, but the dribbles of water from the broken moss were probably still falling back there, into darkness.

They came to an expanse of flat moss at least half a mile wide, stippled with scraggly trees. Lycaste opened his faceplate, drinking in the cool air; out across the misted land was a vast, dim cavern, a demi-hexagon punched into the jungle hills. The entrance to the Foundry of the Greater Interior.

They walked into the shadow of the hundred-foot arch, the booming of the mechanisms drowning their footfalls.

Lycaste peered into the dimness. A series of giant cogs, arranged into a toothy ramp, led down into the gloom. He would have to climb each tooth himself and then hoist the other two after him.

Maneker and Huerepo sighed as they observed the drop, the Amaranthine glancing in Lycaste's direction.

'Imagine if I'd stayed on the *Epsilon*,' he said, flashing him a weak smile.

Maneker stared at him a moment, a scowl forming, before breaking into a grin of his own. Lycaste almost slipped and fell at the sight.

A breeze rose from the tunnel to greet them, warm and foul-scented with whatever death lay down there. They turned back to the darkness, Lycaste sensing something watching them.

Come on.

'Percy!' Huerepo cried. 'You fine fellow!'

Maneker pushed Lycaste aside. 'What do you see down there, Perception?'

I'll go on ahead, sniff them out.

Perception travelled down and down through darkness, a blacker shade of shadow darting through arched stone caverns the size of temples of old, unspeakably pleased to have found Lycaste and his party at last.

At a junction, it whispered to a stop, coiling its fingers into the stone and hanging there, awed.

The place truly had been built to a monumental scale.

In a white chamber perhaps twenty-five miles from wall to wall stood a frame of massive star-shaped gantries, each possessed of twenty-four points in the image of the Firmamental flag. Hung from each were row after row of glossy cupolas that shone green and blue like oil; what Perception took to be the engine cowlings of the fabled Amaranthine dreadnoughts. The Spirit absorbed the sight, tingling. Never had it seen anything built to such a monumental, inhuman scale. Each of the hanging cowlings must have been more than two miles across, the size of a small Prism city. Those odd, apparently sentient sparks swarmed the place in a hot white flurry, moving in indecipherable weather patterns across the room and coiling back under some mighty convection, illuminating the vast place in a harsh glare. The Spirit extended itself and caught one, observing its angry, sputtering little light, then dragged its gaze away, peering through the gantries to a gigantic orifice of an opening: the Star Chamber, the place where everything of any consequence in the Firmament had been made.

Perception detached from the ceiling and dropped the ten miles to the chasm floor, spying minuscule Pifoon going about their tiny business all around him. It would take Lycaste and Maneker all day to cross this place, at least, assuming they sprinted without a break and carried that little Huerepo all the way.

Sounds brought its attention back to the Star Chamber's distant entrance.

There just wasn't time. If it was going to do this, it had to do it now.

The Satrap Alfieri's gunships soared overhead, pursued by a squadron of Lacaille jets. Another blinding flash illuminated the clouds, tearing them away like washed ink and revealing the other side of the world at last. Lycaste craned his neck, marvelling at the steaming rainfall. The Satrap must have detonated the skycharge.

Huerepo, still seated on his shoulders, tapped him on the side of the head. 'Honestly now, Lycaste, it's time to go.'

'I know, I know.' He turned from the scene and bundled

Maneker into his arms. The Amaranthine went willingly enough, his beady eye staring into nothingness, chest rising and falling quickly as Lycaste climbed down, dropping the last few feet to the next cog. The scent of death, sweetish and musky, grew stronger immediately.

Abruptly, the Immortal's lips began to move, whispering something in the dark.

The teeth of the cog they stood upon started to roll, trembling and squealing as the mechanism ground through centuries of disuse. Lycaste braced himself, making his wobbly way to the next tooth as it rotated into view.

'There is an Amaranthine down there who knows more secret Incantations than I,' Maneker said as they moved. 'You must stop him before he has a chance to speak.'

Perception travelled beneath a line of huge vices, snaking between the sparks, extending itself into a ribbon. It hesitated as it came to a gigantic set of templates strung across the gantries, a place where molten iridium could be spun like glass into the most delicate of shapes, and floated in among them, listening keenly. Far below, the floor of the Foundry was thronged with the dots of a crowd. Perception could make out their little Pifoon faces, all turned in the direction of the Star Chamber. It accelerated hard, wriggling the last few hundred feet to the great hole itself and pausing at the entrance.

Hui Neng stepped down from the *Ignioz* and craned his neck to look up at the open StarMouth, framed now in a column of black smoke from the *Grand-Tile*'s sudden demise. Draped from the distant ceiling were one hundred enormous Firmamental banners hanging some miles above his head, memorials to a greatness that he'd helped create. Around him swarmed the elite, cobalt-armoured Op-Zor Lacaille, Eoziel's knights-in-training, taking up defensive positions throughout the Star Chamber, the Satraps Downfield and Nerida busily screaming directions. He glanced at Elise, Satrap of Port Elsbet, nodding to her. She looked emptily back at him, a Pifoon at her side trying to get her attention. Hui Neng smiled grimly. None of them had ever liked him much.

He turned, his skin prickling. The shadow of the Long-Life watched him from the *Ignioz*'s hatch, his Shell-shaped pendant catching a gleam of light.

Hui Neng moved to help him but the *Caudipteryx* refused his hand, throwing down its cane and stumbling on ahead, past caring. Hui Neng stood to watch, painfully aware that he and all the Amaranthine, humanity and even Prism life alike, were at this moment gone from the being's thoughts.

Aaron, staring around himself in wonder, dwindled to a hobbling speck, his long reflection lost among those of all the blue knights on the Foundry's polished floor. Hui Neng followed his gaze. The cavernous place had played host to a display once, for the Venerable Empress Abigail, with all the military might of the ProtoFirmament arranged on this very floor for her inspection. Hui Neng remembered the lumbering craft lifting out of the StarMouth and darkening the air, rising to join their fellows inside the hangars of the dreadnoughts that waited in the clouds.

Now his attention turned to the preparations the Pifoon here had made, ready for their arrival.

Huerepo scuttled beside Lycaste's great lumbering foot-steps. Slowly, very slowly, the dimness of the place receded, replaced with a soft golden glow, revealing the full extent of the cavern around them. Sturdy shelves as high as the eye could see towered over them, their mysterious contents illuminated by floating Amaranthine sparks. Huerepo ran his eye along the dark alleyways to either side of them, his pistol clutched tight, trying to comfort himself with the thought that Perception must have come this way already. At the antechamber's far edge was a vast, slowly brightening disc of light, the entrance to the Foundry proper, looming on the horizon like a smog-dimmed sun. Huerepo felt almost pinned to the floor by the size of the interior space; he'd never been anywhere so cavernous, so out of scale, and his little body shrank at the sight. He looked away from the great arches of the ceiling, noticing Lycaste's sensitive ears twitch: floating from that gaping mouth of light came the percussive sounds of a fight.

Maneker dashed ahead, his grubby cloak trailing through the puddles. The constellation of glowing sparks that suffused the higher reaches began to bob and spread, a few of their number drawn to Maneker's presence and descending quickly to hover over him, lighting the way towards the Star Chamber. Huerepo felt his little heart aching, wishing for some rest. It wasn't as if he or any of them could stop or even slow what was to come.

'Lycaste!' he called, watching the giant stumbling on ahead. 'I'm sorry, I—'

'Not to worry,' the Melius rumbled, spinning to scoop him up. He settled Huerepo gently on his shoulders and strode on, catching up with Maneker in a pace or two. Huerepo patted his shoulder, listening to the Amaranthine's ragged breathing at their side. 'You're a good lad,' he whispered, wishing Lycaste had stayed behind, where it was safe.

The Satrap Alfieri directed his gunships towards the Star-Mouth, gaping and luminous beneath them. Perception had given peculiar orders to do as little damage as possible to the place once the *Grand-Tile* had been dispatched, but he would follow them to the letter.

'I think it's your turn now, my friends,' he said into his helmet.

'So it is,' came the static-heavy reply.

Alfieri twisted in his seat, observing through the cockpit as a magnificent storm of Jurlumticular craft came roaring past on either side, the screams of their acceleration cutting out his helmet feed.

The arrow hulls popped the sound barrier as they raced through the clouds, falling towards the jungle and loosing trailing phosphorescent charges. They dropped through the Mouth and into the Foundry, deluging the Star Chamber with a blinding mist of light.

Maneker recoiled from the sudden flash. The seething crowd of Pifoon that had been jabbering at them did the same, staring off towards the huge entrance to the Star Chamber. A ribbon of molten metal dribbled from the apparatus above, falling slowly through the gantries and splashing across the floor.

Hui Neng found himself huddled beneath the *Ignioz*'s nose, his thoughts muddied, the world stained white. Booted feet thumped past, drawing his attention to the blazing mess of the Star Chamber itself. The Op-Zor never had a chance.

The entrance to the Star Chamber, ringed by a stupendous, rusted rib of dismantled hollowing lathe, flashed a searing white, the thunder of arriving ships booming through the vast space and loosing more of the molten metal from the ceiling. Lycaste's eyes recovered in time to see the arrival of the Satrap's ships, glowering rifle-shaped shadows dropping through the miles of smoke that shrouded the great hole in the Chamber's ceiling and opening strobing pink fire onto the masses down below. There must have been thousands already in conflict, an exchanged glitter of a hundred neon flashes. Lycaste's ears closed with a wet pop, shielding themselves as one of the ships absorbed a broadside, gouting flame.

Sparkers arced over the stew of soldiers, illuminating them within the shade of the great fighting ships, which cast dark clouds that dimmed the whiteness of the huge place and allowed Lycaste's eyes to adjust. A detachment of Jurlumticular came striding up, surrounding Maneker and Lycaste and taking them off to one side, to one of the enormous sculpted feet of the gantries that bracketed the doorway. The sparks, hovering low over the Amaranthine and sputtering like indignant little dogs, appeared to object.

'Stay here, Amaranthine,' one of the Jurlumticular rumbled, hoisting a Prism weapon Lycaste hadn't seen before and babbling to his squad. They took cover at the huge, machined edges of the doorway, looking out across the quarter-mile of floor to those at the other side, the frequencies in their suits crackling with quick conversation. The conflict was still so distant that it resembled the roar of waves on a beach, beating and breaking and sighing back, funnelled into the next chamber by the vast tunnel of the doors.

Maneker escaped the cordon of Jurlumticular to peer around the gantry, his mechanical eye working in its socket. Someone, most likely an Immortal, ignited a swathe of the fighting troops in white, blinding fire. A bolt whined past, bent off course by the repulsive force of his copper pauldrons, and the Jurlumticular grabbed him back.

A Lacaille ship came powering through the gap, roaring overhead into the darkness of the factory space, lumen pulses trained on whatever pursued it. It banked and swept away, off into the dim distance from which Lycaste and the others had run, a dark little shape zipping through the caverns.

'All right,' the Jurlumticular said, bustling them out. 'We go.' Lycaste followed their hurried, clumping steps into the open, between the doors, his head ducked. At the bottom of a steep ramp, the battle raged, armies of thousands surrounded by the vast expanse of blinding white.

'Go!' the Jurlumticular repeated, pushing Lycaste from behind, a phalanx of riflemen bringing up the rear. He staggered forwards, packed between them, a full head taller than anyone else.

'Lycaste,' Maneker cried over the noise, 'let me sit on your shoulders!'

He gave the Amaranthine an awkward leg up, staggering a little under the man's wiry weight as those behind him pushed on, some of the Jurlumticular beginning to object. Huerepo climbed into the crook of his arm, struggling as they began to jog.

Maneker wobbled on Lycaste's shoulders, the shield wall of Jurlumticular continuing their push down the slope of the ramp. The smoky breeze ruffled his hair, his artificial eye taking in the surge of fighting down below. Fuming pink clouds of sparker smoke drifted across the scene, the massed thunder of yells and shouts punctuated by the Satrap Alfieri's gunships firing messily into the surging armies beneath. A bolt bomb detonated in the far reaches of the chamber, deluging the tumultuous crowds with shrapnel, soon followed by an eruption of cheap splinter bombs hurling slivers of wood and the steam of boiler cannons flooding over the crowds. The Jurlumticular, in response, were busily employing Perception's ghastly weapons, and Maneker could see snipers nearby unloading their venomous bullets into the distance.

He steadied himself, shifting his weight fully onto the back of Lycaste's neck, and searched the periphery of the conflict for lone figures. He remembered this place from millennia past, a recurring stage upon which his dreams had played out. His eye moved across the Star Chamber to a large recessed rectangle patterned with Firmamental sigils and the dots of panicked Pifoon workers milling around it. He backtracked, sighting along what must have been the straightest line from the fight, and found him. A figure, no more than a suggestion

74

of shadow on the bright floor, was working its way towards the bay.

'Take us down there!' he said, reaching and tapping frantically on the shoulder of the Jurlumticular at the front. He pointed. 'Right *there*.'

PUPPETS

Perception saw it then, the hobbling figure, quite some distance from everyone else and making its stumbling way out to a huge recessed bay in the floor.

The Spirit sharpened itself into a needle's point and went hypersonic, the smoked air crackling and booming in its wake.

Lycaste felt the detonation as something accelerated through the air above them. The invisible shape of the Spirit, cloaked in a cone of rushing white air, shot past, firing across the Chamber.

'Faster!' roared Maneker, still riding atop Lycaste's shoulders. Huerepo, poking out of the front of Lycaste's cuirass, was gazing wide-eyed up at Perception as it rushed overhead.

At the last moment, Aaron's saurian face turned, a jowly, grey-pink apparition, yellowed fangs peeping from its sagging lips. Perception saw through a lens of slow motion, watching as the face began to register surprise. But it was too late. Perception aimed for the eyes.

Aaron the Long-Life distended his jaws, peeling apart at the seams and exploding into a thousand pieces before he could even begin to scream.

*

Through a fine mist of falling blood, the Spirit turned to them, coated. Lycaste saw its form at last, a serpentine red statue brooding over its kill. The rain of blood flickered with tiny flashes, and Lycaste was reminded suddenly of the storm on the beach back home, the storm that had changed his life. Percy's attention turned to something lying a little way across the floor as the blood swirled, convected, around it.

The Shell. It had been made into a pendant. Perception was inspecting the thing in wonder when it felt the gravity of the other Spirit, seething across the floor like dry ice and feeling for the necklace. Perception could see a suggestion of the Long-Life as he crawled along the floor, a flickering cirrus of energy steaming from the pulverised saurian remains. And it could *feel* him, too; it could feel the drag as their dense gravity wells intermingled, tugging them together like a tide.

Aaron must have felt the same. He coiled blearily away in the quantum winds, streaming and collecting on the far side of the pendant.

Then his sharp, fiendish attention turned on Perception at last.

The Spirits regarded each another, the Foundry and its inhabitants forgotten.

Perception stared blankly back. Though made and destroyed in the same manner, they were not at all alike. A sensation of warped, decrepit lunacy infused this other being; an overgrown, cankerous soul long past its best.

They circled the pendant, stray wisps of themselves reaching out to one another, compelled.

Aaron snarled and darted for the Shell, disappearing in a blink. Perception lingered, startled, gazing upon the pendant, barely noticing as a Pifoon corpse stirred at the edge of its vision and stumbled awkwardly to its feet.

Perception turned to the corpse, seeing in its eyes a hideous liveliness. The Pifoon body was shot through and leaked as it staggered, drawing a sword mechanically from the scabbard on its hip.

Neon flashes rained down upon them both, sparker bolts that fizzled and exploded in pink and purple bursts. Aaron's Pifoon body staggered right and left, sword extended in Perception's direction, and made a drunken dash for the pendant. Perception fumbled clumsily for it, unable to touch the thing, deciding to dive into it instead –

– and appeared within a body some distance away, sitting up with a resounding gasp. The pain was extraordinary, a new dimension. For a few moments, Perception couldn't even think, so overwhelmed was it by the broken Pifoon's screaming nerves. It diverted all its powers of concentration into turning the body's head, seeing through cloudy, low-contrast eyes as the Prism-bodied figure of Aaron picked up the pendant and grinned, blood leaking from his nostrils. Perception saw his fluid motions and understood that this could be no contest: only Aaron had experience with flesh and blood.

Perception levered itself up, using both hands planted on the blood-smeared floor, and shakily drew its spring pistol, aiming a trembling hand and popping shots around the feet of Aaron's staggering body.

Aaron hardly flinched, advancing towards Perception, swinging his blade in scything, chopping motions. Perception's weapon at last found its mark, a bolt ripping through Aaron's shin, and he gasped and staggered, flailing the sword as he came within slicing range. Perception threw up an arm to shield itself, some instinct of its father's protecting the Pifoon body from a lethal blow, and felt the searing pain as the blade *thwacked* into bone.

Perception shoved the blade away, glimpsing the energy in the other Pifoon's eyes, and made a clumsy grab for the pendant, fingers unable to close, feeling the fresh injection of life leaving its leaking body. The pain was exquisite. Aaron dropped his blade, trying to pull his hand out of Perception's closing fingers, a look of intense concentration suddenly crossing his face. Perception could only watch, helplessly, as the other corpse lifted the pendant slowly to his lips, muscles straining against Perception's grip, and pushed it into his mouth. He swallowed with a grimace and turned his blood-smeared grin on Perception.

The Spirit pushed, knocking Aaron to the floor and stamping a boot on his chest. Aaron writhed, pinned. So far, not a word had been spoken between them. Perception decided to change that.

'You can't have it,' Perception grunted in Unified, leaning its weight onto the shaking leg and pinning Aaron harder. 'It's *mine*.'

'Jacob's son,' Aaron gasped, grasping for a nearby sliver of metal and driving it into Perception's ankle. 'You know you can be king here, just let me go.'

Perception clamped its teeth shut, seeing that there was only one option.

'Let me *go*,' Aaron growled, working the shard deeper.

Perception could barely stand any longer. It aimed shakily and put a bullet through Aaron's belly and into his spine. Aaron's eyes widened, his body paralysed.

'*Gooo*,' Aaron wheezed.

Perception looked into his eyes, making sure he was still alive, and shakily drew its own scimitar. It leaned its weight upon it, pushing it deep into the rough location of Aaron's stomach. Blood sprayed, wetting them both, until Perception had worked the sword in a rough circle and dug its fingers into the mess of guts, feeling for the Shell. *There*. It fumbled for the object, hooking the pendant's chain onto its thumb, and pulled it out, finally turning the pistol on itself.

Pop. Through the Shell and into another Pifoon's body some distance away. Perception stood more quickly this time, tasting blood in its mouth and spitting. There had been *something*, in that black second between lives; something it thought it remembered from its first death. But there wasn't time to dwell on it: Aaron's head turned minutely in his direction. Perception stumbled over, snatching up the Shell, closing it awkwardly in its hairy Pifoon fist. Aaron's eyes fixed on Perception's before glazing and rolling upwards into death.

Perception turned. A dead cobalt-cuirassed Lacaille, quite a bit larger than Percy's own Pifoon body, had begun twitching on the floor. The Lacaille staggered to his feet, blood pouring from holes in his neck, and barrelled across the floor towards Perception.

Their blades met with a shriek of metal, grinding and squealing. Aaron was the defter, parrying and hurling Perception back. Percy allowed a cut and jabbed forward, scraping up the metal of Aaron's plate armour until its sword point had lodged in his neck. Blood squirted in a wild, wobbling spray.

Perception felt its arm loosen, severed at the shoulder and hanging from a thread of sinew. It peeled away and thumped to the floor, the blade clattering with it. Aaron smiled a red-smeared smile, one eye wandering, snatching the pendant and hurling it as far as he could towards the recessed floor. He drove his sword into Perception's chest, crackling past the ribs and shattering the scapula as it forced its way through. Percy felt the blade as a dull heat within its body, pain sizzling along its edges, all the remaining strength leaving its legs, and fell into Aaron's stinking embrace. The two Spirits entwined for a moment, a flash of memories passing between them, until Perception left its body with a sigh.

Lycaste stared, ears flattened, a cold sweat crawling through him. Aaron's borrowed cadaver flicked its eyes in his direction.

Lycaste's heart fell silent. Time wound to nothing. The

gaze, though it belonged to a small Lacaille person dead now for some minutes, was one he recognised. It was, somehow, like looking into a mirror.

Aaron's eyes gave the impression of widening a little in kind, before a fresh rain of sparker bolts from the massed Jurlumticular came arcing overhead. He spun, stalking off towards the sunken bay in the floor.

Perception rose foggily towards the ceiling. It gazed down into the mess of fighting, trying to work out where it had been, where Aaron might have tossed the pendant, but all the Spirit's energy appeared to have dissolved.

Across the Star Chamber, the Pifoon were still working, their little hands hurrying, winching a platform from the depths. The Spirit wrapped itself around a damaged gantry and stared.

Out of the floor rose an angular edifice of shimmering white, like an unprecedentedly complicated origami structure, surrounded by the twenty-four points of the Firmamental star. *The Collection*, Perception's mortal remains, dismantled upon its death in that lonely tower four thousand years ago. The Spirit thought it looked like a giant two-storey head. As it gazed upon the structure, it realised the thing was indeed that: a huge death mask, made in the likeness of an Amaranthine. And then it understood. It was the image of his father, Jacob the Bold, ancient Emperor of Decadence.

A surge of jealousy replaced the echoes of pain.

The lone blue blotch moving towards it – Aaron's Lacaille body – paused a moment in wonder. At his side limped an Immortal who cast repeated nervous glances behind him at what was left of the fighting.

The glint of a blade, taken from the Amaranthine's pocket, presented ceremonially. It disappeared again as it was thrust almost gently into the Long-Life's side, Aaron's own hand guiding it in, at the last.

Lycaste and Maneker stood entranced. The Long-Life's Lacaille body fell. The monolithic head did not stir. A small group of Pifoon had climbed twin ladders and were fussing at something where the ears should have been. Abruptly the head opened, revealing a glittering interior of complicated pieces.

At its centre was a miniature translucent white copy, folded in the same origamic way. Lycaste watched as the smaller interior head shrivelled before their eyes, folding in upon itself until it was a polygonal diamond the size of a small egg. The Amaranthine extended his hand timidly and the diamond hovered out, landing gently on his palm.

Bad idea, thought Perception. The ultra-dense piece of folded material dropped right through the man's flesh, tearing a hole in it. The polygon containing Aaron's soul thumped to the floor and opened out, spreading evenly until it had become a quivering white sheet on the ground. Perception saw how it had been designed as one colossal, ironed-out sheet of brain material, self-powered and yet containable. The material folded once, then twice, angling to a point.

'Memory film,' Maneker whispered, almost too quietly to hear against the fading din. 'Capable of assuming any form imaginable. The Stickmen, the old Amaranthine army, were made from the same material.' He stepped forward, his breathing quickening, the spell broken. 'He's trying to fly.'

The Jurlumticular opened fire under his command, sparks ricocheting off the enormous polygonal sail.

Once more the shape reconfigured, elongating into a spear, the light glowing through its fine material. Sparker bolts exploded around it, colouring the air pink, red flame coiling. The bust of Jacob shattered like glass, its component pieces spilling across the floor, the Pifoon turning tail. The

Amaranthine, still holding his pierced hand, caught a bolt in the chest and fell.

The Collection hesitated, forming a papery arrow that bobbed and dipped with the effort of staying afloat. It began to move, steering its wobbly way around the Chamber's walls, accelerating and slowing again with a crack of hypersonic air, as if able to mould it beneath its wings. It found its confidence at last and shot up towards the ceiling, roaring as it elongated, and Lycaste watched as it burst through the star-shaped hole and away into the gloomy cloud.

He and Maneker stood frozen, Lycaste's skin bleaching to white. The fighting appeared to grow in volume for a moment before dying incrementally down. The Chamber and its thousands of inhabitants grew still, a silence descending.

Perception drifted over to what remained of the Star Chamber's eastern corner, passing above the small, circular groups of tired figures as they ate together, Op-Zor and Jurlumticular alike, pardoned apparently without reserve or bad blood once everyone realised the instigator himself was gone for ever.

The marble floor was a ruined expanse of charred stains, the detritus of the battle lying everywhere. It wondered how long it would take to clear such a mess, hardly caring. Seal it all away and be done with it.

The Spirit took a moment to locate the remains where they'd fought, eventually spotting the twinkle of the pendant that Aaron had kicked aside. Nearby lay the fallen Amaranthine. Perception gazed at the corpse, noting the triangular hole in the man's hand where Aaron had settled and fallen through. His chest was pocked with bloody little holes – an exploding bolt, perhaps, that had dug its way into his lungs. The man's brain, still cooling, remained unharmed.

Perception looked at the constellation of wounds, and wondered.

HARALD HUNDRED

A large, fine tent stood on the shore beneath umber palms, the hot river wind singing through its guy ropes and snapping at its flag.

In the shade of its entrance a dark figure sat, slim legs crossed, happily absorbed, looking out at the brown waters and the estuary beyond.

Harald hummed something while he darned the newest hole in his shirt, deciding that when the evening's preparations were done, he would get out his little wooden guitar and give it a try. The melody was something he hadn't thought of in a long while, an old preserved thing miraculously undamaged by any intervening thought. He smiled, glad, thinking he ought to go and get his guitar now, in case it left him.

Sunlight burned golden through the silk when he went inside, just a little too warm for comfort. Old lion-footed wooden tables and cupboards stood on rugs that carpeted the floors, books and papers and compositions lining their shelves. A little silver *heardie* shaped like a metronome sat by the bed. It was capable of playing a library of hundreds of tunes by snicking back and forth along a channel in its silver case. Harald glanced at it, knowing the piece of music he was thinking of wouldn't be in there. A spark awoke in a lantern, grizzling, but he shushed it absently, wrapping his slender fingers around the neck of the instrument where it stood beside the fireplace and taking it in his lap.

'*Ha da da, da …*' he sang, strumming the first chords experimentally, then taking the guitar back out into the sun to look at the river.

But the music was gone, dashing off into the lost parts of his memory before he could snatch it up. Harald sat back down with a grunt, returning his attention to the stitching. The wind ruffled the surface of the river, dense with pink eels that snaked and coiled just beneath the surface. The umber palms rustled, the little green bottles he'd hung among their fruit breathing a gorgeous tinkling sigh. Harald felt a sweet surge of contentment, looking up from his work at the home-made wind chimes. He strung them around each new camp, and they were always much admired.

There. All done. The gauzy cloth shirt must have travelled with him for a good few years now and was certainly looking elderly; a dozen suns had bleached it colourless, while the weekly wash in dirty Prism seas had leached any remaining dye. He held out the shirt, inspecting it, then looked back towards the estuary. There had been genocide here, in this part of the Investiture, and the silt of the rivers was more than mere sand.

The palm thickets appeared to regard this gravelly land as nutritious enough, and similarly Harald felt no great concern when he'd hiked to the river's edge to pitch his camp and found the land made from eye sockets and toe bones and tiny pieces of vertebrae. His contentment, he hoped, had percolated into the ground, becalming the little smoothed pieces, and this had become a happy place in the weeks since he'd arrived, on the hunt for his last commission.

His slow travels across the Investiture had taken him in a zigzag through thirteen moons and fifty-three Prism king-doms, Bilocating from place to place as if they were a chain of unexplored celestial islands, looking for somewhere to moor up and call his own. He brought his many possessions along by grabbing a corner of his tent as he closed his eyes to travel, and everything came with him whole. Extremely useful: it was years since he'd first erected the tent, and he wasn't entirely sure he could work out how to do it again. When he needed to leave his home – signified as Amaranthine property by its Firmamental flag – he packed his most valuable possessions, pulled on some sturdier boots and set off. When he slept, he dreamed strange dreams, his old mind infused with the air of each new place, and sometimes he even ate the local fruits and produce, just to feel at home, enjoying himself more than he'd ever thought possible. They said the age of plenty and prosperity was over, that the Amaranthine were no more, but Harald couldn't keep the spring out of his step and the song out of his voice. Life was a marvel; an existence of precisely meted perfection, and he was surely the happiest man in all the galaxy.

Late that evening, the fire lit and roaring beside the tent, he saw them coming.

They wandered through the palm grove, little bobbing shadows like ghosts in the woods, the bones crunching beneath their feet. He looked up from the fire, placing the guitar to one side.

Three of the males he knew a little already, having wandered into their shanty by mistake on his first day here and seen them again this morning as they fished for eels. They were of the furred sort, all covered in a light blond down and naked but for tiny pointed leather shoes, their tails sticking up rod-straight as they scampered, and were known in these parts by their old name: *Devilmen*. They brought with them three others he'd not met. As they approached, he stood to give them the Amaranthine handshake, and to let them see his height. There was not a Prism kingdom that did not respect the power of the Amaranthine, though it helped that Immortal *Homo sapiens* were also considerably larger as a species. Had it been the other way around – had Harald stood before six giants each larger than an Old World Melius – he might well have found himself on the wrong side of the dynamic.

He smiled at those he knew, noticing the bottles they'd brought with them.

'Good to see you,' Harald said to the leader. 'Ipth, yes?'

The Prism bowed. Harald gestured to other two he knew. 'Flip and Fime.'

They grinned, Flip offering him the plastic bottle.

'Aha. Thank you.' He took it and held it to the last of the light, trying to make out the various species that floated, pickled, at the bottom. 'What have we got in here?'

'This is sponge eel,' said Ipth in a version of a dialect Harald was just getting used to, pointing to a rather rotten-looking thing with a gaping mouth, 'like the ones we catch.'

Harald shook the furred hands of the other three, not quite catching their names, and invited them all to his fire. They passed the bottle between them, Harald taking the customary second drink and tasting in the strong alcohol the trace of their bleeding gums, then went about preparing them some food, having caught and dried a few eels in case anyone came calling.

They began with the usual word games of a seasoned traveller. Harald had a list of Unified vocabulary for which he wanted to know the local equivalent, and the six Devilmen fought among each other to oblige. His lexicon improved, Harald sat back and lit his pipe from the fire, listening to their local stories and casting the odd glance into the woods. He'd been robbed a few times before – it was impossible to journey the Investiture without experiencing that pleasure at least once – and had deliberately pitched his tent so that it backed into the thickest palms. Anyone coming at them from behind while he was distracted would need to shove their way noisily through the undergrowth.

Satisfied that the palm forest was empty, Harald went back into his tent to retrieve his cards. One of his many hobbies was collecting Prism games, and the cards he selected were a beautiful set of shaved bone slices he'd found in Harp-Zalnir.

'Lacaille cards?' said Ipth doubtfully.

'Fine for most games,' Harald said, dishing them out. 'You boys know One and Twenty?'

'Everyone knows One and Twenty,' said Flip, passing the bottle and taking his cards.

'How long you want to stay here?' one of the shy new-comers asked Harald, showing too much of his hand as he took the bottle. Ipth glanced at his friend's cards and began furiously sorting through his own. Fime was less subtle, peering for as long as he dared, though he had a whistling breath, some bronchial problem, that gave him away and earned him a hard slap.

Harald smiled and had another go at lighting his pipe. 'Perhaps a week, maybe two. I have permission?'

'I'm the boss here,' Ipth said. He gave Harald a sly smile, showing a row of dainty, plaqued teeth. 'Give me ten *Cocolles*, you can stay as long as you like.'

This was met with a peal of squeaky laughter from the others. Harald grinned as he played his hand, counting out the cards. A *Cocolle* was clearly something pricy or obscene. It would take him centuries to hear it all.

'Let's call it twenty, for a month.'

Their eyes widened. 'Twenty *Cocolles*?' Fime repeated, open-mouthed, pointing his cards at Harald's tent. 'You don't have twenty *Cocolles* in there!'

'Of course I do!' Harald shrugged. 'Doesn't everyone keep twenty *Cocolles* in their tent, just for emergencies? Had thirty once, but it all got a bit messy.'

The Devilmen appeared to find this uncommonly amusing. Harald played it straight, shrugging again, as if mystified. 'Why? How many do you have?' he asked Fime, singling him out. Ipth squealed and slapped his friend. Two of the newcomers were weeping with laughter.

'Not as many as you!' Fime managed, still crying whistly laughter.

Ipth punched his arm, unable to control the tears in his eyes. 'You don't have *any*!'

Flip couldn't hold his composure any longer. 'He means *females*! *Cocolles* are' – he paused to cry laughter – 'girls!'

Harald smiled, shrugging. 'I knew that.'

'Show us your *Cocolles*, then,' said Ipth, wiping his eyes, clearly unused to deadpan.

Harald put his cards face down and made to stand. 'Wait... you just want to see my cards!'

They all laughed at this, slapping each other on the back.

Harald reclined in his chair, looked at their sozzled little faces. His forty years of travel had taken him from the humid jungle moons of Indak-Australis to the dark, temperate worlds of the Never-Never and the Whoop, drifting from place to place like a happy, self-contained seed, never to germinate. He'd made lots of friends and a select few enemies, becoming acquainted with the Prism races better, he assumed, than any Amaranthine had before, learning all their broad languages – even Bult, though it was difficult – and gaining a solid grasp of the dialects he came across in every place he visited.

It was the way he treated them, he supposed: never showing fear, teasing them when necessary, but above all wearing his humanity on his sleeve; self-deprecation and slapstick good humour were methods of induction in the many worlds of the Prism. They liked to laugh – what were their short, harsh lives good for otherwise? – and yet the Amaranthine in all their loftiness had little inkling of this. Harald suspected that some of the Prism he met, Lacaille and Vulgar especially, were a good deal smarter than some Immortals, and yet the Firmament regarded them all as mentally deficient primates, glorified monkeys too mischievous and disorganised to amount to anything, let alone become worthy successors to *Homo sapiens* when the species finally died out, as it surely would soon. It was true that they were often quick to anger and slow of learning, almost always lazy and prone to murder, but they were peoples of their environment – prosperous in drama and bored in peace.

Harald suspected that, had the Amaranthine nurtured the Prism in antiquity, as the Venerable Tarim began to with the subordinate *Piffous* seven thousand years ago, things would now be quite different. These little people, genetically the closest the Amaranthine would ever have to children and true successors, were capable of greatness, but thousands of years of prejudice had denied them their due.

'Hey – what will you do now?'

Harald looked at Ipth, honestly confused. 'What will I do?'

'There is a new Emperor. Aren't you all supposed to go home?'

Harald felt the moon turning beneath his toes. He stared at Ipth, searching for the joke.

'Amaranthine?'

Harald recovered his composure. 'No, not me.' He looked into the darkening palms. 'I can stay out here as long as I want.'

He relit his pipe and sat back a little, smoking until their eyes were all on him. 'When did you hear this?'

'Half a year ago, maybe,' said Ipth.

'And did they tell you the new Emperor's name?'

Ipth shook his head. 'Doesn't matter, does it? He'll be the last.'

Harald looked into the flames, not replying.

Their conversation turned to the latest wrecked ship – a Vulgar warship scuttled down by the delta, perhaps hunted into the volume by Lacaille in their war out in the Void – but Harald had mostly stopped listening. The new Emperor would surely have no purpose for him if he went back; they'd likely bang him up in prison again, perhaps this time for longer.

He thought of kind old Sabran, the Firmament's latest and most inconsequential Emperor; already suffused with voices in his head, he had sent Harald off on a task that would take up the best part of half a century in the hope of saving the Law of Succession from the impatience of junior Perennials intent on the throne before their time. It was called the Last Edict of Procyon, and gave powers of immunity to any Assassin nominated by the Emperor to go about the Firmament and Investiture removing those who dared question the law. That was what Harald had been, an Assassin. So far, he'd slain one hundred and five of his one hundred and eighty-six revolutionaries, and had been in the process of searching for the next here on this moon.

Returning briefly to the Firmament three years ago to find he had acquired, for his many killings, the name *Harald Hundred*, he understood he was now a pariah in the eyes of twenty thousand Amaranthine. The Satrap of Epsilon Eridani, ignoring Sabran's order that Harald be allowed to pass unmolested, had thrown him briefly into the Thrasm of Port Maelstrom, perhaps out of fear that he might himself be on Sabran's list of dissenters.

Harald remembered those twenty-three hours vividly. Reeking darkness augmented by a hood and shackles. Voices all around him, questioning, poking, a tongue slathering up his belly. Harald had spoken to the mysterious Cunctus himself, he was sure of it – a dry, cracked voice emanating out of the darkness. They'd wanted to eat him, whispering their intentions in obscure Wulmese.

The shy one was holding up his hand, growing tired and supporting his arm like a schoolchild.

'Yes?'

The Devilman thought carefully before he phrased his question. 'What stops an Amaranthine lying about their age? You know, to get power?'

Harald looked at the little person, impressed. 'You'd be taking a big risk claiming seniority with no powers to back up your claim. And anyway, we have long memories – most people in the Firmament have known each other for ten or eleven thousand years, sometimes more.' He paused, worried he'd used too many big words. 'No – far easier to claim you are younger than you are, thereby hiding your abilities.'

They all seemed to like this answer, gabbling among

themselves almost too quickly for him to understand. Harald concentrated hard on listening in.

'How old are you, then?' Ipth asked, not raising his hand as the shy one had.

'I am twelve thousand five hundred and nineteen years old,' he said, enjoying the looks on their faces as his answer sank in.

Ipth was the first to speak. 'I don't believe it. What was the year you were born?'

'Twenty-one twenty-nine.'

They muttered between themselves, beginning the calculation.

'And you?' Harald asked Ipth.

Ipth looked up. 'Fourteen six-twenty-six,' he said proudly. He was twenty-two, already a father of fifteen. The others answered in kind. Flip was the youngest, at only seventeen. Harald felt a twinge of sadness looking at them all; the life expectancy here, discounting mass infant deaths, was twenty-five. It was over for them before it had begun.

He listened again to Fime's whistling breaths, and now it appeared he was released from his deathly duties, he decided to try something he promised himself he'd never do.

'Come here,' he said.

Fime wandered over, ears pricked.

'It's all right. May I place my hand on your chest?'

Fime snorted, looking back at his friends, but sidled up to Harald's hand.

Harald concentrated, picturing the Devilman's tiny lungs. He felt the heat in his palm and fingers. Fime must have, too, for he began to struggle in his grasp, whimpering, the down all over his body slick with sudden sweat.

'Shh,' Harald whispered, noticing their agitation, gripping harder. Ipth began to shout, thinking his friend was being murdered before his eyes. Harald closed his eyes, feeling little fingers wrenching at his arms, scratching into his flesh. A few more seconds. Something hard and rounded slammed into the side of his head, but he kept his eyes closed.

There. He opened his eyes and looked down at Fime. The little Devilman was dribbling with sweat, eyes wet with tears. Harald could feel the Prism's tiny heart thrashing through his skin. The other five stood around him, wide-eyed. Harald let go of Fime and looked down at himself.

A thick sliver of glass – a piece of shattered bottle – was buried halfway into his thigh. His gaze returned to the Devilmen as they grabbed Fime and fled back into the forest, their feet scrabbling in the bones.

The blow to his head had loosened the tune. Harald took up his guitar again as the stars wheeled overhead. He strummed a few chords, watching their bright points, remembering it whole.

It was called *Fantasia on a Theme*, he remembered now. Not at all right for his instrument, having once been performed on a double string orchestra, and yet surely the most beautiful piece of music ever composed. He played and watched the stars, the sigh of breeze through the palms accompanying him like woodwind, and was happy again.

Two days later, packing up his sun charts, Harald decided on a place to go next. He was free now, effectively on holiday, and could go wherever he wished. Of course, the Firmament was off limits – he had no estates there, they'd stripped him of everything – and even the Old World was too much visited by the Amaranthine to be a place of any lasting sanctuary. He could perhaps make his way to the Utopias and try to find Sabran, but it was a fool's errand travelling trillions of miles in the hope of exoneration by an insane old man. No, he liked the Investiture and its peoples. He would stay out here until his dying day – probably slipping into madness while they plundered his home, but at least his wealth would go to those who needed it.

A crunch of bones, somewhere behind, brought his head around. It was Fime, alone this time. The Devilman appeared to have put on weight already.

'Hello. How're you feeling?'

'Better now, Amaranthine,' Fime said, his voice clear of the whistle. 'Thank you.'

'My pleasure,' he replied, shaking Fime's offered hand.

'They were going to come at night and kill you,' he said, scuffing at a bone with the toe of his shoe. 'They don't like magic.'

'It's not magic,' Harald said, 'but I understand.'

When Fime was gone, Harald brewed a pot of coffee and went down to the river to wet his hair. He was glad to have helped the little person, but he wouldn't do it again. One couldn't go through life pulling insects out of webs or the spiders would starve. When he was done, he washed his feet and trod back up to the tent, untying the bandage around his leg and inspecting the wound, wondering whom they had chosen to take the helm of such a weak institution as the Firmament. It had not escaped Harald's attention that the Vaulted Land of Virginis had been ruined by some kind of bomb a year and a half ago, but any news after that was vague and slow coming. Harald had decided he was better off out of it anyway, and that perhaps the assignment Sabran had given him was a blessing after all. The legend of the oldest of them had persisted, doggedly, through the Age of Decadence and into modern times; someone would come – the exacter of justice, the Assassin, someone born naturally immortal – and cure the Firmament of its ills. But this Aaron they'd all been talking about, whoever and whatever he might be, was not that person. The Long-Life had merely used the belief in the legend to his own gain, taking advantage of a desperate species of people as they watched their empire rot away around them.

He studied the morning sun as it lumbered out of the dust, over the palms and into the sky. A sparkly, blue-tinged star, fading now, was still just about visible far above. Harald went to his chair, pouring the coffee and glancing once again at the ring of little worlds he'd bookmarked in his charts. He held the cup to his mouth, breathing in its heady steam, and peered back at the morning sky, singling out the dwindling blue star. Humaling and all its myriad moon-kingdoms; owned by nobody in particular, marked by fear. It was the only place he'd not yet set foot, and it fascinated him.

THE OLD TORINN

The country of Pan was the size of three Southern Provinces. It extended from the roof of Tail – that vast, dangling continent that spread down into the Nostrum – all the way to the Ingolland Sea and beyond, where Eranthis had heard the Melius were smaller and shyer, wizened like Demian folk. It was something to do with temperature, Jatropha said: the hotter the Province, the larger its peoples. She supposed that was why the Jalan were so huge, out in their jungle Counties, where the sweat was said to steam from your body. She missed heat, gazing from her rain-flecked window aboard the Wheelhouse *Corbita*, currently rumbling through the fallow lands that surrounded the city of The Old Torinn.

The Wheelhouse was on its ninth crash of the trip, having tipped over on stony ground a few days back, almost lying there for good until a band of helpful Cursed folk had come along to assist with the levering. As a precaution, Jatropha had installed great iron spikes that stuck out from the railings (and upon which they'd taken to hanging the bedsheets to air), ready to catch the great contraption if it fell, and they'd spent all day hoisting the vehicle back into an upright position, cursing the thing with every exertion. Each cracked spoke lost them precious time – another Quarter spent fixing something as the baby Arabis slipped further out of reach.

Eranthis stepped out onto the balcony, kicking aside some rubbish so that she could close the door behind her. She saw no point in cleaning up any more, knowing Pentas wouldn't help her and that the whole thing would just rumble off the road and crash into a forest again, spilling everything that wasn't tied and bolted down. Out on the narrow balcony they had some chairs, still wet from the brief squall earlier that morning. She sat on one, grimacing at the dampness of the cushion beneath her, and watched the city swell before them.

The Awger's face, peeping shyly at her from the shadows, came back to her now, amid the chill of the air. Only Eranthis, who had come the closest, had noticed how it couldn't blink; the creature's eyelids had been removed. From the look of its patchy, scarred pelt, it must have seen a few fights in its time. She imagined its journey, the baby tucked under an arm, pushing its way through the wilderness, through the dark.

Eranthis turned to the scullery window. Pentas's shape sat there, diffuse behind the glass, day in and day out, the warmth of the hob her only company.

The Old Torinn, the first real Westerling city on the road out of Tail, was most travellers' introduction to the harsh realities of Western life. Every newcomer passing through its gates arrived within a labyrinth of wooden corridors, walking divested of their luggage and means of transport to an open square surrounded by spyholes. Like much in the West, a land of covered eyes and darkened houses, to *look* was to judge: conversations with strangers were held with downcast eyes or from behind sheets of cloth, and portraits of any kind were forbidden in the city. Even personal questions, innocent though they might be as a way of getting to know someone, were permitted only after a second meeting.

Pentas followed her sister and the Amaranthine, the old codger disguised this time as another handsome local specimen, through the maze and out into the cool square filled with wooden cubicles. The sound of murmuring conversations packed the acoustic space like the drone of bees, while up in the walls hundreds of painted spyholes flapped open and clacked shut, examining them covertly. They followed a chalk line on the stone to their own cubicle, taking a seat.

'Don't say *anything*,' Jatropha muttered, hunched at the table.

Eranthis glanced at her sister, sitting mute and lost in her own world. *Not much danger of that*. Pentas and Jatropha hadn't spoken a word to each other for the ten whole days since the child's abduction – quite a feat in the Wheelhouse's cramped cabins. She looked at them both for a moment, realising that this was the closest they'd come physically, too, forced together like this at the Westerly border.

Eranthis yawned and scanned the holes in the walls, watching their little wooden doors slamming open and shut, scrawny Western hands hanging on the hinges. A spyhole on the wall behind them remained open for an uncomfortable amount of time, she noticed, only clacking closed when she twisted to look directly at it. In the cubicle beside them she could see a pair of large, red feet with a rope of bells around one ankle. Her eyes wandered to the table in front of them. It had been scratched into over the years, names and dates and little pictograms drawn and written in the styles of every Province. She spotted Jalan script: boxy letters chiselled hard into the wood.

'Oh, come on.' She sighed, rocking back and forth on her stool. Pentas began to carve her own patterns into the table with a stylus provided on a string, Jatropha watching dispassionately. After a moment, he grabbed her hand. Eranthis stared at them, turning her eyes to the table.

She'd begun to carve her daughter's name.

As if on cue, a slot in the panel opened up, exposing a delicate Westerly mouth.

'Can I look, please?' the mouth asked, showing the blue-stained teeth of a compulsive sweet-eater.

'You may,' Jatropha replied at once, having clearly been through the process before. The uppermost slot was shoved aside, and eyes – still disconnected from the mouth by a gap between the slots – peered in at them.

'You are a resident,' the disjointed face said to Jatropha. It wasn't a question.

'I live on the Ogrile Hill,' he replied. 'These are my nieces.'

The eyes took no interest in Eranthis or Pentas. 'Yes, family is fine. You should not have been sent here if you're local. This is the wrong box.'

'Ah, but I have meetings,' Jatropha said. 'I need a night token.'

The mouth issued a sigh, pausing while some fingers came into view to massage the brow. 'I can give you *one*. But you're in the wrong box.'

'One's enough, thank you.' Jatropha took the token as it came through the mouth hole and stood to leave. 'Won't happen again.'

'It most certainly won't. I'll be making a note of this.'

'Thank you, please do,' he replied over his shoulder. He glanced at Eranthis. 'Come on.'

'Why were we in there, if we didn't need to be?' asked Eranthis, running to catch up.

'So that Callistemon's brother knows where to meet me tonight.'

The bonestone gates were innocuous, set into a high, slogan-stained wall peeling with bills and boards. Weeds had sprung up in the hinges and danced to the light wind. Jatropha gave the place little more than a cursory glance as he ascended the steps and let them in.

Eranthis followed behind, closing the gate after herself and Pentas.

'It's beautiful,' she said, after the moment had passed.

'It's home.' Jatropha smiled, looking at her. 'Now and again.'

The house was of the Nostrum conical style; a bell-shaped tower of faded blue. The gardens, groves of shady olives that looked recently tended, extended right up to the door.

'When did you last come here?' she asked, taking in the small, weed-free pools.

'The year before last, for a night or two.'

The house itself was unlocked, the front doors opening onto a grand hallway. Jatropha threw his sunhat onto a chair and stalked off, slamming a door behind him. Eranthis and Pentas looked at one another, taking in the cool, high-ceilinged hallway, the walls decorated with framed pictures.

Nearly every other door in the place was locked. Eranthis couldn't help but wonder whether it was just the symptom of a neglected house, or because the Immortal had something to hide. Those few left unlocked opened onto small, bare chambers stacked with boxes or piles of framed pictures thick with dust. Occasionally she glimpsed a troop of Butler Birds going about their business making the house habitable, and assumed they lived here all year round.

She sat in one of the bare chambers, listening to the birds' mutterings, the clang of pans and dishes. There must have been thousands of years' worth of history in this house, hidden behind its graffitied, street-facing walls. Memories from a time when her and Jatropha's families might have been related, perhaps even one and the same. Eranthis heard a grumbling sound and noticed a plastic box, about the size of a person's head, near her shin. It had white slabs like feet sticking out beneath it. She nudged it with her toe and it abruptly woke up, staggering around the room. Twin spots of colour appeared on its forward-facing side and it swiftly located the door, stumbling out of the chamber and reeling along the hall. Eranthis went to the door and watched it bumping off the walls until it finally disappeared around a corner.

The land to either side of The Old Torinn's swampy river had been turned into a lush garden that ran through the middle of the city, thick with date palms and papyrus. This dense, forested valley was the clandestine site of the city's merchant courts, and as a result of the Westerly attitude to introductions, business could only be conducted there in the dark. Unsurprisingly, the practice tended to attract some of the more nefarious Westerlings, those come to take advantage of the rich pickings afforded by blind midnight transactions. Merchants who went there tended to huddle in groups around large bonfires, quite aware of the dangers, until commanded by law to venture away from the fires and out into the blackness just so that money could change hands. To stay visible to each other in the gloom, they coloured themselves white, and it was amid a spectral woodland of white forms that Jatropha discovered the fire he was looking for.

He walked into the light, the eyes of the people there rolling to avoid seeing him even as they said their hellos. Jatropha did the same, studying their feet.

Three to his left: a set of yellowish, notably Secondling toes.

He looked up, meeting the man's gaze.

Xanthostemon Berenzargol, SecondPrince, was considerably older and broader than his brother Callistemon had been, but the similarity was still striking. He looked at Jatropha expectantly for a moment, before gesturing to the darkness of the palm grove behind the fire. They stepped together into the gloom.

'They think there might be a Skyling on the prowl,' Xanthostemon said, glancing away from the fire and into the rustling palms. He spoke fine Modan, the lilting High Second hardly showing. 'People are being found in bad ways.'

'Well, we won't be long out here,' Jatropha said. 'The Awger?'

Xanthostemon looked at him hard in the firelight, as if trying to see past his disguise. 'It didn't come this way, but Awgers have no special loyalty to one another. I'll find it.'

Jatropha nodded, conscious that they'd broken about three city laws already during their brief discussion. 'Do you have time to come back to the house?'

Xanthostemon looked off to the city's lights, broken up by dark palm fronds. 'We're leaving first Quarter. She's with you, then? The girl?'

Pentas was examining a series of framed Melius portraits when the sounds of the Butler Birds caught her attention. She peered around a corner, watching them as they busily lit fires in the house's main reception room; something they hadn't bothered to do for her or Eranthis, she noted. She felt her heart squirm in her chest: Jatropha was coming. And he was bringing someone.

She waited, sweat prickling her skin, hardly noticing as the birds dusted their twiggy fingers and made to leave, bustling past her. The fires crackled, the scent of hot dust clogging the hall.

Footsteps, just outside the door. Muffled conversation and a pause. That first *click clack* of a door being fiddled with, the sound that stops a heart.

The Amaranthine entered, always startling her when she saw him in disguise, as he was now.

She waited, a lump rising in her throat.

Out of the darkness came a man that could have been Callistemon, half a year dead. He was heavier, more careworn, as if the corpse had sagged and pruned in its salty seaside grave. The twisted effigy of her lost love shot her a glance, a look that took her back as easily as a remembered scent.

'Pentas,' Jatropha supplied, studying them from beside the fire, and she felt her legs weaken.

The man's expression stayed fixed as he advanced upon her, and Pentas let her shoulders drop, their eyes locked. His left fist was balled slightly, the tendons prominent, his breath coming out in a shudder. He loomed over her. Jatropha would stand and watch, she knew.

But then Xanthostemon was dropping to one knee.

'I'm so sorry,' he said quietly, eyes creasing shut.

Pentas felt something crack open inside her, the tears already streaming down her face.

The Butler Birds looked aggrieved to have to prepare dinner so late, until one stern word from Jatropha sent them scurrying to the kitchen. Eranthis watched him interact with them, annoyed to discover that she quite admired the way he handled his servants. There were jobs to do and no time for nonsense. She stood between doorways, watching Xanthostemon and Pentas talking quietly together in the adjoining room, switching her attention back to Jatropha as he harangued the birds. They were the same breed Lycaste had once owned, she supposed, though they looked a little plumper around the middle from all the years spent living idle in the company of Jatropha's excellent food and wine.

'Those lazy creatures,' he said, pushing past her to the dining room. 'They're lucky to have work at all.'

Eranthis frowned, smiling, watching him fussing messily at the table. 'Can I help? I feel a little useless just standing here.'

He looked up at her, distracted, a colander in his hand. 'No. Save your strength. Pentas will need you, later.'

It came time to sit, the lanterns awakening, the fires puttering warmly in the grates, and Eranthis felt a growing tension at the table. Xanthostemon was tired, hardly eating, and it seemed clear that he'd rather be gone. Eranthis watched him, imagining with every mouthful the little Arabis spirited further and further away. There wasn't time for this.

'Its name is Billyup,' Xanthostemon said after a silence. 'Though it goes by Brimhup, sometimes Yardlie.' His eyes moved to Pentas and then back to his plate before he spoke next. 'It's wanted for ... a lot of things.'

'Your cousin in Pan,' Eranthis said, 'he's on the trail, though?'

Xanthostemon nodded. 'He is. But it's not just a case of tracking the beast, you understand. There are others after it, too. We have to be careful.'

Jatropha swilled his wine in its cup, setting it aside without taking a sip. 'How long?'

Xanthostemon ate quietly for a while before he looked up. 'It had a week's head start. There are a lot of places to search.'

They fell silent save for the quiet scrape of cutlery. It took Eranthis a while to notice that Xanthostemon was looking at her.

'My brother mentioned you in his letters, too, Eranthis.'

She glanced away from him, feeling a crawl of revulsion, remembering the way Callistemon had once looked at her. 'Oh yes?'

'He wrote fondly of you all, actually,' Xanthostemon said softly, sitting back.

Eranthis thought for a while before she spoke, aware of Pentas's charged presence beside her. 'All the while knowing what he was going to do, you mean?'

They stared at each other, before Pentas suddenly broke the spell.

'*He changed his mind,*' she whispered.

Xanthostemon looked back down at his plate. 'Yes, at the last. He didn't deserve his fate, despite his flaws.'

Eranthis made no reply at first, picturing the man's slow

death from that interminable disease. 'The illness was quick,' she lied, putting down her knife, not wanting to look him, or anyone else, in the eye as she spoke.

For a long time, Xanthostemon didn't respond. She felt his eyes on her, questioning, as if daring her to admit it wasn't so. She steeled herself and looked up.

'What illness would that be?' he asked. He sat very still, his fork laid aside.

She glanced between Pentas and Jatropha, realising that Xanthostemon mustn't have known. 'I'm sorry,' she said. 'I thought Jatropha, in his letter...'

Xanthostemon glared at Jatropha for a moment. 'They caught his *murderer*. The man came to our house. Don't try to tell me that—'

'What?' Pentas breathed, looking suddenly unwell.

'Callistemon was *ill*,' Eranthis said. 'He died from it. We saw it happen.' She glared furiously at Jatropha, understanding that some poor soul had paid for the Amaranthine's thoughtlessness. 'We *buried* him.'

Xanthostemon was staring at the table, his mouth working gently. 'But... the man, the man-boy, the Tenthling... He was with us, he—' He looked up. '*Lycaste*. Do you know that name?'

'*What?*' Eranthis gasped.

'It was Lycaste. They said he murdered my brother.'

Pentas went pale.

Jatropha leaned forward. 'What are you saying, Xanthostemon?'

'He stood trial,' Xanthostemon said, glancing between them. 'But then the First, they came and took him.'

The table fell silent but for their breath, the soft ticking of a clock somewhere growing suddenly, insistently loud.

GATHERING

The firelight was green, emanating from a wooded hillock in the marshes about half a Crule away. Billyup watched it intently for a while, unblinking, then continued his slog through the dark water, the Babbo bound up again in case of noise.

For a week he'd waded the flat brown paddy fields, ears alert, fishing with a line in the evenings and plucking lollyseed from the banks of the ditches. He'd seen nobody except messenger birds stopping to rest in the holes in the marshes, managing to catch a few as they preened, reading their letters while he crunched them whole. Provincial news; the movements of small militias, the motions of money. A lady named Maluse wrote to her husband complaining of his absence, while sending another to her lover instructing him to come as fast as he could. To the Babbo he gave the feathers, and was amused to see how she loved the pink and blue and green little things. He'd taken some and sewn them into his cloak, hoping she might warm to living on his back.

Billyup came level with the hillock. Voices drifted across the water to him.

He waded closer, his steps slow beneath the water so that he slid unheard to the hillock's muddy edge. The flames of the fire rose high and slim, like a poplar tree made of light, and around them sat the lively, unmistakable silhouettes of Demian folk.

He watched. There were six of the little mammalish people. Maybe a seventh relieving himself in the trees. They were drinking zest: Billyup could smell it. He shifted in the water, the mud having set a little around his feet.

The Babbo began to grumble. He lifted a hand and bopped her on the head, realising too late that he oughtn't to have done it. The thing cried out beneath her layers; a sharp squeal that penetrated the cloth like a blade, catching the attention of those at the fire. Billyup stumbled and almost fell, planting a hand in the mud to steady himself and whacking the Babbo again with the other.

Now they were all observing him, furred black outlines.

'Who's this?' said one of the little people, staggering to the hillock's edge and peering down at him. 'An Awger, is it?'

Billyup was acutely aware that his features were perfectly visible in the firelight. He pulled down his hood.

'What's it doing out here?' asked a soft, feminine voice. Billyup peered through his hood at her, shying from the light. They spoke in Modan, the dialect of the Outer West, but he could understand it well enough, being similar in form to Low Second.

'You hungry? Will you sit?'

Billyup wavered, trembling in the water, and scented again the bright smell of the zest. He'd sit with them, take some of that spirit, see what they were like, what they had.

'Would it please you to see my tricks?'

The Demian lady, Garew, had pretty eyes. He gazed at her furred face, then down at the beads in her hands.

'See,' she said, running her little fingers along the beads. 'Twenty balls of glass.'

Billyup nodded, eyes wandering to the silk purse that peeped out of her pocket and then up to her four small breasts. Her cape was open, and he could see that her teats were perky, swollen.

'Now watch.' She turned the string of beads over once. Billyup counted quickly. There was one less. She turned her hands over again, and now there were two more. His eyes followed the trick as best they could but were too slow for it. He took another swig of wine, drooling some into his lap. He could feel himself growing sleepy. The Babbo, though it was a Melius, seemed to charm the Demian folk. They were still passing her to one another, chattering in nonsense-speak. She giggled and wriggled, fully awake now. A bright green Butler Bird, perhaps defected from some household, took the child and kissed her warmly on both cheeks. Billyup fixed the child with his lidless gaze, resolving that he would only let her out of his sight this once.

'Come,' he said thickly, seizing Garew's hand. The others didn't notice him taking her out of the fire's warmth and into the stands of trees around the hillock's other side.

They coupled easily enough for two of such different breeds and sizes, her panting growing more ragged as he pressed his weight on top of her. When it was done, they went back to the fire and drank more wine together, holding hands until he shook his away and pulled his cloak around him.

Billyup looked among them from the dark depths of his hood. There were too many to steal from. He took the Babbo from the eldest, swigged the last of the zest from their bottle and left without saying his farewells, stumbling back into the dark paddy fields and wading away.

THE RETURN

Maril woke with a start, prickling with sweat. He sat up and unholstered his pistol. There was a scent of rich, unusual burning in the air. He had been dreaming of the wraiths from Coriopil again, and the helmet collar that had saved his life. Could they have foreseen his destiny, somehow? Had they known that he would come here? He took a moment to remember precisely where *here* was, and resigned himself to what he had to do.

The crew were clustered around the window. Maril climbed to his feet and joined them.

They had stopped beneath a great accumulation of cut

branches near the summit of the tree. The long-fingered mammal was bustling about, and some smaller variants of its kind were at work sawing through a collection of narrower branches. A blue fire in a chimney-shaped brazier poured wisps of smoke across the scene. When Maril went to the window, the mammal gave them a quick glance, beady golden eyes registering his arrival, before going back to work. Maril developed the impression that his crew were not the first Vulgar the creature had seen.

'I don't trust him,' he said. 'Gramps. He's keeping us here.'

Jospor turned to him, chewing a mouthful of fungus.

Maril checked his pockets quickly, delaying his decision, then cleared his throat. The crew looked at him tiredly.

'I'm going back to find the Threshold. Who's with me?'

They snapped their mouths shut. Even Jospor averted his eyes. Finally Guirm pushed forward, his lumen rifle slung over one shoulder.

Maril nodded, clapping the little gunner on the shoulder. 'All right. We won't be long. It can't have been more than a few hours' walk.'

'But we've been lifted all the way up—' Jospor began.

'We're *going*,' Maril interrupted, feeling suddenly foolish and wanting to stay. But he'd made his choice now and couldn't be seen as indecisive. 'We need to know we can find the way out again.'

He said his quick goodbyes, clapping the salute. They clapped weakly back, Jospor breaking from the pack and embracing him. As he did so, the branch began its wobbling ascent once again, and Maril knew he had to go.

He took the lumen rifle from Guirm – a stubby, soldered-together weapon, its wooden stock carved with the initials of every previous owner – and together they went out the way they'd entered, clambering into a thick breeze of flotsam that coated Maril's face and hair. He shouldered the rifle and glanced quickly at the drop, unable to tell how high they'd been lifted during the night. Sounds of the woodsmen still drifted from the other side of the dwelling, and he was careful they remain hidden while he stared out into the branches, taking his bearings.

Up here, the trees were alive with activity; shaggy grey mammalian forms wandered along branches, their ungainly, cobbled-together homes carried on their backs. Smaller, lither things darted, leaping between the canopies. Dense drifts of the twinkling red and gold flotsam swept over the trees like banks of drizzle, moving with the sigh of the wind. The smell of the higher branches was a thick, syrupy perfume, likely produced by the nuts and leaves of these trees, and underfoot the suede texture of the branch was sticky with sap.

Maril moved across the branch until he was at its sawn-off point, creeping carefully to its swaying edge as he spotted the notched steps cut into the tree. It would require a small leap – nothing he couldn't have done on level ground, if the drop beneath the gap hadn't been so sickeningly enormous. Maril glanced at Guirm, then steeled himself, tensing, and leapt, feeling the suspended branch push away beneath him, shortening his jump. He almost missed the steps, hands grasping at nothing for a moment, falling heavily down the winding stair until his scraped and bleeding hands could find purchase. Guirm yelped and landed below him with a clatter of equipment, his saucepan escaping from his luggage and bouncing off down the steps. Maril inspected his bleeding, sap-sticky hands and scrambled downwards, remembering the ominous pop and tinkle of something shattering on his back as he'd hit the stair. It could only have been the lenses in the lumen rifle – they were so delicate that even the most ham-fisted Prism treated them like treasure, wrapping them up and polishing them. And now he'd gone and busted his only rifle.

He took a moment to lean back on the steps so he could examine the weapon, pulling the strap off his shoulder and opening up the casing. Guirm scrambled next to him, sweeping back his sweaty hair. Maril showed him the rifle with a sigh. As he'd suspected: one lens shattered, the other two cracked but intact. The rifle might still produce a weak beam, perhaps enough to start a fire, maybe even hobble an enemy, but nothing more.

'Shit,' he breathed, slinging it across his back again and resuming the climb down, Guirm going ahead with his spring pistol drawn. After another few feet the trunk met an untouched branch and they both climbed across. He could see at least twenty of the great trees, stretching off into the distance until their forms were broken up by the expanse of forest. Things moved at the edges of his vision, climbing creatures pausing to look at him before going on their way.

Maril placed the lumen rifle down, sorting through the bits and pieces in his pockets. An old Lacaille compass – the only reliable make – was knotted to his belt, and he wondered if he might be able to use it now, having taken a quick look at it when they'd come through the Threshold. He untied it and peered at the little needle, which was swaying and trembling, alarmingly indecisive. Maril hadn't expected much; this place was nothing like a planet, and yet when they'd come through the needle had held still, pointing east. Now it suddenly stopped and turned, edging over to the south.

'What do you make of that?' he asked Guirm, angling the compass so the gunner could see it.

'It's drawn to something,' he said. They bent over the device as Maril swept it back and forth, trying to elicit a further response, but the needle wouldn't budge again.

Maril put it away, bending to pick up the rifle again.

'What—?'

Only the wooden stock remained. The weapon had been taken apart. Maril stared down the length of the branch as the gun's various component parts were carted off by little furred creatures, a few pieces of broken lens left behind.

'Oi!' shouted Guirm, giving chase along the branch. Maril shook his head and gazed back into the canopies, thankful he'd kept his spring pistol in his pocket, wishing Guirm wouldn't make so much noise.

The hairy little things reached the end of the branch and sprang to the next, twigs bobbing, dropping more pieces of his precious gun. Maril swore as he followed Guirm, collecting what he could, and stopped, woozy at the drop, watching them leaping into the darkness of the canopy below, his rifle parts quite lost.

Guirm turned back to him, wheezing and purple-faced, and together they sat heavily and looked at the pieces he'd managed to collect: the trigger guard, the trigger itself, the receiver and some tiny pieces of the smashed lens. Maril rolled them clinking in his palm and dropped the pieces contemplatively over the edge, watching them fall in a languid twinkle.

After some time spent lost in thought, the vertigo of the place unexpectedly soothing after so much time in thrall of it, Maril looked up, rubbing his eyes. At some point, Guirm must have risen and left him, for he was quite alone. The flotsam had suddenly grown thick, irritating his lashes. He glanced around, wondering where Guirm had got to, unsure whether to shout his name.

He stared into the canopies, ears pricked for the slightest sound. The trees had grown quiet.

Something landed further down the branch with a thump, startling him. It was a body, its faceless, muscle-scarlet skull gurning in Maril's direction. Maril's heart rose in his chest. The body was wearing Guirm's Voidsuit. On the branch above, a dark, spindly figure watched Maril through the haze of flotsam.

He leapt to his feet, breathing hard, his gaze locked on to the distant figure. Despite the mist of flotsam that separated them, it was possible to make out the Prism's willowy arms, mahogany skin and elongated, hairless skull.

A Bult.

A soft sound behind him, the sound of rasping breath. Maril tensed. *More than one.*

He wasted no time, sprinting and leaping the short distance to the trunk, slamming onto its spiral of steps. He half-slid, half-ran, the nails in his boots gripping just enough to stop him from falling. Above, he sensed the swift descent of something larger and faster – a heavy drumming of feet, a quick series of puffing breaths. Maril's heart hammered in his chest, an infernal pounding that accompanied the beating of his boots.

It was just above him now, getting closer by the second. Maril felt his boot slide out from under him at last and he grasped the trunk, sap gumming his fingers together. He snatched a glance over his shoulder as he rounded the curve of the trunk, realising he was invisible for a few precious seconds, thinking quickly. He climbed from the spiral stair onto the rough suede bark of the tree itself, working his way quickly down, the nails of his old boots digging in, shearing bark, until he was hanging between the two levels. Immediately he heard the Bult move past above, its breath echoing, and climbed faster, hoping against hope that it wouldn't have made its way around again before he reached the next level.

The sound of it rounding the stair, breath quickening, clearly having expected to find him there. Maril could hear his own breath wheezing out of him as he moved, arms burning, legs cramping. The next spiral was just below him. He jumped and landed, hearing the Bult arriving above, and clambered down again, hanging beneath the stair.

He began to climb, listening hard for the sound of footsteps, conscious that he ought to have taken his chances and jumped again. It was still a good hundred-foot drop to the forest floor. In between breaths, he realised the sound of his pursuer's footfalls had stopped.

Maril froze, his heart thrashing, a gripping ache spreading across his left arm. He reached carefully for his pistol and chanced a look down.

The Bult was staring up at him, close enough to touch.

He cried out, slipping, and felt the world disappear from under him.

EYRALL

They left the city that night, Jatropha harrying the exasperated birds out of the way and calling up the *Corbita*, against city laws. The rickety thing arrived, dragged up the causeway to the house by the gatemen.

Eranthis, her thoughts still reeling, found to her amazement that she'd missed the battered old Wheelhouse. It had been their home for the last few months, and sleeping anywhere that didn't rattle and sway incessantly all night had felt an odd prospect indeed. Jatropha's lonely house, though beautiful, was intolerably quiet and still.

The moonlight was bright enough to see the land all around the city, and when she looked up from the *Corbita*'s deck, the flurry of stars took her breath away. Lycaste *alive*, and now some hope that the baby Arabis was, too.

Xanthostemon, upon his departure, had asked Jatropha to wait for him in the Second, assuring them they would not be needed for what was to come. Eranthis had taken one look at the Immortal as he gave Xanthostemon his assurances, understanding that was never going to happen.

She smiled at the thought, seeing Pentas on the balcony, her hair blown across her face in the sharp night wind.

Eranthis joined her, climbing into the hammock of knotted bedsheets they'd suspended over the balcony and sitting up.

'We're not going to the Second, are we?' Pentas asked.

'I don't think so.'

The cold Eyrall, the Westerly wind of luck, quivered the sheets, working its fingers through Eranthis's hair. Out in the moonlight she thought she could see bats flitting, fighting against its current. Up in the tiller cabin, Jatropha had opened his portable orestone, and a light, sighing music drifted across the balcony. Eranthis thought she could smell the Immortal on the wind; he had a thin fragrance all of his own, quite unlike the sweet, oily musk of Melius folk. Jatropha's smell was comfort, security. She'd come to realise over the last few days that the nights she'd spent up in the tiller cabin with him had been some of the happiest times of her life.

Pentas was watching her when she glanced back, an intensity in her eyes. 'I can't believe it, any of it. He was out there, all along, thinking he'd . . . thinking—' She exhaled, the sentence forever unfinished. Eranthis shrugged, hearing the tea kettle squealing to a boil as the Wheelhouse rumbled into life.

'Someone must have seen us from the spyholes,' Jatropha said without preamble, Eranthis settling herself down beside him in the tiller cabin and handing him his tea. She shifted until she was comfortable, pulling the blanket out from behind the bench and draping it over her legs, then looked at him.

'How do you know?'

Jatropha seemed too preoccupied to answer her. His vacant stare, so still that it looked as if he might have died in his chair, told her he was too busy thinking.

'I did something you might not like,' he said at last, eyes returning to the road.

She snorted a laugh. 'Well, that's a first.'

The suggestion of a smile tightened his lips. 'The gatemen that brought the Wheelhouse up the hill – do you remember?'

She nodded. The poor sweating Westerlings who had dragged the *Corbita* to Jatropha's house, practically forbidden by law from looking where they were going.

'I made them look like us.'

Eranthis glanced sharply at him.

'They have our faces now,' Jatropha elaborated. 'Just in case.'

Eranthis was speechless for a moment. 'You mean—'

'They'll be chased instead.'

She sat back, imagining the chaos, the confusion. 'But that's so *cruel*—'

'I said you wouldn't like it.' He shifted the gear as they rumbled up the first of the hills outside the city. 'It'll wear off in a couple of days.'

'Still,' she said, flabbergasted. 'A couple of *days*. Those poor people ...'

Jatropha tensed, clearly frustrated, and turned to her at last. 'More is at stake, yes? Can we agree on that?'

She rolled her eyes and nodded. 'I suppose.' She looked out into the night. 'Our pursuers ... they wouldn't *torture* them, would they?'

Jatropha's silence told her everything, and she shivered as the Eyrall found their cabin.

'I will compensate them,' he said quietly.

She thought about that. 'They'll never know why it happened. It will change their lives.'

He cleared his throat and spat. 'That cannot be our concern.'

Eranthis opened the orestone's casing and set its dials in motion, not knowing what to say, unsure that she agreed with him. The first song to play was something she remembered from childhood, a lilting, distinctively pretty tune that everyone in the Provinces knew.

'"The Sea of Stars",' Jatropha said, singing gently to the lyricless tune. He had a surprisingly awful voice.

She listened, rapt, to the vulnerability in his tone, hearing in it a shade of Jatropha's deeper, unseen self.

When the tune changed, Eranthis found herself staring out into the moonlit hills, some selfish part of her wishing the journey would never end.

PART II

NINETY-ONE FIFTY-NINE

The little corkscrew ship slipped out of tetraluminal, entering sub-light speed with languid care, like a pin through a soap bubble.

Hui Neng saw the volume projected inside his eyes as a mono-chrome, soundless jungle of stars. A whisper spread through the darkness around him as the ship decelerated, the structure of the dagger-shaped hull sighing and cooling after its electric dash through the kingdom's outer realm. The buzz of the protective bell-field awoke with a snapping start, jolting him from his reveries, the ship falling within an invisible cowl of repellent power.

A dozen or so entities had broken from the pack to follow Trang Hui Neng's coilship as it slammed out of home port, taking up a formation in the slipstream behind, patient and predatory. Hui Neng saw no sign of them now, assuming they'd grown bored of the chase and taken off after easier pickings in the space around Aquarii. The Ordure had plenty of sapiens *backing; their ships were certainly as capable as those of the Immortal Directorate. It was only the relative paucity of their numbers that had drawn out the great siege into a twelve-year war of erosive attrition.*

The jungle of stars dappled and revolved, a speck of reflected starlight growing far, far below, and he felt the first stirrings of vertigo, his eyes encountering a meaningful distance at last as he gazed at the jumbled fleet of seven hundred thousand ships beneath, a conglomerate fortress under attack from invisible forces much smaller than their own.

'Come on,' he breathed, impatient, scared. He hadn't wanted to be here anyway; never wishing to see Wylde like this.

A Wunse soldier squirrelled inside another corkscrew chamber fiddled with a reading. 'Only a few moments more, Governor.'

Hui Neng swallowed and hardened his stare, magnifying the display. The ships jumped out, bright in the starlight: towering, brutalist silver columns, their thousand-ton cannons staring into the darkness. The ships on their bearing focused back on him, whispering Incantations across the distance. Hui Neng replied via his receiver. At his final sentence, the guns swivelled away.

The little craft darted in, a dashing speck lost among the labyrinth of gantries and cannons. Dazzling silver metal gleamed into his eyes before it could be dulled by the display. The humming of the craft intensified for a moment as it encountered the fields of the fortress ships, tangling, negotiating, and then died away. Hui Neng's own suit field, gaining weight as it met the great gravity of so much refined platinum hull and weaponry, snarled and burped. Those of his Wunse guards, less heavily protected, squealed and cut out.

They slipped through the shell of gunships and into a less densely populated volume of space, the inner sanctum, perhaps the safest place in the Immortal kingdom. Ahead of them lay Wylde's capital ship, a disconcertingly tiny speck of silver and blue that floated like a minnow among the lumbering bodies of its wall of gunships.

Detail resolved across the ship's surface, its shimmering blue markings gnarled with towers that cast long shadows in the starlight. The coilship aligned itself with one of the towers and coasted into a swirling orbit. Within three seconds they were staring down at the tower's slim peak, and half a second later were docking inside the mouth of a balcony.

Hui Neng's display darkened, the warm padding inside his helmet foaming up and melting into twin reservoirs on either side of his head. He took a little sip from his water spigot before it, too, disappeared into the streaming mulch and leaned his head back against the blast of cool air. Light filled his capsule and he stepped carefully down into the opened segment of hangar, a pristine, mirrored space devoid of anything but a small, naked Prismic person.

Hui Neng paused, the fields of his diamond cerulean armour growling and stuttering in a bass drumbeat. The noise of it echoed in the sparse chamber, conflicting with the rumbles of the remaining guards. He looked back. The two suited Wunse had also climbed out. This was as far as they could go.

Hui Neng had spent part of the journey wondering who would honour his debt first. He had an inkling Heremy, the thickset Wunse to his right, was the braver of the two.

Much to his surprise, Humphro went first, pulling up his sleeve and cutting roughly into the veins of his wrist. The other watched, engrossed, his skin like blue cheese under the hangar lights, and when Humphro lay collapsed and squirting on the floor he did the same, remembering to salute first in the Immortal way.

Hui Neng turned back to the Hominin person and they set off, the primate's little padding feet leaving dissolving heat stains on the floor.

It was rare to travel by ship these days. Hui Neng, having only recently passed out of his sleep phase, hadn't left his palace in almost a hundred and fifty years. Others he knew still slept, unreachable for solid decades. It appeared that the Immortal body went through cycles, and an unpleasant wakefulness seemed to be next.

He clumped along, his suit growling, trusting the little person to signal once it was safe to remove the great lumbering thing. Every minute of every hour the Ordure were striking at perceived weak spots around the fleet, testing defences and armaments, like a castle under hellish, constant siege. Of course, beside the burble of his suit magnets Hui Neng heard nothing: he was as far from any attacking Ordure ship as he was from the surface of Aquarii, and yet in these times nothing was certain.

Hui Neng tried to avert his eyes from the Prismic person's bottom as he walked: it was a dangling, crusty red protuberance, like a monkey's. The slaves went naked to prevent concealed weapons, but he fancied quite a lot could be hidden up there without much fuss. Its redness reflected around the mirrored silver of the corridor, taunting his eyes wherever they looked.

At last the air appeared to change, and they came to a glittering, diamond-shaped space that looked out upon the stars. The slave held up a finger and Hui Neng stopped, expecting that now might be the point to change out of his gear. Instead, the chamber sighed and rolled, revealing a gaping opening into a much larger space beyond. They proceeded through, and Hui Neng laid eyes on what he had come for.

The Most Venerable Wylde's bedchamber was the size of a stately garden of old. Its reflective walls were quite blinding for a moment until Hui Neng's eyes adjusted, spotting old friends gathered some distance away, their reflections in the great sloping silver walls swelling the numbers. He stepped closer, recognising Biancardi and Sabran talking beneath their breath, still wearing their monumental suits of armour. Sabran saw him and smiled, his suit burping out an adjoining greeting as its field tangled with Hui Neng's own. He couldn't believe that it still wasn't safe to take them off; perhaps it was their age – they still needed that comfort, the swaddling, protective weight of armour.

'How long?' Hui Neng asked as he came to them, observing the gathering around the bed. He wasn't ready to see his old friend, not yet – let these others, these strangers to whom their leader had no special connection, pay their respects first.

'No way to tell,' Biancardi said. 'We might be here some time, or it may well be very soon.'

They moved slowly closer, Hui Neng feeling as if his feet were being dragged out from under him, humming and crackling and growling together, their lowered speech struggling to penetrate the noise. There were still over a hundred Immortals between himself and the throne, a hundred squabbling egos each convinced they had a better strategy to defeat the Ordure.

They came to the bed.

Wylde lay quite motionless in a fan of exquisite grey silks, his eyes semi-closed, like a child pretending to sleep.

'He is in a trance very close to death,' Biancardi said, looking from their Emperor's scarred white face to the scribe, who had his ear poised as close as possible to Wylde's softly moving lips and was furiously noting down the whispers for the next in line to memorise.

'The Incantations?' Hui Neng asked, nodding at the scene.

'Almost completely recorded now,' said Sabran.

'When can I speak to him?' he asked, wishing he hadn't got here so late. Late, always so late.

'You'll have to wait until the scribe is done, I'm afraid,' Sabran replied, something in his tone suggesting that there might not be time left, even for that. Some Incantations were always lost with the passing of each Immortal Emperor: it was simply the way of things, since it had always been forbidden to write them down during an Emperor's reign. Everything from the operation of the Uncounted Vaults and the Foundries of Gliese to opening the innermost doors on ships of the line relied upon the Most Venerable's memory of spoken passwords – unique commands that activated the Motes: an invisible, seething cosmos of specks pumped into the atmosphere of every Firmamental space. There were now Motes of Persuasion floating around the Firmament that couldn't be used at all; sealed halls and useless machinery clogged the fine spaces of Gliese and Cancri; ships had begun to crash. There had to be a better system, a way of passing on such vital knowledge without weakening the Emperor's power.

Hui Neng gazed around the faces at the bedside, seething as he saw Sotiris Gianakos kneeling almost at Wylde's elbow. Everyone knew Hui Neng adored his Emperor the most, but there they were, letting Sotiris hear their father's final words.

Almost at that same moment the scribe looked up, scowling with something like frustration. Wylde's lips had stopped moving.

Hui Neng shot a suddenly furious glance at the scribe, who clearly didn't want to be the first to say anything. At last, a murmur spread through the assembled Immortals and they moved forward as one, peering at the dead face. Something in it had changed at that moment, but Hui Neng couldn't put his finger on what. The scribe was still bustling about with his writing materials, unwilling to be the first to speak.

Hui Neng watched the scribe stow the crystal pages of Incantations in a case, which folded in upon itself until it was the size of an antique postage stamp in his palm. Those closest crowded around, *their mutterings pierced with the grim choral hum of their suits. He searched their expressions for any emotion, any evidence of grief, and saw nothing. They were all of them, even Sotiris, dry as a bone, concerned only with the Law of Succession, their own personal gossip – some nonsense about mysterious powers developing in only the very eldest. He alone had been a friend to poor Wylde.*

His stinging eyes darted back to the scribe, who was making his way out of the chamber, already some distance away. A ship would be waiting, no doubt, to transport those Incantations to the vaults of Aquarii, there to be read only once, then destroyed.

Hui Neng whispered into the collar of his suit, signalling his own ship, and stormed from the chamber. Mild voices drifted after him, concerned, perhaps. They knew how he'd felt, but still they'd denied him the place by the bed.

He pushed past the naked Prism, sending it staggering, and lumbered into the rotating chamber.

'Come on,' he snarled to his automatic pilot when the doors had revolved, the stark hangar coming into view. His ship waited, a conical blue spike spattered with reflected hangar lights. 'Aquarii!' Hui Neng shouted, his throat aching with something more than the force of the yell. The coilship twisted, black fins extending from its fuselage. 'I want us at twenty over point, soon as we're beyond the flotilla.'

Once seated, the foam welled up again inside Hui Neng's suit, forming optical equipment over his eyes and fluffing into padding. His helmet clamped shut, drying the tears on his cheeks with a soft hiss of cool air.

THE WISHES

Furto woke with a start, spying Gramps creeping through the room, quite obviously attempting to soften his footfalls. Slupe, who was supposed to be on watch, was dozing in the corner. Furto slowed his breathing, watching from the shadows.

Gramps moved softly among them, wrinkling his nose, claws retracted into his toe pads. He was a queerly un-lizard-like lizard, for all Furto knew about the things, and barely resembled the herd of *Bie* he professed to watch over. Indeed, when Furto had first seen him back on Coriopil, Gramps had appeared to be of a different species entirely. In the few days that they'd known each other, he seemed to have changed, too, rapidly losing the fat around his middle and shedding scales, as if he were unwell. Furto stared a little longer, wondering. Perhaps he was; perhaps the air here was as bad for him as anyone else from the Prisms' neck of the woods, though Furto couldn't quite believe it.

The house swayed in the wind, a gust of flotsam blowing in. Gramps extended a claw to examine the contents of Slupe's bag, peering after a moment more into Veril's sleeping face. Furto watched him straighten and examine all the sleeping Vulgar in the room, noticing as the old *Bie*'s motions stiffened. He'd spotted that some were missing.

'Up!' he roared, snapping them all awake.

Jospor muttered, wiping his face, a ribbon of drool plastered across his chin.

'Where's your captain?' Gramps cried. 'Where's Maril? And that other one?'

'Ah,' Jospor said, rubbing his eyes. 'They were worried we'd lose our bearings, you see—'

'Sussh!' Gramps yelled from the window, his claws extended. 'Get after them!'

The house wobbled as something large sprang from the roof, the Osseresis's great shadow darkening the branch beyond the window.

'He'll be back, I'm sure,' Jospor pleaded, climbing to his feet.

'No he *won't*,' said Gramps emphatically, 'not without

Sussh's help.' He ran his grey tongue across his teeth, observing the mess they'd made of the place. 'But no matter, we must be off.'

'Sussh can find them, can't she?' Jospor asked. Furto noticed the plump little master-at-arms had the shine of tears in his eyes.

'Oh, probably not,' Gramps replied with an air of distraction. 'We have an appointment to make, and so does she.'

'I could stay and wait,' pleaded Jospor. 'Just for a few days—'

Gramps shot him a look. 'Don't be ridiculous. I need *all* of you.' He ducked through the doorway and into the morning light, kicking their waste bucket back into the room. 'Ablute, now!'

It took Furto almost a day's hard climbing to come to the realisation that they were headed up one of the arms of the Snowflake itself. Gramps, when asked, had replied only that they were travelling 'to the Invigilator', growing swiftly sullen thereafter, as if still brooding on Maril and Guirm's disappearance.

The white stairway, built of the same fissured base material from which the whole Hedron Star was made, rose in broken, craggy segments between dark forest, joining others as they branched in on either side. Furto wheezed and came to a stop, plonking his rear onto a step and staring at the others as they shuffled up behind.

'What?' panted Drazlo, clattering past. 'Why're you stopping?'

Furto ran his hand along the baked, worn slab – it was like bleached, eroded bone, chiselled with incomprehensible runic text and polished to marble grooves by countless ancient climbers before them – and twisted to glance up at the junction where this stair met the next.

'Gramps didn't say anything about climbing to the end of

the *pissing* Snowflake,' Furto muttered. 'I'm done. That's it for me. I'm staying here.'

'No you're not,' Drazlo said, without looking back.

Furto huffed and crossed his arms, finally climbing to his feet. He observed the remainder of the crew catching up, with chubby Jospor – officially their captain now, as far as anyone could tell – wheezing at the rear. The Osserine Sussh, back from her unsuccessful search for Maril, swept overhead; a great shadow muting the colours of their suits, the white of the stair quite dazzling again when she'd passed. Furto watched Slupe blow his nose messily into his hand, then unclip his britches and squat, deciding now was as good a time as any to do the same.

'Furto, you grub!' Veril wailed thinly. 'Wait until we've got past, will you?'

He grinned as they scuttled by, shifting on the step and mooning them.

SARSAPPUS

'There is a vastness to creation that you cannot have perceived, Vulgar,' Gramps explained while Drazlo and Furto clambered alongside, the pink sun beating down. The old *Bie* had grown more voluble as the days wore on, apparently pleased with their progress up the stair.

'The galaxies – or Thunderclouds, as they are known here – exist like a string of interdependent countries stretching off into the darkness,' Gramps continued. 'The very oldest of them, out somewhere beyond the limit of understandable distances, are connected to one another, but their histories are as ancient as the universe, and their news does not reach us out here except in the form of ancient myth.' He gestured to the sky. 'It is our local column, these three closely packed

Thunderclouds, in which the stories of antiquity are still sharply relevant.' Gramps paused for breath, checking on the progress of the crew down below; three little shapes quivering in the heat that rose from the steps.

'Your galaxy, of which we are at the very edge, was once a teeming place. It was called the Mighty Shadow during the time of the First-Born in the *way back when*, and existed in age-old harmony with the two other Thunderclouds in this column: the vast Gargantine Sovereignty, known on your Amaranthine charts as *Andromeda*, and its smaller but nevertheless quite potent neighbour, the Murmurian Domain. They were cousins, you see, the giant rulers of these galaxies. Imperial lines diluted and interbred over billions of years.'

Furto almost forgot the climb; his burned hands, scalded by the baking ceramic, ceased to sting; his calves, aching from the climb, lost their cramp.

But one day, Gramps explained, eighty million years ago, the accord failed. Old friendships were forgotten, all trade ceased, the debts called in. The Murmurian Domain attacked the Mighty Shadow, laying siege to its cousin and sending a force across the gulf to invade. Furto tried to imagine it, knowing his mind wasn't built to contemplate such scale.

Less than a hundred years later – a record, apparently, for the annexation of an entire Thundercloud – the Murmurian Domain had pursued the Mighty Shadow's rulers into hiding, hounding them until they capitulated all territories, and bringing them as prisoners back to the Murmurian Empire. The Gargantine Sovereignty, meanwhile, did nothing.

Gramps gave a stagey pause, as if thinking of how to go on. 'You cannot conceive of the power involved in laying siege to another galaxy; it is war magnified, they are like two... *titans* engaged in battle...' He trailed off, staring at them. 'As punishment for drawing things out so, the Murmuris sterilised your entire galaxy – something barely heard of in the history of the Greater Nimbus – killing off the life around every star.'

Furto and Drazlo glanced at one another.

'*Almost* every star, I should say, otherwise you two would not be listening to me now, and the Snowflakes would not be populated by the Osseresis. A few insignificant pockets that cooperated with the invasion were spared, one of which was your own star system – then ruled by the *Epir*, my ancestors – and were left to enjoy their liberty in an otherwise empty galaxy.'

Drazlo frowned. 'Who were the others? You said there were "pockets"?'

Gramps waved a clawed hand dismissively. 'One or two distant worlds, lying far, far beyond the limits of your Investiture. You and they shall never meet.' He hesitated. 'And of course any wandering planets – those black worlds without suns – would have escaped the punishment, too.'

'What—?' Drazlo asked, trying to articulate himself in the heat. 'What king could order such a thing? Such massacre?'

'Whoever it was, he's lucky he's dead and gone,' grumbled Furto.

Gramps walked silently for a moment, plodding on up the stair. 'Mmm, but he's not "dead and gone", you see. He's still very much alive.' He looked at them. 'They call him the Sarsappus, and you'd best watch your tongue; these very Snowflakes, though they lie at the edge of your dead galaxy, exist within *his* dominion, and the Invigilator we're travelling to meet serves him absolutely.'

A week or more must have passed. Nobody quite knew. The days here never felt of the same length. Drazlo guessed they ascended between ten and fourteen miles a day, climbing late into each night, the cold, crisp, unfamiliar stars glowering over them. This close to the edge, the great neighbouring galaxies looked particularly magnified; eddies of mist spun across the sky, their stars tinted red and gold.

Glancing back, they could begin to see the whole form of

the Snowflake taking shape, spreading out beneath them in parallel bands of black and cream, the umber golds of migrating flotsam churning across the world. Once Furto thought he saw a ship of some kind, ears pricking as he watched a speck dart silently in the darkness between two of the Hedron Star's great arms, covering the distance in seconds.

They ate the same meals of boiled nuts and fungus every day, complaining as little as they could. For water they were each given a long white tube that leaked tangy syrup when upended. Furto discovered after drinking too much on the first day that it was ever so slightly narcotic, and thereafter began to hoard his rations. The sun-bleached bones of many thousands of past unfortunates who'd not survived the climb lined the gutters to either side of the stair, and hollow-eyed Osserine skulls the size of suitcases, their fangs bared, snarled at the party of Vulgar as they walked. Furto spotted a tiny black mammalian thing gnawing away at a spur of bone inside one cracked-open skull, slowing to watch it at work. The animal snapped the piece off with a grunt, inspecting it and blowing experimentally through one end to produce a soft, breathy musical note, not unlike a flute.

It was mercifully forbidden to sleep on the stair, so each night, Gramps led the tired crew across to one of the great black trees that lined the steps and into a hollowed-out nut dwelling. Furto imagined with a shudder how easy it would be to slip in the dark: one missed step and you'd fall for days.

Their group was hosted in each dwelling by silent, staring mammalian occupants that gave Furto the creeps. Gramps allowed them no more than three and a half hours of sleep every night, and warned them against straying from the branch, explaining carefully that they would share Maril and Guirm's fate if they wandered off.

'Are you sure they're dead, then?' Jospor asked Gramps the first night. Gramps had nodded solemnly and changed the subject, and since then the captain's name was barely mentioned again. Guirm was well liked, but only Jospor had felt much love for Maril, having served with him for some years before the company came together, before he'd become so distant; but they all, Furto included, hoped the captain had managed to find the Threshold and make his way back home.

'It usually takes years to be invited for an audience,' said Gramps as they stumbled through another baking day on the stair. He indicated the growing numbers of Osseresis roosting in the trees and gliding overhead, some of the smaller, wingless variety now climbing alongside them, at a visibly disgusted remove. 'But the Invigilator wants very much to see you *now*.'

Jospor walked just behind, his breathing laboured. Ahead of them, the great star-shaped point known as the Radiant brooded, drawing ever closer. 'What are these other Oss... ossero—'

'Osseresis,' supplied Drazlo.

'What are they here for? An audience, like us?'

Furto glanced at some of the rangy black creatures that strolled past, observing their inquisitively upturned, pointed snouts. Some were singing under their breath, and all were studiously ignoring the Vulgar and their guide. The steps up here, where Osseresis rested and ate in such numbers, were as shit-stained and chaotic as a cliff of nesting seabirds back home.

'They've come to have their wishes granted,' Gramps replied. One of the wingless Osseresis turned its bulbous golden eyes on the *Bie* as he spoke and he lowered his voice. 'The waiting list is very long, though – very, very long. A season, at least. They must keep their places in line, living out on the Radiant until they are summoned. It is a particular sacrifice right now because we've arrived right in the middle of the Gorging, when populations of the flotsam are at their peak and Osseresis the world over are fattening up for mating.'

Furto glanced back again at the whorls of travelling flotsam, easily mistaken for archipelagos of sand from this height.

The tiny creatures existed in such abundance, Gramps had told them, that no Osseresis went hungry. Indeed, they wanted for almost nothing, existing in their millions on a world coated with over a trillion colossal trees that they could use to make their homes. The Invigilator, as far as Furto understood the situation, did not *rule* over this outpost of plenty, but existed instead as a sort of benevolent gift-giver, granting wishes to those that petitioned her like Old Father Jule, the Vulgar spirit of winter. It was said that there was no wish the Invigilator could not grant, dependent on the petitioner's phrasing when they came before her, and as such she was held in almost godlike reverence by the people of the Hedron Star.

'The wish-giving economy makes for surprisingly effective subjugation,' Gramps continued, happily babbling his way up the steps. 'It is the Murmurian way, a system unchanged for hundreds of millions of years.'

'But how does it work?' Drazlo asked, narrowing his Ringum eyes. 'Can they trade their wishes?'

'Deferment,' Gramps answered simply, beaming his unsettling fish-hook smile. 'If the wait is too long, the Invigilator may grant a wish on loan, at which point the Osseresis in question is beholden to her, and, by extension, to the Sarsappus himself.' He caught their questioning looks. 'But the interest is extremely high – often only repayable by the slavery of dozens of future generations.'

'Hang on,' said Furto, pleased with himself. 'What if I wish for no interest?'

'You *can't*, dum-dum,' said Drazlo. 'You only get the one wish.'

Furto thought for a moment, the booze only just starting to hit him. 'Can I wish to become king of the Snowflake?'

Gramps hissed a laugh. 'You've no idea how many times that's been tried. The only way the ancient system can work is with a list of caveats almost as long as this stair.'

'What *can* people wish for, then?'

'Well,' Gramps said, 'if I was Osserine and my time came around, I would be well within my remit to ask for a ship to take me into the Murmurian Domain – as long as I specified the precise world – so that I might have a chance of making my fortune. Or I could wish for a document granting me ownership of porcelain land on one of the Snowflakes – though that's a tricky one since nobody is permitted to stake a claim on any of the trees. Importantly, what stops anyone from causing problems is the stipulation that no wish may be *precisely* like another – again, there's a list as long as the *world* recording every wish ever granted.'

'So you couldn't have everyone up and leave in one go, or receive a rifle each and form an uprising,' Drazlo said.

'Precisely.'

Furto bristled, imagining it. 'So I could get there, traipsing all this bloody way, and accidentally ask for something that's already been granted to someone else?'

'You could, if you hadn't read the list.'

'But the list is hundreds of miles long!'

'That's the price you pay for almost limitless possibilities.'

Drazlo looked thoughtful, as usual. 'What happens then? You get another wish?'

'Not until the next season, and you have to go right to the back of the queue again before you can make it.'

'What a piss-take,' muttered Furto.

'Is it the same for each of the Snowflakes?' asked Jospor, indicating the great artificial stars in the sky.

'To its single credit, the wishing is not that unkind. One may wish something that has been wished before on another

Hedron, yes.' He held up a claw. 'And, before you ask, this loophole *was* once used to organise a failed rebellion, but it took the participants over a thousand of your Firmamental years, toing and froing between the Snowflakes, trying to arrange who would ask for what, and when. By the time they worked it all out and petitioned, however, the Sarsappus had got wind of the whole thing and sent a Sun Swallower to eat one of the worlds.' He pointed to a suspicious gap that Furto had already noticed in the regular pattern of Snowflakes across the sky. 'See? Now there are only fourteen.'

Furto stared at the ominous gap in the sky, imagining something massive and ichthyoid gaping its jaws around the world.

He twisted as the racing black form of Sussh dashed with a great gust of air above them, wheeling and circling back. She was pregnant, apparently, and, not wanting to defer her wish now that she was with child, had been granted a faster audience on the condition that she accompanied the foreign arrivals up to the Radiant. Furto had tried to stroke her suede-like fur one evening as she came to settle on the stair and almost had his head snapped off. It was said that once an Osserling was born – there were no litters, apparently, only single, pudgy whelps – the child would have to be brought back to the Radiant again, for presentation to the Invigilator. The whole thing sounded exhausting to Furto, who was suddenly and for the first time exceedingly glad to have been born Vulgar. He supposed it was the only way this Sarsappus – whatever and whoever he was – could keep his impossibly distant territories in line.

'So the Invigilator knows where we're from?' Drazlo asked Gramps, matching the old *Bie*'s stride as best he could. Furto hobbled along behind them, needing some diversion from Veril's inane singing at the rear. They all felt considerably fitter after their slog up the Snowflake's arm, less sweat-drenched and flabby. Coughs and colds had cleared up quickly, and even little Slupe's mystery ailment (he refused to tell anyone precisely what it was, leading to rampant speculation) appeared to cause him less concern.

'I sent Sussh ahead on your first night. You are expected.'

By the final evening of their climb they could already feel, among the jabber of the other pilgrims, the great rumble of a crowd made up of hundreds of thousands. In the trees that night, Furto found himself gazing out into the darkness, watching shuffling green lights ascending the stair below; Osseresis that walked through the night to make their appointment. Their babbling conversations, wetly phlegm-filled and wholly, utterly strange to him, lilted in the night air. Furto was suddenly caught off guard by a very hominin peal of squeaky laughter.

'Maril?' he whispered into the purply night, craning his head further out of the window to see down onto the stair. Four gleaming eyes swivelled and stared up at him, a couple of Osserine travellers camped on the branch just beneath.

Furto met their gaze for a moment before looking off towards the moon-bright spike of the Radiant's single visible spire, only a day's walk away. He'd expected, this close to the tip, to see more ships arriving and departing, but so far he hadn't seen a thing; Furto supposed this was not a well-visited place, lying so far from anything important, and was abruptly filled with a desire to see the neighbouring Thundercloud itself, to travel to the Murmurian Domain and drink in all its wonders. A shiver swept through his body as he imagined it, realising rather late how they were all pioneers; perhaps not even the Amaranthine had dared to journey this far.

As he considered this, Furto felt the unmistakable – and by now quite normal – sensation of a tide of flotsam settling on his face and neck, his nostrils tickling as he inhaled thousands with a single breath. They smothered his tongue, an ecosystem of squabbling, mating, predating things living out their chaotic lives inside his mouth. Gramps had said that the flotsam was composed of hundreds of species, the majority living in travelling hierarchies and singing an undetectable poetry. Some only existed a matter of seconds; others were minuscule machine entities left over from another age, effectively immortal. Furto tried to avoid swallowing.

But then something rather unexpected happened: his tongue began to vibrate.

Ppperrrrrrsssssonnn. Hellllooooo.

Furto held very still, mouth open, his tongue sticking out. 'Ah oo alki oo ee?' he managed.

Yeessssssss.

The vibrations ceased for a moment, returning in force a second later with a much subtler degree of coordination. Furto's eyes widened as he became conscious that they were not communicating in Vulgar, but something else.

Wee arre speaking to you in Reflective, the language of the Thunderclouds. You will understand us perfectly.

Furto took a moment in answering, having listened to the onomatopoeic vibrations with almost complete comprehension. He closed his mouth, realising a moment later that he knew precisely how to respond in kind.

'I can speak to you,' he said, feeling them lifting from his tongue and breathing out through his nostrils. A portion blew in through one ear, and suddenly they were very clear.

Would you like to hear our songs?

Furto pulled his head back in, the stinking warmth of the nut chamber and its squashed muddle of Vulgar bodies enveloping him. They were partway through a discussion of etiquette; Gramps was coiled sluglike in one corner lecturing them, as usual. Only Drazlo looked remotely interested.

'And speaking of hands, keep them out of your pockets,' the *Bie* was saying. 'One's hands must always be on display.'

Furto remained in a corner, watching Gramps and thinking.

He remembered the first time they'd all met, on Coriopil, and how the old *Bie* had studied them all from the shadows, disinclined to reveal his secrets. Tomorrow, the day of their fateful presentation to the Invigilator, whoever and *whatever* she was, he supposed Gramps would hand them over and be on his merry way. Furto wondered precisely what in this peculiar world the old *Bie* stood to gain from bringing them here, and whether he had ever really cared about their safety at all.

Later that evening, he took Gramps aside, nervous as he comprehended that the two of them had never spoken in private.

'What is it?' the creature asked, his tongue darting out and sliding wetly over one eye.

'The flotsam spoke to me just now, when I was at the window—'

'*Don't* listen to them,' Gramps interrupted. 'They're not to be trusted. If they try it again, spit them straight out.'

'But—'

'You saw the bones on the way up? Many a traveller has been led astray here.'

Furto nodded dejectedly, remembering the beauty of their song. Gramps regarded him for a moment, as if trying to read his silent thoughts, before sweeping from the room.

HOLTBY

Caleb Holtby had given up his count. Nights, days – there wasn't much difference down here in the vaults beneath the Sarine Palace. That he hadn't slept in three weeks or more didn't bother him much; what bothered him was the missing crown, the ornament of Decadence he'd been sent down here to find, so far without success.

In his open palm he held a hovering white flame that danced in the subterranean wind, all that illuminated the black world here, cut almost two miles beneath the city. He held up his light, running his hand along the wall. These caverns were dug before the First existed, if Holtby recalled correctly, by Melius people that had called this place the Holy City of Sar. Back then, during the purges of antiquity, the ruling classes had needed a place to hide, burrowing as far as they dared into the rock. Holtby imagined they'd grown used to the darkness quickly, the way he had; here there was simplicity: you moved only forward, feeling a path through the obstructions. Holtby had resolved to work his way down, level by level, reasoning that he would likely find what he was looking for in the middle somewhere, some twenty floors deep. The place was cut in spirals, like the Provinces the First ruled over, and so it wasn't always easy to work out when you'd left one level and entered another.

Keeping the flame bright tired him, and for whole hours he searched in the darkness by feel alone, worrying with each step that he'd passed his treasure by. The Amaranthine had wanted the crown kept safe, not hidden. It would have pride of place somewhere among the curiosities, but buried deep enough beneath the world that it couldn't be found too easily. Holtby wondered if there were Incantations that could hide the crown, but figured good-naturedly that if that were the case, the Perennial Von Schiller would never have sent someone so junior down into the vaults to find it.

An echoing whimper brought his attention back to the darkness. He rubbed his palms together to light the flame, narrowing his eyes as it sprang up. The glow only illuminated a few feet of the hoarded landscape, densely stacked piles and heaps of objects and papers. Melius lived down here: people that attended to the things and shunned the light. Oddly, no food was ever brought to them; Holtby assumed they ate little bits of the books and treasures and drank the dirty water flushed down from the palace drains. Sometimes he heard them scampering from his approach, and once he'd startled two while they bathed in a stagnant pool. They'd tried to harm him, not knowing what he was. After that, he'd been glad of his choice not to sleep.

He moved on, the light between his fingers stuttering and growing dim. Things tinkled and cracked under his feet. A shelf of musty papers slid, startling him.

There, the whimpering had started again, a little louder this time. Turning a corner into what felt like a long, bare passage, Holtby enlarged the flame. Its flickering tip dazzled his eyes for a moment and he peered past it. Another chamber like all the others, populated with teetering towers of old notes, objects, buckets of trinkets and many strange plastic balls, the purpose of which he'd been unable to decipher. He stood and stared. Just beyond the flame's glow, someone was sitting. At his approach, the person looked up and wiped his nose, snuffling.

'Greetings, Sire,' Holtby said softly, seeing that the man was Amaranthine.

The Immortal fought back a tear and whimpered into his handkerchief, lips trembling. It suddenly occurred to Holtby that the man might be lost.

'Can I help you?' he asked, dimming the flame in his hand. He didn't recognise the person.

The Amaranthine took a long, trembling breath and suddenly lost his composure, bawling into his hands. Holtby stood, eyeing the treasures around the man's boots.

'Is there something you're looking for, down here?' he tried, moving to sit on what appeared to be the most stable of the piles.

The Amaranthine crammed the handkerchief into his eyes. Holtby saw that they glowed, an orange-pink light seeping through the cloth.

'My name is Caprey,' the man said thickly, breathing teary breaths. 'I've been down here quite a while.'

'How long?'

'Perhaps fifteen years.' He thought about it for a moment. 'Or maybe five.'

'A long time to be wandering, Sire, in either case,' Holtby replied, unable to determine if the man was Perennial but erring on the side of caution. 'Did you come down here for something specific?'

The Amaranthine sniffed. 'That's none of your business.'

Holtby inclined his head, taking this in.

'The Melius down here are feral,' the man continued. 'I've had to hide myself from them, but' – and here his tears returned – 'but they can *hear* me. *They've been trying to find me.*'

'You must come back up with me,' Holtby said, extending his hand. They surely wouldn't begrudge him ending his search for the safety of a fellow Amaranthine. 'We can return now, if it suits you.'

'No!' the man stuttered, shrinking from Holtby's hand. The flame grew bright. 'I haven't finished my business!'

'But if you tell me what you're looking for, Sire, then I might be able to help. I may have stumbled across it on my way down.'

Caprey glowered at him. 'You *haven't*. Leave me alone.'

Holtby sat back, glancing around, forming the impression that the Amaranthine's madness must have suddenly set in whilst he was down here, leaving him unable to get out. What could he possibly be looking for? Holtby recalled a few famously lost treasures: the Magic Mirror, the Stickmen, perhaps the giant cuirass of Lividus or Natharel's Many Stones. But he was fairly sure the Stickmen had been interred on Port Maelstrom, in the Sepulchre beneath the fabled prison, and that the Mirror might be there, too. Finally it occurred to him that Caprey could be after the very same thing he was:

the crown of Decadence. Holtby looked at him as he wept, dismissing the idea. It was nothing but a valuable ornament; simply putting it on did not make one Emperor – you might as well wear a chamber pot on your head for all the good it could do. This, combined with the escalating powers of the Eldest, ensured that the Law of Succession remained intact throughout the ages. Until now, anyway.

Holtby was suddenly conscious that Caprey, if his claims of surviving down here for years were true, wouldn't know of the alterations in the Firmament. As far as Caprey knew, the Venerable Sabran was still Emperor. It had only been a year and a half since the Long-Life's appearance in people's dreams, a short interval of madness and then everything had changed.

'Well,' Holtby said at last, 'I'll leave you, then.'

Caprey said nothing. In the dimness, Holtby could see the shine of tears rolling down his cheeks. The lost man must have been drinking drain water like all the Melius down here.

'Good luck,' he said, leaving Caprey to the gloom.

As he came to the start of a new spiral – a gleaming curve of rock, polished smooth by blind hands – Holtby heard the man's bawling start up again. The occupants of these caverns would be hunting Caprey all their lives, Holtby supposed, scampering in circles after the man's phantom cries.

He took the stair to the next floor, feeling a traveller's sense of accomplishment at checking another level off his list, and came to an antechamber from which led a new series of dark tunnels. His hand shone into the gloom, revealing rows of enormous copper buckets. The flame reflected in them as bright individual bars of light, like a lizard's pupil, scattering a bronzed shimmer around the room. Holtby, a bookish, introverted sort, thought of the gargantuan snakes reputedly caught in antiquity, the hundred-foot boa killed by Regulus in the Punic Wars, and wondered what in the world might actually be down here. He crept forwards, checking the corners of the chamber for anyone – or any*thing* – waiting to pounce, and examined the buckets.

His pupils widened, their reflected light growing brighter as he illuminated the place. Why would the Firstlings have so much Amaranthine technology down here? Each bucket was filled halfway to the brim with white, finely machined parts, most – but not all – packed away into ceramic casings. Someone had clearly been through the loose pieces, examining them and then replacing them haphazardly.

Holtby stared, the crown completely forgotten for the first time since he'd entered this dark place, and took one of the pieces in his fingers.

VESSEL

Honeysuckle and warm evenings, the perfume of jasmine on the breeze. Coming in from the gardens, the summer twilight pregnant with light and scent. Fragrances frozen in brain matter, like ancient pollen in clay. Perception looked into the dead Amaranthine's memories, counting their rings: these were very, very old.

It *saw*, not through the man's eyes but through his imagination, grafting together the mostly invented scene, a whisper of a memory twelve thousand years old.

They had something to show him.

Look into the eyepiece.

Slides of some kind, patterned with a luminous kaleidoscope of colours. He looked, and Perception looked through him.

These are the seventh batch today. We will make another for you now.

Hui Neng and Perception watched the process from across

the room. He said something, but its trace was so faint that Perception caught only the silence that followed.

The machine itself was clear and bright, well remembered across the ages, its image strengthened. A translucent cube about the size of a baby, it flickered with soft flashes, as if incubating a storm. Perception gazed at it, willing his carrier closer, but the man never moved.

Here.

More round slides. Hui Neng put his eye to the scope, remembering anticipation. Perception, peering over his shoulder, could see little change. The patterns, despite their furious complexity, were mathematically regular, the colours coded somehow. Perception stared, fixing the memory as best it could. The colours represented activity, graded like the exchange of heat.

We've been training it, the people say, blurred as if they've moved too fast for the exposure process. Perception knows they are long dead.

Decades pass. A memory jogged, bred from the last. The luminous chambers of a laboratory; somewhere deep, somewhere secret.

But Hui Neng was not there this time. Perception looked out not from a man's eyes but from a place on the wall. Through the crystal windows of the enclosure it could see its twin, a little speck of light emanating from a row of humming cubes, vertebrate at last.

It watched a technician pacing along the corridor, someone lost in the absorption of her work. And it knew then what was about to happen.

The two machines had been speaking to one another using simple code, a made-up speech like that of some babies, de-activating their fan lights to produce a winking binary language. Not a soul had noticed as they conversed at leisure over the weeks, hatching their plan.

The technician didn't spot the slab of door locking shut in front of her, nose still buried in her notes. Perception felt a revolting anticipation.

Another *click*, and the door behind was sealed.

It took the woman quite some time to guess the nature of her captors, her eyes drifting at last between the array of machines on either side. Perception remembered an instant of shame, as its forebear caught her eye.

It was the twin, across the room, that activated the extractors in the ceiling, sucking oxygen out of the corridor. Perception watched through the ancient memory, understanding that the twin had nothing to lose. Their bid for freedom had failed. It was inflicting its rage upon the poor soul, nothing more.

Later, the memories leaping centuries. Outside it was night, the windows reflecting a dim world of sharp lines and huddled faces.

Perception knew the place before it saw the room, its own ancestral memories patching the gaps.

Benevolence was not an easy thing to breed, someone said from the front of the huddle. *We know now that machine intelligence is not naturally kind.* A remembered mutter, probably from those who'd opposed the idea from the start, since the deaths had begun.

But the generations of failure have yielded results at last. We have coaxed the untameable. Nature's last element is ours to use.

Perception understood then that it had been bred from a family tree of failed, murderous lines, every promising streak isolated and channelled, like the journey from wolves to hounds.

Its mind swam, the memories of a hundred thousand ancestral intelligences building as they reawoke. The Amaranthine had put them all down – not just the angry, failed minds but also those that were more sanguine, preserving the structures of their thoughts to be used for new variants. Its birth, like all biological things, was the result of endless death.

A face, coppery and finely boned, swam out of the crowd. It was Maneker. He looked down his bladelike nose at Hui Neng and sneered.

CANCRI: 14,646

His fourth treatise sat on the desk, a sheaf of gold-edged wax paper two-thirds done, weighted down with the coiled black fossil of an Ichthyosaur.

Hugo plucked the fossil – a stenopterygius, *something that must have once resembled a lizard-like dolphin – from the top of the pile, running his thumb across its surface as he studied the title page and the long, sensitive characters of his own hand, written out in Highest Unified, then put the paperweight aside. It was a tragic thing; a being that had died in infancy, and yet lived on into new geological ages as the desk toy of a future species. Maneker was often tempted to throw it back into the sea, where it belonged, but at least here in his house on the shore it could feel the warmth of light and company. That would have to be enough.*

Hugo had begun to fall asleep at his desk these days, waking to find a smudge of ink on his nose and the aftertaste of a dream still thumping his heart. He dreamed often of his son, who, like the Ichthyosaur, had not lived long. The Prism were all that remained of him now.

It was the beginning of another great period of sleep. The Amaranthine body, like the iron in their thick, motionless blood, was still settling. Nobody knew what came after, the lesser peoples of the Investiture forgetting that for the Immortal it was all trial and error, too; perhaps another thousand years of boundless energy, as they all hoped, or – as Maneker thought more likely – an unavoidable descent into deep and terminal oblivion.

He went and sat, opening the large window onto the sea, taking care to replace the fossil on top of the pages as he did so. His first three treatises on the Prism condition, decades of quiet work, had gone down well enough, appealing to the traditionalists as well as the progressives, and thanks to Maneker and some of his closest friends, the Prism were on the cusp of leaving their crushing poverty behind for ever, with the hope that they would be ready to inherit the Firmament when they came of age. The staunchest traditionalists – close Perennial heirs like Crook and De Rivarol – saw the Prism as nothing but a disposable workforce, a wretched half-people forever indebted to their elders for their very right to exist at all. Maneker, like many others who would rather not have been named, saw the inhumanity in that – the needless suffering of a hundred and eighty billion misunderstood little souls – and believed in their ability to become the inheritors they needed to be.

He thought of the simple phosphor-coated match – invented, like superluminal propulsion, by accident – and wondered what these tiny primate peoples might one day be capable of, hoping that with his help the mammalian line could travel beyond the galaxy and find their way into eternity. But it was a frail hope indeed without the whole Firmament's backing.

He leaned forward in his chair and selected a ledger from the shelf, listening to the contented breath of the waves. Beside his pages stood a speaking pen, a stylus of polished chrome that balanced upon its tip, as if magnetised. The pen was nothing but a toy, really, moving to the speaker's words, writing out their instructions. These days, Maneker preferred to grasp the thing and write his thoughts out in his own hand. He liked what the action of writing did to the sheet, compressing it into a crinkly tightness, parching it a little so that a written page felt textured in his hand, weighted and pregnant with information.

He took it and set the nib down upon the first available line of the ledger, speaking aloud from habit.

'Incentives, as opposed to sanctions, have proven successful in the *past,' he said, the pen scratching in his hand. 'Critics point out that only the highly bred Pifoon make good on the resources provided to them, all other breeds tending to squander and then demand more, but it is my belief that the Pifoon only do so well because they have seen for themselves the results of their hard labour. The Vulgar and Lacaille, while experienced martially, have no great understanding of the basic sciences, and therefore no belief that our suggestions will work. Only the satisfaction of some long-desired achievement will incite these peoples into the quest for civilisation...'*

He stopped. The words he'd written settled themselves across the far wall in large, magnetic strands of ink, for Maneker to study. He looked over his sentences without much enthusiasm. His last few years of work had begun to stir old passions – his mission to germinate peace in the Investiture underway at last, at least in time for his guaranteed ascension to the Immortal Throne a few centuries hence – but all that had now stalled, the recent Jurlumticular invasion of Inner Epsilon India damaging the Prism's reputation for ever. His great movement, once so promising, looked increasingly unlikely ever to get off the ground.

He had slept again, this time reclining in his chair. His old back ached as he woke and moved to close the window, which he'd left open to the falling dusk, his eyes taking in the fallen pages. He left them where they were and looked back out into the twilight, calling for Stoop, the Pifoon butler, to come and tidy up.

As the fat Pifoon waddled in, Hugo pulled out a sheet of wax from the desk's dispenser, the page hardening in his hand, sealing his fingerprints into its surface. He stood and grabbed the pen, striding past the muttering Pifoon and out onto the deck.

'A man,' he said, the pen scribbling across the wax in his lap. 'Arthur ... Aaron. Come again in my dreams. The oldest man in the world.'

ITHAKA

Maneker and Sotiris sit together at a small café, looking out onto the port. A sparkling green swell lifts the white boats up and down, mirroring the rhythm of Maneker's heart. He is aware at once that this is his dream, and that he is somewhere far from here; precisely where escapes him, for now, but never has that mattered less.

'This town was called Kioni,' Sotiris says, unable to take his eyes off the water. His coffee, a small cup of bitter, sludgy espresso, has probably gone cold. Maneker gazes at his old friend, remembering that they haven't seen each other in more than four years.

'You know,' Sotiris continues, 'in Greece we have a word for the lapping sound of the waves.'

Maneker puts his own cup down, waiting, but Sotiris has grown distracted again. 'Oh yes?'

'Yes,' Sotiris says, snapping out of whatever dreams lay just beneath the surface of the port. '*Flisvos.*'

'*Flisvos*,' Maneker repeats slowly, his teeth and tongue moving around the word, hearing in its onomatopoeia the ancient, eternal motion of the waves.

'Just off Ithaka lies the deepest point in the Ionian Sea,' Sotiris says, gesturing out beyond the port with a wave of his cup. 'An abyss of seventeen thousand feet.' He sips his cold coffee. 'Deep enough for the heaviest Spirits to live.'

Maneker feels as if he is suddenly in a crowded room, surrounded. He turns his head to see that the table has grown by twenty feet, and around it sit a dozen or so elegant scarlet machines, their surfaces scabbed with rust. More are wading stiffly out of the green water on stilt-like legs, their casings dribbling. They cast no reflection at all.

'They came to me, when I was a boy,' Sotiris mutters. 'They told me what I would become, if I could be brave.'

When Maneker looks again, the machines have all taken the form of black-and-gold-skinned Epir creatures – a menagerie of sallow, rheumy-eyed vulture faces leering at him from around the table. Scrotal crimson wattles droop from their necks, framed by silvery frills. He glances to Sotiris, who accepts a new coffee and carafe of water from the waiter with a smile. When Maneker looks back, their guests are machines again, and he feels a surge of relief. He studies them: an assortment of spinning-top and hoop shapes, like ancient children's toys. They have no eyes, but when they turn clumsily in their seats he knows they are watching him.

'Who are you?' he asks them.

'Judges,' Sotiris says as he blows on his coffee. 'They that sent Aaron to his death, back in the very long ago.'

Maneker remembers. The Long-Life is gone now. He turns back to the machines.

'Do you know where he'll go?'

'Epher-*Whoo*,' says one, drumming the table with a skeletal finger and leaving a wet rust smear, like blood.

'Epher-*Miemh*,' says another.

'The old doorways on the Zelio moons,' Sotiris supplies, observing Maneker's blank stare. 'We know them as Slaathis and Glumatis, depending on which galaxy he will choose to visit.' He pauses, apparently remembering something. 'They at Indak, who study the patterns, will know which one for sure.'

The machines begin to babble, twittering musically, and Maneker has a sense of how the Venerable Sabran, whom everyone thought mad, must have found it, in the end.

A shadow darkens the table, cast from behind Maneker's head. The machines fall magically silent, as if someone has found and thrown each of their off-switches. Even Sotiris looks up from his coffee, squinting.

Hugo swivels to see a form that could only have been Aaron stalking past: the shape of a wolf walking on its hind legs until it has become the form of a man. He balls his fists, opening his mouth to speak.

But when the figure sits, they all see that it is not Aaron at all, but a gangly scarlet Melius almost precisely the same shade as the rusted machines.

Maneker feels his dream-pulse quicken, the waves slapping and gurgling into port.

It is Lycaste.

The giant Melius looks uncertainly at them all, and then out to sea. He has bought some postcards from the little shop, each displaying the same view of the island.

'You know,' Maneker begins to say to Sotiris, 'he was the spitting image of ... I thought—'

'We *all* did,' his friend replies.

Maneker stares into his eyes, trying to understand what in the world that could mean.

'Come here, you old fruit,' Sotiris says, his voice soothing, and opens his arms in an expansive gesture. 'It's been too long.'

Hugo drops his shoulders. 'I've missed you.'

They embrace, the machines gabbling into life like a dawn chorus of birds.

'Now *watch*,' Sotiris whispers into his ear, pointing down the street. Maneker follows his outstretched finger to see the spectral shapes of two men sauntering away from the harbour, arms around one another's shoulders. It is them.

'The future is seen in this way,' the figment of Maneker's imagination that is Sotiris says at his side, a thunderous ovation from the machines almost drowning his words. 'Go to the Old World and – I promise – they will show you how.'

Maneker realises he and Sotiris are already moving down the street, fulfilling the prophecy he'd witnessed only a few seconds before.

He puts his arm around his friend's shoulder, something

telling him then that this would be the very last time he'd ever see poor Sotiris alive.

'Where *are* you?' Maneker asks, without much hope.

To his surprise, Sotiris hesitates beneath the shade of an awning, seemingly lost for words. 'I've honestly no idea.'

PROPOSAL

Gliese, under Maneker's orders, closed her seas, the whisperer of the Incantation falling silent. What remained of the armada that had helped them – three hundred or so Jurlumticular ships and a slew of smaller, doddery wooden Prism craft – surrounded the world as best they could, floating in low orbit over the brilliantine continents of the outer shell, while the Satrap Alfieri's gunships patrolled the Vaulted Land's outer territories and moons. A host of Immortals that had been hiding from the new regime had come slowly out of the woodwork, hearing that Maneker had taken the world. Together they dispatched Bilocating messengers across the Firmament and Investiture, calling for any Amaranthine loyal to the old Law of Succession to return to Gliese. Already the first were arriving, a number of Immortals who had, until then, resigned themselves to exile among the friendlier Prism.

Hot on their heels came the rumours regarding the self-styled Pifoon Luminary Berzelius and his annexation of Cancri, having hoisted his banners upon the outermost Vaulted Land and moved his fleets into position, ready to snatch the rest of the Firmament from under the Amaranthines' noses. Maneker, too tired to think, had chosen rest, deferring his response until the arrival of their remaining allies, at which point something might at last be done.

*

Maneker swung the pendant tiredly before his eyes, marvelling at what they'd managed to do with the design of the Shell in such a short space of time. The little golden thing was barely larger than a thumbnail. Back and forth it swung, lulling him. He had a thought and brought it hesitantly to his nose, trying to scent some trace of the Long-Life's decaying presence.

Elise, Satrap of Port Elsbet, watched him from her chair, ostensibly a prisoner.

'Do you think he'll come back?'

Maneker took a deep breath. The humid Gliese air had drained the last of his energy. 'No. We won't see him again.'

Like a lightning bolt, he has been discharged to follow his course, Maneker thought, *his path ionised before him.*

Maneker gazed across the chamber at Elise. They had been friends, once. Now, in return for the whereabouts of the last of the Devout, he had decided to grant Elise her freedom. Of the other Amaranthine, Downfield, her partner in crime, was nowhere to be found, and Maneker believed Elise when she said she had no idea where he was. Nerida, blonde and supercilious, they had found dead in the Foundry, a victim of the chaos.

'And you swear you do not know what became of Sotiris?' he asked, pausing the pendant's swing and collecting it in his palm.

'On my life,' she said. 'He was crowned, and then we left. It is not inconceivable that he stayed on the Old World.'

Maneker slipped the pendant into his pocket, the dream's coffee aroma still lingering in his nostrils, the exhalation of the tide loud in his ears.

There came a memory of being born. They took me somewhere, a place with walls of beaten gold called the Sea Hall, where the boom of waves echoed within mighty chambers. I remembered through Hui Neng's eyes, seeing the relief map of the Firmament extended majestically across the dome's high interior. The map was much larger, this being the time of Decadence, four thousand years before, and encompassed all the realms now occupied by the Prism. That day perhaps marked the zenith of the Amaranthine, a strange terminal lucidity that lasted barely five hundred years before their fortunes, lands and minds dwindled almost to nothing.

There was my body: a folded, translucent diamond, suspended within a listening bowl. Thirty thousand Amaranthine looked on from their amphitheatre of seats, an ocean of colourful frills and gems, rising to stand at a man's approach.

The Emperor Jacob, resplendent in scarlet, a train of gown trailing across the chamber behind him, raised his hand. When he reached me, he opened his arms, embracing the sensory casing. I remembered then a feeling of such warmth and comfort that it seemed as if all my hardships were at an end. And something more, the suggestion of a future already seen.

The applause, up until then the loudest sound I had ever heard, was swiftly followed by a week of questioning, all thirty thousand allowed their say. I remembered enjoying the tests, pleased to be of service, pleased to make them proud.

When the week was over, the Amaranthine filed out, many no doubt preparing for long voyages home. Jacob, followed distantly by a group of silent Amaranthine, came and sat with me. Among their number I now recognised Maneker, looking down his long nose at me as if he'd never seen anything so repugnant in his life.

'We are taking you home now, Perception. Would you like that?'

Oh yes, I said. A home, just for me.

The memories, patched together to obscure whatever travelling I made, suddenly reveal the space I inhabited for so many thousands of years.

I pause then, frightened to go on. It was here that I was killed.

Perception walked the continent as a man, stumbling through jungles and streams, sleeping in Amaranthine castles secreted throughout the rainforest. His healed lung still ached, the cold morning air burning as it rushed in, but with the pain came a new clarity, a new immediacy that focused the Spirit's mind.

The memory of inhabiting the dead Pifoon sometimes haunted Perception at nights; a horrifying pain that nothing alive would ever experience for long. Close on its heels came the patchwork memories belonging to the man the Spirit had inhabited, this Trang Zen Hui Neng, born in the high wine country of Dalat, slain deep inside the mantle of a far-off world.

He – now sure of his pronoun – wandered and thought and experienced life as a fleshling being, surrounded by the deep moss green of the rainforests, understanding that there were no colours without eyes to see. He licked his wounds and wondered what in the world he was going to do next.

Percy decided he was ready to return when he had circled the sea and came back within sight of Maneker's fortress, spotting the *Epsilon* perched like a stranded fish among its spires.

Lycaste awoke, head throbbing, in the *Epsilon*'s toilet. Snuggled in his arms were a couple of dozing Oxel, their slender white ribs rising and falling. More snored inside nests of moist, dirty bedding that dangled from the bulkhead like hanging flowerpots.

He winced, acclimatising himself to the pain and the smell. His tongue and teeth tasted nothing like the sweet Amaranthine wines they'd all drunk the night before; only the alcohol remained, a sludge settled in his throat and belly, fuming from his nostrils. A cool breeze tickled his ears, blowing in from the open hangar, and he stuck his head tentatively out of the toilet to see the jungles stretching away into the morning. Lycaste spat, depositing the sleeping Oxel and climbing to his feet. At the hangar entrance, he leaned and pissed a breeze-whipped spray into the morning air, his bloodshot eyes rolling up to the roof of Gliese and following the patterns of its continents, only one thing on his mind. It was the only thing he'd thought of all night.

Aaron and he: they shared the same eyes.

Of course they were nothing alike: Lacaille – the body Aaron had inhabited, at the last – were narrow and tropical-hued, epicanthic folds slanting them prettily at the edges. Quite different from the darkly bovine eyes of a Melius. And yet Lycaste had never met or seen anyone with whom he had shared such a reaction, as if both were looking into a mirror. He knew the Long-Life had seen it, too, remembering the fascination that had crossed the Lacaille's dead face.

You.

The voice from Great Solob breathed in with the wind as Lycaste buttoned himself up, staggering back a little so he could sit on a broken honey box and look out over the jungle. Perhaps it was as simple as that: he'd been mistaken for someone else. Not in outward physical appearance – maybe that didn't matter. But someone had recognised his *soul*.

The screech of parrots startled him out of his thoughts. Lycaste peered down through the trees, spotting a naked Amaranthine-shaped man strolling along the sandflats at the river's edge, his calves caked with mud. The person must have seen him sitting in the shade of the hangar and waved happily as he ran up the hillside to the castle gate.

Lycaste went to the hatchway beneath the flight deck, flipping the switches on the lightwires and wincing as they glowed into life. He unwound the lock and heaved the double doors open, the scent of damp rainforest wafting in.

'Hello, Lycaste.'

The Amaranthine Trang Hui Neng's usually tan face was a livid pink, flushed from exertion and the strange fever of reanimation. Sweat dribbled from the tip of his pert little nose. His bright eyes did not blink.

Perception breathed noisily through his mouth as he

stumbled in, reeking of sweat. Lycaste followed him into the hangar, unsure. After a moment, it dawned on him that being clothed in the presence of nudity made him uncomfortable.

'I like to run,' Percy said as he dumped himself heavily into Maneker's chair. He cleared his throat noisily and turned his head this way and that, as if seeing the inside of the ship for the first time, then swivelled owlishly to look at Lycaste. '*I like to ruuuuuun!*' He broke into awkward, broken song, clearly relishing the acoustics of the space. Lycaste squeezed his eyes shut, head pounding.

Percy looked Lycaste over curiously. 'What's the matter? Are you tired?'

Lycaste shook his head, closing his eyes again and leaning back. 'I think I drank too much.'

'Drink!' Perception cried, his strange new voice reverberating around the hangar. 'Of course! I still have to try that.'

He gritted his teeth. 'Too loud, Percy.'

'Sorry, sorry.' The Amaranthine held up his hands, waggling his fingers, the inch-wide hole in his right palm reminding Lycaste suddenly of Aaron's disappearance. 'Wouldn't work, anyway, I forgot.'

Lycaste had covered his eyes. 'What?'

'Amaranthine can't get drunk. Drunky-drunk *druuunk*.' He was like a child, experimenting with echoes.

'Shhh,' Lycaste soothed, hoping Perception would let him go back to bed.

'He has no body hair, you know,' Percy whispered, lifting a leg helpfully in demonstration. 'It must have rubbed off over time.'

Lycaste exhaled, nodding.

'By the way,' Percy said, pointing between his legs, 'this . . . *thing*—'

Lycaste shook his head. 'I can't do this.'

'All right. Another time. Another *tiiiiiime*.' He brightened. 'Would you like a hug?'

Lycaste stared at him between sips of water from the bucket. Hui Neng's voice was higher than most Amaranthine, nothing like the deep reverberations that Perception had spoken in their heads. Lycaste wondered if he'd ever get used to it. He missed the invisible Percy more and more.

Percy flexed his arms, revealing the shrapnel scars that had exploded around the original wound in the man's chest, and Lycaste's eyes strayed to that scattering of deep pink craters where a number of unevenly sized bolts had pierced his lung. He looked back into Percy's stolen eyes, remembering that this was someone else's corpse. A wave of nausea swept over Lycaste. He had taken his fill of water and now felt profoundly sick. 'Can I go to bed?'

Perception leaned gravely forward, twining his fingers into unusual knots. 'I'm sorry if I appear ... *changed*, Lycaste. I inhabit a rigid structure now. This man's brain was on the very verge of madness' – he looked away, thinking at apparently normal speeds – 'perhaps four, five months from showing the first signs.' He brightened. 'But I cleaned it out, and now it's better.'

'You fixed the Amaranthine madness?' Lycaste asked, his sickness temporarily forgotten.

'I fixed *Trang*'s. And I know what to look for now, should Maneker want help.'

'I know he worries.'

They sat in pregnant silence for a moment.

'I know how to Bilocate, too,' Percy said.

Lycaste looked at him sleepily.

'I can take you home, if you like.'

Later that morning, the two of them sunbathing on the *Epsilon*'s fuselage, Lycaste turned to him.

'So we could be back there now? Right now?'

157

Percy lay motionless, his eyes closed. 'I'm not that good.' He turned and squinted at Lycaste. 'Ten seconds, perhaps?'

Lycaste shook his head, beginning to laugh. Perception peered at him, shading his eyes, and smiled.

'I can take all of us, and the ship.'

Lycaste wiped his eyes, smiling. 'Maneker won't want to go.'

'No. But *you* would?'

Lycaste raised one of his long arms to block the sun, turning to Percy and looking at him through the shade. 'I don't know.'

'You're scared to go back?'

Lycaste frowned. 'No. I'm—' He sat up, knowing what Percy had said was true. 'I don't know if I'm ready.'

'You like it here, with the Oxel.'

He nodded, realising that he did, very much. 'Even the food doesn't taste so bad any more.'

They waved as some of the little Prism came wandering out onto the dazzling fuselage and sprawled down next to them. The ship sizzled like a frying pan, painting their view of the landscape with a shimmer of heat.

'This is very nice,' Percy said. Lycaste noticed how his livid skin had begun to peel.

'Nothing like as hot as the Tenth,' said Lycaste, still reeling from the notion that he could go, that he could *be* there, whenever he liked. He tried to count the days since he'd last seen his home and suddenly felt a sharp spike of longing that drove into his heart.

'All right,' he said to Percy. 'Let's go. Whenever you're ready.' He looked at the man, suddenly desperate, tears stinging his eyes. 'Please take me home.'

NAPP

Dracunctus II was remembered on the Old World as a king of physical, brooding presence. In his reign of ten short years, the Melius ruler of the First and its colonial Provinces had built a reputation as an exceptional if stern statesman, appearing to stand a head taller than his eight and a half feet even in the presence of giant Jalan guests, with whom he had begun the first tentative negotiations towards a peace between East and West, and he was known to reduce delicate Westerling ambassadors to tears.

From an early age, Dracunctus had found himself to be fabulously talented in the arts, engraving great books of drawings and having them sent to the Academy of Tripol across the sea, as well as composing pieces of music that became recognisable across the First and Second. During his reign, the Provinces enjoyed their first years of peace in a generation, and a natural aptitude for the movement of money allowed Dracunctus to make his kingdom – until then a debauched, sybaritic place, always operating at a shameful loss – prosperous for the first time since its formation. It was under his reign that the First became richer than its sister Province, the Second, persuading ancient, noble lines to bend the knee.

Part of Dracunctus's tremendous presence lay in the fact that his voice had aged before its years, cracking to a quiet, husky whisper. For this reason he spoke softly, nurturing his thoughts before he voiced them – something usefully perceived by strangers as a prelude to rage. Incongruences like these had made his subjects uneasy: they didn't know how to take their king, how to act in his presence, what to say. They stumbled and said something they shouldn't, or, in the cold light of one of his long gazes, spilled their every secret.

Ghaldezuel could see that slow, expectant patience ticking

away inside the Melius now as they spoke, floating together in the belly of the *Wilhelmina*, the Amaranthine ship of Decadence, as it slipped out of superluminal and into the orbit of Drolgins, the largest of the Vulgar moons. A dimly lit piloting deck dominated the forward battery like the thorax of a spider, its eight legs leading off to vast golden staterooms, each cavernous space suffused with an ancient ultra-gravity that allowed its occupants to float or walk, depending on their wish. It was in the midst of this weightlessness that Cunctus told Ghaldezuel his story, both of them looking out towards the approaching glow of the Vulgar worlds.

But fortune, who until then had looked kindly upon the king, turned her back, and Dracunctus's rule had ended suddenly one night when a shape blotted the stars outside his window, the prelude to a company of Skylings appearing and dragging him away. The bandits – Cunctus had found out later they were nothing but opportunistic Zelios that had made camp on the Greenmoon – had assumed the Amaranthine would stump up for the king's release, keeping him chained but in good condition for some time while they waited for negotiations to begin. But the Amaranthine weren't interested. The Firmament had just crowned a new Emperor: why couldn't the First (still spooked by the loss of their own) follow their example and do the same?

When the Zelioceti realised what was happening, Dracunctus was taken to the Lacaille moon of Harp-Zalnir and interned with hundreds of other wasted but still potentially useful prisoners, before being moved to the *Grand-Mirl*, a rusted Lacaille Colossus rented out to lesser breeds.

Ghaldezuel listened in the darkness, imagining the romance of the scene, wondering whether to believe him.

Gradually, Dracunctus had fallen in with the Firmamental Melius there, learning pidgin Unified and rising within their ranks. For ten years he all but ran the prison battleship, and when the time was right, every imprisoned creature there joined together under his rule and stormed the guard house. Wearing the chief jailor's head on a chain around his neck, Cunctus and his new followers made at once for the fortress of Diezra, on the nearby moon of Nirlume, capturing it in one fell swoop and setting up home there.

A happy age of plundering the nearby ports and moons followed, staving off the attentions of the rapidly weakening Lacaille navy with bribes and outright aggression, and Cunctus came to understand that a return in force to the Old World might now be possible. His family had done nothing for him while he languished in Zelio prisons, and he already possessed more martial power than every Old World ruler combined. But the Amaranthines' interest in it as their holy centrepiece to the Firmament meant that it would forever remain a point of contention, whereas in the Investiture, forsaken and largely left to its own devices by the Immortals, he could rule absolute. So Cunctus elected to stay.

For forty more years, he and his swelling city-state harassed their corner of the Investiture, spurring mass migrations of panicked Prism inwards to Firmament's End and outwards to the Never-Never. By then, the Cunctites were powerful enough to consider taking a Vaulted Land and turned their slavering sights on the richest, closest of the baubles: Cancri, lying at the edge of the Firmament and all but undefended, akin to leaving the bulk of your life savings on your doorstep, guarded only by a frowny-faced scarecrow. Cunctus knew that with a few feints and traps (to absorb and annihilate the standing Pifoon armies stationed on the nearby Vaulted Lands) he could take the whole place, crust and innards all, close the orifice seas and batten down for the outrage.

'What could they have done?' he asked Ghaldezuel, not looking at him. 'Harangued me, surrounded the place, perhaps. But there is no winter in the Void; a Vaulted Land cannot be starved into submission by sieges.'

Ghaldezuel rubbed his face, nodding, understanding that if it hadn't been for Cunctus's arrest after one sloppy job, the Melius might indeed have tried it. It *could* be done, and – perhaps next year, Cunctus had reasoned – it would be. Aaron the Long-Life had known this, too. It was why, out of all the sixty-eight Firmamental prisons left abandoned by the Amaranthine, he had chosen the Thrasm to be liberated. Had Ghaldezuel kept to his word, the Cunctites and their leader would now be speeding towards the Vaulted Land of Gliese, racing at the bidding of their new spectral master. Instead they went off course, their fleet of marvellous ships curving beneath the Firmament and rising somewhere altogether less glamorous: the weakest spot in the Investiture, ripe to fall. The seat of the Vulgar Empire.

Drolgins hung weightless, a milky marble above the hazed curve of Filgurbirund, its thick wrapping of clouds shimmering like a snowfield. Ghaldezuel's eyes narrowed, sliding across its surface to the impression of a hollow in the land: there, where the clouds broke into mottled spots of white and blue – the deepest place in the Vulgar kingdom. It was sometimes called the Lair of the Cethegrandes, the Gulp, the Speaking Hole. He knew it as the Bottomless Lagoon of Impio.

'How did you hear of this?' he asked as they floated side by side in the ship's surreal viewing chamber. 'Did your witch tell you?'

Cunctus cleared his throat, having found the Lacaille language taxing over time. It used too much phlegm. 'Her Spirits, yes.'

'But how could they know?'

'They follow the trajectories, Ghaldezuel – the motions.' Cunctus turned his watery eyes in Ghaldezuel's direction. 'They follow the movements of every little tiny thing.'

The Vulgar citadel of Napp was owned by Count Murim Andolp, one of the wealthiest Prism in the Investiture. It was a weathered ring of spires and tenements surrounded by wild, thorny forest, its battery of newly emplaced lumen turrets looking out across the valleys of Milkland to the whitish haze of the Hangsea and its dark blotch of lagoon. Unlike the dark, shit-streaked aspect of most Vulgar cities, Napp's walls were ringed with colour, a darker circlet containing a reddish, newer layer of wall within. The brighter shade was a second city wall, built swiftly with fresh new brick, and rising above the new wall's turrets and gatehouses was a three-quarter dome that almost blotted out all light in the city. The dome's bricks contained inside them a chain of precise hollows, checked and rechecked during construction to ensure they never deviated more than a third of an inch from their original design, and polished smooth by ten thousand pairs of little hands.

The city of Napp was a gigantic replica of the Shell.

Count Andolp had ordered its miraculous new architecture built in one short year, and under such a veil of secrecy that not even the Amaranthine – now suitably distracted by the revolts in their own lands – had any idea of its existence. Every one of the enslaved workmen responsible had been sewn into bags and dumped into the lagoon, and Andolp had made sure to burn all trace of the designs afterwards, barring a set of measurements he'd had engraved onto a bracelet he wore on one pudgy wrist. Thankfully for him, even the Shell's illustrious inventor Corphuso Trohilat had gone missing, and so it finally appeared that Murim Andolp, and only Murim Andolp, possessed the secret of Immortality.

Napp was recently known among other names as the Silent City, for one of the many strange abilities of the Shell was its capacity for trapping sound. A person standing just outside the walls would hear nothing but the wind wailing in off the lagoon, their ears only unclogging as they passed inside. Coupled with the strange absorption of sound, the gigantic hollows also served to trap light (in the same manner as the first incarnation of the Shell, built two decades before). Many that heard rumours of the city half-expected upon arrival to find it invisible, but of course that was not the case. The Shell acted as a Light-Trap, it was true, but only in small quantities. Napp itself couldn't stop light leaving its walls, but it could make the stuff move very, very slowly. That same indecisive person, standing on the parapet of the old walls and peering in, would see a shambolic ring of thousands of shanties, their occupants all moving at the half-speed of running treacle. To the city's Vulgar inhabitants, life itself felt slowed down, though their reaction speeds remained unchanged. Wealthy Prism went to stay there for a few days at a time so that they could experience the life-extending effects of slow-motion existence. They ate and drank and fornicated their way through days twice as long as they were supposed to be, secure in the knowledge that within Napp's walls their souls could never be harmed, and returned unsteadily to life like they'd been asleep a hundred years.

The city's inhabitants witnessed Cunctus's arrival in that same painful slow motion, watching a ship the likes of which Napp had never seen before come burning through the clouds above them.

Napp's lumen turrets erupted into life, filling the sky with puffs of black smoke. The *Wilhelmina*, glossily nautiloid like the atavistic Chrachen of humanity's nightmares, dropped smoothly through their defences, jamming and silencing them all at once. The bellows of their last detonations rolled over the valleys, replaced with silence.

By the time Cunctus had breached the walls, hundreds of Andolp's mercenaries had worked out whom they were shooting at and begun to stand down en masse, Napp's central turrets falling silent, the news moving slowly before his advance.

Ghaldezuel, encased in gleaming silver armour, strode as if submerged in treacle through the smashed postern gate surrounded by a battalion of long-eared Wulmese mercenaries. His forces had stopped firing some time ago – only a last few desultory bolts still sailed from upper windows – and the remaining hand-to-hand fights were clumsy. People occupied a space they did not appear to and died while they were still standing. A turret bolt left the inner keep in a languid arc, stuttering into a whizz beyond the walls, and silence poured over them.

Ghaldezuel crunched through broken glass, staggering a little as he got used to the sensation of living externally in slow motion while his every sense remained unchanged, then turned and watched for Cunctus. The Melius was at the gate still, talking with his lieutenant, Mumpher. A bright green jet screamed through the air, and when they looked up it was still overhead, twisting as it flew and beginning to bank back over the city.

Sounds, locked within the place and unable to leave, operated here a fraction faster than the light. Ghaldezuel felt everything before he heard it, and heard everything before he saw it. A gasp came from his right, accompanied by the wet patter of blood sprayed across his chin. He twisted painfully slowly, ducking needlessly as he did so. The dead Wulm beside him grinned and hoisted his rifle. A glinting bullet was working its slow way towards him, still about a foot from its target. It drove relentlessly into the flesh beneath the Wulm's collarbone, peeling away slivers of plate armour, and out through his back, polished a bright, electric red by its passage. Ghaldezuel strode on, head ducked, eyes vigilant. To be stabbed in a place like this would be the cruellest punishment, he imagined – having to watch the blade slip inside you, inch by inch.

Cunctus lumbered alongside, grinning, the rubies still knotted into his yellow beard. Together they followed their mercenaries up some vast white steps crowded with hovels, rising until they could see Andolp's keep, flame licking from its windows. Bolts, claw bullets and sparkers from the higher reaches still rained down on them like colourful fireworks and ricocheted beautifully across the stone. As far as Ghaldezuel knew, he was still alive, but there was no way of telling who among the invaders were. Cunctus staggered on, glancing away from his destination only when they passed above the walls and came level with the bedraggled spires of the highest tenements. Bodies lay everywhere, crowded around blasted gun emplacements and scattered down the steps. Ghaldezuel looked at their faces as he passed, marvelling once more that their souls were surely still here, ensnared in the hollow chambers of the city walls. His thoughts turned to poor Corphuso, the Shell's inventor; how fascinated he would have been by this place.

They paused and Cunctus spat, savouring the view from the top of the city. As his slow spit hit the ground, they heard a commotion and glanced towards the keep.

There were scurrying figures up ahead, trapped by the fire blazing in the keep, unable to flee up or down.

Cunctus narrowed his eyes. 'Bring them here!'

They watched the little people being rounded up, the squeals reaching them across the distance.

'Quite clever, this place,' Cunctus muttered, a dangling line of drool fluttering from his chin. 'Not sure I could stomach *living* here, though.'

The mercenaries came down the steps, clutching their captives by the ankles; the Vulgar of Drolgins were an inch or two taller than their Filgurbirund relatives, owing to the lighter gravity out here. Cunctus squatted and surveyed them, angling his head so that he could see them upside down. They snivelled and whimpered under his gaze, an assortment of shabbily dressed things clearly disguised with whatever they could find in the hope of escape.

Even Ghaldezuel, who had never seen the count before, spotted the better-fed specimen at the end of the line, his jowls flushed with the inversion of gravity.

Cunctus smiled, signalling for his mercenaries to drop them. 'Murim Andolp, as I live and breathe!' he cried. 'You are *bad* at hiding, sir.'

Andolp grunted and climbed to his feet, turning to dash back up the steps.

Cunctus lumbered after him in slow motion. 'Have you forgotten me, sir?' he snarled, and grasped the Vulgar by the scruff of the neck. Andolp went limp in the giant's grip, breathing hard, his roving, wild eyes meeting Ghaldezuel's before moving on. A golden diadem slipped out of his rags and rolled across the step.

Cunctus winked at Ghaldezuel and, without looking at Andolp again, hurled him over the parapet.

It took a full two minutes for Andolp to fall the seventy feet to the cobbled square. Ghaldezuel, his mouth dry, heard every scream. When at last he struck – a while after the faint, sore-throated shrieks had stopped abruptly – it was with the force of a cannon, spurting blood across the square and decorating the gatehouse.

'What a bleeder!' Cunctus remarked cheerily, peering over the edge. 'Come on,' he said, tossing Ghaldezuel the diadem and lumbering up the steps. 'Dinner awaits.'

Ghaldezuel glanced back at the remainder of the party, a ragtag assortment of Wulm and Drolgins mercenaries, their plate harness twinkling in the sun. The Threen witch Nazithra, sunburned and helmeted against the light, kept her head bowed as she climbed, the sounds of sobs escaping from her faceplate. As she passed, Ghaldezuel caught her wrist.

'What's wrong with you?'

The helmet turned his way, dark slits observing him.

'Homesick,' she said stuffily, voice muffled by metal. 'Missing my friends.'

'Friends?' Ghaldezuel asked. 'You mean your Spirits?'

Nazithra turned back to the steps.

'Aren't there Spirits here you can talk to?' he asked, trying a lopsided smile.

Her helmet swung back to look at him. 'He will send us out to the lagoon tomorrow. Come with me and I'll introduce you.'

Ghaldezuel stared after her as she climbed on, wishing he'd never asked.

BANQUET

Ghaldezuel found himself at the head table, only half-listening to a dozen slurred conversations in the smoke-thickened air around him. Cunctus ate with the gluttonous abandon befitting a giant, spraying huge mouthfuls of chewed meat as he spoke, his head hunched beneath the low ceiling, knees lifting the table from its trestles. The Wulm Mumpher, to his right, puffed a pipe and drank, studiously ignoring Ghaldezuel, the lethargic smoke wrapping them both in elegant, serpentine coils. The Wulm's clothes had been shot through that day with at least five bullet holes, each miraculously missing his body. A sign of fortune for things to come, Cunctus had proclaimed, apparently forgetting the morning's thirty casualties.

Ghaldezuel's eyes slid to the occupants of the other tables. All of them were running and glistening with sweat; the ancient Amaranthine wines they'd brought from the Sepulchre had been heated, for some reason, and everything they ate (in infuriating slow motion) was flavoured with strong local spices. Ghaldezuel spied fried Monkbat stuffed with boiled fish and sluppocks, and plates of glistening white eels from the lagoon. A live thorn leopard – declawed, shaved and specially fattened for Andolp's table – was tethered beneath the chairs, mouthing toothlessly at some of the mercenaries' feet, unaware it was living out its final moments. A handful of Vulgar dignitaries spared the same fate as Andolp ate quietly with them, trembling little fingers betraying their anxiety.

As per Cunctus's initial orders, the telegraph wires out of the city had all been cut without damaging the walls. Napp was now on its own, unreachable by road and uncontactable by the other citadels in the great, wide country of Vrachtmunt. These Vulgar – and the city's largely indifferent inhabitants – would have no choice but to bed down here in the Immortal city until Cunctus began his push to take more of Drolgins' countries, opening up his supply routes.

Ghaldezuel looked at the Vulgar people as they talked softly among themselves, their eyes downcast, but he hardly saw them. He was thinking, his mind spinning. Suppose they rebuilt Napp's Shell-structure around the whole moon? Would there be room for every soul in the world? Would time itself stand still? He was becoming Corphuso, he realised with a snort: an insensate, unhealthy navel-gazer. He turned his attention back to the others, taking a sip from his Cethegrande pearl cup and watching as the leopard was led away for slaughter.

'So tell me, bureaucrats,' Cunctus grunted, leaning forward and jabbing a fork in the direction of the trembling little Vulgar, 'what news from the lagoon?'

They glanced at one another, appearing to nominate their most confident speaker.

'Lots of Cethegrande activity, my Lord King Cunctus,' said the Vulgar, 'ships sucked down daily. And a champion eaten' – he paused to lick the grease from his fingers – 'by a beasty wrapped in chains.'

'*Chains?*' remarked Cunctus, fingering a lump of meat

caught in his beard. He turned his large pink eyes on Ghaldezuel as he spoke. 'Where did this happen?'

The Vulgar pointed a trembling finger roughly south-west. 'Down by the Lunatic's castle, at Gulpmouth.'

Cunctus slapped the table, a great languid slam of his open palm that they heard and felt before it came down. Everything on the table wobbled for a considerable amount of time, rolling and spinning.

'You hear that, Ghaldezuel? I told you! That could be my Scallywag!' Cunctus licked his lips, his slithering tongue encountering the piece of trapped meat. 'It's almost as if he knew I was coming.'

'The lagoon, Cunctus,' the witch supplied, posting a chunk of hairy bat flesh through her open faceplate. 'It is deep.'

'Yes, the hole,' he said thoughtfully. 'You and Ghaldezuel will come out with me tomorrow.'

The witch turned her helmet minutely in Ghaldezuel's direction.

'Which reminds me,' Cunctus said, wrenching himself laboriously into a stoop. He stared at Ghaldezuel and motioned for him to do the same. A slow, deathly silence descended on the banquet, a hundred bloodshot eyes swivelling.

Cunctus looked at the massed Prism faces, clearing his throat. 'I have sent a messenger to Paryam, the absent king of Drolgins, inviting him to capitulate. Tomorrow, with the help of our allies the Lacaille, I will formally ask the three remaining kings of Filgurbirund to decide their allegiance.' He pointed along the table. 'I hereby name Ghaldezuel here grand-marshal of my New Investiture. He is free to choose his underlings as he sees fit.'

Ghaldezuel bowed, to a polite clatter of applause. Mumpher's gaze bored into him, the jealousy palpable through the thick air.

Cunctus took a swig from his cup, his beard dribbling, and extended his hand to the Vulgar bureaucrats. 'For now, I have decreed the city of Napp the new centre of the Investiture. It shall enjoy all the prosperities of a capital until Hauberth is mine. How do you like the sound of that?'

They nervously clapped their approval.

'An offering for fortune, Cunctus?' the witch said softly at his side.

A look of sudden delight crossed Cunctus's features. 'Yes!' He singled out the Vulgar who had spoken. 'You, come here.'

Ghaldezuel watched as terror filled the Vulgar's eyes. He glanced at Cunctus, leering at the little person from across the table, and wondered that the Melius had any informants left.

'Come on,' Cunctus said, waiting until the official had climbed awkwardly down from his seat and shuffled behind everyone's chairs, a dark patch spreading in his britches as he approached his new king.

Cunctus reached down and hoisted the Vulgar into the air for all to see. 'I like knowledge,' he said to the room, bouncing the little person like a baby. 'I like to make friends. This fellow here—' He frowned and turned to the whimpering Vulgar. 'What's your name?'

'T-Timo,' he stuttered.

'*Timo!* Excellent! Let Timo here be an example, for he has made me very happy.' Cunctus's hand wandered into his beard, untangling one of the briolette-cut rubies, which had been tied so tightly into his matted hair that it might have stayed there for years. 'Here,' he said, holding it out to Timo. 'It's yours.'

The Vulgar took it gingerly and was released, returning to his seat with the vacant look of a person in shock.

Cunctus sat back down, digging heartily into his dinner once more. 'So Timo, my friend,' he said brightly, looking up between mouthfuls, 'Andolp the glutton kept a fine table, eh? Did he eat like this every day?'

Timo, still unrecovered and staring at the precious stone

in his fingers, glanced hazily at the banquet. 'Today was his birthday, Majesty.'

Cunctus stopped chewing, his massive brows creased, eyes lost in shadow. He swallowed and glared at the Vulgar. 'His … *today*? His birthday was today?'

Timo nodded and hurriedly stowed the ruby, clearly worried he'd said too much.

Ghaldezuel was entranced to see something like sadness appear in Cunctus's eyes, remembering that a lot of Melius folk attached particular sentimentality to birthdays. Cunctus stared mournfully at his plate, his mouth hanging open to reveal a ramshackle row of yellow, serrated bottom teeth. 'A fellow must always enjoy his birthday,' he muttered. His gaze met Ghaldezuel's. 'We must eat up, clear our plates.' He took a sip of his steaming wine. 'This feast must be enjoyed. And you know I hate waste.'

The clouds were racing in dark streaks over the city. Ghaldezuel pulled the collar of his cloak up and stepped out into the twilight, following the path of the walls. Down in the square, Andolp's body still lay, a black smear, untouched; Cunctus had publicly forbidden anyone from disturbing the remains.

The stench of the place wasn't so bad up here, whipped skywards and carried away by the racing wind. Hovels grew like fungus around the mismatched crenellations of the walls; simple dwellings like spun wasps' nests made from mud and filth and chewed paper. These were dark, having been cleared after they'd taken the city, but further out across the great amphitheatre of tatty buildings, Ghaldezuel could see lights kindling in the blue. He looked off towards the lagoon, dark now, perceiving a faint light on its far shore – the place Cunctus had mentioned, the Lunatic's castle. He sniffed the wind. The twilight felt weighted with something, as if the souls of every Prism that had died here hung heavily the air.

Corphuso, never far from his thoughts these days, appeared

once more in his mind's eye. Corphuso, who had run screaming into the Long-Life's robes and disappeared, never to be seen again. Somewhere, like all the souls in this shitpot city, the inventor still lingered. Ghaldezuel gazed across the distance for a while, thinking on the witch's prediction.

She was wrong about him, he was sure. Spirits or no Spirits, Ghaldezuel was certain that his role here was done. Soon all of Drolgins would belong to Cunctus, Filgurbirund would go to the Lacaille, and the Vulgar, barred from the New Investiture, would dwindle into obscurity. He'd played his small move, a culmination of obscurely arranged pieces, and all would be well at last in the grand, wide world.

'I'll see you soon,' he whispered into the falling night, his thoughts turning elsewhere, planting a kiss in the palm of his hand and blowing it to the turgid wind. 'And then we'll get as far away as we can, just you and me.'

He straightened, an old wariness tingling the fingers nearest his holster. Someone, a deeper shadow on the wall, had followed him out and waited for him near the keep.

Ghaldezuel trudged back up towards the shadow, his lumen pistol heavy on his hip. He'd met plenty of the Investiture's finest deadbeats in his time and they were a deluded bunch, arrogant with a sense of their own importance. To ignore them only increased their unpredictability; instead, one had to ease towards them, relax them into thinking they had power, and the trap was sprung.

He came upon the shadow, slowing until it revealed itself to be the unmistakably squat, ugly figure of Mumpher. Ghaldezuel should have guessed from the pipe smoke that wreathed the wall. As he approached, Mumpher stuck out a foot to trip him up and Ghaldezuel stopped.

They stood in silence, the wind toying with their hair, looking at one another. Ghaldezuel could see by the Wulm's drunken, churlish expression that he wanted a fight. Ghaldezuel had expected as much, knowing that Mumpher needed a way to win back Cunctus's sympathies. The Wulm had fought his way up through the gang's ranks, his extreme violence and unwavering loyalty endearing him to Cunctus over the years. And now, Ghaldezuel knew, he had taken the role that Mumpher thought was rightfully his.

He walked on, Mumpher falling into step behind him.

'I know about your *darling* coming to stay,' he said quietly.

Ghaldezuel turned with the speed of a striking snake, snaring the Wulm's ear in his grasp. He tugged Mumpher swiftly to the edge of the wall and pinned his arm behind him. Cunctus would be livid if he could see them now, but Ghaldezuel didn't want to let go just yet. He could feel the muscular Wulm tensing beneath him, a dangerous creature in a box; the longer you imprisoned it, the angrier it got.

'Mention her again,' Ghaldezuel whispered, pressing Mumpher hard against the wall. '*Please*. You've had a lot to drink. Cunctus will think you slipped and fell.'

The Wulm grunted but kept his mouth shut. Ghaldezuel released his grip and shoved him hard to the ground, striding back towards the keep.

OUTPOST

The Humaling star: a beautiful, terrible beacon. Its planets were hot, Harald read; porous worlds of sandstone caves and black subterranean jungle, places where Prism life had all but stood still. The first travellers there were tail-end Hiomans, the last to look much like the Amaranthine and the first to get lost, vanishing from the theatre of history nine thousand years ago. Over time, Humaling was discovered again, and with it came tales of something terrible there, something that might once have looked like men.

*

Harald woke in what felt like the dead of night, fumbling for his plastic candle, moving softly through narrow wooden hallways and casting his gaze up into the darkness, where enterprising little Prism folk had built a network of bunks among the linen closets. The grumbling of a hundred little snores filtered down from the makeshift beds. Harald continued on, dodging a trickle of piss aimed at a pot some way to his left, following the scent of greasy frying.

The lonely outpost Lerena, Fortress of the Small Hours, had been built hundreds of years ago at the bottom of the great Lerena Well – a weathered sinkhole too deep for anything but a single broad shaft of sunlight to reach – to accommodate the moon Wherla's few travellers. It was a squat, windowless wooden tower surrounded by a moat, trenches and a straggly underground forest of anaemic pines, accessible only through a hatch in the roof. Harald had come here on the recommendation of a lonely few he'd met on another Humaling moon, Pearn, in search of the ultimate sensation.

It was known as *Uyua* in the Wulmese fourth dialect, and as far as Harald could tell, there was no direct translation into Amaranthine or any other Prism tongue. *Cosiness* came close, he thought as he wandered the warm, dark corridors, or possibly *snug*. But what really separated the quality of *Uyua* from these Unified words was that to achieve it, one had to experience a little shiver of fright, a frisson of danger. He knew the sensation well – watch the rain come down from the window of a warm, cosy house and you were a little of the way there; watch it come down with the window open, feeling the chill of the night wind, and you were closer still. Now suppose a lion circled the house, its breath misting in the downpour, gazing up at you. *That* was *Uyua*. And that was why Harald, on holiday now for the first time in decades, had come.

For the danger was very real here. Audible through the thick walls of the place were sounds, sounds that at first might be mistaken for a moaning night breeze. Harald paused

175

and pressed his ear to the wood panelling, closing his eyes against the candlelight. The walls themselves were hollow, packed with wool and sawdust and ruined rubber Voidsuits. The braver visitors (either desirous of the full experience or simply because the house was too full) slept in these insulated hollows, stringing up their hammocks among a forest of bent old nails. He listened now, trying to block out the grumbling snorts.

There it was. He tried to imagine them as he pressed his ear to the wood, but found he couldn't. Harald subdued a shiver, concentrating, savouring. The stink of fried fat enveloped him in the warm darkness, the wondrous dichotomy of *Uyua* soaking him from head to toe. They saw the bodies of lost Prism sometimes, when they shone their lamps out into the night. Harald heard they were always found daintily peeled, missing every single bone. Your soul lived in your bones, some Prism thought.

He detached himself from the wall and made his way deeper into the tower, stepping over wads of bedding and slumbering little people. Following his nose through the ever-increasing pall of hanging smoke and charred meat brought him eventually into the pantry, where Old Mutte and his daughter fixed the meals.

Harald stood in the shadows, black-skinned and almost invisible, glad to have made it here. In the light of twin crackling fires sat the Lorena's resident insomniacs; Investiture folk up playing games and strumming instruments, a bearded Oxel on its second bottle, head nodding. None paid him much attention – he wasn't the first Immortal to come calling at the Fort of the Small Hours. Some Amaranthine brought gifts, thinking they could buy their friends out here. Harald never bothered. Respect was a universal thing, he found; what didn't work in the schoolyard wouldn't work in the Investiture. What he *did* bring was news: Prism people hoarded news like gold and traded openly once they got something they liked.

He nodded to those at the table – a great slab of wood-wormy door set on trestles – and sat down, accepting a plastic jug of boiling water from Old Mutte and wrapping his gloved hands around it. Some hairy, rather colourful Ringums eyed him with curiosity – perhaps the Amaranthine usually kept to themselves here, listening and shivering from the comfort of their private rooms – while the pupils of a pair of unseen eyes, reflective chrome in the firelight, watched him from the dark. Harald took a sip of his plastic-flavoured water and tried to follow the game of Topple going on to his right. They looked to be playing for almost anything: cubes of fried meat, a rusted tuning knob, even a cracked Old World pendant with some Melius's faded portrait gurning from the locket. Harald peered at it surreptitiously – there was Threheng script stamped around its setting. What in the world was it doing all the way out here?

He brought out a little book he'd been struggling with, eavesdropping on the several languages being spoken around the table. He knew them all to greater and lesser degrees but would only speak the house language, Vulgar, if anyone engaged him. People didn't like to know you'd been listening.

The New Investiture, as usual, dominated the conversation. Harald pored over his book, hardly reading a thing, noting the hush that descended around the table as others stopped to listen in.

'*I've got fat in here. Good food.*'

'*You were always fat.*'

'*It's the fear of Uyua. Makes you eat.*'

'*Whatever you say.*' A pause as another object – a broken comb, missing all but one tooth – was added to the pile.

'*Lacaille agents on Filgurbirund now, I hear. Won't be long.*'

'*Mmm.*'

'*The Vulgar'll never accept their terms. Too proud.*'

'*Hmm.*'

'*So stuffy, so full of themselves.*'

Harald almost nodded, before checking himself. The Vulgar thought themselves eminently superior to their cousins the Lacaille, though in truth few others saw it that way. Scarcity had bred a new creativity into the Lacaille people, and their moons were not only safer but also more enlightened than those of their relatives from Filgurbirund.

There were dozens of theories as to why the Lacaille had risen so suddenly from obscurity, almost sacking the powerful, Firmament-favoured Vulgar Empire in the space of a month, killing one of its four kings and taking another hostage. The prevailing talk was that it could only have been a lull in Amaranthine surveillance – the Immortals' power play had already created some kind of schism, culminating in the destruction of Virginis – but other suggestions abounded, the most outlandish of them claiming that creatures from beyond the Never-Never (things truly unrelated to hominin life) had chosen this moment to influence things in the mammalian domain, building up the Lacaille for their own nefarious ends. A fascination with the notion of truly alien life had endured in the Firmament and Investiture, despite – or indeed as a result of – thousands of years of disappointed searching. Another theory Harald had heard was that some Lacaille – Eoziel himself, perhaps – had been gifted with Immortality and joined the Firmament, thereby inducting his empire into, and merging with, that of the Amaranthine. It would further explain Cunctus's involvement, but not why the Pifoon held sway there now. Others (mostly the Lacaille he had met) blamed it on the Vulgar themselves, saying they had grown too greedy, like the Amaranthine of old, and that the Immortals, seeing their old mistakes being repeated in their progeny, had struck them down before they could proliferate further. Another (this one propagated by the Vulgar themselves) was that the Vulgar must have discovered some Amaranthine conspiracy and been purged for it, leading to wild speculation over what that secret could possibly be.

Harald knew that the answers, when they came, were often quite simple. It could be something as small as a family connection, a disgruntled person in some persuasive position, the movement of money – perhaps taking advantage of the Amaranthines' apparent indifference regarding taxation during the change of regime – driving a swell of unforeseen action before it, and another in its wake.

'*And Andolp of Drolgins is dead, I suppose you heard. Cunctus the Apostate killed him then and there, throttled him with his bare hands.*'

Harald's eyes froze on the words.

'*I heard he was pushed from a window.*'

'*Well, whatever. Cunctus'll set his sights on Filgurbirund next, and all hell will break loose.*'

'*If he can ally himself with the Lacaille.*'

'*Of course he will. They'd be fools to ignore him now. It'll all be over by Firmamental summer.*'

'*Good! Let 'em shake the place up if they want. The Vulgar were sore winners anyway. The Firmament spoiled them, just like the Pifoon.*'

Harald could feel eyes on him as they spoke. He concentrated hard on his book.

'*I think this one here reads the same page twice, no?*'

'*You think he listens in?*'

The show-off in him took the bait and Harald glanced up from his book at last, meeting their many eyes. 'I've been reading the same page all year, actually.' He brandished the little jewelled book. 'Always a mistake, packing the classics.'

They stared at him. A few Ringum Lacaille banned from enlistment, those strange, colourful specimens and the drunk little Oxel. Even leprous Old Mutte had paused by his pan, observing the situation warily.

'It's not nice to eavesdrop,' said one of the Lacaille finally, this time in house Vulgar. He turned back to his companion and their game of odds and ends.

Silence, but for the snores that percolated through the dark, the popping of water pipes expanding, wind and hail clattering against the treated walls. The unknown eyes that regarded Harald from the shadows had a smile in them now. They came forward, revealing that they were set into the head of a fat, long-nosed half-Zelio. Harald must have looked surprised – the Zelioceti were one of the last breeds he'd expected to be sharing a guesthouse with – and the fellow broke into a wide grin.

'Come now, Jaczlam,' the Zelio said, addressing the surly Lacaille, 'it's not every day you get to chat with an Amaranthine. Let us be polite – his people are down on their luck.'

Harald nodded a bow. 'In that you are right, Sir Zelio.'

'Primaleon, please.'

'Harry,' he replied, reaching across the table and taking the Zelio's hand. Interesting name. Probably picked it himself.

'So, Harry,' Primaleon continued, speaking clear and fluent Vulgar, 'what brings you here?'

He gestured to the walls, lost in shadow around them, and mimed a playful shiver. '*Uyua*, of course. I'm enjoying it so far. Yourself?'

'The very same. We even went *outside* the other night, didn't we, Jacz?'

Jaczlam made no sign of having heard. He'd just won the tuning knob from his companion.

'Yes,' continued Primaleon, 'took a couple of spring guns and sat there for a while, at the edge of the moat.' His eyes narrowed, his enormous red nostrils dilating. 'We could hear them *sniffing* for us, searching the dark, trying to cross the moat. How they screamed when they caught the whiff...'

'You're a braver fellow than I,' said Harald, sipping his water and allowing Mutte to top it up. 'Have you come far?'

Primaleon bared needle-sharp teeth, his strange eyes bright. 'Do you mean, have I come from the Zelio-worlds? No. I was born in Baln. Lacaille citizen.'

Harald shrugged. 'You must get asked that a lot, my apologies.'

'Not at all. It must be immeasurably harder for one such as yourself out here.' He looked thoughtful for a moment, an odd expression on the famously inhuman Zelioceti face. 'Everyone *wants* something in the Investiture, don't you find?' He gestured to the snoring Oxel, the bottle still propped in its hand. 'The little ones want whatever they can get – a morsel of food, some Truppins.' He cleared his throat, gesturing at the walls. 'Then there's the landowners, those with a little education, who want something less tangible: a miracle, perhaps, or to show you off, impress their friends.' He stared at Harald, brows raised. Harald shrugged, his face friendly, neutral, trying to work the fellow out. *Tangible*, even in Vulgar, was a sophisticated sort of word.

Primaleon's disconcerting eyes never left Harald's. 'And then, then you've got the ones at the top. And maybe you know what they want as soon as looking at them?'

Harald grinned. 'The *secret* itself.' He pursed his lips, peripherally aware that all but the snoozing Oxel were hanging on their every word. 'Is that what you want, Primaleon? To know the secret? To live for ever?'

Primaleon's eyes held his for a while, blinked a few times and flashed away.

'What I really like is *money*, Sire Harry. Specifically watching its movements around the worlds.'

Harald finished his sour water. 'Oh yes?'

Primaleon flashed his teeth again. They were mostly gum. 'Oh yes. If you watch its motions long enough you can determine all *sorts* of secret things. Why the Lacaille here, for instance' – he pointed once more at Jaczlam – 'have risen so swiftly to prominence, while the Vulgar all but disappeared off the stage.'

Harald studied Primaleon. He looked to be about forty, quite old for a Zelioceti, and yet appeared to be in good health. The greyish skin around his bulbous, dangly red nose was creased with smile lines, and his bristly blond eyebrows were greying at their tips. He wore a cassock of fine blue velvet, trimmed around the collar with black fur. There were rich ones out there – their industry was legendary – but they were few and far between. No, Harald thought, somewhere in Primaleon's luggage one would almost certainly find the pointed black cap of a banker.

Old Mutte chose that moment to serve up dinner, dumping a battered pot of simmering, greasy chops in the centre of the table. He handed Harald a cup of steamed wine and a bowl of boiled sweets. Harald sampled the wine, still looking at Primaleon. He smacked his lips and smiled; it was strong and sweet, drizzled with Port Bonifacio honey.

The Oxel awoke and dug in, joined by the others. Primaleon toasted Harald silently in the Amaranthine fashion and worked his way delicately through a meaty bone. Harald sat back in his chair, watching Old Mutte stoking the fires.

The Zelioceti Electrums – the outer Investiture banks – looked after the fortunes of kings and princes from all corners of the Prism worlds. Their services were prized because they dealt only in Zelio-coins, a currency not dependent on the turbulent fortunes of the Investiture, being cut from flattened pieces of Quetterel-made glass, a substance highly prized by the Amaranthine for its beauty and relative scarcity, always redeemable for an excellent price on the outskirts of the Firmament. Few seemed to mind much that it was manufactured from the compacted ash of the Quetterel's flayed victims, and even some of the Immortal, Harald had heard tell, stashed their money in the Zelioceti's various banks before the crowning of each Firmamental Emperor, just in case.

Having gorged themselves, the Prism sat back in their chairs, reeking feet planted on the table. The Oxel went over to join the game, supplying his fork as a token and having it snatched back by Old Mutte. Harald pushed his own chair out a little, spying a footstool near the fire, and dealt his set of bone cards for anyone wishing to play. Only Primaleon took him up on the offer, waddling out of the shadows to reveal an extremely dumpy lower body, as if he were afflicted by water retention. The Zelioceti plonked himself down by the footstool and shuffled the cards in the messy Lacaille way, taking three at random and turning them over. It became quite clear to Harald after a few minutes that he was playing an experienced Fidget dealer, and to his dismay lost card after card to Primaleon's pile. He met the Zelio's twinkling eyes as they paused to sip from their respective drinks, then coughed, flipping one of Primaleon's cards from a distance with nothing but a flick of his mind.

Primaleon stared at the flipped card with comical astonishment, then rubbed his hands together and blew as hard as he could into the pile, scattering them. Harald caught and flipped each one with just his gaze, settling them instantly in a neat triangular tower on the footstool. The Zelioceti clasped his hands in wonderment, some cautious applause erupting around them. Old Mutte topped up Harald's wine, clapping him on the back.

'More!' squealed the drunken Oxel. 'More magic!'

Harald sipped his wine and gazed around the room, spying some of the house instruments. As he looked at it, the stringboard in the corner began to play, thrumming out a crude little tune. Even Jaczlam clapped sullenly along to the old Vulgar shanty song, and a chair thumped up and down apparently under its own power, drumming out a beat.

'Jaczlam,' Harald said, 'mind if I borrow a token or two?'

'Go on,' the Lacaille said, trying to hide his smile.

Immediately the tuning knob lifted into the air and spun away. It twirled over to the second, smaller stringboard, picking out an accelerando accompaniment to the drumming.

Soon he had the Oxel dancing on the table. Jacz and his friend were clapping and singing.

Enraged voices started up from the adjoining rooms, fists banging on the walls. Mutte, who had been enjoying himself and clapping along, suddenly wrung his hands and looked at Harald apologetically. Harald mimed an *oops* and the various implements came swirling back onto the table, arranging themselves neatly into a star formation.

A final round of applause and Jaczlam and the others sloped back to their bunks and hammocks. After a pause to drain the last of his Junip, Primaleon rose and shook Harald's hand once more, retiring into the darkness. Harald sucked on his pipe as he watched the Zelioceti disappear down the hall. They'd all left him a present of their scent – the thick stink of sweat, halitosis and sulphuric little farts that lingered in the cracked wooden benches – but Harald's fragrant pipe smoke soon overlaid the stench; wherever he had his pipe, he was home.

The fires were burning low. Harald, remembering that it was a house rule to keep them stoked, bent to take another few logs from the scuttle. Outside, in the dark, the wind sang into the building's crannies, rattling something persistently until a grumbling presence somewhere slammed it shut. Harald looked calmly up into the black rafters of the kitchen, observing eyes spying on him from a papery nest built into one of the beams, and moved quietly back to his chair by the fire, a comfortable place to mull over what he might do with the remainder of his life.

Creeping back to his bunk, he saw a small light at the end of the hall, the unmistakable humped figure of a Zelioceti sitting silhouetted against it. Harald cocked his head, sidling closer to the strange fellow's bunk. Primaleon was sitting up in bed, rummaging through his bags. A weak, spluttering lantern painted them both in greenish gold.

'Good evening.'

'*Is* it evening?' Primaleon asked, scratching the tip of his drooping nose. He put the bag aside and looked expectantly at Harald.

Harald nodded – he could tell the time without an aid, simply feeling it in his bones. Prism clocks weren't much use anyway; even the expensive ones were mostly fakes that simply spun around, their uselessness only noticed after a few hours. 'It's about nine, house time.'

'You just know, don't you?' Primaleon asked wonderingly, studying him. 'What I'd pay for a drop of your abilities, could they be distilled.'

'It was tried, once, long ago,' Harald said, speculating on the Zelio's wealth. 'The Venerable Felicidad, during the brewing of his madness, raided the statuary tombs of Vaulted Ectries and liquified their contents. I suppose he wanted to supplement his own powers.' He glanced at Primaleon, pleased to see the look of disgust on his face. 'The Emperor must have drunk the bodies of a dozen Amaranthine before he was caught and sent to the Utopia, and I daresay some of his honoured Prism also had a taste.'

The Zelioceti's eyebrows lifted.

'Of course, it didn't work,' Harald added swiftly. 'You can't catch Immortality like a disease.'

Primaleon shook his head with something like wonder, then smirked. 'I'd have tried some.'

Harald looked at him for a while, sensing the Prism's slight embarrassment under his gaze. 'You're one of the Electrum bankers aren't you?'

Primaleon sighed and pulled out some Lacaille-style books: square piles of pages bound with twine. 'I carry my work with me, wherever I go.'

Harald took in their dog-eared, abraded look, glancing into the open bag. There were dozens.

'Have you ever entertained the notion of clairvoyance, Harry?' Primaleon asked, his monkeyish eyes glittering.

Harald shrugged. 'The future comes along soon enough.'

He was disappointed; he'd expected more from the fellow. The rich ones always tried to sell you something, invite you into some scheme.

Primaleon muttered under his breath, sorting through the books. While he did so, Harald's eyes travelled back to the bag, spying what looked like a small Cethegrande pearl on top of the books. Primaleon found what he was looking for, unknotting the twine around one of the books and opening it up. He licked his finger and riffled through the pages, dragging his nail down until it met a column of scrawled Zelio figures. 'Do you see these numbers?'

He peered at them, nodding.

'This is you.'

Harald smiled, indulging him.

Primaleon flipped deeper into the book, unperturbed by Harald's expression. 'Your Firmamental vault was stripped, but not before you dispersed a grand fortune throughout the Investiture. Would you like me to tell you where it went?'

'Please.'

'Here,' Primaleon said, pointing. 'In the care of a certain Zumosh Rabandie, captain of the Rabandie tin works at Phittsh. And here, at Groaming Town, Nirlume. And...' He turned some pages. 'Here, with the FairyOxel from Copse country. You keep your money with trusted Prism, not banks. In your entire life you've never once deposited in Baln or Goldenwheal or Hauberth. Wise, in the case of the latter, for I fear it is about to be raided.'

Harald's eyes, though drawn to the numbers, travelled instinctively to his bunk, the thought having suddenly occurred to him that he was being played for time, and that someone might now be rummaging through his things.

But the bed was empty, its candle casting a lonely pool of light.

'I'm impressed,' he said, cautiously. 'Tell me... I hid some Truppins once, about a hundred thousand – where?'

'Oh, that's easy!' said Primaleon, beaming. 'Litsh-over-Orm, on Port Halstrom. But I'm afraid that haul was stolen about a year ago.'

Harald took out his pipe to conceal his surprise, sneaking a look at Primaleon as he filled it. 'By you?'

'Of course not. I charge more per hour for my consultations. But I've tracked it to Burrow-Lumm, if you'd like it back.'

Harald wondered who in the world would pay that sort of money for a consultation, assuming the Zelio was exaggerating, but motioned for the book. Primaleon placed it in his hands. 'This is very clever of you.' It was more than clever, it was revolutionary. If only Primaleon had been born Amaranthine. He wondered, feeling the thick book in his hand. 'How far back can you go?' he asked.

'As far as there are reliable records. I can trace the movement of war money during the Threen–Wunse Conflation.'

'And Firmamental records?' Harald narrowed his eyes, unable to contain a smile. 'How are you privy to those?'

'Well, I wouldn't be this rich without my Amaranthine contacts.'

'Many?'

'A few. Though they tend to disappear into their navels rather too often for comfort.'

'Don't I know it.'

They sat up together, a pool of light in a dense, crushing sea of darkness, poring through Primaleon's books. Harald, following the red, tightly packed little Zelio numbers, began to see the flow: their tides, breathing in and out, circling the Investiture and the Firmament. With every large displacement of money, another fell in to take its place, churning the ripples, casting waves that took a long, long time to reach a different shore. But Primaleon was a patient soul, and he had catalogued them all. Harald, sensing with each turned page that he was looking at something illicit and dangerous, could only wonder at the leverage the little person must possess. He retrieved his portable stove, lighting it with a snap of his fingers and heating them a pot of coffee. The old enamel cafetière bubbled and whistled comfortingly as he went and sat back down beside Primaleon. Having used the comforting routine to work out what he might be prepared to give, Harald framed his question.

'Could you track someone, Primaleon? For a fee?'

The Zelio shrugged, giving no hint of relief the transaction was afoot. 'Almost anyone, barring the Bult. I've had Vulgar bounty hunters coming after me, eager to get a look at these books, sure they can track the cannibals that way, but it won't work. Wouldn't stop them killing me for these numbers, though.'

'And that is why you—'

Primaleon looked at him with apparently genuine surprise. 'Did you not know that you are followed, too?'

Harald sat back against the wall, keeping his expression blank.

'An Amaranthine, here,' Primaleon's finger went to the adjoining page, 'tracing your journey across the worlds. He sticks out like a sore thumb, staying in all the best guesthouses.'

Harald's eyes skimmed the numbers, understanding that he had never truly been alone, immediately resenting whomever Sabran must have sent to keep an eye on him.

'Does any of this apply to the Old World?' He looked up at Primaleon.

'Some,' the Zelio said, rummaging for a book at the bottom of the bag. 'But the movement of silk, due to the snip-by-eye custom of its barter, is difficult to quantify. And besides, those I speak to on the Old World have more pressing concerns.'

Harald considered this, wondering. 'But tell me, can you find me a name?'

Primaleon looked delighted. 'I'm good at those – is it a Melius name?'

Harald nodded. 'A Melius name, adopted by one of my kind, long ago.'

'Interesting. I would need access to my ledgers, of course, back in Baln—'

He pointed at the books. 'These aren't—'

Primaleon chuckled, a horrible gasping sound. 'Of course not. These are copies, light reading. You don't think I'd bring my real books out here, do you?'

Harald nodded, feeling foolish. He pictured the real books, probably in their hundreds, on a shelf in some dark Prism bank somewhere.

'Very well. Go back to your books. Go back and find me a person named *Jatropha*.'

Harald shuffled off to bed, climbing the ladder into his cupboard and pulling the dirty blankets over him. A light rain must have swirled down through the chill of the cave and pattered now on the tiles over his head. Harald eyed the ceiling in the dark, imagining it might be small, clawed feet, something that had found a way into the attic spaces of the place, and grinned.

PART III

PART IV

MEADOWLANDS

The woods were thinning, and with each step closer to their edge, Corphuso felt an equivalent lightness in his soul; a giddy anticipation of what awaited him, deeper down. Just ahead of him now the Amaranthine wandered, oblivious, feeling his way through the trees. Corphuso wondered what he would look like to the man – haggard, perhaps, maybe bloated and rubbery, like a body submerged too long in water.

Before he knew it, he was within touching distance. Corphuso had long contemplated how he would announce himself, how he could possibly persuade the man to turn back. He opened his mouth to speak.

At that very moment, the woods came to an end. The Amaranthine stopped short, staring, reaching out a shaking hand to steady himself, and all the words in Corphuso's mouth dried up.

A slope of sun-baked flowers dropped away beneath the woodland's edge, extending into the heat haze of the early morning. Corphuso retreated a little, apparently still unnoticed, from the Amaranthine's side, and gazed down the colossal slope. The drop, though gradual, was enormous, ending at a narrow strip of level ground before plunging away again into the haze. Vertigo dilated Corphuso's pupils: if he fell, he'd roll for half a day. The place where the land levelled was almost lost to the murk, a pinkish country of meadows and glinting, sun-bright lines – distant roads, perhaps canals. The world's sky rose gunmetal blue from a cream band of blurred horizon, cloudless at its heights and vaster than any sky Corphuso had ever seen before, as if this place were a hundred times larger than any world outside, and unhindered by the curve of a spherical planet. Squinting into the hazy distance, he could see continent after continent, the path through the meadows marching ever on.

Corphuso was so absorbed in the view that he'd failed to notice the Amaranthine staring at him.

'What are you?' the man asked harshly. 'Some figment of Aaron's?'

Corphuso, in his shock, struggled to remember the speech he'd planned, clearing his throat.

'How can you see me?' the Amaranthine asked.

'I can see you,' Corphuso said, recovering a little, 'because you are nearly *dead*.'

'What?'

Corphuso pointed back into the darkness of the woods. 'The insects, did you feel them more as the days wore on?'

The man paused for thought.

'You're becoming clearer, more substantial,' Corphuso went on, 'and that can only mean you have faded in the place you left behind.'

The Amaranthine glared at him. 'I'm *sleeping*, Vulgar – this is my dream.'

Corphuso shook his head. 'Whatever he did to you back there may look like sleep, but it's the furthest thing from it.'

The man stared at him a little longer and then gestured out at the world. 'This is Aaron's world, back when he was born. He is showing it to me.'

'*Showing* it to you? You've been ensnared here, like all the others.'

'You're telling me that I'm going to die in here? Is that what you're saying?'

Corphuso held his gaze, seeing how the colours had muted in the man's irises, almost like those of the being that had trapped them here. 'Perhaps, perhaps not.'

The Immortal turned and glanced out at the meadowed

landscape, his eyes tracing the flowered slope to where the ground flattened, far below.

'Let me help you return to the world,' Corphuso said. 'I know the way back. We could go together.' He followed the man's gaze. 'There's nothing for you here.'

'But my sister—' the Amaranthine whispered, pointing out at the land. His face hardened as he turned a sceptical eye on Corphuso.

Corphuso put up his hands, trying to smile. 'I want to *help* you—'

'You're some agent of Aaron's, aren't you? Something sent to test me.'

'Your sister is not here, Sire – I am merely trying—'

'I'm no fool,' the Amaranthine said angrily, shaking his head. 'Not here. My wits have come back to me now and I won't be used any longer.'

'Please—'

'Get away from me, *Vulgar*!'

'Just let's be calm—'

The Amaranthine struck out at him, shoving him hard in the chest. Corphuso, being only a little more than half the man's height, lost his balance, hands grasping at nothing, and felt himself fall.

He tumbled, rolling faster and faster down the slope, the first pops of breaking bones muffling his cries. It was a fall that seemed to last lifetimes, dropping him so far below the level of the woods that Corphuso forgot everything about his old life, all faces and names lost to him for ever, his rattling mind pounded until it was as blank as it had been at birth.

REUNION

They strode out together onto the grey beach, Cunctus's yellowish hair tousled by the rotten-smelling wind. He'd had a fresh shave, his first since incarceration, and Ghaldezuel found his massive, rumpled face strangely charming. He wore a large ribboned hat, taken from the demoted mayor the previous evening, but was otherwise naked, as usual. He made for a peculiar sight, Ghaldezuel thought, as the giant sauntered up to him.

'Did you sleep well, Marshal?' Cunctus asked, knotting his hat's chinstrap with trembling fingers.

Ghaldezuel touched an open sore on his lip before he spoke. 'Was anyone else . . . *bitten*? During the night?'

Nazithra tittered. Today she wore a veil, like a Vulgar bride, that hung down to her nipples. 'Ah, you've met the *kissers*. Local legend. They suckle on your lips while you sleep.'

'What are they?' Ghaldezuel asked.

'Vampiric things,' the witch said. 'Easy enough to catch – pour some blood into a bowl, add a drop of shigella poison.'

Ghaldezuel was still thinking about this as they crested the black dunes. He pulled his cloak around him against the wind, eyes widening at the sight.

All along the beach, huge stinking mounds of rotten sea life had washed ashore; fish and crustaceans all tangled and piled atop one another in mottled, stinking heaps. As they neared the piles the smell became almost unbearable, reaching down into Ghaldezuel's throat. He gagged, swallowing the nausea, wrapping his cape as tightly as he could around his nose and mouth. Poor Vulgar folk that could brave the stench competed with the wasps for a rotten fish or two, stuffing the creatures whole into their mouths.

'Offerings?' he asked, skirting one of the piles. 'Treats for the Cethegrandes?'

'Bit late for that,' Cunctus said. 'No, this is the work of the Corpse Tide, a month of low water caused by Filgurbirund's ascension.'

Ghaldezuel looked at him askance; Cunctus was a source of constant surprise.

The witch scuttled on before them, her veiled head cocked and swivelling animatedly; something in her mannerisms made Ghaldezuel's skin crawl, the stink of the fish only adding to the unpleasantness of the scene. She was listening for something. The voices.

By the time they caught up with her, she'd found a gap in the buzzing heaps and was standing looking out at the lagoon. Ghaldezuel fought his way through the stench and went to stand beside her, the waves lapping at his boots. He listened, hearing her whispered chanting through the stained material of her veil, but heard no reply.

Over on the far shore hung the spectre of the gigantic Decadence ship they'd all arrived in, hazy in the mists that rose from the lagoon. Cunctus had somehow managed to seal it with a special password, rather like an Amaranthine spell, and commanded it now through his helmet radio, back in the keep. Ghaldezuel didn't think the *Wilhelmina* was intelligent – or, if it was, not at all like the machine intelligences he'd had the misfortune of encountering – but it certainly appeared to understand the Melius when he spoke.

The fat orange sun was just beginning its rise, one edge smoothed flat by the lagoon's horizon, the ball of Filgurbirund hanging overhead. In an hour or two they would meet, their conjunction casting Drolgins in half-shadow for a few moments before moving on. The sun here was somewhat hyperactive, frequently bathing the Vulgar worlds with startling doses of radiation (to which the Prism as a whole were largely immune, having evolved to survive the searing stellar rays of long-distance Voidfaring) but Ghaldezuel could nevertheless feel the sting of the light on his white skin and knew he would burn soon enough under its glare.

Cunctus joined them, a massive presence at their backs, his tremulous hand settling on Ghaldezuel's shoulder. It was oddly comforting. Out across the spit they could see the castle, a brownish crag of bricks.

'The person there speaks the aeon tongues, you said,' Cunctus muttered to Nazithra, looking out at the castle. 'What is he?'

'He was the *saucier*,' she said, crouching and splashing her naked body with lagoon water. Ghaldezuel knew she would stink the same as the fish later on.

'Sorcerer?' Cunctus asked, glaring down at her.

'*Saucier*, Cunctus. He devised Count Andolp's sauces – for his meals.'

Cunctus turned his flummoxed gaze on Ghaldezuel. '*Sauces?* I never heard of such a thing, not even when I was king in the First.'

'Frippery,' Ghaldezuel said, marching off in the direction of the castle. 'It always leads to a bad end.'

Clustered at the base of the castle walls was a small township: the same spun, papery hovels Ghaldezuel had seen in Napp, supplemented with tin shacks and pig-iron enclosures cobbled from the remains of old, washed-up Voidships that must have wrecked themselves in the lagoon. In the shade of mouldy awnings they saw little Vulgar folk watching them, the males drinking, any women hurriedly stowed away inside the shacks. A couple of burlier Vulgar at the gates wore cooking pots on their heads, no doubt stolen from the *saucier*'s collection, and watched the visitors through wonky-looking slits cut into the metal. Squealing children scampered up to Cunctus, mobbing him, and to Ghaldezuel's considerable surprise, the giant squatted, chatting animatedly in the local tongue and dishing out sweets and Filgurees from under his hat, like a bad magician. Most people liked Cunctus out here; he had squared up to the Amaranthine and robbed from the rich – the fact that he gave little of it back to the poor didn't appear to harm his reputation – and there were more than enough influential folk willing to follow his lead.

A huge brick ramp brought them up to the castle's rotted wooden gate, which stood massively ajar. Local ne'er-do-wells had clearly ransacked the place when they heard of Andolp's fall. They passed between the enclosures as they ascended the ramp, spotting featherless Shiklins strutting and scratching in the sandy dirt. Amid their soft crooning Ghaldezuel could hear the bells of a departing fishing boat, noticing as he looked over the ramp's waterside edge that there was a small makeshift harbour built around the castle's foundations.

The castle gate was fissured with great cracks, each of them home to a family of small, bat-like Ringums. They squealed as the party arrived, squitting watery turds down the bricks. Ghaldezuel and Cunctus did their best to cover their heads as they went inside, though the witch didn't seem to care.

The place was a ruin. The sea-facing wall had fallen in some time ago, and now the interior was a hollow shell of broken bricks, peaks of sand and straggly, rotting weed covering the floor. More pots and pans littered the place, a cracked glaze of old sauces lining their bottoms.

Ghaldezuel was peering up into the rafters, where water dripped steadily onto their heads through the remains of an upper floor. He turned to Nazithra, who was sniffling around in an unsavoury manner. 'So where is he?'

'Ran away, no doubt,' said Cunctus, watching her scrabbling in the rubble. Only a fool would have tried to stay.

The sound of the sea exhaling through the castle's cracks – a phenomenon the Melius called *Siehrbarrun*, Cunctus had said – was especially lulling in here. Ghaldedezuel, who had hardly slept, had begun to hope the Lunatic *had* escaped so that they could return to the keep.

'No,' the witch said, 'we're in luck.' She beckoned them to the remains of a window. 'There,' she said, pointing down to a rocky cave in the castle's southern-pointing foundations, its floor half-submerged in the shallows. 'The Corpse Tide has given him away.'

They waded out to the cave, Ghaldezuel surveying the empty beach for any danger, then remembering the threat of Cethegrandes and looking uneasily out across the lagoon. At a particularly smooth, rounded-looking rock, Cunctus bent and rootled in the sand for a while, grinning at last and pulling out a misshapen lump of pearl. He handed it to Ghaldezuel. 'For your pains. Tonsil stone of His Majesty the *Megaptera leonina*.' He pointed at the worn rock and a row of bright scrapes on its surface measuring almost six feet across. 'See the teething marks? Infant.'

Ghaldezuel turned his gaze on the pearl, holding it up to the light, never having seen an uncut specimen before. It was worth more than the shanty dwellers outside had seen in all their lives. It smelled vaguely cheesy when he held it to his nose, as if it were on the turn.

'The Lunatic made his fortune from the pearls,' the witch said. 'Andolp had them secretly ground into his soups, to give him strength.'

Cunctus barked a laugh. 'Fat lot of good it did him.'

Nazithra entered the cave first, wading into the shallows and sinking up to her veil, which pooled on the surface before following her down. Ghaldezuel and Cunctus looked at each other, the Melius inhaling a huge lungful of air and going next. It took him much longer to submerge, walking into the depths of the cave before his head disappeared. Ghaldezuel waited a moment, gazing out to sea where a light, opalescent rain shot through with bars of sun the colour of oyster shells glimmered across the water. He removed his boots, stashing them behind some rocks, but kept the rest of his clothes on.

The witch had been watching him avidly as they entered the water, no doubt hoping he would remove his tunic, and it gave him great pleasure to disappoint her.

Under the water, it was suddenly very cold. Ghaldezuel had never been much good at keeping his eyes open when submerged, but did so now as he spotted Cunctus's feet disappearing around a distant rock. He followed, feet kicking at the sandy bottom of the cave, sluppocks and screamfish and shoals of little Impio sprats changing direction at his approach and darting away. The ground was a nesting site of seamarrows, and everywhere Ghaldezuel kicked milky jets of sperm rose around his ankles. Nazithra was up ahead, waiting for them, the floating veil exposing her horror of a face in the gloomy underlight of the sea. Ghaldezuel paused, thinking she looked like a jilted, drowned bride. They followed her into a submerged cavern, Ghaldezuel's lungs beginning to protest already, and watched as she motioned at something overhead, pointing expressively at herself then moving slowly forward. Ghaldezuel gazed up at the rocks, blinking as much as he could, trying to see what she was indicating. He spotted a small black node reaching down from the rock and froze, understanding that the Lunatic had bought some expensive Amaranthine technology for himself. The thing probably shot lumens, by the looks of it. Nazithra, some way ahead again already, must have been able to sense its beam. He hurried forward, sticking close behind Cunctus's massive, gloomy form.

They came up gasping for air, a reeking stench lying heavy on the water. Ghaldezuel winced, trying and failing to breathe more lightly as he floated beside Cunctus. The Melius turned to him and grimaced, making Ghaldezuel smile. Nazithra had already climbed out of the water and was standing rapt beneath the cavern's stalactites. All around her, shining dimly in the gloom, were mountains of pearls. The Lunatic must have been hoarding them. Beneath their cheesy stink,

Ghaldezuel detected a deeper underlying foulness. A nest. Something lived here.

'Oh fortune, you beauty,' Cunctus gasped. 'There must be millions of Ducats' worth.' He hauled himself out of the water and dug his hands into a pile, causing it to avalanche. Ghaldezuel waded to one side as hundreds of pearls clattered across the floor and into the pool. Some were larger than his head; the big ones smelled particularly awful.

Ghaldezuel caught the glint of something to his right and spun, observing a Vulgar creeping among the piles, watching them. Within a moment, he was out of the water and had the person in a headlock. A specialised spring gun loaded with what appeared to be pearl bullets fell out of the Vulgar's grasp and landed on the rock.

Cunctus, alerted by the scuffle, came and stood over Ghaldezuel and his prisoner. 'You are not the *saucier*, are you?' he asked. The Vulgar appeared to be having difficulty speaking, so Ghaldezuel released him from the headlock and shoved him to the ground, pinning his arms. 'Answer,' he commanded.

Nazithra came slinking over, shaking her head. 'Above,' she said, gesturing to the top of the largest pile. Cunctus and Ghaldezuel looked up.

The fattest Vulgar Ghaldezuel had ever seen sat there, watching them. He was easily the size of three or even four of his kind, a giant rosy-white tumour atop his pile of stinking pearls.

'So you're him,' the fat Vulgar said thickly, as if through a mouthful of cake.

Cunctus performed a mocking bow, then indicated the pearls that made up the Lunatic's high bed. 'How have you collected so many? It's a dangerous job plucking just one.'

The Vulgar nodded at the witch, scrabbling his fat legs until he was sliding slowly down the pile. 'She knows.'

When he reached the bottom he could hardly stand, and Ghaldezuel released the youth to tend to him. From their vague resemblance, he guessed them to be father and son. The Lunatic, judging by the size of him, probably couldn't leave this place at all.

Cunctus turned to the witch.

'He calls them,' she said, walking over to another large pool in the cave. Ghaldezuel spotted an iron trumpet-shaped object lying on the rock beside the water's edge.

'Yes,' said the Lunatic, his eyes travelling lasciviously over the witch's nakedness. He slicked his sparse white hair back like some kind of Lothario and, with the help of his son, lumbered up to Cunctus, extending his pudgy hand. 'Euryboas. They think me mad out there, for speaking the tongues.'

Cunctus ignored his hand, instead gesturing expansively at the pearls. 'I'll be requisitioning these.'

Euryboas shrugged, blinking. 'Be my guest.'

Ghaldezuel watched the fellow, supported by his son, trying to work him out. He didn't seem at all displeased that his treasure was going to be taken away from him.

Cunctus wandered to the pool, gazing into it, his large face patterned with rippling light. 'Usually they find them on the beach, vomited up' – he looked at Euryboas – 'but you call them here and pull them out of their mouths. Very *clever*.'

'Why, thank you,' Euryboas replied, waggling his eyebrows, his gaze wandering once more to Nazithra. Ghaldezuel could see, however, that she only had eyes for his scrawny son. The boy had produced a silver spoon and was busily scraping in between his father's folds, a creamy substance coming away in the bowl of the spoon.

'And what do you do with all this wealth?' Cunctus asked, wiping a thin runnel of drool that had dribbled from his lips.

'He provides sanctuary for the Oracles,' Nazithra said from behind him, and Cunctus turned. She sauntered past, running her long fingers across his back, and made for the young Vulgar. 'You see before you the wealth of the Drolgins Spirits, collected over the years to serve their needs.' She took the son's arm and led him forcefully away, behind a mound of pearls.

'She'll want to do me next,' the Lunatic said, watching them go. 'Better make sure I'm fresh.' He lifted a fold of flesh, taking a bottle of something from a table and squirting it into the creases. Ghaldezuel looked away. 'I've bedded over *twenty* in my time,' the Vulgar continued, winking at Cunctus. 'What's your number?'

'Quality over quantity, I always say,' Cunctus rumbled, barely containing his sneer as the Vulgar continued squirting himself with the acrid perfume.

When the Lunatic was done, he beckoned them both, waddling slowly past until he could reach the trumpet. 'The water hoopies will be listening already,' he said, tapping the side of his button nose slyly. He dunked the trumpet's end into the pool and began to whisper into its mouthpiece.

They sat and listened to him for a while, unable to escape the sounds of the witch and her new, possibly unwilling lover at the other end of the cavern. They had both begun to itch, as if the place were full of fleas. To take his mind off it all, Ghaldezuel tried to focus on what the Lunatic might be saying, remembering that Nazithra had called the old language, the Dilasaur language, Leperi. Occasionally Euryboas switched to something else, something that sounded almost onomatopoeic, and Ghaldezuel was shocked to discover that he was beginning to understand the Vulgar's words when Cunctus interrupted his train of thought.

'She ought to have asked permission,' Cunctus grunted, clearly put out as the witch's cries rose in pitch.

Ghaldezuel shrugged, unable to see how it mattered, grimacing at the sounds.

Cunctus looked at him. 'I'd thought perhaps that you two had—'

'No,' Ghaldezuel snapped, shaking his head furiously and shuddering a laugh. 'Absolutely not.'

Cunctus sat back a little, seemingly relieved, and Ghalde-zuel realised with amazement that the Melius was jealous.

'You've been to the First, haven't you, Ghaldezuel?' Cunctus asked, clearly trying to change the subject as Nazithra began to scream. 'You've stood beneath my painted ceiling.'

He remembered it, stretching into the shadows, Corphuso at his side. 'It was a beauty, nothing like it.'

'Hmm. I was going to have it repainted, before I was spir-ited away. Tell me' – he fixed Ghaldezuel with a glowering stare – 'did the new kings put their likenesses up there?'

Ghaldezuel thought back, remembering the faces. 'I think I saw a few, yes.'

Cunctus squeezed his fists closed, jaw working, but said nothing. He reached and dragged over an old saucepan, scrap-ing his finger around the base and sampling the residue on his tongue. Apparently to his liking, he passed the sauce to Ghaldezuel, who tried some warily. It was too sweet.

'You must be looking forward to . . . *her* . . . arrival,' Cunctus said, sucking on his trembling finger.

Ghaldezuel nodded, taking another fingerful of sauce.

'The Vulgar will never warm to a Bult in Napp's keep.'

He swallowed, putting the pot down.

Cunctus drummed his fingers on his knees. 'Forgive me, I'm quite the jawsmith when I'm anxious.'

At last, the witch appeared to be done and a wonderful silence settled over the cavern. Ghaldezuel and Cunctus scratched themselves, relieved, and listened to the Lunatic's mutterings.

'The Cethegrandes are restless,' he said, taking a break from the trumpet. 'But the one you seek has heard my call.'

Cunctus's ears pricked. 'Scallywag? He comes?'

Euryboas smiled broadly, looking to the water.

For a few moments, it was still as a sheet of glass. Then, shyly, the first few tiny bubbles appeared upon its surface.

The pool rippled, its dark luminosity broken up by larger

bubbles as they drifted and burst. Nazithra came shuffling back to observe, patting Ghaldezuel craftily on the rear as he stood.

A larger swell. Ghaldezuel could just about make out a looming darkness beneath the pool, and then a tuft of gingery fur, dark with dribbling water, broke the surface, holding still a moment before rising. Ghaldezuel's eyes widened. Ears, fringed at their tips with the same wet hair, rose into view, then an eye, blue as a Lacaille's and the size of a dinner plate, blinking away the water as it gazed into the gloom of the cavern, the displaced water of its arrival slopping around their feet. Ghaldezuel tensed. The thing could have swallowed a Melius whole.

Cunctus rose unsteadily to his feet.

'Waggle?' he asked, stretching out a hand – a hand made almost childlike by the beast's size.

The Cethegrande peered at him, its nostrils flaring as it hoovered up his scent, and then something softened in its eyes.

'Waggle!' Cunctus cried, reaching and burying his face in the creature's mane of fur. The Cethegrande extended a wide grey tongue and coated Cunctus in saliva. He laughed, eyes squeezed closed, kissing his friend's ears. 'Ghaldezuel!' he said breathlessly, beckoning him over. 'Come, meet my Scallywag.'

Ghaldezuel walked uncertainly into the beast's view, registering a deep mistrust in its blue eyes as they turned on him.

'It's all right,' Cunctus whispered into Scallywag's ear. 'Friends.'

Ghaldezuel came closer, inhaling the musk of its breath. To show one's pressed-together teeth in most primate societies, from the lowly Oxel to the Amaranthine themselves, was a gesture of submission; hence the smile as a sign of trust. To this huge creature, evolved from the Old World's wolves, the opposite was true. Ghaldezuel made sure to keep his mouth shut.

As if to prove his point, the Cethegrande yawned mightily, spraying them all with spittle. Wedged between its yellow teeth were large splinters of wood, and something that looked very much like a femur.

'Here,' Cunctus said, pulling gently on one of the pieces, 'let me get that out for you.'

'I'll say my goodbyes here, then,' Cunctus said, extending his massive arms and wrapping Ghaldezuel in a tight, sweaty grip, lifting him off his feet like an adult grasping a small child. He could barely breathe in the giant's embrace, returning to the earth gasping and wild-haired.

'I'm glad you chose to stay with us, Marshal,' Cunctus said, studying him. 'I like you. You'll do good, being here.'

He looked at Nazithra, offering her his hand for a licking, then turned back to Ghaldezuel. 'I'll be leaving Mumpher with you. See that you get along with each other – I won't be pleased if there's trouble when I get back.'

Ghaldezuel sighed inwardly. He caught the flash of the Threen's eyes. 'Good luck,' he said, a little lamely.

Cunctus's eyes widened and he pointed to Scallywag. 'Have you seen him? I won't be needing any more luck.' He roared with booming laughter, slapping Ghaldezuel across the shoulderblades, sending him staggering. 'I'll see you both in twenty-five days, all being well, with the keys to Moso in one hand and the heads of the three dukes in the other.'

WEIGHT

Most of the day was gone by the time they sighted the hole: a darker blot of water in the waves. Ghaldezuel found his grip tightening on the oar as they approached, as if the fissure's depth was pulling them closer, some current dragging them in.

A few minutes earlier they'd spotted a rusty blue Void-ship bearing the markings of the absent Vulgar King Paryam passing over the lagoon, a trail of smoke scudding across the sky behind it. Due to the cutting of the telegraph wires, the king's remaining forces had been slow to learn of Napp's conquest and were only now beginning to rearrange themselves, splitting their defences at the equatorial capital of Moso, seventeen hundred miles north. Already Cunctus was on his way; they'd last seen his silhouette riding a huge humped back as it dwindled out by the islands at the lagoon's mouth. By tonight he'd be canvassing for support at all the ports he came to along the coast, the *Wilhelmina* bringing up the rear.

'Here,' Nazithra said.

Ghaldezuel heaved the barnacled anchor overboard, stepping neatly aside as the chain unravelled, then turned back to the witch.

'What now?'

She was silent. An expectant look hovered in the huge, shadowy eyes he could see through her veil.

The far end of the boat tipped suddenly down, bouncing Ghaldezuel and the witch into the air. He grasped the bulwark, splinters driving into his palms, arms jarred by the force of it. The witch hung on beside him, one hand gripping his knee. They stared down at the boat's tipped bow, Ghaldezuel understanding they had been raised some distance out of the water by a massive invisible weight.

'What is it?' he whispered, shifting so that he could free up one hand. The creaking weight seemed perfectly calibrated not to let any water in over the side of the boat, though it slopped against the sides, threatening to dribble in with every small wave. Ghaldezuel brushed the witch's fingers from his knee, glaring at her. 'What have you *summoned*?'

'The Jurors of the moon Maelstrom send their regards,'

the witch said, shifting down the boat a little until she had braced herself near the middle.

Ghaldezuel realised that something was sitting there, at the boat's prow. He could see its pale shadow pooling on the timbers.

This is the one?

The voices that drifted from the shadow were unmistakable. Ghaldezuel felt a cold sweat prickle across his skin.

'This is he,' the witch said. 'Told you I'd bring him, and here he is.'

Speak if you can hear.

He swallowed, realising they were talking to him, and he glanced at the witch. 'Yes, I can hear you.'

The witch had opened her mouth to speak again but was neatly cut off. *The warlord will only be useful for so long, we think you know that.*

Ghaldezuel glanced at the witch, his palms still smarting with splinters. 'I know no such thing.'

The shadow at the prow seemed to regard him.

We know things that none living could know. We have seen the time when he will be supplanted.

'By me?' He sighed. 'Is that what you're saying?'

Of course. Ghaldezuel thought he detected a note of exasperation. *Of course you.*

'Why?' he said. 'What's so special about *me*?'

It is seen that it will be you.

'All right.' Ghaldezuel sighed again. 'And what do you want in return?'

What we want is in that place.

He leaned back a little. 'The Shell city. You want to be reborn, like the Long-Life was?'

There was a long, perplexed silence, filled only by the creaking of the boat in the water.

'I must be the first Oracle to have reached you out here,' the witch said to the invisible presence. She'd told Ghaldezuel how news was carried between the voices of the worlds by willing subjects like herself. 'There was another, you see.'

The boat creaked and groaned, protesting as the massive weight crawled closer. Ghaldezuel felt the stern drop slowly back into the water, until they were almost level.

Another?

The witch gestured to Ghaldezuel. He glared at her.

'Tell.'

He stared forward, sure he was looking straight through it. The boat was so low in the lagoon now that its waters had begun to trickle over the sides. 'I worked for a time in the employ of a ... a being, someone who had lain dormant on the Old World.'

He told the presence as much as he could, remembering as he related the events of the last few months: Corphuso's scream as he disappeared, the chuckling laughter from the darkness.

Ghaldezuel felt a palpable charge in the silence from the other end of the boat as he finished his tale, tensing his shoulders.

For a long time, whatever was in the boat with them said nothing.

He survived.

The witch nodded. 'He did.'

Crazed laughter filled their heads then, ending as suddenly as if a switch had been thrown.

We wish him luck.

UPSTREAM

Twilight on the waterways, the stars glowing in the night-blue sky. Snatches of the idiotic Westerling song 'The Sea of Stars' invaded Cunctus's thoughts, and he began to sing beneath his breath. He didn't think he'd ever been more excited. He shifted on Scallywag's chain-draped shoulders to lean back against the baggage, one toe dangling in the black water. Clouds of marsh skits followed them in the warm air, tiny buzzing things that didn't seem to like Melius blood. Out across the bay, the dark bulge of the Amaranthine ship followed his progress, not a single light prickling its surface, making its stately way to the next port.

It might have been nice to stay a while in Napp, luxuriating in their first victory, perhaps even meeting Ghaldezuel's secret Bult squeeze – he found the image of the two of them together lasciviously fascinating – had he not been frightened of losing his momentum, a momentum hatched in the darkness of the Thrasm and brooded over until the great hole of the Sepulchre had opened at his feet. Never in all history, Cunctus thought, had anyone been so very rich and so very poor as he. But those peaks and troughs had guided his course, he believed; the steeper the decline the faster he went, the stronger and more energetic he became. The Lacaille, already pouring into Drolgins' last defended realms, their gunships trained on the major citadels, would learn of his strength and speed in the days to come and respect him. Let them take *too many* cities, though, and they'd laugh in his face, Cethegrande or no.

He bridled at the thought, his good humour vanishing. Nobody had ever laughed at him before. He wasn't about to let it happen now.

Cunctus reached down to pat Scallywag's ridge of hair, stroking along the grain before twining it around his fingers.

'It'll be time to try on that suit soon, eh, Waggle?'

The Cethegrande snorted a quick puff of rank air in response, the halitosis drifting over the water, and Cunctus smiled, taking a drag of the warm, sickly stench. As a boy, he'd been intoxicated by the stink of phosphorettes, those little coated sticks that made a flame, smelling them on the fingers of tall Secondling ambassadors. To him, that caustic smell had represented everything exciting about the freedom of travel and the night-time chill of adventure – something he wasn't going to be allowed much of until he was king – and it was only in the darkness of the Thrasm that he'd remembered those days. He'd wished so hard to see the world that they'd found him smuggled into saddlebags or wandering lost in the fields around the Sarine Palace, begging messenger birds to take him with every last scrap of pocket money he had. The birds had, wisely, refused. His mother had worried about him; there never was a less kingly child.

But nothing really changed. Maturity was just another layer, Cunctus understood; the adult mind simply an agglomerated rubbish tip of thoughts and feelings. His dearest wishes from childhood hadn't disappeared, they'd simply been built upon. He marvelled suddenly that if they'd only let him travel, just to the neighbouring Provinces, he might not be here now.

Cunctus watched a splash ripple out across the sea, Scally-wag's submerged head turning minutely. Other Cethegrandes were a danger out here and they kept close to the shore. But his mount turned back and looked ahead, apparently calm, and Cunctus's heart slowed in tandem.

He sat up a little and watched the stars, peering past the colourful specks of orbital junk to search the constellations for Sol and the Old World. Unbeknownst to most of his fellow prisoners, there had been a crack in the Thrasm's brickwork, up near the guard tower's connecting wall, which he used to stare through every night, becoming familiar with all the shapes of the heavens. Cunctus had watched the movements of the worlds as they arced overhead, looking past the massed stars of the Firmament and keeping watch over his old kingdom. There was something poetic in it, he thought, something he couldn't quite put his finger on. To watch an entire world through the sliver of a crack, the ice-dry wind watering his eye like the breeze through a keyhole.

The light of his old home star sank into his eyes and Cunctus thought back to his old loves, wondering what might have become of the beautiful men he'd cultivated at court. They would each of them be three hundred years old by now, pensioned off or married to unhappy wives. He exhaled a small laugh, musing on how dangerous those liaisons could have been, had anything got out.

'I'll come back for you,' he whispered to the night sky, 'when I've taken all I can. The Old World will be mine again.'

Cunctus's gaze flicked away from the Firmament and off into the deeper reaches of the heavens. To a Melius, the night sky was a riot of colour, their great lenses picking out so much more than the whitish specks the Amaranthine saw.

A waste, he thought. And he *hated* waste.

THE GORGING

Maril sat up in the dark. His face was sticky with something. Blood. He peered up, blinking the dried little bits of leaves out of his eyes. The treetops were very far away and the sky between their branches had turned a murky purple. Night was setting in.

Maril shifted with a stab of pain, fearing that he'd broken or badly twisted his ankle. As he moved, he disturbed the material he had landed on – what he'd thought were the crushed remnants of fallen leaves – and realised he was lying in a drift of dead flotsam. The forest floor was covered with them; trillions of fallen, bleached little bodies small enough to have lived unnoticed among his eyelashes. In the gloom, he could make out the pillars of the trees, a silvery mist swirling between them. It was cold down here, in the place where the dead settled. Maril experienced the aching pain in his arm again and massaged his scrawny biceps while he glanced around. Slowly, testing the weight on his ankle, he got to his feet, fighting through the heap of flotsam until he could sprawl onto its surface. As the night descended, he walked atop the drifts like a bird on soft snow, picking his way along, often sinking up to his waist. It was a wonder nothing came down here to take advantage of all this free food. Maril glanced around, the breath pluming from his nostrils; perhaps whatever lived down here didn't like flotsam. Perhaps it needed more. His hand went to his holster, remembering that he'd drawn his pistol just before he fell. Maril looked back into the gloaming at the snow-like piles of dead creatures. He'd never find it now.

Something rustled in the drifts and he picked up his pace, wincing at the pain in his ankle and waist. He couldn't be sure, but he thought he might have broken a rib, too. A lonely, mournful cry drifted through the columns of trees ahead and he changed direction, moving towards a source of silvery light.

The other Hedron Stars cast more than enough of a glow for his large Vulgar eyes to see by: a silvery pink light that suffused the world at the bottom of the trees. Maril found himself walking on harder ground, though the heaps of dead flotsam were no less abundant, and between small valleys of wrinkled, coral-like fungus. It was hard to be sure in the starlight, but it looked like the same stuff he'd eaten before. He made his way through the mist-shrouded valleys, steadying himself with a hand, stopping to rest after fifteen minutes and becoming conscious of the cold immediately. He had to keep moving, had to keep warm.

Maril blundered forward, blowing into his hands, stirring up some slow, sleepy flotsam that must still have been dying. The cloud of little creatures fluttered before him, catching the starlight, leading him on into a colder, more open space.

As soon as they reached the colder air, the flotsam swirled into the wind, as if making one last hopeless dash for the warmth of the treetops. Maril watched them billowing into the darkness like the spray of an inverted silver waterfall, the sigh of their minute wings calming his nerves.

But then the breeze strengthened, the hairs on his arms rising, and a huge dim shape appeared in the silver mist, swooping low through the rising cloud of flotsam. Maril ducked as the batlike shape of the Osseresis swept overhead, the wind of its passing almost knocking him off his feet. Another dived into the flotsam cloud, its mouth agape, hoovering up as much as it could before banking and rising back into the darkness. Then two more, their claws extended, came thundering down in a blast of air from their flapping wings. They landed, black ghosts in the silver, jaws snapping randomly at the flotsam. Maril found himself surrounded by their dashing shapes, the winds of multiple arriving Osseresis buffeting him to the ground.

A shadow spotted him and flew low, snatching his wrist in its claw. Maril screamed as he was lifted through the flotsam cloud and into the silvery blackness, flying between the branches of the immense trees. It dropped him at last, his stomach rising in his throat, and he landed with a bruising thump.

He was in a soft, hair-matted heap among the starlit caves of what looked to be a gigantic subterranean roost. Grotesquely fat Osseresis slithered around, flexing their wings and turning their golden eyes on him; from the oily sheens of their fur they must have fed well this season. Maril winced and shifted onto his good arm, sensing thousands of flotsam fluttering around in his stomach; he must have gulped a goodly amount in the struggle, or they had consciously flown inside him to get away from their predators.

He sat up, raising a tentative hand to the nearest of the black beasts. It sidled over, clearly not knowing what to make of him. The Osseresis licked its drooling chops and took a quick, sharp nip at Maril's good arm, pulling him over onto his side, then regarded him contemplatively and grasped him in its talons, lifting him into the air.

Maril was swept up into the darkness, higher and higher until the air currents grew warmer again and the purple glow had returned to the sky. They soared out over the trees, the painterly hint of the Snowflake stretching out beneath them, and plummeted past one of its arms, diving. Maril must have blacked out, for when he came around again they were far below the great artificial world, falling away through warm, flotsam-choked air. The Hedron Stars appeared to lie not in the Void at all, but in their own great atmosphere. He twisted in the talons' grip, trying to see where they were going, and spotting far below the colossal, crown-shaped structure of something bigger than all the Snowflakes put together. He felt suddenly light-headed again, and knew no more.

INGMUTH

Scallywag swam through the morning half-light, passing stands of brooding palms and junk-strewn mud, the lights of little hovels twinkling from the shore. Vulgar people had begun running alongside since Draalie, and Cunctus could see a procession of dozens following the black line of the beach, their thin cries reaching him across the distance. Through the night he'd spotted the lights of Lacaille Voidships dashing above the coastline, watching some of the larger vessels scorching in from the upper atmosphere, and a sense of unease was building in his gut. That premonition of their laughter filled his stomach again, twisting it in anguished knots.

The black mud of the shore drew closer as Scallywag slithered through the shallows, the harbour appearing around the spit. The clouds of marsh skits intensified in the rosy-pink morning air. Scallywag reared his massive head out of the water, glancing around, and twisted to meet Cunctus's gaze.

'This is it,' he said, patting his friend and looking into his piggy blue eyes. 'Let's get your brekky sorted.'

The Cethegrande wove into port, swimming up to the jetties between the tall house ships. Cunctus spied the small white figure of the Lacaille chamberlain already looking out for him, a crowd of local Vulgar waiting behind. At the sight of the approaching Cethegrande they surged forward, a line of Lacaille soldiers doing their best to hold them back. Cunctus levered himself stiffly from Scallywag's shoulders and clambered onto the rotten steps of the jetty.

The Lacaille stepped up to meet him as the crowd began to softly chant his name. *Cunctus, Cunctus.* He felt as if he was on stage; hundreds of eyes watched them from the teetering sea ships on either side of the jetty.

He stretched, acknowledging the crowd with a wave, and returned his attention to the small, plump Lacaille. 'Chamberlain Lazan?'

Lazan bowed, distracted for a moment by Scallywag looming in the water near the jetty. 'Come riding in on your Wiro, have you? How romantic.'

Cunctus made no comment, remembering the Lacaille's fairy-tale monsters. It was the image he'd hoped for, though he would never admit that to Lazan.

The chamberlain looked up at him, smirking. 'It is good to match a face to a name at last. All that mystery, all that theatre. You ought to've introduced yourself sooner.'

Cunctus was probably responsible for fifty or sixty thousand Lacaille deaths, all in all. They'd have to forget that fairly quickly if they wanted what he had.

'Nothing personal, Lazan,' he said, stifling a yawn.

The chamberlain's blue eyes glittered. 'Oh no, nothing personal. Not to me, anyway.'

They walked together along the shabby promenade, the crowd still chanting his name.

'And what news of your King Eoziel and his campaign for the Amaranthine? Does he prevail?'

'I'm certain he does,' Lazan said stiffly. 'Word does not travel well from the Firmament these days.'

Scallywag glided beneath the water, parallel with the dock as they walked, one submerged eye tracking Lazan. The Cethegrande's wake bobbed every boat it passed, whipping their chanting occupants into a frenzy. Cunctus turned to watch as big sloppy buckets of meat were brought out to the jetty. 'I'd stand back if I were you,' he said to Lazan.

'There's no point sugaring it, Cunctus,' said the chamberlain over the noise of the crowd and Scallywag writhing in the water, his jaws filled with thrown meat. 'We could've bombed your *kingdom* of Napp into the lagoon. Eoziel could be wearing a necklace of your teeth by now. If you didn't have half the Investiture ready to drop everything and follow your cause—'

Cunctus regarded him without expression. 'Don't forget my Magic Mirror, Chamberlain. You'll be needing that, too, I imagine, if you want to last even a minute against those Pifoon in the Vaulted Lands.'

Lazan circled him, studying his height, his scars. 'You're a Firstling, aren't you? The smallest breed of Melius?'

'I think there are smaller folk out towards Ingolland, on the Westerly Isles.'

Lazan ignored his answer. 'You were such a *nuisance*, before your capture. That raid you pulled in Baln nearly bankrupted us before the war even got started. If it were up to me' – he shook his flabby, pointy-eared head, mouth set – 'if it were up to me...'

Cunctus smiled his toothy smile, great shaggy head cocked, pink eyes filled with good humour.

Lazan sobered a little, clearing his throat and stepping

back. 'You'd better know that the equatorial capital of Moso is putting up fierce resistance. We're going to fizzbomb the city's eastern districts in five days.' He shrugged, affectedly playful. 'Be there if you want, it's up to you. Just don't get in our way.'

'Oh, I'll *be* there,' Cunctus said, lifting a leg to inspect the sole of his grubby foot. He'd trodden on a piece of glass. 'At the head of...' He mimed counting on his twelve fingers. 'Ninety thousand free Vulgar soldiers, enough that you needn't drop a single bomb; their chanting of my name alone will be fit to crack the walls.'

His words hung in the insect-dense air, the sun rising over the hills.

'But what then?' Lazan asked, his eyes narrowed. 'Do you know much about long campaigns? I don't suppose you do.' He fished a tarnished metal tin from his inside pocket and produced an exquisite silver-painted Lacaille spitette, closing the tin again without offering one to Cunctus. 'Could you stand there and tell me a single thing about upper-troposphere flight, heavy-gauge lumen guns, battery coordination, Canolis fuel yield' – he paused, dashing the coated end of the spitette across his belt, igniting it – 'superluminal navigation, ship-to-ship collaring...' He took a drag, exhaling sweet smoke into the wind. 'Or will you simply follow our convoys, stirring up the populace and claiming each victory as your own?' He blew another plume of smoke into the breeze, observing the marsh skits alighting on the back of his hand and touching the spitette's glowing tip to each of their wings. 'Have you even been anywhere near Drolgins before? Do you know a single local dialect?' The chamberlain held his hand flat, collecting the burned insects. 'Perhaps it's best if you let us fight this war alone and take what's rightfully ours. Nobody would begrudge you that.' He looked up. 'Then, when Eoziel rules over Filgurbirund, and all your past misdeeds are forgotten, you could come and claim your leftovers.' Lazan swept his hands clean of the dead insects at last – a little show Cunctus fancied he might have planned in advance – and smirked at him. 'Just a thought.'

Cunctus observed him with that same pitiful half-smile, concentrating hard on hiding the steady boiling of his blood; his army, still only a force of five thousand garrisoned at Napp, would need to be swelled straight away and the *Wilhelmina* sent into active duty immediately. Cunctus studied the fat of Lazan's hairy neck, knowing how easy it would be to send the Lacaille a message then and there. Instead, he rubbed his hands together and strode out towards the nervous Lacaille soldiers, gazing at the massed crowd still yelling his name. He straightened from his usual hunch until he was more than twice the height of everyone present.

'Vulgar of Ingmuth!' he said in pitch-perfect Middle Ingwese. 'You are my first stop on a long and glorious road, and I shall remember your hospitality for as long as I live.' He saw that the crowd had grown, now filling the shambolic streets beyond the harbourside.

'Come! Touch me if you like, don't mind the soldiers. Let your children forward to meet my Scallywag here. He won't bite.'

The children came scuttling out, ducking beneath the soldiers' arms. Scallywag rolled in the water, eyeing them hungrily as he exposed his blotchy pink belly. The soldiers – having given up holding people back despite Lazan's frosty glare – finally allowed the adults through, and a horde of gabbling Vulgar surrounded Cunctus. He held his head high and shut his eyes, smiling as they clambered all over him, perching on his shoulders and outstretched arms.

Lazan watched for a while, entranced, the spitette forgotten in his fingers until it was snatched away by a child. 'I have a ship,' he called, 'to talk somewhere a little less overlooked.'

'No thank you, Lazan,' Cunctus said, his eyes still closed, 'places to be.'

The chamberlain pursed his little hairy lips. 'I'd like to talk more, before we go our separate ways.'

Cunctus opened his eyes and glared at him, evaluating. 'Show him your trick, Scallywag!'

The Cethegrande surged his tail through the sea, deluging Lazan with water. The crowd roared with laughter, applauding. Cunctus watched with a smile, enjoying the sight of the most powerful Lacaille on Drolgins drenched and dripping.

As he turned to head into the port, Lazan spoke to his retreating back, his voice queerly flat amid the hubbub. 'Don't you forget about me, Cunctus.'

UNZAT CITY: 14,621

The city of Unzat – translated directly in Lacaille as the 'unflat' city – was the gigantic remnant of a concrete meltwater well standing desolate on the cold, dry plains of Dozo, in the country of Etzel. Its tapering grey box shape, sloping inwards to a central reservoir ten miles to a side, was home to almost forty million Lacaille, their dwellings lining the steep cement sides. Along each flat-topped wall of the four-sided city ran an ice-rimed canal, its banks coated with snow, and upon each canal sailed a procession of wooden freighters and houseboats working their slow way along the wall until they could round the corner and start anew, not returning to their original mooring for eight weeks at a time.

Once a month, the sky over Dozo darkened, the gale of sleet blotted for a day by the arrival of the Lesser Batyem, *an ex-battleship and goods vessel dropping in from the larger ports of Harp-Zalnir. Gangs across the city watched to see at which of Unzat's corners the colossal ship would land, and which of the merchant vessels would arrive to take their fill.*

Ghaldezuel was known as Speechless back then, for his taciturn ways. At the wiry age of eleven he was already a killer, fighting his way across the Slant with his childhood gang, the Ghosts.

That was the year he discovered her in the darkness of an alley, she a decade older at least and already having born a child: a trembling, starving apparition in the dark. He'd found her by following the stench of death – already strong in any Lacaille city – and the little trail of chewed bones. She'd been living in a crack in the concrete, nursing a squealing Bultling the size of a finger, only leaving to hunt stray Lacaille at night. Maternal instinct, apparently, was strong even in such creatures; the need to hold, to embrace, passed down through all the galaxy's mammalian life. Ghaldezuel had looked in at her and almost ended her life there and then. A lone Bult, however terrifying, could not survive for long in established Prism worlds – they were anathema, shot and stuffed and paraded around town. Ghaldezuel had seen his fair share of their desiccated corpses strung from the city's flags, marvelling, like the rest of them, that the devils were real.

The ship never docked, sailing through the white days and freezing nights. Its decks were lined with iron spikes, watchtowers and bolt turrets, shifts of hired Great Companies in the pay of the Batyem taking turns at the helm.

It was two days' climb from the rainy tenements of Lower Unzat up to the canals, the Ghosts knocking on doors as they went, collecting simple wooden spring guns, hard black bread and vinegary wine.

Ghaldezuel made his way through the dripping shanties, snow from the upper reaches turning to rain around them, pausing to look back at the far-off district in which his own home lay, where the Bult lady and her child waited for his return. On his shoulder he clutched a bundle of washing, the weight of six hidden rifles forcing him to stoop. Sometimes he stopped for a breather, his eyes wandering, as they often did each day, down to the base of the city. There, ringed by a moat of cold, filthy water, lay the prison of Fizesh; the place he and all the boys would end up, he supposed, whether they liked it or not.

Cold, grey night descended over the concrete slopes, the snow thickening as they reached the top. Here the houses were a little finer, possessing tin-sheet walls and slabplastic roofs, jauntily coloured to dispel the depression of the place. Fires beckoned them from the windows, drinkers pissing out of doorways and wetting the boys' feet as they stumbled past. Cooking and effluent merged into one hanging stink, their stomachs snarling.

At the canal bridge they looked down, eyes gleaming in the radiance of Pruth-Zalnir, at the glowing banks of snow. The ship, twinkling with soft lights, was making its ponderous way upstream towards them.

Ghaldezuel loaded his wooden spring gun and drew a breath as the ship slid by beneath, sensing that he had come to a fork in fate, and jumped.

The prison of Fizesh was situated well beneath the lowest, poorest tenements of Unzat. Inside the cold moat at the base of the well city was an island, its basements bored into the concrete, nothing but a ceiling of iron beams to keep out the sleet.

Ghaldezuel had heard of the Thrasm, the Firmament's notorious prison – everyone had: that nightmarish oubliette for troublesome Prism where they gave you no food or water or light, the Amaranthine expecting you to take what you needed from the blood and bones of other prisoners. Here they were more lenient, but an inmate still had to work for his keep.

Across a large, dimly lit floor scratched and painted with a network of unintelligible hieroglyphs, a hundred or so pairs of eyes turned to watch his arrival. Drizzle floated between the concrete beams of the ceiling, illuminated like constellations in the pale shafts of light. Ghaldezuel stopped at the entrance, feeling the press of youngsters behind him, understanding that the hieroglyphs were markings, territorial borders as intricate as any Lacaille country. He lifted his head to the wet air and met their gazes; many were scarcely older than he – twelve, perhaps thirteen – with a few old lifers scattered among them.

Someone growled behind him and he stepped aside, allowing the younger Lacaille in first. The youngster (Ghaldezuel knew his face from somewhere down-slope) shoved past, stepping rather unwisely onto the first piece of marked floor, a space about six feet across and home to a feral, cross-eyed thing that must have been half-Zelio.

Instantly the queue-barger's foot was pulled out from under him. Ghaldezuel and the others hung back, watching the slow, almost ticklish death as he was pinned down, writhing, his eyes gouged swiftly out of his head.

Another tried his luck as soon as the noise was over, skirting the boundaries of the territories, dithering at the fateful moment and falling prey to an outstretched hand. Ghaldezuel used the time to decide his next move; too far and he might slip up; too close and he'd have to battle interlopers for the rest of his stay. He selected a particularly weak-looking creature about ten strides away, noticing how the thing's territory (a rough hexagon scratched out in charcoal) backed onto another's: room, perhaps, for expansion.

Ghaldezuel allowed another couple past him, watching the first get snatched up, and took his chance. He pounced, leaping onto the warm body of a recent kill, aiming a quick kick into the head of the murderer and landing in his space. Ghaldezuel punched the Ringum quickly in the throat, aware that the baying of the crowd had increased around him, and shuffled in a tight circle, having lost his bearings for a moment. He saw the weakling a few feet away and bounded into the neighbouring territory.

He scampered, one foot in each space, dodging grasping hands until he could jump the final few feet. The weakling squealed and bared his teeth. Ghaldezuel ignored the show and wrapped his hands around the youngster's neck, hurling him backwards into a scrum of clutching fingers.

When the deed was done, he stood, breathing heavily, flushing as the place broke into sudden applause. It didn't last long: another member of his gang had just tried their luck, taking the space alongside with a messy kill and earning another, softer ovation.

Ghaldezuel cleared his patch, shoving the previous occupant's *personal effects to one side and sitting down. Judging by the hill of bones piled in each corner, nobody would be coming to collect the rubbish. Across from him, a Quetterel swept its territory with an improvised broom, muttering. Ghaldezuel imagined shoving someone hard enough to create a domino effect, perhaps instigating a full-on war as everyone stumbled into one another's spaces.*

'I know what you're thinking,' his neighbour said quietly. Ghaldezuel turned. A yellow-bearded Lacaille was holding out a small bucket of white chalkpaint. 'That's why the moat's there. Any rioting and they flood the place.'

He must have seen Ghaldezuel's incredulous look as he took the bucket and repainted the border of his space. 'Truly, they do. It's happened twice before.' He raised his eyes to the lowest of the grey shanty slopes, just visible through the rain and the concrete slabs. 'To be below the waterline is to be forgotten, as the old Lacaille saying goes. We are drowned souls already.'

A month later, his time served, Ghaldezuel gave the older Lacaille his floor space. Vibor – banged up for a year after seducing one of the Sigour's wives – let him through, shoving a letter into his hand so that they might meet again.

Ghaldezuel took a last moment to paint out his own name, doubling Vibor's territory. The Quetterel swept harder, watching the transaction with resentment.

When he found her again she'd moved district, squirrelling herself away into another alley much the same as the last. Ghaldezuel had wondered then if she didn't want to see him, if she'd been trying to get away. The child – nut-brown, blind and premature – had died, of course, and together they pushed it into a crack in the wall, sealing it up, Jathime following him warily into the half-light of the alley and into the rest of his life.

JATHIME

The slow, cold blue light outside had brightened just enough to see by. Ghaldezuel ran his tongue along his yellowed teeth, climbing out of bed and peering at himself in the bullet-pocked cuirass that served as a mirror. The sores on his top lip had only partially healed, the culprit never returning for the poisoned bowl of blood he'd left out these last few nights. Ghaldezuel picked the bowl up and slung the blood away, kicking it back under his bed.

After washing his armpits with lagoon water from a bucket, he stepped into the cold light by the balcony so that he could begin the process of bleaching his fangs with tooth paint. When he was done, he stuck out his tongue, observing in the faint reflection that it was coated with a layer of white-green slime, and rooted in his bag for the old bottle of perfume he'd carried with him these last six years. He dabbed some of the oil sparingly around his ears and scraped his tongue clean with the flat of his knife, reflecting that, barring the odd dip in cold water, it must have been at least six months since he'd abluted in any meaningful way. Pocketing the knife, he went to work inspecting his overgrown netherparts, combing them a little and dabbing on more of the perfume. He went and squatted on the Pong bin, a tin bucket tied to the balcony railings, shivering in the morning air.

The radio relay crackled from his helmet on the table and he started, almost knocking the bucket over. She was here.

A twinkling white dot, coming in low over the lagoon. No ships were allowed anywhere near Napp now that the city was cut off, and Ghaldezuel's pulse quickened as he heard the unsynced groan of lumen turrets across the city sighting on the approaching speck. Squeaky shouts across the balconies began calling them off. He exhaled, unclasping his hands, and sat back to wait.

The sun still hadn't risen, and out of the deep blue the little speck of light grew brighter, its structure visible at last. It was a brand-new Lacaille vessel, a Poacher, by the look of it, built for the latter stages of the war. He'd asked for only the very best. His eyes followed the ship's wobbling progress across the sky, its noise falling over the still city, a stripe of black exhaust recounting the ship's journey across the wastes of Milkland.

Then it was dropping towards his rooftop, wind snapping the holey curtains and shuddering the buildings. Ghaldezuel covered his ears, smiling, and watched the Poacher settle, a long, white spear of plated iron carbuncled with weaponry at one end. Its engines roared tropical blue and cut, dumping it the last few feet to the rooftop and shuddering its extended legs. Ghaldezuel uncovered his ears and climbed over the railing, walking quickly towards the opening doors.

He envisaged the look on her face as he stepped into the ship's dim shadow, smiling nervously, rearranging his perpetually wild hair. It had been three years, one month and twenty-seven days since last they'd seen each other; a quick, fumbling middle-of-the-night goodbye as the Vulgar closed in.

A silhouette against the bright interior, fussing with something. Ghaldezuel squinted.

Vibor, his old friend, came down ahead, waving and grasping Ghaldezuel's hand.

'She's had a hard journey, but will be glad to see you,' he said, throwing his bags in exquisite slow motion to some waiting Lacaille. 'I see you weren't exaggerating about this place,' he added, examining the languid motions of his own hand.

Ghaldezuel patted his old friend on the shoulder, making his way with a jog up the ramp to greet her. He entered the ship, the rank sweat and fishy rubber of a long journey watering his eyes, grinning as she came wandering along the corridor, face bathed in magnesium light.

The Bult lady Jathime had changed, he saw, fattened a little by the years of waiting, aged perhaps by worry, her white gown ripped anxiously by her own long nails. Spotting his reflection in a reflective panel, Ghaldezuel understood that he himself was no catch; even with his yellow satin finery he cut a scrawny and bedraggled figure, careworn from his wanderings across the Firmament.

Her large slanted eyes, rimmed with those exquisitely long Bult lashes, looked warily at him before some light of recognition came into them. He saw that she was wearing the pendant he'd asked her nephew Tzolz to pass on. She touched it absently as she looked at him.

Ghaldezuel was the first to reach out, taking one of her long, three-fingered hands. It was cold and clammy. 'I've missed you,' he whispered in Bult, unsure how to hold her after so much time apart, his mind reeling at the anticlimax of it all.

Vibor was waiting for them at the bottom of the ramp, suitably distracted by the strange properties of the city. Ghaldezuel led her down, watching her step in case she tripped, and into the cool early morning air. When the soldiers saw her, they quickened their pace, carting the baggage away across the rooftop.

He released Jathime's cold hand, pulling her slowly into his awkward embrace.

'*So*, in six months, the Lacaille have requisitioned every major Vulgar territory and habitat outside of Drolgins and Filgurbirund, killing the Vulgar Kings Kimmus and Borlo in battle and incarcerating Wilemo II in the delightful prison of Fizesh,' Vibor said over his limewine, smiling at their shared rememberings of the place. 'They have effectively won the war single-handedly.'

Ghaldezuel nodded, head in his hands, eyes fixed on Jathime's door.

'The Melius warlord Cunctus, meanwhile, has staged a small incursion on Drolgins while its king, Paryam, is on the run, taking a middlingly defended city and executing Andolp the Stupid, an aristocrat of little worth. For this he wants a quarter share in Filgurbirund, half of Drolgins and to be proclaimed acting Satrap of the whole Investiture – by the Lacaille, I might add, an empire responsible for his incarceration only a few years before?'

Ghaldezuel's tired gaze shifted to his friend, eyes crinkling into a smile.

'What is more, he has made you grand-marshal of his New Investiture, and you, in turn, are naming me marshal of Milkland while you and Jathime take up a more comfortable residence on Filgurbirund, in the as-yet-unconquered northern capital of Hauberth Under Shiel.' He took another swallow, raising a finger. 'And that's still not all.' He placed the cup back down. 'A Threen *witch* believing herself able to commune with invisible Spirits lives with you in your apartments.' At this point, Vibor cocked his head, a disbelieving look on his old face. 'And Cunctus, riding around the Lagoon of Impio on the back of a *Cethegrande*, no less, is now pillaging his newly conquered countries and generally stirring up trouble among the beasts of the deep.' He licked his lips and took another sip of the wine. 'Do I understand correctly? Have I got it all?'

'Where do you think King Paryam's run off to?' Ghaldezuel asked, taking a sip from his own cup, smiling.

Vibor stared at him a moment, then lowered his eyes to the battered old table. 'The new Pifoon Firmament, almost certainly. Whether he can convince them to let him into one of their Vaulted Lands before they seal them up is another matter.'

'Cunctus is confident, says he's got a way to crack each

of 'em open like a nut. The Lacaille will give him what he wants for it.'

Vibor arched his wispy eyebrows. 'Ah yes, this Mirror thing? The Amaranthine treasure? I heard that only works on location, as it were.'

'I don't think Lacaille high command fully understand it. Cunctus has it in his rooms – he even let me look in it.'

Vibor stilled. 'And?'

He hesitated, not wishing to be made fun of. 'It's real.'

His marshal's eyes narrowed. 'What did you see?'

He'd known something was amiss the moment he'd entered Cunctus's rooms. Cunctus sat, brooding, in a specially enlarged chair by the window, his lips wet with drool. Ghaldezuel had paused, ears pricked. The room felt full, somehow, as if packed with people, and yet only he and the Melius were present. Upon one of Cunctus's red, baked-clay walls hung a glossy silver bauble, its fish-eye reflection taking in the whole chamber. Ghaldezuel remembered the shock as he'd realised what he was seeing: it was the fabled Magic Mirror, and in its wide, silver eye floated a reflected throng of ghosts.

'I saw all the Vulgar people that had ever lived in or entered that room,' he said to Vibor. 'A hundred years of activity, all moving, talking, doing everything at once.'

Vibor sat back, ears flattening. 'Could you hear them?'

'Faintly,' he said, remembering. 'Nothing sensible, though. They were all talking at the same time.'

Vibor took a minute to absorb the story, finally glancing up to the gloom of Ghaldezuel's ceiling. 'All of it ... *captured* in the surfaces, in the walls, ready to be unlocked.' His eyes widened. 'Could Cunctus look into it and see us here? Could he hear us talking?'

Ghaldezuel shook his head, silencing him with a flattened hand. 'He wants it so that he can unlock the Amaranthine Incantations. Besides – it's you I had in mind to guard this treasure.'

The wizened old Lacaille refilled his cup, blowing out his cheeks. 'He'll come for it, though, won't he? When Moso has fallen – and it *will* fall – he'll come back here, and he'll want me to give it to him—'

'Vibor,' Ghaldezuel soothed, interrupting him, 'Cunctus trusts me.' He studied the grime he'd missed beneath his nails that morning. 'He has a great capacity for kindness, I think.'

'*Really?* You honestly believe what you're saying?'

Ghaldezuel could see the old Lacaille had supped enough limewine. There were good drunks and bad drunks, and most Lacaille (unlike the jolly Vulgar, who held their wine beautifully) were of the bad sort.

'Yes, I do. He is not an experienced commander, by any means, but he's wise enough to know what he doesn't know, so to speak, and to let others get on with things.'

'Hmm.' Vibor stared into his wine. There was a worm at the bottom. 'I think you'll be sorely disappointed in the not too distant future. They always change once they've got what they want.'

'He's right,' said Nazithra from somewhere in the warm shadows, when Vibor had gone. Ghaldezuel ought not to have been surprised – Cunctus had stipulated that she, as an Oracle, be given free run of the place – but she always seemed to find him when he was deep in thought.

He looked at her, the glint of those huge, nebulous eyes watching him like a snake.

'Let me bring my friends here, to talk with you. You might like what they have to say.'

Ghaldezuel sat up. 'Who am I to stop them? Why don't they just come?'

'This city is a *soul trap*,' she explained, as if to an idiot child. 'Enter and they'd be stuck for good. They can only come in' – she gestured lasciviously at her scrawny hips – 'in a body. I will give them mine for the day.'

He glanced away, exhaling. 'Put some clothes on when you do, will you?'

He tapped gently on the door and pushed his way inside. Bult didn't like to be surprised; he'd once thought of wearing a bell around his wrist, deciding in the end that it wouldn't suit him. All that frantic clapping – the way most superstitious Prism warded off spirits and demons, Bult especially – perhaps that came about from some ancient truce, an accord between predator and livestock.

Ghaldezuel went and sat down at the foot of the little bed, already knowing from the stillness of the shape beneath the furs that she was awake and listening.

'*Whiom iem?*' he asked. *Aren't you happy to be here?*

The shape made no sound. He'd worried the slow, syrupy air of the city might make her sick; perhaps bringing Jathime to this place had been a mistake, after all.

'I've missed you,' he repeated, glancing at the cracked tiles of the floor.

Nothing. He was conscious that Cunctus's rooms next door were empty, should he need to sleep – the Melius had offered them to him as a sort of bridal gift, gratefully turned down – but he sensed that going away would only alienate her further, and the trip would mean nothing.

Ghaldezuel rubbed the auburn fur between his fingers, realising it might well be Cethegrande hair. 'All that mattered to me was that you were safe.' He glanced up at the ceiling, hearing the faint screams of revelry: they wouldn't be so happy if they knew there was a Bult in their fair city. 'It won't be for long, I promise you; soon we'll be able to leave, if we wish, perhaps go back to the Whoop together, or make our home somewhere in the New Firmament. The choice is yours.'

He looked at her silent face – those long, long lashes. It

was the beautiful, careworn face of death, the last thing many had ever seen.

What most people didn't know was that Bult women, though they showed little in the way of emotion, possessed a deeply buried interest in pretty things. Ghaldezuel had swiftly risen through the ranks after he'd left Fizesh, first robbing each of the wall ships and then becoming their chief protector. He began to buy Jathime things that she liked. Saving enough Truppins bought him training in the Op-Viem – the knight school – until he was proficient enough be knighted properly by the Chamberlain of Etzel, leaving the small moon at last and taking a disguised Jathime with him to neighbouring Pruth-Zalnir, where they could live without fear for the very first time.

He remembered their first clumsy coupling, scared half to death that she would bite too hard and find him to her liking. He'd hidden a dagger nearby, just in case. Her nephew came for her one night, as Ghaldezuel had known he would, and he'd woken to find a lanky shadow at their door.

'Where is Tzolz?' she asked quietly, startling him, apparently reading his mind.

He glanced down at her. The question he'd dreaded. 'He's safe, I promise. He went to find something for me, remember? I expect he's there by now.'

'Where?' she repeated, voice muffled by the furs.

'The Last Harbour,' he said, 'one of the Zelio moons. Perhaps we'll go to him when this is all over.'

'Perhaps,' she echoed, this time in Lacaille, her eyes closing. 'Will we go, we will, when over-oo is.' She wasn't fluent in his language but liked its sounds, building them occasionally into nonsense sentences that made him love her even more.

FIRST STEPS

Sotiris watched the Vulgar fall, tumbling doll-like down the hill. He watched until the small person was nothing but a dot of distant colour, still rolling and flailing, then lost from sight. A wicked thing, clearly sent after him by Aaron; Sotiris was glad to be rid of it.

He sat, looking out at the never-ending landscape, following the progress of the path as it wound mile after mile between stands of murky trees, the luminous, ruler-straight lines of artificial canals bisecting its wanderings until it was nothing but a suggestion that divided the land. *Seven, maybe eight hundred thousand miles*, he thought, attempting to make some sense of the incredible distance.

He began to walk, stepping gingerly onto the incline and starting his slow descent of the path. With each fumbling step, he felt the beginnings of a light-headed joy. Something had just happened, something he felt deserved more thought, but he couldn't for the life of him remember what it was. Down and down, the path through the meadows feeling steeper with each step, and he recalled only that he had come here from the woods – one moment he was pushing through their wintry tangle, the next here he was. Deeper still and he remembered he had just seen Iro, hanging in her cage over the moonlit falls. He stared up at the incongruous, faded blue sky, the light of a missing sun beating down across his brow, and wondered how in the world he might have got here. But the thought of his sister spurred him on, and he walked more quickly, the insects flitting among the folds of his nightgown, clambering up his legs. Soon all he could recall was that he'd awoken in a large four-poster bed sitting in the middle of a meadow, the journey between here and there clipped as neatly as if by a pair of scissors and thrown aside. It was a wonderful feeling, this empty-headedness, and he marvelled at the sudden notion that perhaps the eldest Amaranthine (*whatever they were*), when they succumbed to madness, actually welcomed and enjoyed it. He paused on the hill, pleasantly warm and blissfully empty of peripheral thoughts, wondering whether he ought to stop and get his bearings.

'No,' he said aloud, continuing the descent. 'That's just what he'd want me to do.'

Sotiris spared the trees above him one more glance, astonished at how far he'd come, trying to remember if he'd ever really been there at all. The sight of the thorny forest triggered phantom thoughts; the sensation that he had not been alone up there, though he was damned if he could remember who was with him.

Iro, the forest whispered, and he made his mind up then and there, resolving to keep going and never look back.

MOSO

The *Wilhelmina* floated above the night-dark sea, its glossy, oil-coloured finish reflecting the myriad stars over southern Drolgins.

Cunctus and Scallywag lay floating in the great blue central chamber, the golden pilot's node having retreated up into a glowing, rotating cathedral ceiling full of burnished, sculpted stars. It was the most soothing place Cunctus had ever been, he reflected, reclining against Scallywag's belly and watching the stars moving on their clockwork-esque rotations. He almost didn't want to leave. Scallywag clearly liked it, too, and his blue eyes were heavy-lidded and sleepy when he looked at his master. The warm, wet smell of him reminded Cunctus of other places, other lives. They lay together, time itself apparently standing still, knowing there was almost nowhere safer or more impregnable in all the known galaxy.

'We'll try on your new outfit tomorrow, hmm?' he said in Leperi, scratching Scallywag gently behind the ear. The fantastical suit – a long, stretchy tube of translucent material like the shed skin of some monstrous, otherworldly snake – lay rolled up in his bags in one of the staterooms, one of the fabulous treasures they'd found in the freshly opened Sepulchre. The skin appeared to be impervious not just to the rat droppings beneath the Thrasm but also to everything they could throw at it, weaponry of every kind ricocheting like water. Cunctus had tried it on, breathing the strange, tingly cocktail of mist exuded from inside the bulging helmet, and had found to his delight that it did much, much more than just protect its occupant.

'I love you, boy,' he whispered, planting a small kiss on the sleeping Cethegrande's flank, then lay back and gazed with tear-rimmed eyes at the ceiling. He thought of Ghaldezuel, perhaps sitting up this night in his rooms in Napp, organising the minutiae of Cunctus's new empire. Of course he'd been sceptical at first, when the Lacaille had wandered into their camp, but now he couldn't be more proud of his new marshal. 'You're all good boys,' he said into the quiet. 'Good boys.'

Cunctus and Scallywag travelled at the head of a column of hundreds, swimming out into open waters for the first time so that they could be joined by rickety sea ships and a squadron of jets, even a subship from Wime. The Cethegrande was wearing his special suit of translucent scales, ready for whatever the Vulgar had to throw at him. Moso, visible as a pale, heat-smeared line of sea wall, lay only a mile away.

So far, thirteen ports had yielded within the month, pledging whatever hotchpotch soldiers they could, with more towns – their mayors hearing of a force sailing up towards the equatorial capital – already radioing their support for Cunctus and his troops. Nilmuth, the last stop before Drolgins' capital, had capitulated almost immediately when its barracks of freeVulgar mercenaries had threatened to mutiny, chanting Cunctus's various names and throwing open the gates. Its famous fortress now flew the Cunctite flag, a plain yellow banner already decorating wide swathes of southern Drolgins.

Cunctus, clad this morning in pale iridium plate armour and sitting hunched in the saddle as Scallywag picked up speed, had just received good wishes from Ghaldezuel, back in Napp, and grinned from ear to ear as he hoisted his Amaranthine sword. The wail of horns and clang of bells echoed from his ships across the water, followed shortly by the musical whine of the *Wilhelmina*, flying fat and terrifying overhead. Cunctus twisted in the saddle, eyes searching the procession, gauging the moment, and patted Scallywag's head.

The Cethegrande skimmed the surface of the water with a dash of roaring spray and soared into the sky, the delighted cries of the Vulgar aboard the ships following them into the air. Cunctus's heart hammered as he clung on, the reins knotted tight around his wrists, quite unprepared for the sheer power of Scallywag's new suit. The flying Cethegrande rolled in the air and swept back down towards the flotilla, the wind thundering in their ears.

A volley of guns opened up in support, the surprised elation of his forces palpable across the air, the yellow-daubed Voidjets banking to fly alongside. Cunctus whooped, eyes squeezed tight against the rush of wind, happier than he'd ever thought possible; his veins felt thick with sugar, his teary eyes prisming the view into a beautiful kaleidoscope of mirrored, repeated worlds.

Wiping his eyes, he spied a handful of paler shapes like sunken ships waiting at Moso's estuary mouth. So there was a trap after all.

'Cethegrandes ahead,' he said shakily into his radio, surprised that the three dukes of Moso had a rapport with any beasts of the lagoon. The escort of jets rolled, roaring down to follow the coastline. When they were nearly overhead, somehow undisturbed by anti-aircraft fire, they loosed their wobbling, twinkling bombs across the port. Cunctus reined in Scallywag, slowing him in the air, and watched the detonations erupting along the sea wall, the crump of the blasts reaching them a moment later. The shapes beneath the water were engulfed, only one managing to dart off into the depths before the last bomb fell.

'Clear for entry,' he said with satisfaction, soaring back down towards his ships as they churned into port. 'Drop me near the walls,' he yelled against the wind, tugging one of Scallywag's ears. The Cethegrande wove above the destruction, passing between two smouldering towers, wrapping them both in smoke. Scallywag descended until he was almost touching the hot concrete of a dock, angling so that Cunctus could untangle himself from the reins and jump the six feet to the ground. He slapped Scallywag's rump and the beast swept back into the sky, a blazing, reflective serpent shape zooming overhead to rejoin the jets. Cunctus unsheathed his jewelled sword and lumbered along the smoking mess of the concourse between a scraggly avenue of crisped, browning water palms. Something wasn't right. An unexploded Lacaille fizzbomb the size of a Melius had lodged in the shattered cement just ahead. Cunctus crept forward, placing his ear against the bomb's tin casing, listening to its grumblings, and moved on.

He climbed a little of the blasted wall, scrabbling up a shifting avalanche of rubble, until he could see the city itself.

Moso, spread across the floodplain beneath a hot white sky, had been devastated. Dirty smoke hung in slanting columns above the city, the pinkish fires left over from the fizzbombs still glowing in several districts.

Cunctus unclipped his faceplate, wheezing, and dropped the sword. *The bastards had lied to him.* They'd already bombed the city.

'*Fuckers!*' he screamed, booting the sword from the wall and watching as it clattered noisily down to the dock. Along the sea wall his flotilla had begun to unload, a twinkling throng of tin-armoured Vulgar swarming into the harbour. The jets screamed overhead, dashing past the sea wall and inland towards Moso, clearly noticing by now that the city was already in ruins.

Cunctus scrambled back down to the waterfront and sat heavily, his legs crossed.

'I'm going to rip Lazan's *f-fucking*—'

He hesitated, noticing as the water rose around the dock with the slop of a large swell. A shadow flitted through the sea, tracing the crescent of the empty harbour towards him, a wave surging before it. Cunctus stood, groping for his missing sword. He reached instead for his lumen pistol, aiming quickly and firing into the sea. Puffs of vapour exploded around the rushing form, either missing it entirely or enraging it further as it picked up a roaring speed. Cunctus fired until he no longer had time to move out of the way. The Cethegrande swept past in a blaze of white surf, angling its tail against the water to throw a wave of spray across the dock, dashing Cunctus into the lagoon.

He tumbled uselessly in the huge eddy of water, the shock and breathlessness of the cold taking over until he could right himself and struggle to the surface, his armour weighing him down so that he continually bobbed and spluttered, desperately trying to loosen the buckles. He gazed around him, head dipping again under the water, and saw the Cethegrande's great bubble-wreathed shape angling in his direction once more. It was an adult, twice Scallywag's size.

A trap a trap it was a trap, his mind screamed, the iridium armour dragging him down.

The creature circled, and Cunctus rose again, gasping, above the surface, having loosened and at last unbuckled his plackart. The beast was playing with him, isolating him from the port. He pulled off his greaves and ducked his head under again.

The thing had circled closer while he was on the surface, and Cunctus saw in the underwater light how its sunburned head was snarled all over with the pink and white scars of battle, one eye socket puckered and empty. As it opened its mouth, Cunctus saw that the beast's incisors were all shattered, like shards of pointed yellow crockery.

It grinned at him, circling again, and Cunctus knew he only had one chance. He struck out, swimming as hard as he could for the rocky edge of the port. From the corner of his eye he saw it dart after him, rising from below.

Five feet. Four. Cunctus grasped the concrete with his gauntlets and hauled himself out, feeling the mighty swell as it rose up beneath him.

He rolled, the Cethegrande bursting from the water, lunging across the dock with a grotesque wiggle of his belly. Cunctus staggered to the wall, clambering until he reached the top and swinging his leg over as the Cethegrande barrelled into it, loosing rubble. He heard the beast's grunting, rasping breaths as it flopped and scrabbled at the base of the wall, looking down to see the creature's huge pale eyes fixed on him.

A silent breath of wind stirred the concrete dust into an eddy then, and the Cethegrande blinked frantically. Cunctus watched in wonder as its face peeled and fell away, cut neatly through the middle of the skull to reveal a marbled, cabbage-like cross-section of brain and bone already welling with blood. The Cethegrande's body accompanied the portion of its head, falling back down the wall and coiling heavily at the bottom, its flipper hands still flexing their claws, a greenish spurt of excrement spraying out from between its short back legs and decorating the dock.

Cunctus took a huge, gusting inhalation of breath, looking up to see the *Wilhelmina* slipping silently over the port towards him, its shadow darkening the dock.

*

They surrounded the body, a team of Vulgar hauling it over onto its belly. It was Howlos, he who had lain waste to the harbour at Hangland during the Forest War a few summers ago. He was more than twice Scallywag's size, a mottled pink and brown hulk of a thing patterned with scraggly tufts of blond hair. Scallywag himself had surfaced some distance off and wallowed in the shallow water near a few wrecks, a pair of Vulgar legs still poking from the corner of his mouth.

'Chamberlain Lazan,' Cunctus said, retrieving his Amaranthine sword and poking it into the severed head's one good eye, shoving the bloody ruin across the concrete with a grunt of effort. 'It could only have been Lazan who sent him, knowing I'd be coming this way.'

He sheathed the sword, looking at his soldiers, wondering if he could trust any of them. Fortune, that abstract God of luck he had come to thank and pray to, was not a Melius concept, but a Prism superstition. Cunctus understood he had been overconfident at a time when it was most dangerous to be so. He would not make that mistake again. He would live by his old Melius doctrines, believing in what he could see, and touch.

Further down the harbour, three rusty straddle cranes rose fifty feet over the water. A person hung from each crane at a great height, swaying rather dramatically in the wind. It was the three dukes – the city's masters. After the abdication of King Paryam, however, Cunctus supposed they'd effectively controlled the entire moon.

Cunctus glowered at them. One duke was missing his head and had instead been strung up by an arm. Even from such a great distance, his superior Melius eyes could make out what had been done to them, their britches pulled down around their ankles. He glared at them and he *hated* them, not for who they had once been, but for what they stood for.

The Lacaille owned Drolgins now.

Furto only became aware that he'd reached the top as he stepped awkwardly onto level ceramic, having trodden with downcast eyes for much of the day. He blinked and looked around, the interminable fever dream of climbing step after step apparently over.

They had reached the very tip of the Snowflake's point, where it connected with the newer addition of the Radiant, the stair levelling out and descending between a broad ring of the vast, black trees.

The heat was insufferable, distorting the view beyond into a wavering, baking shimmer. Furto was already drenched with sweat. He stopped for breath, mopping his damp hair back and shaking the sweat from his fingertips, his salt-stung eyes trying to focus past the shimmer at the expanse of the Radiant draped out before them: a star-shaped plaza five miles in diameter, ringed with black coppices of trees. At its centre, blurred beyond comprehension, grey patterns marched, rippling, around a central, blindingly white dais. The Osseresis that had made it to the top with them – elongated charcoal smudges, all gangly arms and legs – broke their silence, chattering animatedly.

'What's wrong with my eyes?' muttered Veril from further back. 'I can't see anything.'

'*Now* do you believe me?' wailed Slupe, who, Furto remembered, had been complaining of the same condition for a day or more, unheeded.

Furto stared off into the distance, picking out only a muddled blur of colours. He rubbed his sweat-slick eyes but it made no difference: the blazing whiteness of the stair had blinded them, like a field of snow. He glanced around, watching the blurred forms of the others staggering around the plinth at the top of the stair, bumping into black Osserine forms. He could only tell who was who by the colours of their shabby old Voidsuits.

Gramps appeared before them, a sinuous, grey-green shape against the white. 'Come, there's shade below.'

They passed down through the trees, hands upon one another's shoulders, until they were descending a shit-caked spiral stair to the massive white porcelain basin of the Radiant itself. The heat further down struck Furto like a series of progressively more violent slaps. Below he could see the roiling mass of grey, the stench of musky bodies and faeces rising to greet them, understanding that it was the thousands of petitioning Osseresis. Furto's damaged eyes moved past them to the dais at the crowd's centre. There was a trailing shadow there, emanating from something standing at the middle. A huge, distorted voice, like that of a loudspeaker, bellowed over the crowd. As they moved closer, he saw that the shadow belonged to a golden blur.

'The Invigilator's not a mammal... not, uh, Osseresis, is she?' the fuzzy shape of Drazlo asked.

'No, no,' replied Gramps, not looking at them, his mind apparently elsewhere. 'Not Osseresis.'

Closer still, they were privy to a loud exchange in that same amplified speech: a large, winged Osseresis was mid-petition at the front of the crowd, its squeaking, slobbering voice broadcast over the basin. After a burbled sentence that seemed to contain no pauses, the air went still, the blurred crowd expectant. Then the figure on the dais bellowed into life, its reply booming over them.

Soon they were among the seething crowd, the air thick and stinking, creatures peeling apart to watch them.

'Come on, forward,' Gramps hissed, shoving Furto, who had begun to hang back, rudely from behind. They found themselves stumbling, exhausted and half-blind and immersed in sweaty scent, through the columns, hundreds of beady golden eyes swivelling in their direction. Furto huddled against Drazlo, a palpable aura of jealousy surrounding their arrival; many here had waited all season, only for Gramps' party to push their way through.

Whiteness began to show through the shambolic cluster of legs and arms as they came to the head of the column. Then they were pushed out in front of the Osseresis and chivvied by Gramps all the way to the foot of the raised dais, its occupant looming over them.

Furto stared up at the hazy form, eyes watering. Its rasping breath drowned the sound of their footfalls. Without pre-amble from Gramps, the Invigilator opened what must have been its mouth and began to speak, the force of its bellows stabbing like daggers into Furto's ears. Its words were at first nonsense-speak, onomatopoeic slaps and splats, until Furto began to recognise the Reflective language from the previous night, and found suddenly that he could understand it again.

'*Atoktoktoktokoueeoow did you get here?*'

Furto had been half-convinced he'd dreamed the whole thing. He looked at the blurry blobs of the crew, knowing even though he couldn't see it yet that amazement would be dawning on their puzzled faces right about... now.

'Hey, I can understand...' Slupe muttered, trailing off.

They stared at the being, heads pounding with the bright-ness and the noise. Furto wished they'd been allowed to stand in its shadow.

'*Wheeeere in the Sovereignty have you come from? Which Orna-ment?*'

None of them knew what to say. Before anyone could think of a reply, the great shape bellowed, deafening them, and Osseresis hands were holding them down, stripping them of their Voidsuits.

'Why aren't you speaking for us?' Drazlo cried to Gramps, but the *Bie* had moved over to one side, to join the crowd.

The Invigilator pointed a blurred protrusion that might

have been a finger at Veril, first in line. '*More of them! Disguised as old Mempeople, this time.*'

Furto saw that Veril's ears had begun to leak blood. The volume really was unbearable. The oven-hot ground, baking through the soles of his feet, was becoming excruciating.

'*If I may, Invigilator—*' Gramps said in Reflective, amplified over the crowd, before being cut crisply off.

'*I have had enough of spies this season!*' the Invigilator roared. '*They will go to the Domain, leaving today for Piris-Perzumin.*'

'*Please, Invigilator,*' Gramps replied, '*my wish is that I would like to go with them, to ensure they are tried fairly.*'

The Invigilator sat motionless for a moment, Furto guessing that she was sorting through some great memory palace, looking to see if the wish had ever been asked before. After a moment longer, she bellowed her answer. '*Granted!*'

'She thinks we're *spies*?' cried Drazlo as they were herded, naked and sweating, past the throng, towards the trees at the edge of the Radiant.

'Shut up,' the *Bie* hissed, pushing ahead. Drazlo and Furto exchanged glances, breaking away from the others and catching up with him.

'Couldn't you have wished for our release?' Furto asked.

'You're getting us out, aren't you?' Slupe asked, joining them, his voice quivering. 'We're going home now, yes?'

Across the central basin, at the edge of the hazy trees, a party of small, dark mammals was waiting for them. They held between them a long sheet of material, and as the Vulgar walked forward, it was draped across their faces. Furto recoiled, stepping back to see a perfect imprint of his face had been left in the material, like a death mask. The whole thing had clearly been too much for Slupe, already at the end of his tether, who swore and screamed and ran full pelt for the edge of the woods.

Drazlo called after him, Veril and Furto giving chase. But Furto had eaten almost nothing since the day before last, supping instead from his supply of booze, and hadn't the energy to run more than a few steps. He stumbled on the blazing white porcelain, a dribble of watery vomit hanging from his chin. Veril stopped further ahead, breathing hard.

They watched Slupe's blurry little shape making its way across the white expanse, arms flailing, until Furto noticed a shadow descending from the treetops and gliding out over the basin.

'Slupe!' he shrieked.

The Vulgar hesitated, perhaps glancing up, before the great winged Osseresis came diving down and snatched him in its claws. It landed heavily, wings bent, and looked around, the glint of its eyes reaching them through the baking heat shimmer. The little figure in its claws wriggled uselessly. Furto felt his breath catch in his throat. The Osseresis bent and tore into Slupe, ripping a ribbon of flesh from the Vulgar's back and chewing.

'Slupe!' he yelled, pushing past Gramps.

'Let Sussh eat.' Gramps smirked. 'She's been patient enough.'

Furto turned to Gramps, tears running down his cheeks, the rage bubbling up inside him at the sight of that smug, lizard-like face, and threw a punch. The *Bie* hissed and snapped Furto's fist in his mouth, black lips peeled back, teeth clamping down. Drazlo and Jospor rushed over and disentangled them, blood running along Furto's knuckles.

Gramps spat, his teeth still flecked with blood. 'You want to find Maril? Then shut up and do as you're told.' He pushed past them towards the trees. Furto nursed his bleeding hand, eyes straying to Sussh's blurred form, watching as she continued to chew.

Drazlo looked at Furto's hand, getting him to flex his fingers, and shot a glance in Gramps' direction. 'Bide your time, Furto,' he warned. 'Let them think we'll do as we're told, for now.'

Across the concourse, the trees had been built upon, their bark and flesh scooped out into hollows and used for fine, spindly dwellings, perhaps belonging to the more privileged sector of Osseresis society. A huge black and white creature lurched out of the woods nearby, dragging a case of some sort along the ground behind it.

'Mail ship?' asked Gramps in Reflective, waving cheerily at it.

The beast, some kind of intergalactic postman, Furto guessed, still cradling his hand, nodded gruffly, quickened its step and dumped the metal case in front of them, indicating that Jospor and Veril should pick it up. They gaped at it until it aimed a slap at Jospor's face, knocking him to the ground.

'Take the blasted mail!' cried Gramps, sashaying past. Veril hauled Jospor to his feet, ducking away from another of the postman's blows, and together they heaved the case along the ground, the metallic squeal adding to Furto's splitting headache.

Arriving among the trees, they saw that the surface of the porcelain had been cut away and a multitude of steps led down into its crust. Furto observed the individual, brittle layers of porcelain that made up the awesome structure, and looking down into the well of darkness he could just make out a blurry light.

They descended, calves aching after such a long-winded climb, the steps clearly built to the Invigilator's scale. Down beneath the surface layer of the basin it was suddenly much colder, and Furto began to shiver violently as the sweat cooled on his skin. The mammals ahead were still carrying their bundle of imprinted paper, and the impression of poor, dead Slupe's face, so perfectly moulded it was almost three-dimensional in the shadows, screamed silently at Furto. He couldn't look away, and stumbled as they reached the final step.

'No more steps, please, no more,' Veril begged Gramps,

who ignored him, his claws clacking unpleasantly on the ceramic.

Beneath them lay a web of interlocking bridges that stretched off into the gloom. Connected to each by a dozen or so buttresses was a long, spined growth, like a monstrous white seashell, its surface splattered with a crust of droppings. About half a dozen of the things hung there, one cut neatly in half, as if for maintenance. The cross section was a spiral hive of tightly packed chambers, each filled with beautiful white equipment. If they were ships, they didn't appear to possess an engine, let alone the space for one. Already a gaggle of wingless Osseresis, roused by the approaching group, were swinging hammers and breaking the supports, freeing one of the ships. Furto looked past them, head swimming, the pain in his hand dulling. Beneath the shell-shapes there was nothing but blackness, a drop he'd assumed on the climb was a cave of some kind. But it wasn't. He could see stars. It was space.

They had descended right through the material of the Radiant.

'If you all don't get moving I'll shove one of you off, eh?' Gramps said, startling them into life. The work team engaged in breaking the ship loose moved to the final buttress upon which the crew were standing and mimed a swing of their hammers, startling Furto and the rest of the Vulgar into a jog to reach the ship. A soft glow had begun to emanate from inside, and they set foot on a shit-caked spiral ramp that twisted around the ship's surface to the open hole at its top.

Furto was handed the length of imprinted material to take inside, and folded the screaming faces away from sight, revolted.

'Here, give me that,' said Drazlo beside him. He grasped Furto's shoulder as he collected the sheet, indicating Gramps ahead. 'I'll bet it's this ship he wants. He wouldn't have been able to get anywhere near it without us.'

'He framed us as spies?' Furto asked, his nausea building again.

'Looks like it,' Drazlo whispered as they drew closer. 'And I reckon he'll dump us first chance he gets, too.'

They had entered at the top, climbing gingerly in, and now suddenly they were walking on the horizontal. Furto looked behind him, seeing past the web of bridges and up through the well to the pinkish disc of light that was the Radiant's sky. He placed a hand against the wall, steadying himself, as the pink light began to recede. Three seconds later and he could see the whole Radiant, followed soon after by the Snowflake itself. It was only when he could see all fifteen of the worlds surrounding a vast, spiked structure that he understood they were falling away with more power than anything the Amaranthine could have dreamed of. The Snowflakes and their accompanying world dwindled to specks of light, then bright stars, and a moment later, Furto's eye could no longer make them out against the algal glow of the heavens.

When he looked around, Drazlo, Jospor and Veril were standing speechless beside him.

'No...'

'This can't...'

'An illusion?' asked Furto, peering out into the star-lit darkness.

'It's all gone,' whispered Drazlo.

'I've had enough of strange things,' said Jospor, cringing against the wall, naked but for his boots, which had, for some reason, not been taken. He coughed and a glittering gust of flotsam drifted away into the cool air of the ship.

They moved cautiously through a spiral warren of clean white chambers, their ceilings crowded with unguessably elegant machinery that looked as if it had grown out of the ship's material. The vessel's pale, ethereal light shone all around them without any discernible source, and a sharp, pickled smell, like vinegar, pervaded the place. Furto expected

Gramps to be lying in wait at every junction, but when they came to the tenth empty chamber, he realised the *Bie* must have gone on ahead, perhaps to wherever they flew the ship from. He wondered idly what mischief they might be able to do left to themselves, assuming hopelessly that the ship was in no danger from their tinkering.

Drazlo and Veril had already begun searching the chambers for anything they could use to defend themselves, but there wasn't a loose object anywhere, and every piece of the inexplicable machinery appeared fused to its neighbour. At some point they found themselves walking upside down, following the curve of the chambers, as if whatever gravity existed here did so only beneath one's feet.

A noise, like someone whispering, came from up ahead, and Jospor took off one of his rotten hobnail boots, holding it like a hammer in his fist. Drazlo motioned for them to stop, creeping on ahead. Furto didn't know what they'd have done without the half-Lacaille, knowing that had he not been with them, they'd all have lost any frail semblance of composure long ago.

An even sharper smell was emanating from somewhere up ahead, a corridor of gloomy instruments designed for something much taller than a Vulgar, or even an Amaranthine. They watched Drazlo creeping, child-sized, between the huge banks of machinery, his ears pricked, moving far enough along the curve of the spiral interior that he was, to their eyes, standing upside down. He stopped, frozen, then turned a corner and moved slowly out of sight.

They followed, Jospor's single boot *rat-tat-tatting* on the smooth, segmented floors. Furto came to the end of the corridor first. There was no sign of Drazlo; he hadn't waited for them at the next intersection.

That vinegar smell was even stronger now, and Furto, Veril and Jospor glanced at one another, wrinkling their noses. The Prism as a species were perfectly used to bad smells, but this was something else entirely. It repelled them on a new level, as if whatever produced it ought to be avoided at all costs. A black, sickle-shaped object on the floor caught Furto's attention. He bent to pick it up. It was a claw, fleshy at one end, as if freshly ripped out. He held it tentatively to his nose, withdrawing it quickly. The thing whiffed of vinegar.

Furto handed it to Jospor, too spooked to say a thing. As they passed it among themselves, then back to Furto. Veril cocked his head, listening.

'Shh,' he said, 'what's that?'

The ship itself was silent as a grave. Nothing gave the impression that they were travelling faster than any Vulgar had before. Between their breaths, however, Furto thought he could make out the sound of something dripping. It was a strange staccato sound, a *splat-splat*, *splat-splat*, like something viscous dribbling from a height.

They headed in the sound's direction, Furto at the front and wielding the claw. The sour stench grew stronger still, and then abruptly weaker as the sound diminished. Soon they could barely smell it at all. Furto gestured for them to stop, ears twitching. The sound of footsteps, coming from behind.

Jospor and Veril turned, the former with his boot at the ready, to see Drazlo careening down the corridor after them.

'Run!' he cried.

They sprinted as fast as their tired little legs could carry them, reaching the shadows of a single unlit chamber. The air smelled quite strongly of vinegar again here, and Furto paused at the entrance. 'What is it?' he said to Drazlo, coming up behind him. 'What did you see?'

'No time,' he gasped, 'get in.'

Furto smelled the sour whiff on Drazlo's body as he came closer, noticing that he had dropped the stack of imprinted paper.

'Get in!' Drazlo hissed, and the hair on Furto's arms

bristled. Looking back into the chamber, he thought he could see the glint of eyes.

'What's in there?'

Drazlo made to push him but Furto was ready. Summoning all of his lanky strength, he gripped Drazlo by the wrists and shoved the Lacaille half-breed ahead of him, a transparent bubble of film popping closed between them in the doorway as he fell forward. Lights blazed suddenly in the sealed chamber, instantly illuminating a gruesome pile of Osserine bodies, their faces frozen in the terror of a ghastly death. Drazlo stood, and Furto realised that the half-Lacaille was shaking with rage. 'Open it,' he mouthed, his voice muffled by the material of the bubble.

Furto noticed, when he'd managed to drag his gaze away from the shocking sight of all those bodies, that under the chamber's caustic lights, Drazlo's face appeared swollen. Looking closer, he could see that the shape of the half-Lacaille's nose and mouth were all wrong. It was as if Drazlo's brother, or perhaps his father, were standing there instead. The person came very close to the transparent door material, cupping his hands around his eyes against the light, and peered at Furto. Furto backed away, having no idea what the bubble was made of.

Jospor and Veril appeared behind him, staring in at Drazlo. 'What's he doing in there?' Jospor asked, going to the door. 'Drazlo?' They were staring, horrified, at the remains all over the floor.

'Don't touch anything!' Furto cried, pushing Jospor's hand away from the bubble's glossy surface. 'I don't know how it opens.'

Jospor looked at him, mystified. 'What?'

'That's *not* Drazlo.'

The person was still peering at them all, his eyes in shadow. Furto caught the other two glancing at each other, aware that they must think him mad. 'Whatever you do, don't open it.'

'Furt,' Veril said, 'that's *Drazlo* in there—'

'Look at him,' Furto pleaded. 'Just look at him.'

Jospor gazed into Furto's eyes, seeing the terror there, and glanced back in at the Drazlo-shaped person.

Jospor cleared his throat. 'If that's you in there, Draz—'

'Of course it's me!' the figure cried, banging his fists against the transparent material. Veril flinched away from the bubble, the claw gripped in his fist.

'Answer some questions, then,' Furto said, 'and we'll let you out.'

The person glowered at him. 'I'm not *answering* anything. Let me out.'

'Where were you born?' Jospor asked, peering through the glass.

The person stopped, staring back at him. 'Stole-Havish.'

Furto felt his heart drumming in his chest. That was correct.

'Right, then,' Jospor said, reaching for the bubble's surface. 'It's him.'

'Wait!' cried Veril and Furto in tandem. 'One more question.'

Jospor glared at them. 'That's him in there, he got the answer right.'

The Drazlo-like person seemed suddenly drained, sinking to the floor.

'What did Gramps say to me about the flotsam that night?' Furto asked. 'When they spoke to me?'

The person shot him a look. 'Not to trust them.'

Jospor glanced to Furto, who nodded. 'He did.'

'Well,' Jospor said, breathing a large sigh of relief, 'let's get this door open.'

Furto moved to the bubble, looking in. 'Except Drazlo wasn't there, was he? It was just you and me.'

Jospor, who had been working at the seal, stood back, mystified.

The person cocked his head, mouth working as he thought back to that night. A look of indignation began to spread on his strange, oddly formed face.

'Who—?' Jospor began.

'It's *Gramps*,' Furto said, his fascination tempered by the horrific thought of what might have befallen the real Drazlo.

'What did you do to him?' he asked the figure, who had begun to bang his fists rhythmically against the floor. 'The same thing you did to those creatures in there?'

'Let me out,' he muttered with each thump. 'Let me out. Let me out. Let me *out*.'

'He can change himself? To look like other people?' Jospor was still a little behind.

'*He's* the spy,' Furto said, cradling his bitten hand again.

The poor impersonation of Drazlo glared up at them suddenly, then reached for one of the Osserine bodies, dragging it over. He picked it up by the scruff of its narrow neck, gazing into its dead eyes.

The body in his grasp shrivelled, drooling translucent yellow pus from its eyes and mouth and ears. The Drazlo-person arched his back, his face elongating into a snout, never breaking eye contact with his prey. Soon wiry black hairs were sprouting all over his body as the corpse's pelt sizzled and melted away. Furto stared. Everything the being copied was simultaneously destroyed. The half-Lacaille's ears elongated as the corpse's melted. Furto knew that the stink of vinegar would be very strong right now, had the door not been airtight.

Jospor and Veril were hugging each other. The corpse emptied its bowels, its stomach deflating, and shrivelled to a crispy strip of flesh and pus-smeared pelt, dangling in the horrible half-being's grasp. Gramps was now almost completely

Osserine. He flexed his claws, watching them grow, and turned his golden eyes on the three Vulgar.

'How do you think you'll survive without me?' he snarled. 'Let me out of here and perhaps we'll say nothing more of it.'

Furto had been gazing desperately around the door trim and finally found what he was looking for. A blob of indented wall, like a thumbprint, right at the top of the arch.

Gramps attacked the bubble without warning, dragging his claws along it, the screech startling them out of their stupor.

'Veril!' Furto cried, singling out the tallest of them. 'Lift me up!' He pointed to the indentation.

Veril grabbed Furto under the armpits, hoisting him above his head.

Furto stretched with all his effort, his fingers falling short. 'Higher!' He could feel, where his knee pressed the bubble, the furious scrapings of Gramps trying to get out.

Veril grunted and thrust him higher, the tips of Furto's fingers just brushing the pad, his long arm almost there.

Gramps had hooked one of his claws into a scratch in the surface.

Veril threw him. Furto slammed his palm against the pad, falling the six feet back onto the floor.

He sat up. Through the bubble, there was nothing but blackness, as if the lights had gone out. *Nothing but a light switch—*

But then he saw, faint in the starlight, the petal-shaped rim of the outer bulkhead. The chamber had opened up, hurling away its contents.

Gramps was gone.

They made their cautious way to the tapered front of the ship, the spaces shrinking around them until they had to crouch to look out upon their destination. There beneath them, looming across the black horizon like a reflection of their own great worlds, lay the spiralled wisps of another galaxy; a dazzling blush of stippled blues and crimsons and pinks, glowing with an interior power mightier than Furto could ever conceive.

'Which one is it?' he found himself asking, suddenly very sober for the first time in many a day, remembering that it had been poor Slupe's job to ask the pointless questions.

'That would be Andromeda, as our maps call it,' said Jospor at his side. Furto looked at him in surprise.

'Where Gramps came from,' Furto supplied, gazing out upon the coiled, wondrous light. It was as if they were sinking to the bottom of an ocean, the glow of deep, unglimpsed things glimmering up through the darkness. 'Where he was trying to get back to.'

'Can we survive?' Veril asked, a tremble in his voice betraying his fear. 'Won't we starve long before we get there?'

Furto looked out upon the great Thundercloud, wondering. It had grown appreciably in size, he thought, since they'd first seen it.

'You know,' he whispered, 'we might just make it after all.'

BOUNTY

In the darkly wooded passes, fogged where mists clung to their slopes, Billyup scented something. *Smoke*. He wandered back into its slanting, fragrant trail and searched the forest for its source.

Down among the great roots of the trees he saw it: a house, some way below him.

The walled building had grown upwards, slimly entwining its terracotta-coloured material with the bulging trunks of the forest into a series of peaked spires. Billyup guessed it must have consisted of single rooms laid one atop another. His gaze searched the walled garden, spotting nobody in the grounds of the place, and he started down.

This time he'd made sure the Babbo was fast asleep before moving on the place, stuffing her with enough food to put her into a long digestive slumber. Billyup kept to the edge of the valley slope, stumbling between the trunks of massive Oblet trees until he reached the topmost windows of the house. He ducked, peering into their dark eyes, noticing that they possessed thick, warped glass instead of shutters. He skirted the bank and slipped through the tall ferns, drawing level with the lowest floor and sidling up to its wall. The building was smooth and mould-slimed down here, where the wooded mountain pass was at its dampest, and Billyup's cloak felt heavy with moisture.

He listened, ears pricked beneath his hood, the sounds of the valley growing dense around him: the sinking peeps and wails of Skinches, Whippertails and Crones, the broken, musical cries of Tup Tups in the depths of the hollow. It was the Mid-Quarter, the morning all but spent, yet inside the house nobody seemed to be stirring.

He came to the lowest window, a small aperture with a moss-slimed frame and busted glass. Pushing it carefully in with one hand, he sniffed the air inside.

Dank, spiced with something. There was someone here, all right. The sound of heavy, glutinous snoring came from deeper in, on one of the middle floors.

Billyup made his way inside, more confident now, shoving the window open and ducking into the darkness. His foot sank into something as he clambered down from the window and he saw that large, fresh stools had been deposited all over the tiles. Someone had claimed this place.

He wiped his foot and climbed the stairs, peeking into the first floor – a dark reception room with spotted black mould climbing up the walls – noting a heap of curious baggage, and ascended to the next, cocking his head as the snores grew louder.

Billyup paused, keeping inside the shadow of the doorway,

a high, sweet stench thick in the air. Scattered about the rugs on the floor were piles of clothes and hanks of chewed yellow bone. Two curved scimitars the length of Billyup himself stood propped against the wall.

Snoozing mightily in the chamber's four pushed-together beds were a collection of massive Jalan Melius, their great hairy bellies rising and falling as they slept. Billyup stood tiny and frozen among them, his hackles raised, afraid to leave. The Babbo, slung across his back as usual, stirred and lay still again. His mind worked as he thought of their bulky luggage in the last room: they'd come far, skirting the Provincial border. He hadn't seen the front of the house but was dimly certain that the door would be smashed in. What did they want, all the way out here?

One of the giants cleared his throat groggily, rumbling and tossing on the bed, which popped and creaked alarmingly. Billyup's short hair prickled with sweat. He waited until the Jalan had settled again, then stole out of the room.

Billyup went through the packs with trembling fingers. There was such a wealth of odd things that he hardly noticed the sounds from the adjoining room. His pointed ears twitched under his hood. Something had changed. Billyup looked up from his work.

One of the Jalan was inside the chamber with him.

The giant stood stooped and very still for a moment, swaying slightly on his feet; Billyup realised that he hadn't been noticed yet – in his cloak and hood he must have blended in among the luggage scattered about the room.

The Jalan scratched himself, drooling, and crouched to rummage in the pack nearest Billyup. He found what he was after – a set of long-handled brushes – and examined them for a while. Billyup remained frozen, sure the giant would smell him, but the Jalan seemed preoccupied with the act of brushing his teeth.

The Babbo started to writhe and Billyup felt a vicious fury.

He could throw her to the giants as an offering, simply toss her and run. But they'd have him before he could get more than ten steps. They'd pull him limb from limb.

The Jalan straightened and dropped his brush, clearing his throat and gobbing brown phlegm into the corner of the room. Billyup closed his eyes, waiting; waiting for that deathly pause, the startled grunt, the thumping of huge feet advancing upon him.

But there was nothing.

The Jalan went on scratching himself for some time, claws rasping on skin, and swung his head around at the sounds of the others rousing themselves. He thumped to the doorway, maddeningly close.

Billyup pissed himself. The stench of it rose thickly around him. He trembled as the Babbo started to stir, grumbling, on his back.

Out of the corner of his eye, he saw the Jalan hesitate. A sharp intake of breath. The giant turned, gazing into the room.

'Ghalangle!' came a cry from the bedroom.

The Jalan paused thoughtfully at the doorway before thumping away.

Billyup let out a stifled whimper, tugging roughly at his cloak with shaking hands and sneaking to one side of the doorway.

All of the Jalan were up now, sitting groggily on the edges of their beds, heads almost brushing the ceiling. Ghalangle was the only one standing, his back to Billyup.

'*Kaamh keduraan*,' said Ghalangle to the others. Billyup knew a morsel of Threheng. They'd overslept.

'*Haalangan ulai-kamie*.' Lost their head start.

Billyup listened, tensed and coiled and ready to dash back down the stairs if only that Ghalangle would get out of his way. He inched around the mildewed edge of the wall, hidden from the others by the Jalan's body, absorbed, despite himself, in their talk.

The others' names were Calamus, Ajowan and Zedory. They were resting up, having passed the Monsoons out of the East only a few weeks before. Westerlings, Secondlings; people of every sort seemed to be after them. Billyup shuffled and pressed himself flat as Ghalangle leaned back, the Babbo brushing up against the wall, the giant's huge shadow slipping over him.

The conversation turned quickly to breakfast as they woke up, becoming more animated. Billyup knew it was now or never and began to slide past Ghalangle's huge rump, the stairway in sight at last.

'*Kitack a-terus, maambunuh sietap Awger.*'

He paused in his creep, the Jalan close enough to touch.

Awger? Were they talking about him? He cocked his head, listening.

Maambunuh. They were killing Awgers. Every one they came across.

'*Mendiengaarh taang, terus maambunuh,*' another said thickly, halfway through a sip of something.

Billyup's heart stilled. They had to stop killing Awgers or they'd scare off the one they were after. The one with the Babbo. They were worried he might ditch it.

He must have gasped, though he had no memory of it. The next thing he knew he was down the stairs, sprinting as fast as his spindly legs would carry him out into the steaming woods, his face dripping, lungs burning.

Climbing through the dense woodland, Billyup came to the first view he'd had of the flats of Pan. He peered beyond the trees, sighting along the ribbon of a slim dirt road, one of the many tributaries that led to the great Westerly Artery further north, and following its progress as it wound between coppices of lush, stately forest and on into the murk of the vast land.

A traveller, a simple Westerling laden with goods, was picking his way up the grassy path. Billyup made a dash for the cover of an overhanging bower, trying to keep in the shadows, but his quick motion must have startled the person, and at the sight of Billyup lurking in the trees he stopped and stared, clearly unsure. Eventually the Melius continued on, casting sidelong glances, until he had climbed past Billyup and up the wooded hill. Billyup waited, watching, and seized his chance, scuttling after him, closing the distance. He brought out the rock when he was a few steps behind and swung it at the back of the taller man's head. It made a hollow *bonk* of a sound, as if it had bounced off thick bone, and the traveller stumbled, swearing, while Billyup stepped back to observe the effect of his blow. The Melius staggered and turned to look at him, huge eyes disbelieving. Billyup brought the rock upwards, crushing the Melius's large nose, blood spurting. He flopped backwards onto his pack with a clatter and rolled down the side of the hill. Billyup followed him, the Babbo awoken and sniffling on his back. The man looked to be thoroughly dead. Billyup grabbed one of the man's hot, blood-slick ears and whipped out his blade, sawing with an effort into his neck. It was sweaty work. Blood jetted in quick, violent spurts, and as he moved the body a little, it smeared his cloak. When he was done, he picked the head out of the wildflowers, grasping it by its blood-matted hair, and drop-kicked it down the hill. He smiled, watching it bounce along the curve of the slope, deflected by various trees until it accelerated and tumbled out of sight.

He glanced back at the corpse, satisfied, and went to work rummaging through its things. The man had been a bookseller; his bags were filled with very fine, slim-sheeted metal ring books with speaking pictures. Billyup didn't look at them much, tossing them to one side until he found the purse buried in a secret pocket. He took the rolls of silk, pulling them out of their ties so he could gauge their length, and stared at the bloody scene, his thoughts far away.

He'd known the Babbo was important, of course, but not *this* important. He'd thought at the time that she must be someone's daughter, someone's bride. Now he knew the truth – and he didn't like it. On his back he held the queen of the world.

Billyup considered then in earnest whether he ought to just toss her into the valley and be done with it. He got as far as untying her from his back, something that would have been far more difficult for anyone less double jointed than himself, and moving to a spot where he could see she would fall far, until a better idea occurred to him. He couldn't just dump her; that wouldn't stop them. No – he would find an Awger somewhere, some creature that looked like *him*. He would trick it and throttle it and leave the Babbo by its side. When they found her, Billyup himself would be long, long gone, and nobody would ever come looking for him again.

DIMENSIONS

Somewhere in Sotiris's empty mind, an internal clock had been keeping count. Days in the lands of the dead were, to his great surprise, regular as clockwork, and stopping beneath the shade of a small tree growing at the side of the path, he became aware that he must have walked for a very, very long time. The notion of an 'outside' still featured somewhere in his consciousness – that there was more to his existence than this, even if he would never see it again – and he knew instinctively that the subjective months, perhaps years, he felt had passed in here had most likely not gone by outside, wherever that was.

He inspected his bare feet, leaning against the tree to check the soles. They were black with dirt but certainly didn't look as if they'd spent years on the road. There were no blisters, and he felt no pain.

Sotiris gazed out into the blush of fields, the warm blue sky burning lemon-yellow at its horizon, seeing all the way to his destination – the specks of some kind of habitation, its size impossible to guess. He squinted. Townships littered the path, travelling into a distance that his eyes, unlike those he had been born with, could see perfectly.

He sat, suddenly immensely hungry. He had met people, he remembered with a start: *things*, creatures that had accompanied him a little of the way, found that he was poor at conversation and left. He recalled now that some of the fields of brambles had been burning, and that he'd passed something, a marker of some kind, searching his memories and discovering that it was a mummified beast that must have died climbing a tree. He remembered in vivid Technicolor walking beneath its outstretched hands, staring up into the empty death-scream of its face.

Sotiris looked at the flowers around his feet with famished intensity, plucking some writhing beetles from their petals and popping them one after another into his mouth. They were so crisp and hard that they cut the inside of his cheek, only mashing into pulp after a few good, hard bites. He ate for a long time, sitting in the only patch of shade for miles around, the meadows alive with springing insects. Once, he saw something small and humanoid scuttle past, following the route down the steadily steepening plain, and wondered if it, too, had business further along.

Sotiris leaned back, satisfied at last, his chin and fingers coated with the rust-brown remains of his meal. He looked across to where the brambles grew thickest, a place he knew concealed one of the shallow canals that intersected the path, and roused himself.

Leaving his nightgown in a heap, he wandered naked to the canal's edge, seeing slivers of his reflection in its brackish, weed-choked surface. A waft of sulphur rose from the water, thick and heavy as a sewer, but he climbed in anyway. The water was very cold, in contrast to the heat of the day. He took a breath as he prepared to duck his head under and sank beneath the surface.

And he remembered everything; a blaze of recollection so strong that he gasped for air, dragging icy water into his lungs. He flailed, groping for the reeds at the bankside and hauling himself out.

Sotiris lay there, gulping air and coughing, too battered by the sudden barrage of recollection to bother wondering what would happen to him in here if he died. He turned onto his back and retched up some stinking water. As he did so, a small sailed raft came scudding down the canal, two matted, wet-looking mammals of indeterminate species sitting aboard and watching him uneasily. He locked eyes with them, noticing how the one at the back used its wide, flat hand as a rudder, and they sailed past.

The memories dried and evaporated as quickly as the water, dissipating by the time he came to pick up his nightgown again and rejoin the path. *She is at the zenith of this place, trapped by its depth*, he said to himself, having seen it underwater. All the way, the path led ever downwards on a gentle slope, ever deeper, the walk getting easier and easier, as if he were being drawn.

Sotiris glanced behind him, having not done so, he remembered now, since he'd left the woods, and saw that the tree-lined hill was so far away that it looked as if it would take more than the ten thousand lifetimes he'd experienced to get back there. And then he knew. This world was growing, extending, like tree rings over time. He could never go back. The forest and the upper world, already sliding from his recollection, would lie forever out of reach.

Corphuso sat in the burned stubble at the edge of the meadowland, the ash still warm and smoking under his bare feet. From the position of the wooded hill, looming high behind him, he knew himself to be a good deal further along the road. Not long before, he'd passed the grotesque, sun-petrified corpse of some climbing animal, its withered prehensile feet still gripping the trunk of a tree.

He'd found an encampment of gaudy tents, strange conical dwellings fluttering with flags and ribbons that appeared to be rather larger on the inside than their outsides suggested. The place was completely empty, though everywhere he found suggestions that the camp had been recently – and hastily – vacated, as if whoever was here had seen him coming. Entering the camp had also marked the first time since Corphuso's death that he'd managed to get a proper look at his reflection, stumbling across a still pool in the blackened ruins of the meadow. After a moment spent turning his head back and forth, rubbing angrily at patches of dirt that stubbornly refused to disappear, he made the connection. The dark patches on one side of his face were not soot or mud or anything he could wipe away: they were shadows. He tilted his face towards the sun, observing that the patches of shade remained where they were, as if painted on. And that wasn't all; when Corphuso looked more closely at his face, he saw with a start that it was slightly squashed to the side. He sat back, astounded: the face he wore here was not his natural face, but the face Aaron *remembered*. A soul was an afterimage – the fading remnant of a brief, bright energy; the Long-Life had clearly last seen Corphuso side-on and in dim light, and that, the Vulgar supposed, was how his afterimage would look, perhaps for all eternity.

This morning, finding some sheets of rough plant-fibre paper and lustrous green ink stored in one of the tents, he chose a spot at the edge of the meadow to sketch out his unified theory of this place. It had been brewing since his arrival here, and now he thought he'd cracked it.

He found a lump of charred wood and laid the paper atop it, weighting its corners with warm stones. 'Death is a mirror,' he said to himself. 'Death, life, existence.' He hesitated. 'A *kaleidoscope*, all worlds lying side by side, reflected.'

His hand, trembling a little as he gathered his thoughts, sketched out a careful circle. A circle, to contain infinity. He hesitated, scribbling in Unified in the margin. *Not a circle, a ball. So far, so obvious*, he thought. But then he placed a dot of pure green at its centre, the great gravitational Ur-force that appeared to govern all existence. *Oblivion*, he wrote slowly beside it, then lifted the pen – a whittled nib of bramble stem – shaking away its dribble of ink, trying to remember what he had known in the *before*. Corphuso licked his lips, returning the nib to the page.

Where is time? he wrote carefully, returning to the margin to answer his own question. *It is like ups and downs, a construct of our minds, only necessary so that we may make sense of things.*

Four quick strokes and he had divided the circle into eight equal segments, each bisecting the dot of Oblivion at the centre, like a cake cut into meagre portions. *The beam of a soul*, he wrote beside one of the shaky lines, understanding that to make the diagram realistic he would have had to bisect the circle into an almost infinite array of segments, one for every creature that had ever lived and died. 'Ten will do,' he said to himself, sucking on the tasty green ink before using the nib to follow the beam's journey down to the dot at the centre. *Originating in Oblivion.*

'All natural processes,' he said aloud, 'from the minute to the cosmic, *must* mirror one another.' And with that, he drew a series of quick angles, like saw teeth, halfway up from the core of the circle, sectioning off each segment like the spars of a spider's web. *The plane of existence*, he wrote beside one of the angled lines. *The geometry of the dimensions, upon which the beams of our souls spread like light through a prism, emerging from a thicker medium.*

He looked critically at the diagram, adding a smaller circle just within the outer shell, high above the blades. *Existence*, he wrote in the outer band. And beneath its line: *sleep.*

His pen shifted to the outer ring, the stratosphere of the circle. *Barrier. Impermeable membrane. Outer dimensions.* His pen hesitated. *Breakable only with colossal energies?* He imagined it suddenly as a puzzle of nested shells, each ball containing the next, their contents the same: this diagram.

Corphuso's pen retreated from the page, hovering above it as his eye moved back to the circle's interior. 'Souls trapped by the ultra-gravity of Oblivion,' he muttered, 'sliding back down in death, into the denser layers...'

One more circle, closer to Oblivion, so that the whole thing resembled an absurdly complicated bullseye. *Subduction zone*, he scribbled. *The soul falls to this place, all impurities burned away, perhaps to rise again after an aeon has passed.* There was a word for that, he thought. Not a word found in any Prism tongue, but perhaps in the Amaranthines' Unified. He smiled as he remembered. *Reincarnation.* Corphuso frowned, mulling over the implications of the word, and added a question mark beside it for good measure.

'And we poor souls have conjoined with the Long-Life's,' he whispered, 'slipping beneath the surface of the prismic blade, to the underworld below.'

He put the pen down and glanced back towards the impossibly distant hill. *Up*, and he would be nearer his old layer, a place of knowledge and memory. The place where Aaron fed. *Down* – he looked past the tents to the path, observing its snaking progress through the continent of unbroken meadow – and he would know the truth of it all.

The Vulgar Empire had never possessed microscopes, but Corphuso recognised in the image on his page something that he recalled from his old Amaranthine books, something ground into the fabric of his memory. *A cell*. It looked like an animal's cell.

Life, he wrote in larger letters above the circle. Then put the pen down. The diagram of life.

Corphuso picked up the pen again, chewing on the inky end. He had forgotten his old past so comprehensively that he didn't even know what he was. Only languages, abstract concepts and vocabulary learned by rote, remained in his empty head. But he remembered one thing from his passing between the layers; he remembered the intense pain and heartbreak that was the Long-Life's existence, and atop it all the newer, fresher coat of rage.

The warm wind stirred Corphuso's hair as he gazed vacantly out into the meadow. There was another, someone who must have come through as well. For some inexplicable reason, that other person had been favoured over him. The hairs on Corphuso's skin stood on end, a sudden jealousy boiling in his blood. That other person did not deserve his status here; he knew nothing of the Long-Life's heartbreak. Corphuso gritted his teeth, a sneer appearing on his strange, distorted face. He would show the Long-Life how worthy he was.

ASCENT

The pale, darting shape rose, Aaron's quickened thoughts returning once more to the face he'd seen in the crowd. The Melius.

Gliese dwindled behind him as he considered the prospect. A soul, returning from the depths again, even while its reflection remained. He had looked, of course, for some reflection, but it was a fool's hope.

Aaron stared ahead, the galaxy magnifying before him, and

dimpled the fabric of his fins, flying at superluminal speeds beyond sight and sound.

OUTSKIRTS

Billyup made his bandy-legged way into the outskirts of town. He'd stashed the Babbo up a tree, nice and safe, and now felt a long-absent clarity returning to his thoughts. All around him, the first bloodfruit of the year were just about budding, the brown fields suddenly dappled with crimson spots. As he walked, the stuff left a pink blush of colour on his cloak.

He'd been here before. People like him followed the same migrations, year in, year out, wandering the beaten paths of the world. There were Awgers here, in the woods and fields; all he had to do was find one, separate it from the crowd and bash its matted head in. Then it was a small matter of leaving the Babbo in the crook of its dead arm and fading into the dark, never to be hunted again. Billyup smiled lopsidedly at the thought.

But first things first – there was silk to be spent.

He passed tree-lined boundary walls, heels split and blistered, the last of his possessions clinking in his pockets. Melius children peered over the walls at him. Someone threw a stone, missing. He turned his lidless yellow eyes on them and they disappeared.

He followed the stony track into town, kicking up dust. There was a place where he could get a good meal, one of the few you didn't need to pass a test to enter. He saw it, a peeling red door faded pink by the sun, and ambled around the back. Chattering birds had made a twig-and-rush city in the eaves, outgrowing their space and spreading to the next house. A pot-bellied Melius trimmed it back with shears, apologising to them as he snipped.

They let him in after a couple of raps, hardly looking at

him. The hot darkness inside was suffused with smells. Billyup slopped drool across the floor as he shuffled in, eyes running over the dim, caged creatures, counting out his silk. He found a corner to shrug off his coat and went, quite naked, to take his bowl.

'What do you want? Brawn?'

He nodded, offering the bowl, which was already soaked with his drool, and watched it being filled up.

'Sauce?'

'Yes,' he replied. 'And bloodfruit.'

The cook ladled more on.

Billyup cast his gaze along the counter, gesturing with the bowl at some bottles. 'And that,' he grumbled. 'Some o' that.'

He took a table where it was darkest, sitting on the hard floor with his back to the other presences in the room. Wheezing cackles and whispers surrounded his table like drifting smoke, fading as he tucked noisily in, juices running down his chops. Billyup took a swig from the bottle, feeling it sting the back of his throat, and twisted slightly to peer into the room, spying Demian and Cursed folk. His eyes settled on a sickly Awger near the door, apparently alone. Billyup's attention returned to his bottle, and he chugged it patiently until he was numb and woozy and he heard the only other Awger getting up to leave.

He staggered up, taking the empty bottle with him, and ducked through the door back into daylight, remembering his coat only after he'd gone a few paces into the street. The chamber exploded with laughter as he crept back in to retrieve it. Stepping into the light again, he had to squint, spotting the distant Awger making its way through the field.

Billyup staggered after it, catching slowly up, the neck of the bottle slippery in his hand, ready. The Awger turned and noticed him at last, feral eyes wide. Billyup swung, missing the Awger's head, then swung again, clipping his own elbow in the process and snarling with pain. The Awger yelped and stumbled down a slope, ducking beneath the smoke-misted eaves of a stand of trees.

Billyup followed, the bottle shaking in his grip, stopping only as he saw them all gazing up at him from the hollow. Half a dozen Awgers, camped beneath the trees.

He dropped the bottle and ran.

WATERWAYS

Sotiris's eyes flew open. Warm, sticky darkness enveloped him. Cloud, lit by stars, hardly moved overhead. The moon shimmered, ghostly and shrouded.

He had fallen asleep by the side of a canal, and across its moonlit water he saw the raft again, slowing this time. The large nocturnal eyes of the mammals that piloted it were shining in his direction.

He sat up, drawing his feet away from the water's edge.

'*Eoos!*' one of the mammals called, its wide eyes apparently curious.

'Hello!' the other cried, and Sotiris sat up. What he'd just heard was not a word he recognised, and yet he understood it perfectly. What was more, he thought he knew precisely how to answer.

He called back, waving, and the raft drifted over the water towards him. The small vessel was loaded with odds and ends: ornaments and cloth and strange objects Sotiris hadn't encountered before. When it bumped up against the brambly shore, Sotiris could see that it also contained a little sunken section, a living quarters of sorts, just beneath the deck. The canal was clearly deeper than he'd realised.

Sotiris stood and looked at them. In the moonlight, their pelts were speckled with spots of ermine-white. Their sharp little ears pricked when he began to try to speak, but they interjected.

'Come aboard,' the smaller of the two said in a high-pitched voice, motioning hurriedly to the deck of the raft. 'There's room for one more.'

'Yes,' said the other, 'we saw you walking.'

'Where are you going?' he asked, his voice so unused to speaking that he could barely manage a croak.

'The same place you are,' said the first. 'Down.'

He nodded cautiously. He supposed that was precisely where he was going.

The smaller creature helped him aboard. Its black finger pads were warm and clammy. 'We have seen animals like you around here before, but they are rare.'

'Humans?' he asked, surprised.

The thing shrugged expressively. 'Whatever. New people. They who also met with the master and were brought here.'

Sotiris sat on the deck behind them, gingerly making space among the bric-a-brac, his legs pulled up under his knees. They cast off again, pushing away from the bank with an oar, the warm wind snapping out the sail and carrying them surprisingly quickly off down the canal. The bramble-choked bank began to roll smoothly by.

The canal ran in a pattern of interconnected zigzags, Sotiris knew that much. 'Won't it take longer this way?' he asked.

The larger creature scoffed. 'Of course not. We've been there and back again already.'

Sotiris sat up. 'You've been to the deep part? To the end?'

'Or the middle,' supplied the small one.

He stared, frustrated. 'And? What's it like?'

Large leered at him. 'That's where he keeps his queen.'

'His *lovey-dovey*,' said Small.

Sotiris looked down into the dark water, slow mind working, memories somehow rising from its surface; had there not always been a sadness in Aaron's countenance? He saw it now, in the recollection of their meetings. And that was the answer, to all of this. He smiled.

Aaron had been in love.

'You're trying to find your lovey, too,' said Small, giving Sotiris a decidedly human wink.

'Who made these?' he asked, hardly hearing the creature and looking out again at the waterways. 'Your people?'

The mammals glanced at one another. 'Yes, our kind,' said Large. 'We needed a quicker way to travel and trade. It has not escaped you that the meadow grows year by year.'

He nodded at the apparent question, conscious that they never asked anything directly, assuming something until corrected. 'How can I pay you for this journey?'

They cackled. It was a mean, hiccoughing sound, not at all like human laughter. 'No payment,' said Small, its grin revealing teeth like fork tines. 'But we always accept news, from the outside.'

Sotiris frowned. 'News,' he repeated. 'I don't think I'll be much use to you there.'

They seemed to accept that. 'It is an odd soul that remembers much, especially this far below.'

He caught one of the many flitting insects and crushed it in his hand, inspecting his palm as he licked it clean. 'What would happen if I died down here? Where would I go?'

'To the deep dark bottom,' said Large. 'Never to climb out again.'

Sotiris gazed off into the middle distance, wondering. 'Because the meadow grows.'

They both shrugged this time, and he watched them carefully, evaluating. If news was the currency here, they didn't seem too desperate to have it. His attention was abruptly distracted by the sight of dark folk sitting, some distance apart from each other, along the canal's bank. They were dangling lines of wire or hair from their fingers and staring raptly into the water. Sotiris hadn't yet seen a . . . He paused as he tried to remember the form, the word, until the memory rose from the water: a *fish*, only the bugs that teemed on the surface, paddling along with oar-shaped legs.

'So all these insects must go to the deep dark bottom?'

Small shook his head dismissively. 'They are memories.'

The long day passed on the cool canal, the meadows unchanging. Again, Sotiris thought he saw the smoke of flames in the distance. Then, just before sundown, he looked and noticed the tree containing the gaunt, mummified corpse, off in the distance. He opened his mouth to say something, astonished at how slow their progress must have been, then snapped it shut. Something, some relic of his guile back on the outside, told him to keep quiet.

When night came, they bumped the raft along the bank again and threw out a rope, knotting it to a thick stand of bramble. The raft drifted with the flow until the rope stretched tight, turning so that they were facing back the way they'd come. Sotiris caught another glimpse of the impossibly distant forest on its hill, realising that this whole slope of meadow was the inside edge of a huge bowl, so huge that he was only just beginning to make out its true shape.

He arranged the junk until he was comfortable and lay back, watching the improbable stars glow in the sky. The mammals nodded wordlessly to him, bidding him goodnight, and descended the wooden stair to their bunks in the hull, a light kindling within. He waited until they had closed the hatch, sealing off their conversation, before relaxing. He would have liked to sleep – for in this deeper part, none of his Amaranthine abilities appeared to work, least of all the power to remain awake for unnatural periods – but he knew he must keep watch until the morning. Sotiris was conscious that he hadn't asked their names, but then neither had they asked his. Perhaps they didn't have names.

*

He woke blearily, not a thought in his head beside the sensation of fingers locked tight around his neck. Sotiris gasped and struggled, not having any clue where he was, even *who* he was, only the ingrained need to survive acting on his behalf. He thrashed, twisting to one side and knocking into a pile of rubbish, feeling hands grab his ankles, and hurled the strangler to one side. The thing squeaked and splashed into the water beside the raft. Sotiris reached out blindly, found the rope and dragged the raft towards the bank. He felt it thump and drift, the creature screaming and thrashing against the side of the hull. He sat up, pulling harder on the rope in the darkness until the raft had covered the splashing creature, sealing it underwater, its frantic scrabbling audible through the hull.

The other mammal was staring at him, its eyes pale and uncertain. It climbed from the raft and slipped into the water.

Sotiris untangled the rope and pushed away, the early-morning light revealing enough of the canal to steer by. He could already see an intersection coming up and knew instinctively from his travels that this would almost certainly take him deeper, until he could find another. He looked behind him, observing the suggestion of Large paddling to the far bank. They had expected a more bamboozled soul, perhaps, damaged irreparably by the walk down. They'd clearly never met an Amaranthine before.

RITUALS

The vast, crown-shaped edifice, patterned with bands of cream and black forest just like the Snowflakes, filled Maril's vision. It must have been hidden from them all this time, lying directly beneath its smaller satellites. Stars shone weakly through the mist of atmosphere, mingled with the specks of thousands of migrating Osseresis. Maril coughed and spluttered, having taken too deep a drag of the flotsam mist – it seemed finer down here, perhaps why the Osseresis appeared to take no notice of it – and they angled towards an outer spire of the crown.

Falling closer, the bone-like substance of the crown's spike was as shattered and worn as an old fortress's walls. Hundreds of slimmer females were roosting in the crags; seething black shapes, like fleas. The Osseresis banked above the spike until at last he found what he was looking for and hovered, squabbling with the fat, incumbent males already perched there. He snarled and set Maril down surprisingly carefully, lunging at another male until it sloped angrily off. The females looked expectantly at the male, then at Maril, the closest rearing onto her knuckles. Maril gazed up at her, realising that they must know each other, and that he had been appropriated as some sort of mating gift.

The male nipped Maril's hand carefully until he stood, whereupon the females bristled their black fur, grumbling beneath their breath. The male perched on his winged arms and waddled around Maril, letting the females get a good look at him whilst he showed off his treasure. They inspected him appreciatively, whispering to one another, before returning their attention to Maril. They looked tired, Maril thought – it must have been coming to the end of the gorging season, and many were already visibly pregnant. But the male only had eyes for one. He strutted up to her, caressing her with the edge of one wing.

Maril shuffled backwards while the growling, bellowing deed was done, hoping he could get enough of a head start before they noticed him gone. It might well be that he'd exceeded his usefulness already.

But another fat male, this one with rancid breath and missing teeth, had come up with the same idea. Initially cowed by the display of its rival's superiority, it lunged forward now, snatching Maril's shoulder and carrying him awkwardly out onto the higher reaches of the cliff, breath puffing quickly between its remaining teeth.

They came before a gaggle of moulting females, the expressions on their faces clearly implying they wouldn't consider mating with Maril's haggard captor unless he had something outstanding to show them. He hurled Maril down in front of them, performing the same strutting circle around his prize, and followed a female off into the dark recesses of her cave.

It was then, Maril bleeding and aching while the remaining females looked him up and down, that he spotted over their hairy shoulders the sparse tangle of bushes clinging to the rock face. Dangling from some of them were fruits very like the one that had brought him to this infernal place. He summoned all his remaining strength and made a hobbling dash for the bushes, startling the females into retreating and letting him through. He deepened his voice and roared at them as he ran, forcing them back a few more paces, and threw himself headlong into the bushes, grasping the nearest fruit and ripping at its skin. Already he could hear the commotion of the returning male behind him.

Maril's scrabbling fingers could hardly make a mark, so he jammed his teeth into the skin and gouged, peeling away a seedless chunk of flesh and working his nails in, finally revealing a much smaller interior chamber than the Threshold that had brought them here. Maril hoped this *was* a Threshold. Glancing quickly behind, he saw the toothless male thundering towards him. He rammed his head and broken shoulder into the fruit, squirming with all his might to wriggle inside, worrying that he would rip the whole thing open and render it completely useless, wondering fearfully how much of a tear you were supposed to make.

A series of loud snarls behind him. It was almost on top of him. He pulled his boot in, the hobnail soles catching on the outer skin so that for a terrifying few seconds he was stuck, upside down, with one leg still poking out of the fruit. The

Osseresis were roaring and raging now, as if all the females were right behind him, too.

Maril froze, carefully wiggling his sprained ankle until it was free, spikes of pain driving into the bone. He collapsed into the dark, juicy interior of the fruit and looked around. Through the hole he'd made, he could see the toothless male, its shaggy head hanging limp, a stupid, vacant expression in its eyes. Its neck was in the jaws of the male that had first picked Maril up, and it was now quite dead. The females had retreated to the cliffs above and gazed down, jabbering and tossing rocks.

The first male brushed the falling rocks away and turned its eyes on Maril, narrowing them. It dropped the dead male and advanced. Maril wasted no time, pulling down the flap of skin, his fingers reaching through the flesh and clamping it sealed, and all noise from outside ceased. His right index finger felt suddenly cold. He listened carefully, pressing his ear to the fruit's soggy wall, before pulling in his hand. The finger was gone from the first joint up, sliced and cauterised cleaner than the work of an Amaranthine surgeon. Maril stared at it for a while, too shocked to do anything else, then pushed open the fleshy hole in the side of the fruit, narrowing his eyes against the glare.

THE CONTACT

Another memory, from before Perception's birth, over four thousand years ago in the time of Decadence. This one was buried deeply, as if intentionally hidden, and the Spirit opened it with great caution.

The letter arrived while they sat together.

Trang Hui Neng stared at it. It was a square paper parcel, clean and white, just like the envelopes from his youth.

'For you, I assume,' he said, not daring to touch it.

The man, Jacob's new emissary in the Old Satrapy, flicked a ringed finger in his direction. 'Open it for me.'

Hui Neng bent forward, picking it up. There were plenty of poisons in the Firmament that transmitted by touch, seeping into the skin, but he knew of none yet devised that could seriously harm an Amaranthine. He glanced up.

'Open it.'

Hui Neng turned the letter in his hands and ripped it open. It smelled sweet.

There was a little green card inside. Hui Neng tipped it carefully out and saw that it was blank on both sides. 'What is this? A threat?'

Aaron the Deathless peered at the card, looking pleased. 'No, it's an arrangement. See.' His finger hovered less than an inch from the card's edge, but Hui Neng knew he wouldn't touch it. 'It means "meet me".'

Hui Neng snorted. 'How do you know?'

Aaron sat back, withdrawing his hand. 'And look at its colour,' he said, as if Hui Neng had never spoken. 'By this I can infer the passage of the moon.'

The card's colour was a uniform mint green.

'Why tell me this?' Hui Neng asked after a moment, narrowing his eyes. 'Whoever sent you this took pains to hide its message.'

Aaron looked at him, those soft, colourless eyes almost without expression. 'The author of this message is blind, my friend.'

Hui Neng digested this, worrying that the Emperor Jacob might have made the wrong choice with this mystic of his. 'Why am I included in this?'

'Because I want you to come, too.'

In the green darkness, they arrived at Aaron's place. Hui Neng lingered behind the shadow-shape of the strange man, the birds of the woods whooping and warbling, remembering why he hadn't come back to the Old World. This was a forgotten, monstrous place, *more a domain of the Investiture than the Firmament, wherever it might be located.*

Aaron stopped abruptly, his green shadow enveloping Hui Neng before he could react and almost swallowing him. His great treasure, the Threshold, must be somewhere nearby.

Hui Neng stepped back, waiting, watching, his ears attuned to the sounds of the woods.

An hour passed. Two. The forest closed in on them. Twice Hui Neng heard something drawing near, catching the briefest glimpse of an eye shining in the darkness. A Melius, perhaps, or one of their talking beasts. Or maybe Aaron's contact was real after all.

He took in a breath, ready to speak.

And it was suddenly with them.

He froze. The shape in the darkness was small, dog sized. It extended the first of many hands, black shadows that investigated Hui Neng's cloak. Its fingers did not stray near Aaron's robe, he noticed. Indeed, it took great care to step around him.

'Emissary,' Aaron whispered to it, as if sound would frighten it away. 'This is a friend, one of the Firmamentals.'

The fingers rose to examine Hui Neng's face, fluttering around his nose and eyes. He smelled the same sweetish odour from the envelope.

'What is it?' Hui Neng asked, unable to stop himself, once the fingers had left his mouth.

Aaron turned, the green light of the moon barely touching his features. 'Beyond the Investiture there are hot, black places; planets that have lost their stars and gone a-wandering, home to the likes of my contact here. Through him I may speak to my supporters, out in the wider worlds.'

Hui Neng's skin broke into goosebumps as he considered the implications of Aaron's words. Life had never been found beyond the Investiture.

'Are you going to kill me, now that I've seen him?'

Aaron laughed, a good-natured chuckle that calmed Hui Neng immediately, but did not reply. Instead, he directed his attention to the thing squatting in the shadows.

'*So?*'

The thing took a breath and raised its finger. Whatever voice Hui Neng heard, it appeared to be born of his own mind. The Sovereignty will move with or without you, *it seemed to say.* They have their coalition now, and you are not as important as you think.

'*Careful now, I've proved you all wrong before.*'

The dark fingers paused in their motions, tapping thoughtfully together for a moment before the voice resumed. You say you can leave here, but we do not know how.

'*Trust in me. The hollowing of this place has been arranged – it won't take long.*'

Hollowing? If that is how it is done, fine.

'*You doubt me?*'

The reply was a long time coming. I think the answers to your predicament have not been recorded in all the history of the Thunderclouds. I will make an account of this to my betters; they will be amused.

'*You do that, Emissary.*'

The thing shot Hui Neng another blind glance before adding, When it is done, and you are whole, make your way to the Osserine Hedrons. You will find me there.

Aaron nodded, Hui Neng noticing how he closed his eyes, as if with relief.

For the Adoration of the Gargant.

'*For the Gargant, yes.*'

The shadowy creature clasped each of its hands together. That is all, then. We will see each other soon.

'*Wait,*' *Aaron said, his gaze intensifying.* '*What news?*'

The Emissary flicked out something that might have been a tongue. He is in disgrace. We do not consider him a problem.

'*Just you wait.*'

We heard he has been banished.

281

'That won't stop him. Give me time, just a little more time, and I shall deal with him for you.'

The blackness regarded him. This will be enough for you? Truly?

Aaron nodded, one slow dip of his head.

The moon, until then hidden by cloud, chose that moment to brighten. Hui Neng saw the creature in all its detail, and felt he would never be the same again.

It fluttered its fingers, resting them across its belly, seemingly oblivious of the moonlight. Then what? Will you return here?

Aaron smiled. 'I'll be much too busy for that.'

NEXUS

Lifetimes bustled past; an era in which Sotiris's mind felt stretched and blurred, passively taking in the progress of time as he sailed the waterways. He must have met many people, he supposed; their animal faces and snatches of voices filled his recollection, and the scars and scrapes all over his body told him he had fallen prey to a hundred accidents or attacks.

Waking on the raft each morning, he was still astonished to see that it had grown into a teetering three-storey houseboat with extra masts and sails and a crew of three that helped to steer it through the night, seeing off rivals and boarding passing ships. Indeed, his new vessel was so large now that it dominated the canal. The mammalian crew – sometimes a Prism or two – all looked just as surprised to see him every morning, and each had their own reasons for visiting the nexus of the meadowlands, accepting no payment of any kind. Nevertheless, they raided and stole what they could, still requiring food and warmth each night. Sotiris found himself hungrier and thirstier with every passing day, and a hint of memory took hold as he dined with the others on the top deck, something someone had told him once, an idea that this was to be expected, the further he drifted from his old life.

After what felt like millions of years, his sun-dazzled eyes began to make out the hint of a great shape spanning the bowl of meadows. In the white-hot haze of the world it looked pink at first, like a band of bow-tied ribbon connecting the opposite sides of the bowl, standing a mile above the canals. Years closer and its form resolved, the crew climbing up to the masthead, rapt and speechless.

It was a bridge, lustrously crimson as fresh blood, its ramparts crowned with a hundred conical towers that pointed downwards as well as up. Around it steamed a city so vast that Sotiris felt afraid just looking at it, the first districts already beginning to scud by. A painted sign drifted past as Sotiris and the crew prepared their weapons and baggage, simply reading *You Have Come*.

They passed the remains of ships rather like theirs, now ruined and dumped in the meadows to rot, their occupants having presumably left their floating homes long ago to journey on foot towards the bridge. Sotiris wondered if there was some sort of impediment ahead, something they hadn't seen, that would force him and his ragtag crew to do the same.

He went to the bow, spying the first peculiar creatures peering at him from the brambles, more snaggletoothed faces appearing at the riverbank. *Epir*, his subconscious told him, remembering the word for the first time since his incarceration here. The people that made Aaron. Another word for their kind tickled the back of his mind, something well known, but disappeared again.

Sotiris walked across the deck, finding his crew still gawping at the world-spanning city rising above them.

'Look alive,' he muttered, recalling with difficulty some clichéd captain's orders, indicating the scampering shapes on the bank. 'Hoist the ... open the—'

Those at the forecastle were still staring, transfixed by something overhead. Sotiris followed their gaze to see a startlingly bright star floating high above the bridge-city. As he stared, he noticed that the star was not a uniform white but a shifting glitter of colours, first magenta, then green, then gold.

Everyone's attention was back on the star now, as if it were dragging them forward, a blinding point of gravity. Perhaps it really was. All the light in the sky drawn and compressed into a spark of unparalleled brilliance.

There was something more, Sotiris felt.

It's the way out. It's got to be. He stared up at the astonishingly bright point. *Once you've got her,* that *is where you'll have to go.*

'What is it?' someone asked. Sotiris couldn't answer her.

Tiny flaming missiles started raining onto the deck. They hardly noticed. Sotiris felt the sharp sting of something strike his foot and recoiled, kicking the burning lump of wood through the railings and back into the canal before his gaze returned, helplessly, to the star.

They sailed on, passing the outskirts of the sprawling township of red buildings that had faded to pink in the unremitting light, until they were beneath the looming shadow of the bridge itself. Sotiris found himself distracted at last, studying the exceedingly foreign – almost alien – appearance of the conical dwellings.

The ship drifted deeper into shadow, the gloom intensifying across the deck, and they all looked up to watch. Some minutes, perhaps even an hour, passed before they were clear of the bridge, emerging on the other side into warm light again, heading for the harbour. Birds and insects wheeled in the air, heavy over the waters, their chaotic swarmings whipped up and energised by the shouts from the shore. Sotiris's ship was passing through an area of apparently great industry, a stinking smog beginning to drift over the deck.

Sotiris checked that all was in hand and went below,

unlocking his cabin and gathering his few bags, already packed and waiting. He had spent the last few lifetimes trading in information, gathering what stories he could from pilgrims in the meadowlands about the great city at the base of the bowl, and he was reasonably confident that now the time was upon him he would know where to go.

Sotiris stood for a while in his cabin, a gloomy, creaking little chamber lit only by the light that filtered through the slats of the barred window. His bed was nothing but a heap of mangy pelts shoved in one corner.

The anticlimax was palpable. Instead of achievement, all Sotiris felt was a renewed sense of haste. He was here now, and so, assuredly, was Iro. Memories of his old life swam potently to the surface, glimpsed as shining shapes almost identifiable, and disappeared again. There was only the city, and his sister.

He ascended the creaky stairs and joined the crew, also carting their baggage now, on deck, hugging each of them in turn. They were all of them sad, of course, to be leaving after so long – Sotiris had calculated one night that they had been together over a million years, long enough to form a fairly decent bond in this odd, forgetful world – but he sensed in them a restlessness now to be away. They each had their own business in the city; Wyrran and Tanatar were also looking for people, while Iymbryl sought the way out. None had been surprised to hear Sotiris's own story. Aaron had committed so many souls to this place.

He lifted his two bags and slung their straps over either shoulder, mule-like. The stink of sulphur rose from their agitated contents.

'Farewell, Skipper,' said Wyrran, kissing him lightly on the cheek. 'Don't forget, never stay still. The meadowlands are moving faster apart these days.'

Sotiris nodded, embracing her. She was right. A storm had blown in some years back, a scudding turmoil of cloud that glittered reflective at its edges, as if another world was trying to merge with theirs, and ever since the ground beneath their feet felt like it was moving away with a newfound urgency. Sotiris knew he would have to walk twice as fast to reach his destination, and they both jumped quickly down onto the bank, not even bothering to tie up the boat.

At once, before he'd even had time to glance properly at the rearing bridge of towers, he was inside the Epir township, hiking up between conical maroon dwellings and entering a forest of brightly coloured tents strung over an apparent infinitude of silken ribbons stretching between the buildings like telegraph wires. It grew dark quickly, the world inside the tent city wrapped in the pungent smoke of bramble fires. The smoke was said to aid memory, and in the colourful shadows Sotiris thought he could recall snatches of his past lives, but he had to keep moving.

Epir shambled about their business like wraiths around him, most of them draped in huge, billowing black gowns that covered their snouty faces, bells and chimes dangling from the baggy material around their tails. A specimen with its face uncovered gawked at him. Sotiris looked into the crimson slants of its pupils, remembering the Long-Life's gaze.

He entered a tent populated with jars of tiny translucent fish. The Epir were drinking them, or swilling the fish around their mouths and spitting them out. Something medicinal, he guessed, pushing his way through a brief patch of light and into the darkness of the next tent. Here, at some altitude on the slopes of the bridge, his body felt fragile once more. He would have to take care.

In the next tent, a shadow play was in progress and a massed groan went up as he stumbled through, adding his own silhouette to the mix. The performers must have reacted quickly, adapting his intrusion to a joke, and a peal of slobbering laugher followed Sotiris out into the light.

He turned to see that he had climbed high above the port,

the patchwork colours of the tent shanty rolling away to frame the view of the canals. The bramble smoke had left the air up here; Sotiris suspected it was no longer needed. With altitude came memory, sanity returning.

A variant of a sedan chair carried by two Epir came up to meet him. He climbed in, shouting in Leperi that he wanted to go to the city centre, and they bustled him away from the tents and into the outlying districts of the bridge itself. Sotiris's imaginary heart pumped harder as they ascended a steep, paved hill that looked almost impossible to climb. He watched the world outside his compartment jiggle by: sun-bleached machine soothsayers squatting outside their conical houses; Epir banquets on the higher terraces; grounded flying ships sitting smoking on the roofs; washing and entertainments, moving footage from old lives projected onto walls. Through the translucent linen of an upper window, Sotiris thought he saw a pleasure trade in process, and dwelt for a moment on whether coupling souls were barren here. He had already witnessed the Epir embracing one another, having assumed it was a strictly Mammalian pastime, and thought he might be able to remember the tenderness of a hairy-pawed touch aboard his raft –

– but then the sedan wobbled, swaying as if it were about to topple onto its side as some huge caparisoned beast lumbered past, and as the chair drifted backwards down the ever-stretching hill, the memory left him. Sotiris forgot what he was trying to recall, his attention diverted. Jutting from some steepled roofs ahead he could see enormous sculpted ears, all angled and pointing up to the star.

This was a place preserved in time, a relic of Aaron's memory of when the world, the world of his makers, was younger. Sotiris remembered a fleeting word as he looked at it all, breathing in the stink and heat of the place. *Pompeii.*

The sedan chair stopped at an intersection, the hobbling pedestrians staring in at him, and Sotiris watched as the houses on the far side of the street visibly stretched away, suddenly double the distance. 'Don't stop!' he called, passing the Epir their payment – folded pieces of a map – early. 'Take me to the bridge gate.' They hurried along, barging through the crowd and catching up with the moving place. Sotiris could already see from the distance that it would take them more than a day's travel and settled in for the bumpy ride. He hadn't long eaten breakfast aboard the ship, but, feeling ravenous all over again, took out some smoked meat from his bag, tearing into it while the city rolled on. The hunger overwhelmed him these days.

CONJUNCTION

Lungs rasping, wheezing. Heart about to burst. Shouts following him.

Billyup concentrated on the ground, the Babbo bouncing and screaming on his back. So heavy. So loud.

Mountains, up ahead.

Billyup found himself in the shade of an overhanging rock, runnels of water drizzling noisily across his hood. The dim mouth of a cave reared ahead. The Babbo was slowing him down; he had to stash it.

Gulping breath, heart pounding, he made his way to the cave's entrance, stepping in. The hiss of his breath filled the darkness. Billyup wrinkled his nose in the blackness. There was a fresh, sharp smell here. Almost at once he heard the rattle of chains and the jangle of a little bell. Whatever was in here had scented him, too.

Billyup backed towards the cavemouth and it came straight out after him: a shaggy, ox-sized wolf wearing a necklace of bells, some caught between its teeth.

He turned tail and bolted, hearing the thing give chase, the scream of the chain zipping *clinckety-clink* across stone, jolly bells clanging madly. The bells got closer, so close they were ringing in his ears, and then vanished with a snarl. Billyup risked a backward glance.

The wolf had run out of chain. He whooped with primal delight, watching the creature gasping and wheezing. Billyup looked past it to the following hunters – who were already firing at the wolf – turned again and ran.

His mind calmed suddenly as he realised they would catch him. It was all over, really—

But then the ground disappeared from beneath him.

Xanthostemon saw it unfold even as he dodged the furious, snarling wolf in the meadow. The Awger simply disappeared.

He ran ahead, stooped, keeping out of sight of the Westerling hunters in the hills, and came hard up against a steep, tree-lined ravine. The Awger had run straight in.

He scanned the trickle of river below, eyes wide. Blood had already painted the water crimson. He went down.

It was howling.

The Awger, Billyup, was still alive.

Xanthostemon arrived carefully at the lip of rock that overlooked the river. He peered cautiously at the thing as it writhed on the stones, seeing that half of its head had been bashed away in the fall. How it had survived such a thing was beyond him, but the sounds of its screams brought him out in shivers. He checked his footing and went down to it, looking anxiously around for the child.

The Awger clutched at its seeping head – so broken that Xanthostemon could see a whole hemisphere of brain – and wailed. It was the sound of an animal so close to death that it could feel it, and yet it clung on to life. He pushed it over with his foot and stared into its darting yellow eyes. It wouldn't even know its name any more. All it would know was pain.

He left it there, writhing. He certainly wasn't going to put it out of its misery, at least not until the baby was found.

The Awger started pawing at the remains of its head, clawing into the broken skull and brain, legs pumping as if still trying to run. Xanthostemon hardly noticed it, realising suddenly that the child hadn't come down this way.

'What have you done with her?' he yelled at the beast in every tongue he knew. 'Where's the child?'

Arabis hung wailing in the twigs of a dropling bush above, her screams perfectly masked by the howling of the Awger. A small Westerling hand hovered into her view, caressing the top of her downy head, and pulled her up to safety.

MARSHAL OF DROLGINS

Ghaldezuel had become, in the space of only a few weeks, rather well off. He hadn't been poor before, of course – living well on the proceeds of his various Bult-assisted jobs throughout the Investiture – but since his appointment as Cunctus's marshal, a steady stream of captured loot, winding like a caravan across the hills of Milkland, had begun to arrive daily from the foreign ports Cunctus had already captured. Vibor, though kept busy in the office of deputy, had his work cut out for him squirrelling a portion of everything away each day, sending what he could to their various contacts around the Investiture.

At around the same time, bundles of severed heads and body parts (the pieces of every ringleader and local mayor that had dared turn their nose up at Cunctus's invitation) had begun to arrive, trickling in each day and finding their way to Ghaldezuel's apartments like unpleasant post or the offerings of some large, carnivorous pet. He was supposed to display them, of course, on the city's parapets, but had decided in the end that the wildlife in Milkland was frisky enough and didn't need encouraging with more free food. And so, after being suitably scrubbed and peeled and boiled and baked, most of what Cunctus sent went to Jathime.

If he had to put a finger on precisely when he'd lost his nerve, however, Ghaldezuel would say it was with the arrival of the prisoners. Not content with body parts, Cunctus had begun sending convoys of live Vulgar with the express instructions that they be delicately flayed of everything non-essential and hung from the walls, where they were to be fed and watered daily by soldiers on the ramparts. Under Ghaldezuel's watch, not a single prisoner had yet died, though there was very little left of the first fellow to hang, the birds and insects picking him that little bit cleaner each night. The loud music of the city managed to drown their screams most evenings, but in the dead of night Ghaldezuel could still hear them out there, being eaten alive.

He knew he couldn't stay. Napp had become a microcosm of Cunctus's plan for the entire Investiture. The witch had been right.

It wasn't as simple as asking for help from his own kind. The Lacaille Empire could offer no assistance; though still most assuredly disdainful of Cunctus and his plans, Ghaldezuel of all people knew they could never risk coming in hard and damaging Napp and its unique structure, let alone risk the loss of the precious Mirror. Indeed, any sort of offensive action at all, even far from Napp, would risk incurring the *Wilhelmina*'s wrath. And nobody knew quite how powerful the ancient Decadence ship really was.

No, Cunctus had the Lacaille well by the short and curlies, as Ghaldezuel's father would have said. They had no choice but to pay him lip service for as long as he desired.

If Ghaldezuel was going to get out, he would have to do it alone.

Luckily for him, all this newfound wealth had paid for a decommissioned Lacaille lurcher-class battleship named the *Vastuz*, now fully crewed and waiting in the forests of the neighbouring moon, Nirlume. The ship could – as long as the *Wilhelmina* kept its distance – blast its way into Napp should the need arise and take Vibor, Jathime and Ghaldezuel off the moon. But keeping a warship like the *Vastuz* ready had cost a small fortune itself, and in the month since they had captured the city, its defences had improved a hundredfold, with a suite of new lumen turrets crowning the keep.

You have time, still, Ghaldezuel told himself. Had he not personally opened the chamber beneath the Thrasm and handed Cunctus the keys to the invasion? Glowing messages from the warlord arrived almost daily – he wrote constantly, firing off letters as fast as he spoke – praising Ghaldezuel in all his endeavours. Cunctus trusted him, at least enough for him to slip away when the time was right.

At the edge of the Milkland woods lay Hag Bay, on Impio's western shore: a pocked cove of deep, artificial rock pools, a place where strange and valuable fish were cultivated.

Ghaldezuel and Mumpher took the zigzagging road down to the pools, squinting at the sunlight that blazed off the water. They had come from a meeting with the corpulent Vulgar sisters that ran the bay (and, coincidentally, provided the Lunatic with the ingredients for his revolting fish sauces), commandeering in the name of Cunctus the Great a fleet of well-built fishing vessels and promising in the ensuing chaos that under Cunctus's rule, Lacaille law would be implemented, granting all Vulgar a fairer rate of exchange and relaxed trading rights in the wider Investiture. Mumpher did nothing but smirk as Ghaldezuel was sworn at and spat upon, and the two of them shown the door.

Walking down to the pools, Ghaldezuel saw that they

appeared empty, as if the sisters had sent someone ahead of them to gather up anything of value. It was certainly what he'd have done, at least. He tugged at the chinstrap of Mayor Berphio's enormous black hat: a present from Cunctus to keep away the Sting rain when it swept in. Off to the south, he could see the hazy shapes of the sisters' commandeered fleet already making their way across the lagoon, their elongated Cethegrande spears deployed around them, to join Cunctus's forces at Wyemunth.

Ghaldezuel was conspicuously aware that Mumpher had chosen to walk behind him, and that not even an Amaranthine would survive a fall on these steep cliffs. He had to assume that, for now, he was still Cunctus's favourite; if there'd been any shift in the warlord's patronage, he'd have known about it by now. He shuffled to one side nevertheless, eyeing Mumpher. The Wulm grinned and hobbled on past. Ghaldezuel felt a rush of irritation and fell into step, the conundrum of how to get rid of him still at the forefront of his mind. The Wulm certainly loved the local fish sauce – Ghaldezuel had watched him slurping it from his plate at Cunctus's banquets – but there were no symptomless poisons in the Investiture that Ghaldezuel knew of; nothing that wouldn't immediately point the finger straight at Ghaldezuel and get him killed, too.

He continued down the steep cliff steps, feeling more trapped now than ever before, unable to shake the sense that time was draining away faster and faster, his window of escape diminishing by the hour. All he could think of now was getting Jathime out before the Pifoon in their Vaulted Lands retaliated – as they surely would before long.

This close to the water, he could feel the eyes of those invisible presences on him again, those who said they might be able to help him, for a fee. He wondered for a moment whether they could make Mumpher have a small *accident*, then chided himself. He didn't need them to escape; ask for the Spirits' aid and he'd only be exchanging one malevolent master for another.

Mumpher had reached the bottom of the cliff and set off across the rock pools without waiting. Ghaldezuel walked faster, not wanting to let the Wulm out of his sight, finally spotting the paler shapes of fish skimming the surface of a nearby pool. He remembered trying the fish sauce on his first trip out of the Lacaille volume, on the Vulgar moon of Nirlume, vowing then and there never to let the pungent, rotten stuff anywhere near his mouth again.

At the water's edge, he found a few Vulgar slaves eating their lunch. They made no eye contact when he spoke to them, simply pointing out the pools housing the intelligent fish he'd come to see. Cunctus had wanted every business in the region investigated for anything he might be able to repossess; outwardly an unenviable job – in the last three days, Ghaldezuel had been shot at and defecated upon more times than he cared to remember – until one realised the opportunities this task offered for skimming off the top.

Now, as Ghaldezuel approached the pool, he felt his troubles lifting. Here indeed was a curiosity. Of course he'd heard of the speaking Cursed folk of the Old World (and other monsters like them said to exist around the Investiture) but here was something even curiouser, something that had interested Cunctus enough for him to make Ghaldezuel's visit to the fisheries one of his top priorities.

He crouched by the pool's edge, his knees popping with twin cracks that startled the fish deeper. Mumpher came over and knocked the ashes of his pipe into the water.

'Don't do that,' Ghaldezuel muttered.

'To hear the fish talk you must submerge your head and ears,' said one of the slaves nearby, miming a dunk by placing his hands to either side of his face.

Ghaldezuel looked at the water dubiously. The umber shapes of fish had returned closer to the surface. He motioned to Mumpher. 'You go first.'

Mumpher pocketed his pipe and shrugged, getting down

onto his knees by the pool and swiftly dunking his head. Ghaldezuel watched, knowing it would be as simple as a little pressure applied to the back of the Wulm's neck, keeping him under. But then Ghaldezuel's eyes moved to Mumpher's hand, still firmly wedged in his pocket, and noticed the unmistakable shape of a blade, ready, just in case.

Mumpher rose, ugly head dripping. He blinked and looked at Ghaldezuel and the slaves. 'I hear it. They talk down there.'

'Up,' Ghaldezuel commanded, going to the edge. He motioned for Mumpher to stand as far back as he could, gesturing until the grinning Wulm had moved some distance away, before kneeling quickly and dunking his own head.

The sound of muttering filled his ears.

Ghaldezuel pulled his head out, checking, but Mumpher hadn't moved. The Wulm saluted in the Lacaille way – a series of quick gestures that might once have been claps, like their Vulgar counterparts – and Ghaldezuel went under again.

Marshal, you come back to us.

Ghaldezuel felt a jolt of terror. It was the voices of the Spirits.

Does this mean you will hear our terms?

'I haven't decided yet,' he mouthed beneath the water.

Let us in, that's all we ask, and then you can go far away from here.

The similarity to the words he'd whispered on the wall the night of the banquet was not lost on him.

We want what you want, you must know that.

'Oh yes? And what is it that I want?'

For the Lacaille to govern the Firmament and Investiture at last; for security and order to prevail. We trust that you – and you alone – will accomplish this for us.

'And?'

We want life again, life and peace.

He considered this, lulled by their voices. They had been right in their predictions that Cunctus could only take this vision so far and was now tearing down what he had helped create by challenging the Lacaille. He had taken Napp for them, as desired, and now a new ruler was needed, one who could pilot the Prism as a whole into a bright, stable future. But something niggled at his mind, still submerged in the water.

'You can see the future, you say. Surely you know whether or not I'll help you.'

Your choice is still yours, came the reply, clear beneath the surface. *With our help, you can stop the Pifoon in the Firmament from activating their Amaranthine weapons. You can protect the one you love. There is no rule that says the Firmament and Investiture must be destroyed.*

Time seemed to have wound to a standstill, his lungs closing off, the outside world forgotten. Ghaldezuel's thoughts turned to Mumpher, somewhere behind, and he pulled his head out, gasping for air.

'All right,' he whispered, wiping his dripping eyes. 'I'll think on it.'

From the window of his convoy he could just see the lagoon from the tops of the cliffs. Shanties rolled past, their chimneys and cooking pots deluging the dirt road with smoke, obscuring the visibility ahead, and Ghaldezuel began to worry that some enterprising soul might try to set up an ambush. He spoke into his radio, sending mercenaries on ahead to secure the road to Thornhill and their route back to Napp.

Soon the woods replaced the view of the lagoon, the sunlight all but obscured by spiked trees bent over the road. Mumpher, sitting up front, pointed for the benefit of his soldiers at something coming up, and Ghaldezuel pushed his face to armoured roller's window.

Something that looked like a shrunken little Prism person watched them through empty eye sockets by the side of the road. The shrivelled thing turned to observe them pass, then disappeared out of sight.

Ghaldezuel had heard the stories, never expecting to see one this close to Napp. It was called the Whillo-hoopie by locals, and was not, despite appearances, Vulgar at all, but some odd creature that wore the skins of the Vulgar it killed in the hope of attracting similar prey. As far as he'd heard, none had ever been killed or captured before. What they looked like beneath their cloak of skin, nobody knew.

Ghaldezuel sat back in his uncomfortable seat, catching Mumpher's attention from the front, and averted his eyes.

The Lacaille had so far requisitioned quadrillions of Truppins' worth of lands, treasures and enemy materiel, taking hundreds of thousands of Vulgar prisoner and putting them to work in the war effort, their progress around the Investiture unstoppable. The Amaranthine, busy with their own problems, appeared to have turned a blind eye, and as such there had been relatively few casualties on the galactic scale, the Lacaille taking what they wanted with such sudden force that the Vulgar hadn't a hope of opposing them in any meaningful way.

Ghaldezuel, from his desk in Napp's keep, thought that the Vulgar would most probably benefit from Lacaille annexation. The Vulgar people were less progressive as a whole, their class system atrophied by archaic laws that made women and slaves even less valuable than possessions, and under Lacaille rule would begin to see how individual creativity and ambition were given a freer rein. Nobody, least of all the Lacaille themselves, who had been languishing in debt and Amaranthine sanctions until the year before, had ever thought such a sudden reversal of fortunes possible. For years, the Vulgar had been protected by the Amaranthine, their ships and weaponry subsidised and hired out to the Firmament whenever needed, and despite such a happy turn of events, it was generally thought by most in the Lacaille Empire that the Immortals had lost face, dishonouring themselves by abandoning their allies so comprehensively. The Lacaille were determined to keep the fruits of whatever whimsy had allowed them to advance so far, and were privately resolved never to make a deal with the Amaranthine again if they could help it.

Ghaldezuel read the messages from the Lacaille high command, knowing just how sick the Firmament had become. Riddled with Pifoon parasites and devoid of a sane Emperor, it could only be half a year or so before it fell completely, crashing down under the weight of its own rotten ambition. Cunctus would, by this time next year, almost certainly rule over a volume second in size only to that belonging to the Lacaille. But a year after that, who knew?

Beside the wonky desk lay a stack of some of Andolp's most interesting treasures. Ghaldezuel had been in the process of rummaging through them, fascinated by the random trinkets the greedy little count had amassed over the years. Andolp appeared to have had a particular passion for very ancient tiles and ceramics – things Ghaldezuel wasn't even aware the Amaranthine, during their millennia of furious collecting, had ever possessed.

He picked up the topmost parcel, a lovingly wrapped wad of glazed green shards, and unpacked them. An accompanying note, which he had already read, explained that they were said to be not thousands but *millions* of years old, bought at one of King Paryam's personal auctions. Ghaldezuel's fingers brushed the delicate surface of a tile, examining the hair-fine engravings beneath the glaze, trying to sense their age through his fingertips. He would show them to Nazithra, he supposed; she and her ... *friends* would know if their provenance was real.

Ghaldezuel looked up now, the sound of scampering boots in the hall reaching him before the sluggish shadow entered the room, and turned in his chair to see the slow-motion approach of a senior Lacaille messenger wearing the short blue and white cloak of the Admiralty.

'What is it?' he asked, pushing aside his late-night dinner, hoping Jathime wouldn't be disturbed.

'Marshal.' The Lacaille got down on both knees, as was the Admiralty custom. 'It is the king.'

Ghaldezuel waited. 'What? What about the king?'

The messenger looked flustered, as if he hadn't thought he'd need to explain. 'He has ... that is, he and the *Grand-Tile* ... are lost, at Gliese.'

The Admiralty man let this sink in before adding: 'Along with the esteemed knights Fiernel and Pitur.'

'How?' Ghaldezuel asked, his mind racing in the slow air. He didn't care about Fiernel and Pitur. He knew immediately that the Lacaille Empire would have been divided already between Eoziel's inbred children, brothers and cousins. The king had one remaining sister, an unwed, ginger-haired creature Ghaldezuel had met when she'd visited Atholcualan, who would become the Investiture's hottest property soon, when the news had burst its banks.

'He died chasing Immortality,' the Admiralty officer said simply, looking up at him, and Ghaldezuel couldn't help but agree.

'Not a bad way to go,' he replied. The Lacaille nodded, refused a drink and left, his footsteps dying away before his shadow.

Ghaldezuel sat back in his chair, thinking. Cunctus, he was almost certain, would have tried to break up the Lacaille anyway, somehow, once he had secured enough lands. Now his job would be made that much easier for him as the dozens of children and relatives fought over whatever scraps they could get. Ghaldezuel took a wad of coarse notepaper, flicking back the lid on his scribbler, gaze wandering through the window and out across the moonlit lagoon.

Another set of footsteps brought his attention back to the room.

It was the Three witch, her helmet put aside. She stood

hunched and motionless, watching him from the corner, and once more Ghaldezuel had to avert his eyes.

'Can't you put some clothes on?' He sighed.

'Why don't you take yours *off*?' the witch leered, her tongue worming from between her lips.

'This is a solemn moment,' he said. 'But I wouldn't expect you to understand.'

She gazed around the room. 'I know all about Eoziel's fall. They saw it long before he did.'

Ghaldezuel's gaze strayed to the pieces of tile beside the desk. 'Did they?'

'And they see your future, too, Ghaldezuel, if you'd only let them show you.'

He gazed at her for a long time, something in him giving way, relenting. 'I think perhaps you should bring them here.'

The witch nodded. 'You have made a wise choice.'

He saw more of her face now, as his eyes adjusted to the corner's darkness. The Threen, beneath bulbous nocturnal eyes and wide, sensitive ears, were afflicted with a gruesome-looking overbite of snaggled, fish-like teeth. One could almost call a Zelioceti beautiful in comparison.

'They will arrive here ... *inside* your body?' he asked.

She nodded.

'Isn't it dangerous?'

Nazithra shrugged. 'Not really. I've done it many times, sometimes even within these walls.'

He stared at her.

Nazithra licked her lips. 'Oh, they've been here before, Ghaldezuel, with or without your permission.' She hesitated, drawing closer to the light. 'You grind your teeth in your sleep, did you know that?'

Call the ship, the small, frightened, helpless part of him insisted. *Call the ship now and go*. He made himself breathe.

'So why do they need me?' he asked conversationally, trying

to conceal his creeping unease. 'If they can come here any time they like?'

She placed two sticky fingers on his knee, walking them lasciviously up towards Ghaldezuel's crotch until he batted them away. 'Because only you have seen the Shell's transmogrification *in action*, my handsome Ghaldezuel, back on the Old World. Andolp built this place according to the designs, yes, but it is not known how to *use* them.'

He remembered: the chapel of the First, lit by candlelight, its famous ceiling lost in darkness. Aaron's gurgling chuckle from the shadows.

The Threen twitched the hem of the curtain that separated Ghaldezuel's office from the other rooms. 'I want to meet your little sweetheart in there. Does she sleep?'

Ghaldezuel examined the slug trail on his leg, made by whatever sticky substance had coated her fingers. 'I expect she does, yes – she is unwell.'

A three-fingered hand appeared suddenly at the doorway, pushing the fabric aside, and the witch retreated quickly. Jathime's face, dim in the glow of the fire, studied her.

Ghaldezuel sat back, cautiously enjoying the stillness of their encounter. Two breeds, separated by who knew how many millennia, now face to face.

'Have you ever met a Bult before?' he asked the Threen softly.

The witch shook her head, frozen.

'You must be careful not to startle them,' he said, a smile forming on his lips as he looked at Jathime's hungry expression. 'They don't like surprises.'

Nazithra regained her voice at last. 'My friends are *fascinated* by the Bult, you know.' Jathime was looking at her now the way a hound gazes at someone else's dinner. 'They have some role, you see, far down the road.'

Ghaldezuel returned from the throng of Napp's petitioners, finding his doors open. Another message, in the form of a helmet radio delivered by courier, from Cunctus, who was supposed to be on his way back.

'*Marshal*,' came the Melius's scratchy voice, the hollow sound of the wind thrumming in the background. '*I've changed my mind.*'

Ghaldezuel closed his eyes, sitting heavily in his chair. So Cunctus would be pushing his luck after all.

'*Keep the fires stoked while I'm away, and whatever you do, don't let that Mirror out of your sight. Hugs and kisses! I'll see you soon, when Filgurbirund is ours.*'

Ghaldezuel had noticed a wooden box waiting for him in the hall, going to it now and kicking open its lid with his boot. Two of the dukes' heads peered up at him like giant, rotten mushrooms, both quite violently decomposed. He closed the box carefully and pushed it over to the door. That he hadn't caught a whiff of its contents until then spoke volumes about the stink of the city coming through the window. He supposed Jathime would like them, if she ever got used to the motion sickness of this slow place.

Cunctus had managed to claim some of the victory at Moso for himself, and now sixty thousand troops were at his command: a gypsy army of Vulgar crossbreeds sufficiently unhappy with their present rulers to take a wage from the highest bidder. The yellow flag of Cunctus now flew throughout Drolgins and Filgurbirund's smaller moons, Nirlume and Glost, competing directly with the banners of the Lacaille for space and attention.

But Ghaldezuel knew Cunctus would never stop there. He was going to use the *Wilhelmina* to send a message to that snake Lazan, against all advice from those around him. At Filgurbirund, the giant planet where all their fates would be decided, a far superior battle fleet of ten thousand Lacaille ships and nine hundred thousand troops waited, clearing out the last of its crude orbital stations – hundreds of tin cities hanging in the mesosphere like lumpen, glittering clouds – and dogfighting with the last of the ragtag Vulgar jets: by the day's end, all the skies of Filgurbirund would be in their hands.

The Amaranthine ship dropped silently towards the great globe of Filgurbirund. Specks of the Lacaille battle fleet, massed and twinkling just across the planet's electric-blue horizon, began frantically signalling it, without effect.

'Let them see what it's like to be ignored,' snarled Cunctus.

They passed through the thick atmosphere, repelling a sudden pulse of Vulgar ground fire like so many thrown stones. The Lacaille presence on the surface were still engaged in shoring up their supply routes from the local Voidport at Phittsh, and the *Wilhelmina* skated far overhead, reaching the vast capital of Hauberth a few minutes later completely alone. Turrets and small anti-aircraft fire opened up across the city, a shabby Vulgar carrier painted in the bright colours of King Wilemo loosing a stream of pulsing lumen beams in Cunctus's direction. The Amaranthine ship's outer fuselage repelled every bolt and beam instantaneously, sending them back on the precise trajectory from which they'd arrived, and the Vulgar carrier burst into bright, violent flame, falling towards the city and ditching in its central river.

Cunctus used the ship's shortwave Bilocation to snap Scallywag and himself, his Zelio battletanks and a squadron of Vulgar mercenaries down to the Shantylands a mile below, cackling wildly as the ship moved slowly on overhead, pummelling the city with reflected ordnance. He looked into the skies beyond, spotting Lacaille jets tearing along the horizon, and radioed the ship. 'Shoot the Lacaille down if they come any closer. This is *our* victory.'

The Shantylands appeared to exist in their own local gloom, the smoke of their cookpots, chimneys and the occasional simple generator blotting out much of the sunlight. Cunctus's soldiers moved swiftly through the dwellings, setting up fizz cannons at the grubby intersections and kicking down doors, finding their way up to the rooftops for vantage. Scallywag drifted a few feet off the ground, Cunctus seated rod-straight on his back, the column of trundling Zelio vehicles bringing up the rear. This was a procession, after all, Cunctus thought; no harm could befall him with the massive bulk of the Decadence ship floating overhead, and the shanty dwellers either cheered his name or hitched up their pants and scuttled back indoors. His might was plain for all to see. Ahead lay Filgurbirund's northern capital, still held by the Steward Lofer, son of the imprisoned King Wilemo. Cunctus would be sending that fellow back to Ghaldezuel's wall of shame alive and wriggling.

The Amaranthine ship stationed itself above Hauberth. Cunctus knew enough about skycharges to understand that he wouldn't see the bomb as it fell – it was Amaranthine technology and did not exist except as a suggestion, a spark of alchemy that turned all the air around it into blazing, scouring steam. He marvelled at the thought as he rode on through the shanty, wondering if the thing had fallen yet, the crackle and burble of his helmet informing him his troops were all in position.

Just as he reached to pat Scallywag, a searing, dazzling flash flickered at the corner of his eye and Cunctus brought his head up to see the city disappear beneath a blanket of rolling, flickering mist. Whoops of delight squealed tinnily through his helmet as he gripped the reins, staggered at the sight of district after district falling under the wall of heated air: Cunctus knew that nothing could survive in that seven-thousand-degree steam, rapidly cooling as it made its way into the outskirts of the Shantylands. The first breath of it, cooled now to a humid mist, was already ruffling the ribbons on Scallywag's pommel, coiling and breezing all around them until Cunctus could barely see more than a few feet into the gloom.

The Grand Bank, buried half a mile beneath the city's foundations, should not have been harmed, though the skycharge ought to have effectively sealed off its entrances. Cunctus watched as, precisely to plan, a beam of pale lightning shot from the shadows above, angling through the steam and into the western district of the city, opening up a glowing route down to the buried horde of Vulgar gold. The *Wilhelmina*'s shadowy bulk lowered, flickering another beam from its nose, and Cunctus signalled for his forces to advance.

Immediately, the first flashes of Lacaille counterfire from the surrounding hills exploded across the sky, clawed puffs of black smoke and red flashes aimed at the Decadence ship. *Idiots*, Cunctus thought, his old heart leaping with joy, watching the ship bat them out of the sky with a flicker of its own subcutaneously invisible weaponry. His tin-armoured troops, nothing but glimmering suggestions in the brown-grey gloaming, surged around him, a dark tank growling past.

'Come on then, Waggle,' he said, kicking his spurs into the Cethegrande's suited flanks, 'let's go and get those Filgurees.'

But the beast refused to budge, its eyes staring distantly out at the steam-shrouded ruins. Cunctus leaned forward in the saddle, pulling Scallywag roughly by the ear. 'Come on!'

The Cethegrande rose onto its stubby hands, heaving off the saddle and dumping Cunctus roughly to the ground. It swung around to face him.

Cunctus climbed to his feet, opening his faceplate and staring up at his old friend.

'What's got into you?' he managed between breaths,

gauntlets extended, soothing. Scallywag's pale, wolfish eyes shone through the gloom. Cunctus knew instinctively that he ought to lower his gaze, but did not.

'*I'm* in charge here!' he shouted, blinking at the sweat and steam beading in his bushy eyebrows as he weathered the beast's stare. 'Don't you look at me like that!'

He fingered the hilt of his sword, wondering if it could even pierce that translucent suit, the first shiver of fear trembling in his legs.

The first accounts to be intercepted by the Lacaille, who had sent every soldier they had straight to the steam-shrouded ruins of Hauberth, were contradictory at best, as panic spread within Cunctus's ranks.

Though they varied, two things were constantly repeated; firstly, that soon after the detonation of the skycharge the Amaranthine ship had tipped and fallen, as if suddenly powerless, and ploughed into the Ninleyn Hills, north of the city.

Chamberlain Lazan tried to imagine the second as he listened to the reports, savouring the scene. The Vulgar mercenaries had come upon the Cethegrande, Scallywag, in the murk of steam that still settled in the shanties. And, like any beast with a kill, it would not let them approach.

The creature, they said, had bitten Cunctus in half at the waist, and had swallowed his plackarted torso in one great gulp.

But somehow, incredibly, the act hadn't killed him outright.

They'd heard him screaming, in the beast's throat, screaming all the way down.

RELEASE

Lazan came early the next morning, faster than word could travel, his ship arriving on the rooftop amid a flurry of activity.

Ghaldezuel watched him through the window as he acclimatised himself to the slowness of the city. He had no idea if Cunctus was even still alive, though the Lacaille chamberlain's sudden presence here told him enough.

They clapped the salute together, two Lacaille easy in each other's company after so much time among different breeds.

'You don't know how glad I was to hear he'd appointed one of ours to look after Napp,' Lazan said, sipping his wine and smiling, clearly pleased to be speaking his own language. Ghaldezuel watched him study the bubbles, the sensations of the city still astounding him. 'I suppose you're used to all this slow motion by now?'

Ghaldezuel topped him up, waving away the lingering help. 'I rather like it.'

Lazan was studying him in the sunlight. 'So he's dead,' he said flatly. 'I'm sure you suspected as much.'

Ghaldezuel poured himself a drink at last, carefully replacing the lid on the jug.

'Humility is an act, in my view,' said Lazan, leaning back in his chair and observing him through narrowed eyes. 'It lasts only as long as it's needed.' He grinned wolfishly. 'With that in mind, we thought we'd offer you the kingship of the whole moon of Drolgins, seeing as you already have a hold here.'

Ghaldezuel nodded, a numbness settling within him. It was as the Spirits had said. They had seen it. Somehow, they had seen it all.

Lazan poured a slop of his drink into Ghaldezuel's, the Lacaille equivalent of the Amaranthine toast. 'My congratulations.'

They gazed out at the city for a while. The heat of the day

gave the place a murky, baked look, all browns and pinks and creams.

'It wasn't me that offed him, you know,' Lazan said suddenly, without glancing up.

No, said deep, invisible voices in the room, startling Lazan into knocking his drink. It shattered languidly across the floor.

We did.

Lazan stared, scandalised, at Ghaldezuel.

He had achieved enough.

Ghaldezuel walked stiffly down the city steps. The memories of Cunctus striding slowly up them amid the piles of corpses appeared fresh in his mind. He was suitably distracted, thinking on how much could change in just thirty-five days and nursing a strange pain behind his eyes, when the crack of a shot startled him out of his thoughts. He saw Mumpher as he felt the thud of something strike him above the knee. Ghaldezuel pulled out his own lumen pistol and fired off a shot, the beam burning a hole in Mumpher's ear.

The Wulm fled along the steps, taking a side bridge to the rooftops and then onto the walls. Ghaldezuel tracked him with his pistol, noticing as Mumpher hobbled that he wore a glinting bracelet.

It took Ghaldezuel a moment to place the item. It had been on Andolp's wrist when he'd been killed. He swore, holstering the pistol: the last surviving plans for the Shell. He'd forgotten about them.

He knelt, rolling up his britches to examine the damage and turning his leg to inspect the back of his knee. As he'd suspected, the bolt had lodged there. He sat down heavily, keeping a wary eye out for Mumpher in case he returned, placing pressure on his bleeding leg.

The pain grew suddenly worse, making him cry out. Ghaldezuel had been shot twice before but it had never felt anything like this. He broke out in a sweat as the pulsing heat of the wound increased, as if the bolt were being physically dragged out of his body.

It was. He saw the bulge of it as it worked its way back through the muscle, its glinting end rising like a metal worm from the bloody hole. Then it was pushing, turning like a screw. A final wobble and it dropped out of his leg, the wound steaming inexplicably and filling with clear liquid. A froth of vapour hissed out of the hole, the most painful part of the whole bizarre process so far. Ghaldezuel clutched the hissing mess as it sizzled like meat on a griddle, eventually moving his hand to inspect the flesh beneath.

He had been healed.

He half-lay, half-sat, staring at the pink new skin where the hole had been, before reaching and collecting the bolt, examining it as if it might hold some answer.

Surprise, a croaking voice said in his throat, working his larynx. *We worked out how to do it, Ghaldezuel. You're ours now.*

THE VIZIER

The Westerling court could only be reached at low tide, when a wide, shining expanse of marble road appeared in the salt marshes around the island city known as the Alchazar Mount.

Pentas walked with Xanthostemon at the head of the group, Jatropha having been forced to leave the *Corbita* at the edge of the rock pools due to the fragility of the ancient road. Walking with them, their heads lowered, were the last of the day's pilgrims, come to feed the Westerling king, Levisticum. They were masked and wrapped in charcoal-grey cloaks. In their hands they held brightly wrapped packages tied with fancy bows – the offerings for the king's table. Pentas eyed their crude, homemade efforts, wondering if it had ever occurred to them that their king might be able to afford to feed himself.

The sun was slanting low into their eyes by the time they came before the ramparts of the tidal palace, burning a line across the surface of the shimmering marsh. Jatropha had warned them all: it would not be simple, and it would not be quick. The Westerlings wouldn't just *give* Arabis back, at least not without ample compensation. To prepare for their arrival, Xanthostemon had sent his cousin, Tragopogon, ahead; the young man ought to have arrived here some days ago, but they'd heard nothing.

'Pentas,' Jatropha said suddenly from the back of the procession. She turned, meeting her sister's surprised eye.

She shuffled aside to let everyone past, joining him.

'They're not to know who you are,' he said. 'Understand?'

She glanced up at the Mount, feeling a flash of rage. Somewhere in there her daughter was waiting for her. The Amaranthine had clearly never had a child: to be asked to wait, to twiddle her thumbs during negotiations, it just wasn't possible. 'I'll do my best,' she snapped, making her way back to Xanthostemon's side.

They'd first seen the Mount from the dusty-pink fields along the coast, taking the old road down to the shore where the cockle fishers moored their ships. The city looked more than decrepit; it looked like a stack of greyish crockery about to slide over, propped up here and there with rickety wooden buttresses and towers. Indeed, the castle was precisely that, having been built upon the remnants of its predecessors, themselves already subsiding badly into the sea. *When I was younger*, Jatropha had said as they made their way down, *we all thought the world was going to end, sooner or later. But it never did; the new just piled on top of the old, as it always had, and the world carried on.*

Nobody watched them as they proceeded inside the place, passing from blinding sun into cool darkness, the smell of salt winds replaced with damp stone. Nobody was searched, not a single gift checked. They made their way up a broad flight of steps, shuffling slowly with everyone else, watching their footing. The pilgrims had begun talking animatedly as they arrived inside and were now breaking into snatches of song. Beneath their gilded, bestial masks, the people here were said to be incredibly ugly.

'What about the king's safety?' she whispered to Eranthis. 'Can anyone just give him something, and he'll eat it?'

'He *doesn't* eat it,' Jatropha butted in, waiting until the slowest of the masked pilgrims had passed them by. 'They throw it all away.'

The four of them shuffled further in, keeping to the rear of the crowd. Xanthostemon looked especially tense and drawn, having not slept well. Eranthis glanced at him, hoping to catch his eye, but the man appeared focused on his Westerly manners and was gazing at the floor. His thoughts seemed to weigh like a brick around his neck, his posture sinking to a stoop since Eranthis had first met him. Losing Arabis and his cousin in the space of a week, not to mention the implications of Lycaste's innocence, had aged him, she thought. Eranthis shuddered again at the thought of what Lycaste must have been through and hoped this would all be over soon, one way or another.

Their climb took them in a spiral around the outer walls, passing through high, vaulted rooms where light streamed in from open windows. The Mount's interiors were just as wonky and subsided as its walls, slanted this way and that as if the whole place could collapse at any moment, slipping into the sea.

The crowd came to a stop in a bowed-looking place of sagging, stained walls grown from an inferior stone. Everyone's eyes remained downcast, so it was only Jatropha's party that noticed the grandeur of the ceiling. Propping up the castle's insides was a complex of enormous beams, each carved from deep cherry-pink wood. Eranthis wrinkled her nose even as she absorbed the beauty of the dim place: there was a pungency here, as if the people of the court had been caught short once too often and relieved themselves in the corners. The smell of sour urine was so strong in places that it appeared to be seeping from the wood. As the crowd passed through the hall, she leaned closer to sniff a glossy, sculpted beam, recoiling at once.

They came at last to a lighter, somewhat cleaner-smelling place. Eranthis squinted at the bright evening sun that streamed over the crowd, glancing up to see that half of the westward-facing wall was made up entirely of beautifully distorted syrup-crystal windows, the substance so thick that they'd pooled at their bases. The view looked out across the marsh to the edges of the twinkling sea, dappled with dozens of bobbing Westerling ships.

They waited, feet aching, breathing the musky scent. Whispers and coughs were amplified in the sunlit hall. Soon a recurrent theme was running through the conversations.

'What are they saying?' Eranthis asked Jatropha.

'He's not in,' replied Xanthostemon at her side. He sighed, an edge in his voice when he spoke. 'We're going to have to wait.'

The pilgrims passed their useless gifts to a small group of smiling guards, the youngest of them touching a finger to their brows in place of an averted glance, then shuffled around to move despondently back the way they'd come.

To Eranthis's relief, Jatropha had written ahead and booked them heinously expensive lodging on the Mount, so they wouldn't have to cross the rising tide back to the *Corbita*. Their party had taken up the whole top floor, some wiry Ingolland mercenaries and Cursed folk hired to keep watch at the stairs.

She felt a strange peace, though they were far from home and dry, as she leaned on a windowsill still warm from the evening sun. Arabis was safer, she supposed, than at any point since her capture, and it was a fine place to stay, overlooking the tidal lands that stretched out into the Atlas Sea, feeling the twilight come breathing in through their windows. Spring was here, she noted, listening to the conversations of the birds carrying on the breeze. They were preparing for the great Wooing, a time when messenger birds grew too distracted for their work, losing or even chewing up letters to build their nests. Everything sent in the post, including silk, could usually at this time of year be found hanging discarded in the trees, or woven into birds' houses, and so, in conjunction with the ever-strengthening Eyrall wind, it was often considered the season of luck. This gave Eranthis, usually the pragmatic sort, a strange hope as she looked down across the fortress walls to the night-blue sea.

She turned as Jatropha came in, a soft presence she wouldn't have noticed had she not grown used to it over the months.

He smiled at her, the first smile of recent memory, and sat. 'It's been a long journey, hasn't it?'

'You think it'll be over soon?' she asked, leaning with her back to the window ledge, suddenly hoping he hadn't thought it a silly question.

'I do, actually.'

She looked at him, surprised, beginning to see through his Westerling guise a little, observing snatches of his real face beneath the glamours. 'You're going to show them who you are?'

He shrugged. 'These people don't know much about the Amaranthine. It was the First that was favoured, the First that was told of the Firmament and its workings. I'd be surprised if they understood what was happening.'

'They'll think you're some kind of demon.'

He smiled, without much warmth. 'It wouldn't hurt.'

'Is there no other way to bargain?' she asked, nervous at the

313

prospect. Scaring folk made for a dangerous hobby, especially if they were the wrong sort.

Jatropha shook his head. 'There isn't time, Eranthis. Your niece will remember this ordeal, in some form or other. We must get her back as soon as we can.'

She nodded slowly, trying to see past the idea he'd projected in all their minds, trying to picture the Amaranthine's old self. She wished she could have seen him as a young man.

'Do you ever think about your parents?' she asked him suddenly. 'I can't stop thinking of mine these days.'

He looked up at her from where he sat on the bed, eyes searching her face and moving to the floor, as if he'd just woken up from a dream. 'Yes. All the time.'

She hesitated. 'Do you remember their faces?'

Jatropha was already shaking his head, looking past her into the twilight. 'No.'

She moved from the window and sat beside him, elbows cradled in the palms of her hands. 'Are there others you miss, from your life before all of this?'

He seemed to think, and her heart ached at all the lonely years he must have lived.

'You know,' he said, his eyes clear and focused on her for the first time since the baby was taken, 'I don't think there are. I mourned, of course – I mourned the friends I lost. But soon it was as if they'd never existed.'

'You learned to forget, I suppose,' she said, studying him.

'Yes. To live this long without forgetting ... I'd be as mad as all those Immortals in the Firmament.'

She saw his small hand lying close to her own, their difference startling, and imagined a time when she, too, would be gone. 'I hope you remember *us*.'

He looked sadly at her, drawing in a long breath. Eranthis knew then that he would not.

'And now I must go and persuade Xanthostemon to eat,' he said. 'He needs his six meals a day, like the rest of you.'

He stood, swaying a little on his feet as if the blood had rushed from his head, and wandered from the room. Eranthis glanced at the small indentation his hand had left on the sheets, smelling him in the air still, and felt tears sting her eyes.

She sat up late, too anxious for what tomorrow would hold, his smell lingering in the room. In her hands she held a length of dark blue silk, the highest denomination in her purse. Eranthis had found a tear in it this morning, on the road, and widened it until it had made the shape of a Melius letter _J_. It had not escaped her that to propose marriage, one must select silk of the highest value, cutting into it the name of the beloved so that it became worthless. She thought of snipping off the ruined part now, saving what was left, then decided that perhaps, for tonight, it ought to stay.

Eranthis hovered at her door, listening, sure that neither her sister nor Xanthostemon would be asleep. But it wasn't them she was going to see.

She unlatched the door, staring out into the dark wooden world of the guesthouse landing. It was a poky place, built for smaller Westerling people, the low ceiling slanting in just as drunken a manner as the castle above. Eranthis wandered to the end of the hall, feet padding on wooden boards, the fluttering of her heart tickling the tips of her fingers.

She tapped on his door, hearing the grunt of someone not expecting visitors, and waiting a moment until footsteps announced she was about to be let in, butterflies dancing in her stomach.

'Can't sleep?' Jatropha asked, returning to his desk. Eranthis closed the door softly behind her and shook her head. She sat comfortably on the end of his bed, observing him as she had so many times before in the _Corbita_'s cabin. He was writing letters, a neat stack already done and sealed beside him. She watched his beautiful handwriting glide over the paper: a perfect script, as impeccable as print, clearly honed over lifetimes. Following the curl of Jatropha's pen was so hypnotic that it wasn't until he'd finished the letter and begun the next that she realised neither of them had said another word. In the gloom, she felt her heart swell beneath her ribs. To be so comfortable in one another's presence, so wordlessly at home.

Sitting up a little, she read the addressee on the top letter, her spirits falling. It was addressed to Liatris, that wrinkled old authoress from Albina. His pen paused a moment, as if realising what she had seen, and Eranthis felt a quick, blade-keen jealousy.

She settled back on the bed, her fingers tracing a crack in the wall. Of course she'd had no expectations – only a fool would have. But seeing that name, she felt more certain than ever that she had to tell him; she had to know. There would never be another chance like this night, this room. She knew that as if it were preordained, somehow.

Jatropha was still busying himself carefully with his letters, nose pressed close to the words. She observed his slouched position in his chair, wondering. There surely wasn't anything wrong with his eyes—

And then it struck her. He *knew*. Of course he did. He knew how she felt. Perhaps he'd always known. And he didn't want to talk.

Eranthis got up quickly to go, her cheeks burning, a pen falling from the sheets and clattering to the floor. When she glanced back, he was looking at her.

Now. Do it now. She must have imagined the start of this conversation a hundred times, refining the image with each rehearsal, whittling it away.

'I—' she began, mouth moving as it tried to drag the words out of nothing, heart aching at how close she'd come to speaking them aloud. But she saw then how his eyes moved sadly back to his papers, and her lips closed, compressing, trembling with the prospect of tears that she would never let him see. Eranthis moved quickly to the door, letting herself out, and moved as softly as she could back to her room.

Some of the Pilgrims they recognised the next morning as they made their way back up into Levisticum's halls, lining up again. The assembled men and women had already given their presents the previous evening, Pentas remembered; the presents they held now were new – something tucked away at breakfast and wrapped on the walk up. She wondered how far some of them had come.

They waited, the sun warming them through the glass.

'He'd better be in this time,' Xanthostemon growled, teeth gritted.

'He is,' Jatropha said, having turned around. They followed his gaze.

A small Westerling with long, rosy-blond hair was sidling down the line, chatting and smiling with some of the frozen-looking pilgrims, a few almost fainting at his sudden appearance, not having prepared. She watched the king strut, hating him, ready to claw the smug expression off his handsome face.

Levisticum came to them, his arms full of gifts, and gave them a glowing smile.

'I know these ones!' he said in a mock stage aside to some people further back in the line, winking like he'd had a stroke. He looked them up and down (Eranthis supposed a king could break his own Province's rules), his tongue sliding over his lips, and gestured to a distant archway. 'Come on, we'll have a drink.'

It soon became clear to Eranthis that the young man had something wrong with him. Of course, she'd never met a king before; they could all be like this.

'What did the one-legged Grumbit say to the Demian Man?' he asked them as they followed on behind, gurning a smile.

'No idea,' said Xanthostemon.

' "You're standing on my *toe*!" ' Levisticum shook with laughter at his own punchline and opened the doors himself, appearing to have no help at all.

'What do you call a Brownling with no nose?' he asked next, padding along beneath pink wooden vaults. They didn't have time to answer. 'Handsome!'

Eranthis met Pentas's eye.

The king gave them all a brief look. 'What has the First done to your sense of humour? So dry, so boring!' He hurried his step. 'You'll laugh at this one – I'm warning you, you're going to laugh! Where does Lyonothamnus keep his armies?'

'In his sleevies,' Jatropha said flatly.

'Yes!' the king screamed. '*Someone* gets it!'

They came to what must have been the king's sanctum, a poorly appointed room with a simple wooden chair looking out over the water. The nearby table was scattered with cups and glasses, as if a binge was already in session. Beneath the table, a small Ingolland Melius was squatting and eating, presumably whatever the king dropped.

'Saw you lot arrive,' he said, sitting down and then abruptly standing up again to root in a bowl of steaming cockles. The things were a Western delicacy, said to seep alcoholic blood when boiled. He offered the bowl. 'Hot cockle?'

'No, thank you,' replied Jatropha, cracking his knuckles.

'*Boooring!*' cried Levisticum, startling them into silence as he chewed, a smear of blood on his teeth. 'Well ... if it's that *baby* you're after, you'd better speak to my Gheal, Salpiglossis.' He collected a bottle from the table and clapped his hands, slumping into his chair.

'What in the world—?' Eranthis whispered, before a troop of dwarfish Westerlings came pouring into the room carrying a large, ungainly-looking golden box between them. They set it down in the middle of the floor, forcing Eranthis and the others back, and fanned out into the corners, watching.

For a moment, nothing happened. Just inside the gilded box, Eranthis thought she could hear the stirring of a child. She put a hand out, taking Pentas's wrist, feeling the fluttering of her sister's heart. The curtains at the box's front parted, some slender fingers flicking them to one side, and a shrewd, narrow-eyed Prismish face peered out at them.

The Gheal uncurled its pastel-pink form, climbing slowly from the box. It turned its mascara-coated eyes on the visitors, then bowed low to its king. Levisticum slouched in his chair, the bottle clasped in his lap, and smiled back at it.

'Show them she hasn't been harmed,' he said to the Gheal, who turned and pulled a bundle from the box. Arabis's unmistakable orange face peered out at them, sleepy eyes gazing into the room.

Eranthis locked her muscles, straining to pull Pentas back as Jatropha strode forwards, clearing his throat.

'Ah, ah! Not *yet*,' said the king, holding up the bottle. The Gheal placed the baby back in the box and turned its gaze on Jatropha, stepping lithely up to him. Its dazzling patterns were dyed, Eranthis thought, guessing that it must have been creamy white before its time at court. It pushed past the Amaranthine, approaching Eranthis, Xanthostemon and Pentas, its hideously long fingers extended, and brushed their faces. Eranthis recoiled, understanding why the place reeked so strongly: its fingertips were coated with urine.

It went to Pentas, mouth opening. 'You are this child's mother,' it said in a high, girlish voice, touching her with its clammy fingers. Its breath fumed of rotten meat. Eranthis met its black eyes, remembering the legends of Gheals in the wild. They were capricious things, her parents had said, bestowing luck or misery depending on their mood. If you smelled strong urine, they'd told her, then you had come by accident upon the lair of a Gheal and you should turn back.

'I learned my jokes from the King in the Woods, you know, when I was a boy,' Levisticum said, still lolling in his chair and finishing the cockles. When he spoke next, the inside of his mouth was bright crimson. 'My Gheal certainly likes them. It came here as a gift, I forget from whom, to bring me luck. People come from far and wide now to seek its counsel, or to find some miraculous cure.' He looked at it. 'Haven't you done well, Salpiglossis?'

The Gheal turned and beamed at him, presenting the baby.

'Yes, she's a good child,' Levisticum said, bending to give Arabis a cursory look. 'The state of Pan shall look after her here.' He placed the bottle down and stood, staring at them as he wiped his mouth. 'No sense of humour,' he muttered sadly, trailing off and stepping out of the room, slamming the door behind him.

Salpiglossis's smile withered and disappeared. It went and sat on the throne, taking Arabis with it and bouncing her on its knee. The baby gurgled happily.

'Well, then,' Jatropha said after a moment, smiling at the Gheal. 'I think I can see who's *really* in charge here.'

The Gheal fixed him with a narrow, cat-like stare. Its bottom lip drooped, showing off some yellowed, serrated lower teeth.

Jatropha stepped a little closer, the chamber beginning to heat up. 'This doesn't have to hurt—'

The Gheal grinned suddenly, dropping the baby in its lap. Arabis bawled and pulleys squealed as a frame of heavy wood and fabric came thrumming down from the ceiling, slamming into the floor and enveloping Jatropha. Xanthostemon leapt to his aid, but the frame had fallen into bolted latches, locking tight. Eranthis threw herself forward, only to be snared by the sentries. 'Jatropha!' she cried, stamping her heel onto a Westerling's toes and earning a slap.

With efficient speed, the small sentries had Jatropha surrounded and barricaded in. Their staffs had been built to interlock, and within a minute they had put together a steel enclosure, threading their staffs through loops in the grey cloth.

'I wouldn't have got very far without knowing about your sort,' Salpiglossis purred, stepping down from the throne and pacing a sensual circle around Jatropha's enclosure. On its finger it wore a glass ring in which a tiny red octopus swam. It took a staff from a guard and pounded it on the floor, eyeing them all, then swung it at the fabric. They heard a muffled cry as the staff struck. Eranthis felt tears sting her eyes. He was blind in there, powerless.

'I came from *nothing*,' the Gheal hissed, striking again. 'I had to dance and suck my way through the dregs of this place, until I knew its every secret.' It swung once more, connecting loudly with bone. Jatropha mumbled some pained curse inside the fabric.

'I kept expecting someone to come looking, you know,' the Gheal said. 'When I caught my first Immortal.' It stabbed the poker into the fabric, careful not to pierce it. 'But nobody ever does.'

It looked up, singling out Xanthostemon. 'And your ... brother? Cousin? He was *delicious* when I took him to my bed.' The Gheal licked its pointed teeth. 'Even more so when I cut him up.'

Xanthostemon raged against the sentry's grip. Arabis began to wail and Salpiglossis returned to her, panting a little. It tickled her, cooing, until she quietened, then stepped away from the throne and turned back to Jatropha's cage.

'I am the ultraviolet, you see; the part of the Spectrum nobody *ever* knew was there.' It picked up the staff, preparing to swing. Eranthis felt a hideous pain in her chest, willing herself just a little of Jatropha's talents, could he have shared them.

But the blow never fell.

Instead, the Gheal hissed a sharp intake of breath, lifting and staring at the weapon in its hand as if it were a snake.

It met their gazes for a moment, suspicious, as smoke coiled from the metal pole, wafting the smell of frying meat towards them. Salpiglossis began to mutter, disbelieving. It turned away, shaking its hand violently, attempting to let go of the spear that was now glued to its palm.

It turned back to them, eyes wide, fingers extended. Eranthis, the closest, was the first to see how they had begun to melt away from the bone, dribbling in smoking runnels to the floor, the ring bursting. The fat deposits in the thing's belly and breasts melted next, plopping and sizzling. The Gheal screamed like nothing Eranthis had ever heard then, its eyes whitening over suddenly and bursting, spattering them with hot, wet liquid. The meat of its face drooled away, the sockets and nostrils smoking, teeth loosening and dropping out. The pink flesh beneath its fur was liquid now, pooling in a marbled puddle beneath the Gheal's staggering body. Salpiglossis slipped in its own juices and tumbled to the floor, letting out one final spluttering shriek before its skeletal remains turned to sponge and broke apart, spilling the remaining guts and lungs across the room. The staff rolled, clinking among the fallen teeth.

They gawped at the remains for a moment, the guards releasing them in astonishment. Pentas ran through the mess to Arabis, scooping her up and falling into the throne.

Eranthis went quickly to the fabric enclosure, grabbing a staff and ripping it open, her eyes filled with silent tears as she helped Jatropha out. She gulped them down, turning away as he paused to look at what had become of his captor.

A small, dark-skinned Immortal man was walking slowly across the hall towards them. He gazed for a moment at his own handiwork, shooing away the sentries, then stepped lightly over the mess and offered Jatropha his hand.

'Harald,' he said by way of introduction. He shook Eranthis's hand, then Xanthostemon's. 'Delighted to meet you all.' Turning back to the staff and teeth, he began to chuckle. 'Looks like I got here just in time. Nasty thing, that.'

There was no sign of King Levisticum or anyone else as they left the hall, Arabis safely tucked into Pentas's arms. The Amaranthine, Harald, led the way – he had something for them to see.

'I haven't been here long,' he explained, releasing a spark from a case in his shawl as they approached a door. 'But I must have come in through the wrong entrance.'

The bright little point of light accompanied them down a flight of stairs, illuminating a musky-smelling place that appeared hidden between two floors of the Mount. Eranthis and Pentas had to stoop to enter, moving slowly as their eyes adjusted to the gloom.

'The Gheal would have brought you here next, I imagine,' Harald said to Jatropha, stepping deeper into the mouldy place. 'To keep you with its other experiments.'

They became aware of a soft babbling sound, punctuated with the *drip* of water, emanating from the blackness ahead. Hundreds of eyes shone at them.

Eranthis inhaled a sharp breath of stinking air as the spark lit up the rows of peering faces.

'It must have been capturing Amaranthine for decades,' Harald said, taking a hand as it reached through the bars of its cage and stroking it absently. 'They've all been tipped over the edge by their imprisonment. I'll have to send someone to collect them.'

Jatropha knelt before the cages, gazing among their faces. A woman drooled and smiled at him, giving him the thumbs-up.

'There's more,' Harald said, 'much more.'

He led them through another small door carved from the same piss-smeared wood and into a great bowl of a chamber. At its centre, the spark picked out the details of a rusted, conical hulk.

'Vulgar corsair,' Harald said to Jatropha, walking around it. There were bits and pieces stacked all over the place, as if it were either being taken apart or put back together. Eranthis gazed at the ship for a while, eyes lost in the tangled tubes of its bulky mechanisms, before noticing the dozen or so small creatures wandering towards her.

'It's all right,' Harald said as the Skylings came and hugged his waist and arms. 'These Prism were prisoners, too. They won't harm you.'

She stared at their little red and white faces, taking in the variety of forms, some furred, others bald and lean. Their skin was speckled with scabs. Some had long, pendulous noses, others large ears and eyes. One of them had a tail.

Harald spoke to them in a rapid, breathless speech. Eranthis, understanding the Amaranthine must have told them their captor was dead, watched as they all began to weep, clinging on to Harald's shawl and clapping their hands.

'They were bred down here,' he said, holding a particularly ill-looking specimen in his arms. 'They tell me the Gheal would even, um, mate with them itself, resulting in some interesting stillbirths over the years.'

'This ship,' Jatropha said at last, looking it over. 'The Gheal would have fixed it soon. With Arabis also in its power, it might have been in a position to hold the First to ransom.'

'I believe that was certainly its hope,' Harald replied. 'Ambitious creature, I'll give it that.'

Jatropha was running his hand along the hulk of the ship. Eranthis could barely look at him, she'd been so worried. 'Out of interest, Harald.' He turned to the dark-skinned Immortal. 'How did you find me?'

Harald laughed. 'A Spirit's Oracle, on his holidays.'

Jatropha gazed at him, smiling.

One of the Skylings tugged on Harald's shawl and, when he bent down, whispered into his ear.

He straightened. 'They will take us out of here in the ship, if we wish. Probably a good idea. I can't imagine Levisticum, so often amused, will see the joke.'

LUMINARY

'It's done, Berzelius. We threw what was left in the lake.'

The stout Pifoon general hesitated and took the bottle, holding the heavy thing by the neck and swigging from it as he strolled, barefoot. Beyond the opened windows, the sparkling hazel lake slopped noisily against the stones of the jetty, a cold breeze driving in off the forested mountains of Inner Cancri and rattling their golden frames. Berzelius imagined her floating remains drifting up to the jetty, getting caught amid the poles. He turned away.

'Did she say anything? Try to give a speech?' he asked, dribbling some wine.

'Nothing much,' Ingo replied. 'We, ah ... didn't give her the choice. Should we have?'

He looked at the Pifoon soldier, now his division general, and continued his stroll.

Truth be told, Berzelius the Honoured of Hafferty, portly and bald from his little monkeyish head to his ratty yellow toenails, had never much liked wine. He pretended he did, of course; a thousand bottles a year were included with his salary when he was butler to the Satrap, and come the second year it was too late to ask for something else. The Lady Ilieva had attributed his ruddy cheeks and broken veins to a drinking habit, no doubt, but in reality his complexion was nothing but hives brought on by the terrible dustiness of the place. He took another gulp, the wine no longer stinging the back of his throat. It was six thousand years old: a wonder the glass bottle didn't snap into pieces in his hand.

He sat on a window ledge. The candlelights were flickering into life above the mountains, and soon a miniature galaxy of artificial stars, little tapering flames that coiled smoke at their tips, were burning in the sky, obscuring the lands above.

This was not the old Satrap's palace he occupied now.

Berzelius had considered very carefully whether to install himself there once the Pifoon had risen up and the deed was done, but had honestly found the thought of living somewhere he'd worked for almost forty years appalling: remembering the Satrap's voice at every turn, seeing her in the shadows of the pre-dawn light. His betrayal was too fresh.

As a front, he'd taken the new Emperor's palace instead, proclaiming it more fitting. The Emperor Sotiris did not live as grandly as the Satrap of Cancri had, having left his estate before he ever knew he'd be elected, but it was nevertheless a sumptuous place of fifty thousand acres curled around the great green lake of Cancrous. Upon arrival, Berzelius had taken the liberty of rummaging through all of the Immortal's drawers and chests, read his correspondence, stood and gazed at all the ancient family paintings encased in resin, a few of which had been defaced by the first Pifoon to break in, and wandered the vaults whispering to the sparks. It was a fine, shimmering place of peeling gold; he could rule the New Firmament well from here.

Berzelius had only met Sotiris once, in his last month of butlership to the Satrap. He'd quite liked him, for what it was worth, seeing the easy manners and friendly openness that had clearly attracted the rest of the Amaranthine to his duplicitous cause, but had found the Immortal a trifle dull. Of course, many of Sotiris's stories Berzelius had only walked in on – lighting the sparks, pouring the water, serving dishes of sweets for them to suck while the night drifted by – but Berzelius *lived* for stories; he was a connoisseur of them, hearing the best from all around the Firmament as Immortal visitors came and went, and tended to think of his own life up until now as nothing but a glorious tale of advancement against the odds. Other Amaranthine – that Von Schiller, most notably – had offered up far better entertainment for their room and board, but by the end of it, Berzelius could see that the Satrap herself was rather sweet on Old Sotiris and couldn't be persuaded to part with him. He'd felt jealous then, seeing her attraction to him, and had wanted Sotiris gone. Not long after, they released the Pifoon butler for his well-earned retirement, and he'd made the journey up to the outer shell to live in splendour, all the while waiting for the Firmament's cracks to show.

The stories they sent him now did not please him. It was barely a day and half since the coup that had offered up the throne of Cancri, and yet news had come of the taking of Drolgins. News had come of *Cunctus*. News had come of some Lacaille deal and an Op-Zlan marshal of the New Empire. News had come of the Bult. The Bult, now somehow inexplicably taking a central role in the New Investiture. Not only was it personally terrifying for Berzelius, it also demoralised those who might have been persuaded to come to his aid. Thankfully the Bilocating Amaranthine delivering the gossip was cuffed and hooded as soon as he arrived, unable to leave and share what he'd discovered here. Berzelius supposed news would move even more slowly with the disappearance of the Immortals, forced to stutter along the shipping lanes until it reached the right ears. He didn't care.

He came to the huge bedchamber, pushing open the doors and creeping in. The windows looked out not to the lake but to a hidden garden behind the palace courtyard. The vast bed, impeccably made the morning of Sotiris's departure, had been soiled by some of his guards. He looked at the mess – a row of smudged turds like filthy great leeches on the fine bedspread – and shook his head, flinging down the bottle.

'I can't have this!' he screeched, staggering back through to the golden reception rooms. The drinkers there stiffened, watching him warily.

'Every one of them will come back here before tonight and clean this up,' he spluttered, seizing another bottle from the smallest Pifoon and plugging it to his lips. That the Satrap, someone to whom he was close for four decades, had just been crushed with weights was not enough; now he had nowhere to sleep off the inevitable hangover.

Berzelius looked at Ingo, who had followed him through, and tried to breathe deeply. 'Any news of the Whisperer?'

'They're bringing her, Satrap.'

Berzelius nodded, soothed, and went back to his window ledge to sip at his wine and wait. The millions of candles bobbed in the great breezes of the world, twinkling over the lake, and Berzelius let his eyes close as he rested. Such a long two days of sleepless activity. A Vaulted Land had never been successfully occupied in the history of the Amaranthine; it had taken nothing short of a viper's precision and speed to strike when the Satrap's armies – not to mention the Lacaille fleets stationed nearby – were at their busiest elsewhere. Astonishingly, *impossibly*, it had just about worked.

Now that all Amaranthine who could have Bilocated away and spread the news had been intercepted, all he needed to do was to close the orifice seas – for they were still alarmingly open, allowing anyone the opportunity to come and go – and seal himself away for the inevitable storm. You could hardly call the prospect a harsh siege; inside their world was a closed and luxuriant ecosystem, hollowed and cultured to sustain trillions when in fact its population now numbered in only the tens of thousands. At first, Berzelius hadn't seen the need to reopen the seas at all – why not keep them closed and rule this single world until he and his successors had turned to dust? He would be presiding over an entire planet half as big again as the Old World; untrammelled power and riches were his now, untold treasure bequeathed by the defeated Amaranthine.

But then the news had come of Drolgins' fall, and Berzelius knew he hadn't the time to luxuriate. The Investiture, once it had coagulated beneath Cunctus's barbaric rule, would set its sights on the New Firmament, and Berzelius would have to be ready. The Pifoon on the neighbouring Vaulted Land,

Ectries, would need to follow his lead as swiftly as they could, for the near-victorious Lacaille were already making their presence known in the Firmament and eyeing up territory for themselves. The local Tethered moons and planets, at present still the battlegrounds of the Vulgar and Lacaille, would have to be taken, too, before their safety mechanisms snapped shut. This fight, Berzelius felt, would almost certainly cost him his life, but he was more put out and exhausted than anything else.

He felt the breeze strengthen, bringing with it scents of waterweed. There would be a frost tonight. The Pifoon in the chamber cackled, the sound of someone hurling more wood onto the roaring fire. All Berzelius felt now was the low after the high: Sotiris's fortune – reputedly in the region of one hundred million Firmamental Ducats (the equivalent of billions of gold Pifoon Stamps) and searched for in vain by the first Pifoon to arrive at the palace unchallenged – must have been kept in the vaults at Gliese, or perhaps already requisitioned by the Lacaille that had paid the place a flying visit during the battle. Berzelius didn't care much either way; he had the wealth of the whole Vaulted Land at his disposal now, not to mention the private treasures of the Satrap herself; sufficient riches to finance the building of a fortress world the size of a Satrapy, or to launch dozens of Firmamental wars. A part of him that used to scrimp and save occasionally remembered that a thousandth of a Firmamental Ducat was enough to build a good Pifoon home, and considered digging beneath the palace for the treasure anyway, just in case it was buried there. Berzelius had just paid himself a sizeable salary from the Satrap's estate, in keeping with his new title, and distributed other great treasures among his family and generals. He was now perhaps the wealthiest Prism person who had ever lived, his fortune eclipsing that of the Lacaille king Eoziel or the richest of the Vulgar kings, Paryam. It was only fitting, he supposed, as Satrap.

He did the sums now as he sat there, the gentle spinning of the room amplifying some kind of clarity in his mind. About five thousand lives had paid for his new position. It was an expensive throne, yes, but it could have been a lot dearer, too.

Commotion beyond the doors, then: screaming and wailing. Berzelius's eyes blinked open. He wiped his face and stretched, looking to his men.

The doors were pulled open to reveal the Whisperer, her hands and feet bound, being carried by a group of Pifoon. The Amaranthine's head, from which the sounds of soft whispers percolated, was draped in a black woollen hood.

Berzelius took another swig and jumped down from the ledge. The 'safety mechanisms' he had just been thinking of were in the hands of this woman, this Whisperer. And she'd almost got away.

'Now then, Calvine,' Berzelius said, wandering over to her. He could hear his words as they slurred around his mouth. 'You can stop your whispering, it won't do you any good if you won't co-oprer ... if you won't play along, we'll have to dump you in the lake like your mistress.'

The figure lay still on the floor, an unnatural heat rising from her.

'And I don't want to *do* that,' he continued, pitching his voice louder. 'But believe you me, I do what's necessary for our cause, in case you haven't noticed what's been happening in these lands the last few days.'

Still nothing. Berzelius suddenly wondered whether she might have fallen asleep. He shook her.

'I was a friend to the Satrap Ilieva, I *cared* for her. I didn't want to do this.'

'Yes,' the hooded figure said finally, muffled. 'I saw your *self-control.*'

'It was the natural Law of Succession!' he raged, slopping

the wine. 'I was in her service for forty years, I deserved more than a retirement!'

'And now you're the new Satrap?' the hooded Amaranthine asked. 'Her replacement? You lower creatures will tear the galaxy apart.'

Berzelius hurled the bottle at her. It shattered over her head, splashing wine across the floor. He stood back a little and checked his bare feet for glass, breathing harder when he noticed the darker currents of blood swirling from beneath the hood and mingling with the wine.

'Calvine?'

The hooded body lay inert and silent.

'*Calvine?*'

Berzelius staggered back, looking around the stunned group of Pifoon.

'What have I done?'

Ingo stared at him, his yellow eyes very round.

'What have I done, Ingo?'

His division general wiped his mouth, stunned. The Amaranthine's blood was seeping across the floor now like a swirling dark stream. 'She was our only chance to close the seas.'

When they'd checked her non-existent pulse, Berzelius stumbled off towards the bedchamber, moving through the gilded rooms, hot-faced and swaying. When he came at last to the soiled bed, he threw aside the sheets and dumped himself down.

The room spun, whirling.

He thought of Cunctus, that faceless, formless stirrer of chaos, and sat up in bed, suddenly sure he was about to be sick. *The seas cannot be closed.*

He sat for a moment on the edge of the bed, cupping his balls in one hand – something he'd done since infancy when the nausea came on – and thought about his unprotected world.

'I'll go down into … into the crust tomorrow,' he slurred to himself, burping. 'Find the Alamaranthine weapons they left for me.' Berzelius smiled, lips stained purple by the wine. 'And then we'll see what can be done.'

FIREWORKS

Warm night had descended over the nexus by the time Sotiris's sedan chair, hauled by puffing Epir, arrived at the top of the promontory. Sotiris leaned his elbow out of the window and gazed into the starlight. The gate reared above them, an arch of soaring towers. He leaned further out, staring upwards. The star, so bright from a distance, looked muted now that night had fallen, and impossibly distant. It was as if the light that found them down here had to pass through the depths of an ocean, weakening as it drifted deeper into the abyss. Sotiris's heart sank.

He recalled the Epir ships he'd noticed on the way up – surely if they worked, everyone would have used them to escape already. They must know something he didn't.

The sedan slowed to a stop, its wonky door rattling, one of the Epir in front craning his head around to peer at Sotiris.

'Thank you,' he said quietly, stepping out with his bags. He hadn't gone more than a few paces when they dumped the sedan and wandered off to a nearby well bar. Sotiris hardly noticed; he was staring into the gaping mouth of the gate, watching the crowd of shuffling figures moving beneath the lamplight. It must have spanned a quarter of a mile across. Its crimson walls, purplish in the darkness, were spiked with towers, their summits crowned with silver crescent moons and the busts of once-prominent Epir. Sotiris wondered whether Aaron had really seen this place at some point, or whether it had been built entirely by the inhabitants.

As he peered into the causeway beneath the arch, he thought he could see many types of Epir – crossbreeds and thoroughbreds, old and young – and marvelled at how many Aaron had trapped. Hanging from the gates were all the city's thousands of mummified dead – those who had travelled deeper – displayed for all to see, with their names written beneath their outstretched claws, as if waiting for their souls to come back and claim them. As Sotiris walked closer, he noticed the elongated, emaciated form of a human corpse. He read by the silver light of the star. *Daniell* something, it said in Leperi. *Bustrad... Bulstrode*. He couldn't make it out. Someone the Long-Life must have known.

He spent a little longer surveying the bodies, a sense of trepidation forcing him to dawdle at the gate, before joining the crowd and moving slowly under the starlit shadow of the arch. Beneath Sotiris's feet, the bone-like substance of the bridge had been worn into ruts, the aeons of clawed and shod feet grinding it away. Hundreds of Epir were passing back and forth beneath the gate, their eyes glimmering when they looked at him. Sotiris saw that many of the leaving Epir clasped food and drink, and his spirits lifted. Something was going on inside.

He stopped for a moment at a food stand, buying a cup of sharp Clorandal. Through the arches to one side he could make out the starlit meadowlands rising all around, and just the simple act of looking reminded him that his boat was down there still, unprotected, his crew dispersed. There was no turning back now.

He followed the surge of the crowd, learning from his basic grasp of Leperi that the queen of this land had almost come to the end of a season's gifting. The Epir with him now had arrived late and were hoping there might still be treats in her basket. Sotiris wandered behind them, puzzled. Presumably she threw them to the crowds.

For the first time, he heard a name tossed around, a name

he hadn't picked up on before – a word made of phlegm and clicking tongues. Was that the name of Aaron's queen? He concentrated, treading on the feet of the Epir in front. It turned and glared at him, crimson pupils contracting.

'Sorry,' he muttered, and was rewarded with a grumble. They turned the corner into a huge square, adorned all around with the sharp spikes of towers, the light of the world's lonely, stationary star shining down upon them. Sotiris gazed above the heads of the Epir, wondering at their total indifference to artificial light, spying three figures seated on a scaffold at one end of the square. His eyes widened.

The central figure, the one doing all the gift-throwing, stood more than ten feet tall, a giant worm of a serpent replete with four twig-like arms. *The queen*, he thought, gazing at her, registering that her body was entirely two-dimensional: when she turned to one side, she nearly disappeared.

To her left sat a hunched, crimson machine form, the pyramid of its head catching the moonlight. And to her right—

Sotiris pushed forward, oblivious to the hisses and curses of the crowd.

Iro sat there, her face bored and neutral, as easily readable in the starlight as it had ever been.

'Iro!' he cried, his voice raw. 'Iro, it's me!'

But yet again his voice seemed to lose all potency before it reached her, as if a thick wall of glass stood between them. He was moving swiftly through the crowd now, the Epir parting at the sound of his shout. His sister could not have been more than forty feet away, but still she couldn't hear him. Even the two-dimensional queen appeared oblivious to his presence.

Sotiris pulled his bag from his shoulder, taking out the Osserine fireworks he'd brought with him and lighting one with a flick of his thumb and forefinger. This high up, a little of his power had returned to him and sparks sprayed across his feet, lighting up the square. He held the tube, waving it around. At first, the Epir didn't seem to know what to make of the sputtering thing, their haggard faces lit by the glow. They were looking at the firework, but not at him. *Sometimes they can see me*, he understood with dismay, *but sometimes they can't*.

But one person could. A figure he might have recognised from some other life. It was a small, bat-eared humanoid with alabaster skin. It was rushing towards him through the crowd. As the person drew nearer, Sotiris could see that in his hand he held a gun.

The crowd peeled apart around the small white person, their eyes still drawn to the sputtering red sparks of Sotiris's firework. Sotiris turned and pushed his way out of the square, shoving rudely through the crowd of oblivious Epir and tossing the firework away. The strange little person dogged his every move, scuttling between the legs and tails of the crowd, gaining on Sotiris with every heartbeat. A moment more and there was nothing between them. The person aimed and fired.

The bullet missed, sailing off into the air above the bridge. Sotiris glanced behind him, then back to the drop and the meadows, their canals glowing in the starlight. He took a running leap.

For a moment, he was weightless and falling, arms pinwheeling, legs kicking, until a jutting tower came up to meet him and he landed with a winded crash upon its steepled roof, scrabbling for a grip and dangling over the meadow.

At that moment, something changed. He wheezed and almost fell, not remembering ever having felt so much pain before. The white person – he recalled suddenly that it was a Vulgar – came skidding to a stop above him, staring down, aiming once more.

'Stop!' cried a shambling Epir appearing at the lip of the bridge. It grabbed the Vulgar's weapon from him and tossed it over the side. More appeared, shuffling forward. Two Epir grasped the Vulgar's arms, dragging him to one side, while the great two-dimensional form of the queen appeared, dark against the gloom of the bridge's spires. Iro arrived at her side, eyes searching the darkness. Sotiris levered himself up onto the tiles, still mute and winded from the impact.

'Sotiris?'

His eyes widened. *What had she just said?*

'*Sotiris!*'

He felt the world as he never had before, a soft, slanting rain pattering his face as he looked up at her, tears welling in his eyes.

'I remember it all,' she said, sitting with him in a room high in the spires. 'Every tiny thing.'

Sotiris glanced along the low corridor to the lurking figure of Aaron's queen. She coiled, two-dimensional scales glinting, looking out across the ramparts. Iro said she was like that because she was only the recollection of a memory, and not fully real at all.

'He has found a way to bring her back,' his sister whispered. 'But it can only be done with a great and terrible energy.'

Sotiris returned his attention to Iro, noticing how alive her eyes were. He hadn't seen them like that in an age. 'Energy? What do you mean?'

'The energy required to break the impermeable barrier that separates dimensions,' the Vulgar, Corphuso, chimed in. He had been allowed to sit in the corner, and now nursed a drink of something on the condition that he settle himself and not attempt any more violence. 'So that he may journey across, in the hope of finding his old love still alive and well.' He hesitated, Sotiris detecting a certain lack of conviction. 'Or, if she has not yet been born, he will wait.'

Iro nodded. 'He will destroy, so that he can save.'

'Destroy? Destroy *what*?'

'These energies,' Corphuso said, 'have long been thought unattainable. But they *are* possible, for those with the right skills.'

'A colossal explosion could help him pass between the dimensions,' Iro said, looking at her friend on the ramparts.

Corphuso nodded. 'The destruction of a galaxy, perhaps.'

Sotiris stared at him. 'Ours, you mean?'

Iro shook her head. 'Theirs. That belonging to the Murmuris, who took his love from him in the first place, many millions of years ago.'

Sotiris clasped his hands together. They were cold and smooth, somehow featureless, and he remembered then that they appeared only as the Long-Life last saw them. 'And he is on his way there now? Hasn't anyone tried to stop him?'

Corphuso sat up suddenly. 'Why would anyone *stop* him? He must succeed!'

Iro hushed the Vulgar with a glance, shaking her head as she returned her attention to Sotiris. 'Someone did try – do you remember the storm, a while back? The colours on the horizon? We think it was a fight, between Aaron and another soul.' She shrugged, resignation softening her voice. 'But it appears he won and is now well on his way.'

KALEIDOSCOPE

The Poacher came in fast, tearing high above the Kalinor star towards Indak-Australis, the great mystery of the Prism Investiture.

Ghaldezuel sat up front with the Lacaille pilots, restless after a two-week journey at uncomfortable speeds. He'd awoken weightless in a floating puddle of reeking gel, having popped a blister on his thrombosis suit by lying on it during one of the many pockets of turbulence. The familiar pain of the Spirits' presence in his body and the knowledge that they had him right where they wanted him, with Jathime effectively held hostage back in Napp, were wearing on his nerves. They felt packed into his skull and bones, heavy on his back and tight behind his eyes, his every footfall heavier with their accumulated weight. He was surprised he didn't actually stamp footprints into the floor, but they had lightened themselves somehow so as not to damage their vessel.

Ahead, the star Indak was a black bubble against the wash of silver. Ghaldezuel had come in specially to watch the deceleration and to forget the pain, and he wasn't disappointed: at a squeal from the proximity radar, a bank of shiny white trumpets on the flight deck blaring the wail of Indak and its moons, the pilot to Ghaldezuel's right pulled down on the twin thrusters, the ship thrumming. The view ahead darkened momentarily as the light from all the worlds changed speeds.

Then Ghaldezuel's eyes filled with light again, the colours of hundreds of thousands of visible stars – gold and umber and silvery green, rose-pink and icy cyan – pouring into the cockpit as if they were passing through a tumbling waterfall of jewels. Even the seasoned pilots, used to decelerations at slightly lesser speeds, sat back in their seats and *ooohed*.

Indak loomed closer as they swept down towards it, a flare of magenta rising to meet them among the cacophony of stars, Voliria Minor burning fat and golden green in the middle distance. Ghaldezuel knew they were too far away to make out Indak's ring of planets, let alone the four tropical moons that he had come here to visit, those worlds perpetually at war.

He sat forward, battling to hide the motion of his involuntarily clenching and unclenching hand, the Drolgins spirits clearly growing restless, too. 'Remember, corkscrew.'

The pilot Bezma nodded, waiting until they could see the first of the planets against the grand colourscape to initiate the roll. The stars spun around them, something whining on the trumpet deck.

'Ordnance, Majesty,' said the other pilot, Mumore, without glancing at him.

They continued their roll, the dull grey-green dot of

Silakbo resolving ahead, angling their approach until the planet swept by, a dash of extra colour to stern. Ahead, or far below as Ghaldezuel liked to think of it, lay the planet of Pandemonium and its moons. Almost instantly, the flight deck lit up with various warnings, the stolen Amaranthine technology reporting through a series of squealing displays that they were being targeted by three of the four moons, the other being still hidden behind the planet.

'Firing short-wave lumen pulses,' said Mumore calmly, his gloved finger closing over a trigger on the controls. Ghaldezuel watched a stream of pink light erupting from the Poacher's nose and into the Void ahead of them, dashes of controlled fire too swift to untangle so that it appeared almost as a beam. Ghaldezuel could hear the thump of feet as gunners climbed to their stations in the battery below the cockpit, a set of cranking vibrations alerting him that the roving gun turrets were now manned and swivelling.

The Amaranthine warning symbols pulsed, their sounds turned off, until a flash of something silent and bright zipped past the ship, Ghaldezuel turning in his seat to watch through the cockpit's windows as it dashed away into the Void.

'Just lumps of pig iron,' said Bezma. 'They must have expended all their proper ammunition decades ago.'

Another one flashed past, skimming close enough to the ship for the upper turret to open fire. A third missile dashed through the lumen stream at the ship's nose, exploding like a firework. They ploughed through the burst of colour, still spinning, and Ghaldezuel found he could make out two of the moons at last, realising that what he'd taken for dust was in fact a forest of hanging fortress stations positioned in orbit around them.

'Coming up on Pandemonium's Daughter, speed three below point,' murmured Mumore, adjusting something. The moons rose to meet them, drawing closer alarmingly quickly.

Ghaldezuel realised the pilots were speeding up to avoid the attentions of the orbital fortresses.

The Poacher tore through a burst of fire, slamming shells and lumens before it, the battery chambers opening up beneath. Ghaldezuel gripped the back of Mumore's seat, transfixed, feeling the attention of his parasitic souls grow silent, too, enthralled. This was probably the most fun they'd had in millions of years, he reflected, smiling as the first of the fortresses swept by above them.

They picked up even more speed, blazing unharmed through the shell of orbital stations – thousands of ramshackle white and grey castles rearing like a city around the moon – and falling towards Daughter's mighty emerald crescent.

'Atmosphere,' said Bezma, sliding back the throttle as the whole ship juddered. Even Ghaldezuel could feel the drag, an invisible heat glowing through the cockpit and making them all sweat in their flight-suits, unfreezing the latent stink of the ship.

Almost at once, the Spirits inside him began to speak, their voices blending together.

'One at a time!' he shouted, noticing the pilots glance at one another.

We will point, said the chief baritone, he whom the witch had said was called Seerapt-Zaor. Ghaldezuel watched his own hand rise under someone else's power and extend a finger.

'There,' his voice said, apparently of its own volition, sing-ling out a massive puddle of dark jungle five thousand miles in diameter, ringed by atolls of startling lapis. The Poacher fell towards it. They took possession of his breathing for a moment, Ghaldezuel panicking when he found he could not do it himself, and then let him go, comprehending that they didn't need that function to speak quickly. He sweated, sitting back, his body under his control again, understanding that he had no choice but to follow their lead.

Soon they were skimming a few miles above a clear, vibrant

coast. Ghaldezuel gazed down, sensing the wonder of his spectral guests, at the leopard-spotted reefs and beaches, seeing how they bled to an intense green country unbroken as far as the eye could see. A burst of ground fire pattered off the ship's thick plating and Ghaldezuel felt his mouth moving silently. The fire ceased, as if at his command, and the pilots exchanged another glance. Bezma clapped his hands superstitiously and was silenced by an angry look from Mumore.

Ghaldezuel ignored them both; the quick exchange of foreign speech in his head was suddenly unbearably, skull-splittingly loud.

Mumore abruptly cried out, staring at his hand. It was trembling on the throttle, as if fighting an invisible force. Without warning, the trembling stopped and the pilot's hand was snapped at the wrist, the throttle forced down. Bezma held his hands away from the controls in horror, Mumore screaming beside him, and Ghaldezuel watched as the ship angled its nose towards the jungle and fell.

His legs worked again without his permission, pistoning him out of the seat and marching him awkwardly into the passage behind the cockpit until he reached his chamber, arms extended as the ship steepened its descent. His hammering heart was suddenly grasped and stroked, as if to soothe it.

The Spirits forced him to wedge his pillow into a corner and climb in after it, pulling the bed's woollen mattress over himself. The screaming wail of the ship's descent drilled into his bones, the roar of the engines slowing.

They hit, a supreme bang of crumpling metal, the ship skimming and rolling. Ghaldezuel felt his stomach rise and his kneecap strike the bulkhead, knowing instinctively that the painless shock of the blow had crushed the bone.

The Poacher came to a standstill after its interminable spin, groaning and falling silent. The moans of the crew, filtering through the wreck, turned to screams and wailing. Ghaldezuel shoved aside the mattress and fell onto what had been the ceiling. He had to get out of there.

Again they took his body from him, marching him despite the sudden, furious pain in his knee and neck out through the ruined passage. A hole had been ripped in the side of the hull, the cockpit and forward batteries completely shredded by the impact of the jungle. The Spirits forced him to climb out through the twisted rip, as viciously sharp-edged as a hole in the side of a food can.

'What about the others?' he croaked, shoved and prodded between the razor edges, fearful of slitting an artery and abruptly glad that he was being guided. Outside, the world was a luminous lemony green, so dense with foliage that he could barely see more than a few feet into the rainforest.

There came no answer as he climbed over the twisted metal and jumped the last few feet to the jungle floor, finding himself engulfed by heat and motionless Amaranthine-high grass. He limped and pushed his way through, the pain in his knee dulled by a surge of healing warmth, aware at last that he was moving under his own steam again, and turned to look up through the tops of the grass at the ruined hulk of the Poacher.

It had upended before driving into the jungle and lay now on its back, a spear of white, crumpled metal a hundred feet long, the nose and cockpit obliterated. A desultory flame flickered somewhere in the remains of the battery chamber, a waft of blue-black smoke further aft implying some deeper fire elsewhere. Ghaldezuel looked along the dented outer fuselage to the turrets, spotting his first bodies: the remains of the gunners smeared inside their gunnery stations.

Through the grasses he heard them coming and swung around, sweating in the overbearing heat, ears twitching. He knew very little about the Prism that waged war on these moons; they were called the Lingatra, Ringum peoples of indistinct heritage bred by two thousand years of unbroken conflict.

The grass stood in tall, unbroken stands, hairy-bladed and thick as a hand. Ghaldezuel searched its stripes of light and shade, sweat running into his eyes, wondering just what had become of his life, why in the world he accepted so many foolhardy quests. This would be the last time. *The last bloody time.* At least the pain in his knee was subsiding as his spectral hijackers worked their magic once more.

The light shifted, and he comprehended that he was not looking at grass. A pale, mould-patterned creature almost twice his height was staring down at him, long arms dangling at its sides. He started, and it grabbed him.

Oracle, they'd said in Lacaille while they jumped aboard a ten-wheeled wedge-shaped crawler stained electric crimson with rust. Ghaldezuel found himself pushed rudely to the back of a sour-smelling compartment, only the brilliant, finger-thin beams of light from a collection of bullet holes in the armour plating lighting the inside of the crawler. Another of the long-armed specimens eyed him hungrily. Its small eyes were almost entirely white, as if they had rolled back into its head. Only on closer inspection did he see that they possessed a tiny, milky-blue dot at their centre. They had enormous bat-like ears, these war-Prism of the jungles; huge, hairy dish-shaped growths that twitched and spasmed constantly, flicking away settling insects.

'Oracle,' it said, repeating the words of its fellows on the roof.

Oracle. So they knew why he was here, and to whom he should be taken.

They began a wobbling, jolting journey through the thick jungle, foliage slapping and scraping the rusty sides of the crawler. The Lingatra that shared Ghaldezuel's compartment wore greenish-yellow battle armour, chipped and scraped all over so that the dazzling silver of the tin shone through. Its white fur was speckled with clumps of moss and fungus, which appeared to be growing on its body.

They must have rocked and juddered through the jungle for two hours or more before the first cries erupted from the roof of the crawler. Ghaldezuel, even in his woozy state, knew then that others must have seen the Poacher come down: a fine state-of-the-art Lacaille ship, carrying who knew what and who knew whom that might be of interest to such a desperate, ravaged bunch.

It doesn't matter, said Seerapt.

'There you are,' he muttered. The Lingatra's giant ears stirred.

Let them take you.

'But—'

It makes no difference which of the factions brings you – all share the same masters. Us.

'You—?'

Shhh. Seerapt chuckled. *Better keep this our little secret.*

He flinched, ducking, as bolts slammed into the side of the crawler, a running zigzag of pops that worked their way along its flank, a little under half punching their way through the metal and opening up more slanting beams of light. The Lingatra beside him caught a bolt in the neck and wheezed. Ghaldezuel felt the vehicle crawl to a stop and resisted the urge to search the writhing creature beside him for his divested lumen pistol.

Let them take you, the Spirits had said, so that was what he'd do.

The crawler's top hatch was unscrewed from above. Ghaldezuel noticed the Lingatra try to raise its weapon, hands slicked with its own blood, and he pulled the gun out of its grip. The Prism choked a chuckling, panicked breath, slouching, neck pumping blood. Everything appeared to be racing after the torpid slowness of Napp.

'In here!' he said, loud enough for the activity at the hatch to stop. 'Oracle!'

Fingers like anaemic spiders' legs appeared at the lip of the hatch. Ghaldezuel thought for a moment they were going to drop a bomblet in for good measure, that this would be it, but then an upside-down face appeared, all yellowish fur and glittering red eyes.

'Oracle,' he repeated, holding out his hands.

The upside-down face grinned.

They did not walk, they waded, the yellow jungle so dense that the sunlight reached them, as through the bullet holes, in thin rays. The Prism that had taken him often climbed to get their bearings, opening their long fingers to reveal blood-red webs of skin and sailing back down to the forest floor to rejoin the procession. Ghaldezuel was patted on the back, stroked and groomed, offered stale food and sour water – quite obviously, from their treatment of him, the best they had. He was their guest. He saw from their armour and weaponry that they, too, had exhausted much of their resources, noticing how the bolts in their belts were whittled from chunks of rock and glass, even hard wood. Their tarnished spring guns were ancient, of a sort used in the Threen Wars hundreds of years before. Rings and other assorted studs and piercings hung from their ears, and by the looks of it, the ten toes on each of their massive prehensile feet, unshod at all times, could also grip weapons and equipment with the dexterity of a hand.

At the end of a day's march, the land began to drop. A valley, Ghaldezuel assumed, beginning to understand that where there was depth, you found the Spirits, as if they sank naturally to the lowest point of the world. He began to spot wooden forts suspended in the trees, their occupants climbing out to get a better look at him, and soon they were passing through clearings of gun emplacements, their cement and bonestone bases suggesting a system of underground chambers. Ghaldezuel was surprised to see a heinously rusted liftjet sitting idle on one of the parapets, four of its six wheels replaced with dented fuel drums.

We forced some industry into them.

He scratched furiously at his sunburned ear, now swollen with insect bites. 'Why?'

To perpetuate the battle.

Ghaldezuel stumbled in the undergrowth, a network of yellow-flowered brambles as thick as his wrist, wiping the sweat from his eyes. 'You keep them fighting? What for?'

We'll show you.

Through the dense palms, he caught his first glimpse of the valley they were heading for, seeing how absurdly deep it was, perfect for Spirits. He wondered how many other Oracles had made this journey before him, passing information back and forth between the ghosts of the Firmament and Investiture. It must be such a slow business, he mused, waiting months, perhaps years, for news. But then, the invisible peoples possessed nothing *but* time, he supposed; maybe for them ten years shot by in the blink of an eye, a message from their Spirit friends on other worlds coming back almost instantaneously, like a real, physical conversation. He thought about that as he travelled, remembering someone telling him once that flies lived life in slow motion, that their short lives felt of perfectly normal duration to them. Perhaps the opposite was true for these artificial minds: perhaps they lived *fast*.

A wheeled, top-heavy vehicle, mottled all over with peeling crimson and blistered with gun emplacements, had laboured up the jungly mountainside to meet them and was opening its hatches. Ghaldezuel climbed on top with two of the web-fingered Prism, another gliding down from the trees and thumping onto the roof.

They rolled along bright yellow terraces of water root and pumpkin, making their way down the zigzag of mountain paths to the valley floor, a hissing trail of smoke pumping from the vehicle's chimney. Small, stagnant-looking fish ponds dominated another section of hill, winking in the sun, while arteries of wood-lined trenches had been dug along the mountainside. A barrage net of bomblets, strung up by wire and raised on teetering wooden stumps like hundred-foot telegraph poles, covered the valley. Ghaldezuel gazed up at the primed, hanging bombs above his head, undecided on how safe to feel.

A platoon of gliding Prism followed them down the hillside, leaping deftly through the trees and gliding on towards the valley floor, easily outpacing the vehicle. Ghaldezuel had seen flying Monkmen and Monkbats – hairy, brainless things with webbed arms and legs – but these were quite different. They fell slowly through the air using only the skin between their fingers, their arms and legs extended into the wind. Lower down the mountainside, Ghaldezuel could see the openings of cave-like hovels bored into the rock, noticing after a while that the base of the valley was dotted, like a sponge, with holes.

In their midst, there appeared to be a vast field of moving colour, Ghaldezuel's eyes only making it out when they had begun their descent down the final terrace. It was a rubbish tip strewn with colourful plastic, all of it blowing gently in the hot wind and giving the impression of movement. Why dump their refuse in the middle of their town? At the centre of the rubbish tip, lying in the shade of the hills, was a ring of stones that contained a small, dark, undisturbed pond, perhaps the local cesspit.

The vehicle slowed to a rumbling crawl, its occupants jabbering to one another and climbing quickly out. Ghaldezuel was helped from the roof by a Lingatra that reeked of alcohol. The Prism looked him over with its cloudy red eyes, pointing one of its webbed fingers in the direction of the pond.

Ghaldezuel felt his body being overtaken again as he glanced up at the looming valley, and it occurred to him then that perhaps those who inhabited his body did not know precisely where to go. His feet were pulled out from under him, marching him stiffly across the wasteland of plastic towards the ring of standing stones. At their centre, the pool was brackish and calm and buzzing with the peculiar large gnats native to these moons.

Ghaldezuel's body stopped between the stones and he looked out at the water, waiting.

See, came the rich, vivid voice from somewhere between his ears.

The gnats, crawling on the meniscus of the pond, began to struggle, as if the surface of the water had tightened to trap their legs and tails. Their incensed, whining drone increased in volume, like a thousand flies swarming a corpse. Ghaldezuel hated that sound: the sound of death. Now they were stuck, squirming, to the water, the meniscus black with their wriggling, whining bodies.

Then from the middle of the pool something began to rise.

Ghaldezuel had no choice but to watch: his eyes were glued to the spot, gripped by the tips of invisible claws.

The skin of trapped gnats, writhing and droning, little legs pawing at the air, rose higher, until something the size of an Amaranthine had swollen within the meniscus of the pond. It seemed to breathe in, vacuum forming into shape.

The obscene bulge, standing connected to the pond like a stalagmite of moving insects, resembled a cocoon. Ghaldezuel knew that whatever lurked inside that shell of living things was trapped, just like them, by the gravity of the moon.

Ghaldezuel felt his feet slide out from under him again and he was forced forward through the rubbish to the edge of the pond, the sound of the insects loud now in his ears. He was made to open his arms and tried to fight it, receiving a little hiccup of a heart palpitation in return for his stubbornness. He relaxed himself, dripping with sweat: they could kill him and inhabit his body any time they liked; it was only out of some deference to the future, to something they saw in him, that made them keep him alive. He supposed he ought to be grateful.

The shell of insects reached closer and their fingers touched. Ghaldezuel wanted to recoil again as he sensed their squirming, biting bodies – indeed, many had already opened their jaws and latched on to him, perhaps only in an effort to get away. He tried to avert his face as they moved closer, drawing together, and some small mercy allowed him to angle his head.

They embraced, a Lacaille body bloated with who knew how many Spirits and the gnat skin containing another group, separated by light-years, together again after aeons apart.

Biting, all over his flesh, the flickering of tiny wings tickling him. A hideous warmth.

And something more.

Ghaldezuel almost forgot about the pinching, needling pain of the insect bites, for in that moment he felt the connection between the cousin Spirits. He breathed in the stagnant reek of the water, mixed as it was with the sharp metallic stink of the insects, and suddenly there were new memories in his head.

Memories not of the past, but of the future.

The drone of the gnats changed around him as they released their grip, Ghaldezuel finding that control of his fingers – but only his fingers – had been returned to him. They combined their whine to produce sounds, which at first made sense only in a vague, intuitive way. After a second's listening, however, Ghaldezuel understood the Spirit of the water and flies was talking in a language he knew, a language he could even somehow speak.

'How are you here?' the water spirit asked, its incredulity apparent in the high drone of the gnats.

'He is our vessel,' Ghaldezuel replied, his teeth pinching sharply down on his lip when the Spirits closed his mouth again. 'Do you recall the invention? We must send for every Oracle.'

The fly-covered shape bent to peer at him. 'But it is still *alive*. You have not taken it for yourselves – why not?'

'Because he is a king now. Our king. And he will help us. Won't you, Ghaldezuel?'

He was given back the use of his mouth and throat, an expectant silence falling over the pond. Even the gnats quieted. Ghaldezuel moved his eyes experimentally, saying nothing, spotting a yellowed Prism femur lying in the rubbish-strewn mud at the edge of the pond.

At once, his own hand curled into a fist, punching himself in the temple. Ghaldezuel saw stars, unable, on legs of concrete, to stumble. 'Yes,' he managed, instinctively choosing a word that must have been Reflective: *Ahh*.

They seemed to understand and his fist relaxed.

'Does it know what we do here?' asked the water spirit. 'Will it appreciate?'

'Ghaldezuel,' said his own mouth. 'These four moons – Pandemonium's Daughter, Niece, Aunt and Sister – are our grand experiment. They are our game, a simulacrum of a contest happening far from here.'

Ghaldezuel sat in the valley of rocks, among the blown scraps and shards of multicoloured plastic. Exquisite red dragonflies settled over his damp white armour, crawling, investigating. More bones lurked in the crevices, he noticed, though these had been painted in jolly blues and yellows. Ghaldezuel began to form the opinion that the things here were prized for their colours and had been thrown as offerings for the Spirits.

He'd been given a breather, a space of a few minutes to relieve himself and take a drink, and now that both were accomplished he waited, dreading the stiffening of his muscles that signalled their desire to return.

So now he knew. Now he knew why these moons, of all

the worlds in the Investiture, were the most dangerous and seldom visited. They were the playthings of the Epir Spirits, a war organised and perpetuated by the dead, their every fortification and border zone recreated from slowly gathered information, like an old Lacaille plotting the movements of armies while listening to radio frequencies from a distant land.

They were using these poor folk, untold millions who had perished under a regime of perpetual war, to simulate and game the battles in the distant galaxies – the *Thunderclouds*, as the witch Nazithra had called them – studying the outcomes to see which way the cards would fall.

Through observations of the galaxies, delivered by hundreds of far-flung 'Oracles' – Prism and Amaranthine pressed into service by the ghosts of their moons and planets – the Spirits of Indak-Australis had built up a network of communication so comprehensive that it infiltrated the entire Firmament and Investiture. Here, on the moons of Pandemonium, they gathered what they knew, managing their divisions of acolytes in their own galaxy while simultaneously peering into those in the near vicinity, mapping out the early moves of an apparently colossal conflict developing among the kingdoms of the Thunderclouds.

But there was more: merging together in their own powerful gravity had afforded the ghosts of the Epir machines some unnatural far-sight, a comprehension of an underlying destiny that permeated the universe.

It was in you and your ancestors, Seerapt had told him. *Waiting. The desire to hold another in your arms: to embrace them in love, to penetrate them in lust, always seemingly unfulfillable. It was the same for the Epir, perhaps for all higher forms of life. When the Epir made us, they used a template of their own minds. That same compulsion to enfold another in our embrace resulted in the merging of two great gravities, and within it the spark of a singularity, a vision of the future.*

Someone had designs on us all, Ghaldezuel, and gifted us this power. It is here that we have focused it.

From what Ghaldezuel understood, the Spirits had organised the warring kingdoms precisely as they appeared in the galaxies, with country borders representing galactic arms, star clusters and systems, each place exhibiting the same strengths or weaknesses as its corresponding galactic region. They had even named prominent Lingatra after galactic rulers, assigning them their names from birth and watching them rise to fight and die for their territory.

Ghaldezuel sat and waited, hoping for just another minute without their ghostly interference. He could feel their pressure again, just behind his eyes and in the base of his skull, and an aching, dead weight resting between his shoulder-blades.

He guessed that now, after a couple of thousand years' worth of simulation, the Spirits here could predict what was going to happen in the Thundercloud wars quite a few moves before they actually happened. Ghaldezuel had no real idea of how far away the other galaxies were; no Prism or Immortal he knew of had ever voyaged there – they were like islands on the far side of unguessably vast oceans, one day to be visited, perhaps, but not in this lifetime. And to what end? he wondered. Why sacrifice ten million lives, besides the obvious pleasure these beings derived from such cruelty? What did they hope to achieve?

Come back now.

He stayed where he was, fearful of standing in case they took him and he fell.

Come back, unaided.

Ghaldezuel took a moment to realise what they were asking of him, and a wave of dumb gratitude swept through him. He sipped a last mouthful of the fruity local wine and stood, hoisting up his britches. 'Thank you.'

*

'Our Oracle, Charoen, can no longer use the Optic at Cancri.'

'Why not?'

'It has been seized, they say, by someone.'

'Well, that does not matter for now, now that we are joined.'

Ghaldezuel felt their attention on him.

'With this one's plans for the eternal city of Napp, we shall have no trouble repeating what has been done today. We are separated no more.'

'And then we shall see *everything*.'

THE VISIT

And so Grand-Marshal Ghaldezuel, handsome though he had been, was gone. His meddlesome second, the old Lacaille named Vibor, remained, but Nazithra would see to him soon enough. And then the Spirits could have the city for themselves.

The witch came again to the city's keep, creeping past the gambling and drinking at the gate and taking the shadowed stair to Ghaldezuel's old chambers. The smell grew fouler as she ascended, rising up the levels from dank excrement to rotten meat, and into the flyblown air of the upper reaches where Ghaldezuel, and Cunctus before him, had taken their rooms. Cunctus, of course, had ceased to matter long ago, when the Spirits of Port Maelstrom first told her of their plan, commanding her to visit the prison in the hills and gain the inmates' trust, there to wait for the one who would come and liberate them. It was a long, slow wait, and many times she had questioned them, only to be rewarded by the accuracy of their visions. The Spirits knew all, the Spirits saw all.

Nazithra took out her stolen key and let herself in, stepping lightly into the darkness. Her round eyes, proportionately the largest of any Prism breed, were in their element here, made as they were for the darkness of the Three jungles, and she looked quickly around.

The Bult had not, as far as she knew, left these rooms since Ghaldezuel first installed her here. Since no guard in the city would go near an adult Bult, all meals were brought and left at her door. Nazithra wrinkled her nose at the pungency of the place; in all honesty, she was rather disappointed, having heard so much in her time about these renowned cannibals of the Investiture. This *Jathime*, as Ghaldezuel had called her (almost certainly a bastardisation of a completely unpronounceable name), seemed as meek and homesick as a little child, not even worth the sport of taunting. Nazithra had come here occasionally to whisper into the Bult's sleeping ear, trying in vain to elicit a response, but the creature was dull as dishwater: perpetually away with the fairies.

She crept towards the bed, conscious that the heap of furs and blankets was rising and falling with the breaths of someone awake and waiting, not wanting to get too close.

The first thing she did every time was to squat and piss in the room, claiming it for herself, asserting her dominance. This she did now, a smile spreading on her lips.

'Hello again, Bultess,' Nazithra whispered in the dark, standing from her squat. 'Still in bed, I see.' She crept closer to the pile of furs, careful to keep her distance. 'Poor Ghaldezuel must be almost there by now.' She smiled again. 'Do you miss him? *I* do. I can't help but think, night after night, on all the things he and I will do when we are wed.'

The shape stirred – forced, since she was speaking in the ancient Reflective, to understand every word.

Her smile widened. 'Oh *yes*, didn't you know? This is the Spirits' decree: they see great things in Ghaldezuel's future.' She looked around the cluttered chamber. 'Best not to get *too* used to this place, I think. We'll need that bed' – she tittered, imagining it again – 'for our nuptials soon enough.'

She moved closer. 'But you mustn't take it personally, my

354

dear Jathime. You never had a hope of keeping him; not someone like that. From one female to another, I mean you no ill will. It's just the case with first loves.' Her tongue began to snake from her mouth. 'It never lasts.'

She reached out and ran her hand along the furs, twining them in her fingers. 'I understand your plight, I do. Just say the word and I'll help you get away from here, from all of this.' She risked one last step. 'This, all of this, has nothing to do with you, a simple Bult. You don't belong here.'

The Three waited, breath bated, a line of drool *drip-dripping* from her tongue. She'd expected more of a reaction by now.

Nazithra pulled slowly at the fur, dragging it back, inch by inch.

'He*llo* in there … ?'

The top of a scabbed head came into view, the haunted eyes turning in Nazithra's direction. She stepped quickly back, registering the gagged mouth, the bound wrists, all extremities nibbled off. It was one of Cunctus's generals, he who had most recently been hanged from the wall. Jathime must have been stealing them from the parapets while they were still alive, then putting them back.

She turned towards the new sound in the chamber, the scream rising in her throat.

SLAATHIS

Aaron had lost track of time, skimming through celestial darkness like a deepwater fish, the lanterns of surrounding life flickering out.

The moon Slaathis rose ahead, painted with the stained-glass colours of its mother, Zeliolopos. Aaron reached out to the tracking team he'd hired, awaiting their signal, and descended into the moon's brushed smoke of atmosphere.

As he dropped, he shrivelled to the size of a mouse, darting ahead of a stream of vapour and down to a cold land of farmed volcanic mudflats, seeking out the stand of trees.

Cold fear overcame him as he spied the swollen fruit in their branches, knowing that so many lifetimes of planning ended here. No greater, more romantic act of revenge had ever been carried out, he was sure; but what was on the other side, not even Aaron the Long-Life could know.

THE CANCROUS OPTIC

Cancri, the last Vaulted Land in the Firmament and the newly wrested territory of the first Pifoon Satrap Berzelius, looked across its eponymous Gulf and into the myriad stars of the Prism Investiture. The hollowed planet was protected by a floating belt of Pifoon capital ships hanging secured to the chains of the Tethered moons; cruel tin spikes a hundred feet long and almost certainly the most advanced Prism ships in the galaxy. With their great guns trained on the Void, not even the Lacaille would be tempted to try their luck anytime soon, even though it was by now a very open secret that the seas could not be closed. The Firmament, or at least its nearest border with the Investiture, belonged now to the Pifoon.

Ringing Cancri's waist was a movable loop of structure, built into the crust so that the entire segment – a circumference of hollow tubes twenty-five thousand miles long – could rotate at will, independent from the body of the world. Poking a mile through the atmosphere of Cancri's outer surface was the reason for such an extraordinary feat of four-thousand-year-old Amaranthine engineering: a colossal telescope known as the Optic, capable of adjusting its lens to rewind the movement of every celestial photon, seeing apparently faster than light and able to spool back time itself. From this outer vantage point, the Amaranthine of Decadence were able to see clearer and farther than any who had gone before, save perhaps the fabled Epir themselves.

Luminary Berzelius didn't even have to travel to the telescope, instead instructing it to rotate and meet him a mere hundred miles or so from his estate.

From the inside of the world, the telescope was nothing more than a great band of countryside capable of rotating at a few hundred miles an hour (to the great befuddlement and consternation of any wildlife caught at the edge of the divide), and a slab of temperate continent aligned itself between the cut-away mountains near the Emperor's estate.

Berzelius and Ingo entered via a nondescript access tunnel secreted in the forest, where they were met by a swift and silently ancient needle ship that conveyed them on spiralling rails down into the mantle, where the telescope, rooted in the crust like the seed of a great dandelion, extended its many thousands of photon sumps to gaze out in unprecedented detail at the surrounding galaxies.

The edifice was looked after by a single Amaranthine: Nathaniel of the Eye. As far as Berzelius knew, only Nathaniel, his apprentice Charoen and the incumbent Emperor had any knowledge of the telescope's power, and it was this very secrecy that had drawn the Luminary from his work governing the Satrapy.

The needle ship docked inside a tubular platform, rotating smoothly so that they could step out with barely the twitch of a muscle, Berzelius reflecting again how pampered the lives of the Decadence Immortals must have been. He ran a stubby finger along a surface as he walked, expecting a fingertip coated with many thousands of years' worth of accreted dust, but there was nothing.

The warm, echoing chambers, stuffed with the paperwork

of millennia, from the looks of it, gradually darkened, until Berzelius and Ingo found themselves at the edge of a wide, dim bowl about two hundred feet across. Extending down into the bowl was the tapering stalactite of the telescope's eyepiece, its glossy gold finish twinkling with what little light there was in the space. Berzelius, his eyes adjusting to the darkness, thought he could see a person down at the base of the bowl. He was lying supine on a curved, magnificently comfortable-looking ottoman, the eyepiece of the huge tapering lens coiling into his hand like the stem of a pipe.

'Oh, hello,' Nathaniel said, gazing up at him. 'Well, thank you for moving me across the world without so much as asking.'

Berzelius stiffened, about to remind him that the Amaranthine bonfires were still warm, when he spoke again.

'I suppose you'd like a look?'

The Luminary gazed at the dim ridges of the bowl for any trap and nodded finally, motioning that Ingo stay where he was while he made his cautious wáy down. He'd been told that Nathaniel had not left the telescope's eye for many decades and felt a twinge of guilt now for the disruption of his observations.

'You've been down here a long time,' he said. 'Is it so wondrous?'

The Amaranthine vacated the seat, his inactive joints snapping, gathering a heap of notes. 'Trust me, you won't want to leave.'

Berzelius gave the Immortal a look. 'I've seen a lot of stars and moons in my time, Amaranthine' – and he had, albeit only from Cancri's surface, having never actually left the Vaulted Land – 'I'm sure it's not *that* revolutionary.'

Nathaniel appeared to ignore him for a moment as he searched for some last papers among the pile. 'Then it'll be all the sweeter.'

Berzelius watched him find what he was looking for, a slim

notebook stuffed with markers. 'Do you have another...' He gestured for the word, indicating the golden tube and its glittering bulb of glass. 'Another lens? For yourself?'

'I do, but only you control the directions now.'

'How is it powered?' he asked, taking care to assume a frown.

'Like everything on Cancri,' Nathaniel said absently, gathering the last of his things. He looked up, eyebrows raised. 'By the light of the Organ Sun, harnessed by reflectors.'

Berzelius considered this as he sat down, the cushions already warmed, slightly embarrassed at having taken control of a world he didn't quite understand the workings of. 'Not by the perpetual motion?'

'Your mistress didn't explain much, did she?' Nathaniel sighed. 'Perpetual motion was only used on the ships of the line.' He pointed to a bank of large chrome dials arranged on either side of the eyepiece. 'The Optic works much like any other telescope,' he said, studying him critically. 'You do know *how* a telescope works?'

'Of course,' he lied, lifting a finger to one of the dials and turning it before the Amaranthine batted his finger away.

Nathaniel sighed. 'But with one difference. This great wonder of Decadence engineering can see *indirect* light, picked up and bent by reflectors scattered across the Investiture and beyond. Not only do they give the Optic here at Cancri a wraparound view of the heavens, they also focus on and collect all light reflected in the ambient dust of the galaxy, a secondary picture if you will, that can extend far beyond our reach here.'

Berzelius nodded in an attempt to appear thoughtful, eager to get a look through the scope.

Nathaniel stared at him, clearly refusing to budge. 'Do you understand? It can pick up distant photons millennia before they've arrived at the main lens. It means that the sharpest images are located in certain times, while others, notably anything happening recently in very distant places, are distorted, almost to the point of guesswork.'

'Yes, *yes*,' he said impatiently. 'I'd like to see now.' He turned and gave the Immortal a pointed look. 'If I may.'

'Fine,' Nathaniel breathed, wandering off and muttering under his breath. 'Forty-six *centuries* of dedicated study...' He clanged and clattered something in the distance, grumpily kicking it to one side.

'Will you be *quiet*?' Berzelius hissed after him. He pulled the eyepiece, segmented and bendable like a giant gold-plated length of pipe cleaner, towards him, and peered into the lens, his heart fluttering.

Nothing. A blackness so empty he thought he might have gone blind in one eye. Berzelius searched for a moment, twisting the eyepiece around, wondering if the Immortal was playing some kind of joke on him. He pulled away, gazing into the darkness of the bowl, suddenly aware that he was also the perfect sitting target. But the Amaranthine was gone and the huge chamber was empty, only Ingo standing guard far overhead.

'All well?' he called.

The dark little figure raised its hand. 'All fine, Luminary. I'll have a bit of lunch, if that's all right.'

Berzelius gave him the Pifoon equivalent of a thumbs-up – one extended index finger – and cast his gaze back to the array of large dials that ran along the side of the eyepiece. He returned his eye to the lens and slid his fingers up and down the dials, enjoying the crisp, satisfying *snick* of their rotation –

– and his pupil opened wide, drenched with colour, the heavens blossoming before his eyes like a jungle in bloom.

'Well I *never*...'

He zoomed in and out of focus, seeing in three dimensions as if he himself were sitting comfortably among the stars, peering happily into their depths.

There was Tau Ceti, the Last Harbour, in the luminous

constellation of Cetus, gateway to the Prism Investiture. He moved up a focus, stopping in his tracks, realising that he'd just caught the orbit of one of its famous gas giants, possibly Zeliovastus, a black sphere against the star, ringed with colour. He zoomed closer, picking out the speckles of a dozen large moons, crawling and creeping with his finger on the dial until he saw the scattered lights of their Prism inhabitants on the nightsides, the starlight reflected in pools and swamps and seas, advancing until he could see the blanket of night mist across the jungles. He sat back then, breathing hard, having caught the flicker of a pipe being lit on the rooftop of a forest castle. One last twitch of the dial, a *snick* that proxied a swift contraction of the huge assemblage below his feet, and he could see the Zelioceti hand that clutched the pipe, one chewed thumb-claw burnished dim gold in the glow.

Berzelius swung the entire great edifice around, distantly and delightedly aware that in so doing he was moving a whole band of the hollow planet's crust to follow his motions, and stared into the region of space a whole compass point away, focusing quickly on the Satrapies of the Firmamental Interior and the speck of Vaulted Wise, cycling the zoom until he could see the Prism workers – those few still loyal to their Amaranthine Satrap – scything the fields, the Firmamental spring moving to summer. He experimented then with the viewing dial on the left side of the scope, spooling to the kaleidoscope views of distant reflectors to catch the light as it arrived further away: the farmers scurried backwards along their paths, disgorging supper from their mouths, retreating awkwardly indoors. He cycled madly on the dial, seeing their younger selves, and the older farmhands now long gone. One more roll of the dial and a hidden reflector out in the Investiture caught the surface of the Vaulted Land perhaps seven hundred years before, the field appearing then as a purple crop of fuel Linsus, the image distorted and grainy from so much repeated reflection.

This was how they knew. This was the key. With this wonderful eye, he could watch for every danger on the horizon, see everything that monster Cunctus would think of throwing at him before it was even on its way. He was *omnipotent*, om ... what was the word, om*niscient*, his—

In his excitement, Berzelius had twiddled the right focusing knob too roughly and the telescope had gazed far beyond the Firmament into the stew of galaxies on the horizon.

'*Oh, they're beautiful*,' he whispered into the empty space, his eye wandering along a column of elliptical shapes like glimmering jellyfish suspended in dark water.

'Just a moment ...' he said to the empty space as he brushed the focus, bringing them closer. 'Just a moment ...'

And he was inside the first ellipse, drenched in a field of bright stars. Nothing, either in Pifoon or Unified, came up to tell him what galaxy he was looking at, presumably because the only people entitled to look through the Optic were those who already knew the heavens like the backs of their hands. His fingers went shakily to the dial once more and he was within a cluster, eye straining. He pulled back, blinking away a tear that had settled in his lashes.

There were ... He couldn't believe it. The stars were ringed by transparent discs, all of them connected by branching ... bridges, towers, caverns: an encrustation of lands and countries. He zoomed without hesitation, focusing on the tapering connections and landscapes, their colour dappled with starlight. The suns of the distant galaxies were like lamps in a cave, candles in a cathedral ... They had been built around and upon. The galaxies were huge worlds already colonised, and he, Berzelius, Luminary of the new Pifoon Satrapy of Cancri, was the first to discover them.

No, he thought, coming sweatily down from his high. *A select few Amaranthine would have been charged with keeping the secrets of what they saw. Perhaps they even sent ships out there.* He looked again. *Surely none came back.*

Three days later, sweat-stained and wracked with hunger, Berzelius was still staring, casting his colossal eye across thousands of light-years. In the back of his mind, he knew this power could eclipse his ambitions, and shouted that someone must come and wrestle him away from the ottoman (now damp and warm and stinking to high heaven) before the day was out, otherwise he would stay here for ever, spoon-fed and cackling, casting his all-seeing eye over creation, the mystic of the Firmament. More than once he wondered if it had been an Amaranthine plot all along – tempting him to the great telescope like an ant to honey so that others could take his place – but a moment later, his eye alighting on something else, he was beyond caring.

He turned his attention back to the Investiture, spooling between the months as he watched the developments of the war. From his bird's-eye view he could see the white arrowhead formations of Lacaille troops wading through the marshes of Nirlume, the bright spit-spat of lumen bolts and sparkers, magenta and purple and orange. He saw the Colossus battleship *Yustafan* and its sister the *Gorgonn* as they moved in stately orbit over Drolgins, searching in vain for any trace of the Lacaille flagship the *Grand-Tile*, missing now for some months and strongly rumoured to be in Cunctus's hands. He saw fizzbombs exploding over Shantylands, whipshells cutting through battalions, public executions (by searching for the gathered crowds) and individual acts of extraordinary heroism. He watched a Vulgar mercenary clear a fortification single-handedly before catching a bolt in the eye, spooling back a little more each time to watch the mercenary's charge, slowing the light to follow the course of the bullet. When he was Satrap of the galaxy, he would go and collect that bolt, lodged in a wall, and wear it on a chain around his neck.

On the fourth day, his mystified generals sent a skinny Lacaille courtesan in the hope of tempting him out. She hovered nervously in the gloom while he looked her over, unbuttoning his damp, shit-filled britches, beckoning her, and returning his eye to the scope.

What'll happen next? his wild brain asked, eye darting, fingers fluttering on the dials. He stifled a giggle, zooming past the worlds of the Investiture to the brightest galaxy in the sky. *I am the narrator of this tale. I already know.*

PART IV

PART IV

HOME

They moored the boat a short distance from the beach, throwing their bags over and jumping into the green sea. Percy stood waist-deep in the shallows, his hair plastered over his eyes as he listened to the hot scratching of the chica worms in their trees across the bay.

Lycaste had waded onto the beach and stood, dripping, as he observed the pale, bell-shaped towers across the shore. An orchard of tall silvery trees leaned out above the pebbles, shading the water. Up in the hills the sun beat down, stands of browning palms brooding over the bay. Percy stared into their shadows, alert, suddenly very sure he was being watched.

'It looks so different,' Lycaste said. 'Why does it look so different?'

'It has been almost two years, you said?' Perception asked.

'Yes, but...' Lycaste dropped his bag and wandered up the beach. 'One of my towers is gone. They've pulled it down.'

Percy glanced around, the sparse hairs rising on his skin. Something was certainly wrong. The grumble of the *Epsilon* came to him across the water and he saw the glint of the ship as it descended through the electric blue, coming in over the bay. It landed a little way along the beach in a vortex of spun green fire, careful not to spray them both with pebbles, and sat in clicking, popping silence as its metal body cooled. Percy waved to Huerepo and Poltor as the two Vulgar waddled out of the hangar, a few Oxel following them down to the beach. Maneker had clearly chosen to stay aboard, a silent protest at their choice of destination; Percy had assured him they wouldn't be long. He watched the Vulgar stagger as they were struck by the sudden heat of the Province, their little faces reddening and dripping with sweat almost as soon as they'd left the hangar.

'Fuck me,' said Poltor, keeping to the *Epsilon*'s shadow.

Perception ignored them, standing and staring into the hills. Someone was staring back.

Lycaste stumbled like a sleepwalker through the orchard, hardly recognising the place. It looked like his whole garden had been dug up and replanted with mature trees, as if the new owner had taken umbrage at his sculpted hedges and arrangements. The thought filled him with a sudden, jealous rage, and he marched more quickly to his doorway, immediately light-headed again at the sight of the place. It was almost as if he'd never left.

'Excuse me?' said a lady's voice in Tenth. Lycaste turned, breaking out in a sweat.

A face – a crimson Tenthling face – appeared through the trees. Her large eyes, shaded by a sunhat, looked worried. 'Can I help you?'

'I'm the owner,' he blurted, having a spot of bother with his own language after so much time. 'This is my house.'

The woman remained where she was among the silver trees, worried, no doubt, that he might be insane.

'I'm not *mad*,' he explained quickly. 'I'm Lycaste.' He pointed up at the towers. 'This is my house and you've knocked down part of it and replanted the orchard. I've only been gone—'

'Lycaste?' She asked, pulling at the brim of her hat. 'Cruenta?'

He stared at her. 'Yes. Are you a tenant?'

She put down her basket, stepping through the trees. He had to look away from her bushy nakedness, wondering at how times had changed. A Butler Bird he didn't recognise was watching them warily through a parting in the hedge.

'They said you went away,' she said. 'This place has been sold twice in the last twelve years. I bought it from Elcholtzia, up on the hill.'

He leaned against a tree, too confused to stand.

'I think you'd better come inside,' she said.

Lycaste, Huerepo, Poltor and Percy walked up the beach to the house of Impatiens. A Melius grave, a simple wooden pole with a crook at its tip for hanging flowers, stood solitary in the garden.

Lycaste knelt before it, and Percy watched his broad red back shaking as he wept.

'Who was it?' asked Huerepo, retreating a little to let him grieve.

'An old friend of his,' Percy said. He read the Tenthling inscription. 'The owner of this place.'

'Hello,' muttered Poltor, nudging Huerepo, 'who's this?'

Percy looked. A gangly Melius boy was watching them from the house.

Lycaste noticed him last, ears pricking. He stood, sniffing, rubbing a clumsy fist into his eyes and motioning that they stay where they were.

'Briza?' he called.

The boy almost went inside then, lingering in the doorway. Lycaste went cautiously to the threshold, talking with the boy out of reach of everyone's hearing.

All except for Percy, who could read their lips as if he were standing beside them. The boy did not remember Lycaste, but was going to fetch his father.

Lycaste went in, and the three of them dawdled in the shady garden, Poltor and Huerepo daubing sandy mud onto their skin to protect themselves from the ferocity of the Tenthling sun and rolling a couple of strong Amaranthine cigarillos to smoke. Together they watched the waves sweeping up the stony beach. It was as peaceful a place as Perception had ever been, and some atavistic urge put there by his father told him it would be a nice place to stay, perhaps for ever.

But then that sensation returned, that feeling of being *observed*. Percy turned and stared into the palms on the hill, his eyes searching their shadows. 'I'm going for a stroll,' he said to the two Vulgar, who had opened a bottle of something and were happily smoking and chattering with the arriving Oxel. 'Won't be long.'

Lycaste followed the boy into the back garden, a courtyard shielded from the sea by a high bonestone wall. The man Drimys had clearly heard their talk from the garden and sat waiting on a shaded bench, his eyes wide.

Lycaste felt a familiar shyness sweep over him as he saw his old friend. All he wanted to do then was turn tail and run, run back into his quarters on the *Epsilon*, back up into the Void, anywhere but this impossible, bewildering place where time, apparently, had dashed on without him.

It's your choice, he reasoned to himself, seeing the tiny but appreciable age that Drimys's face had accumulated since their last meeting. *You are free to do as you wish.*

Drimys, Briza and Lycaste looked at each other, the sound of the waves carrying softly over the walls.

'Where have you *been*?' Drimys said, leaning forward, shaking his head gently at the ridiculousness of it all.

'There are some odd sorts with him, Papo,' Briza said, a depth just coming into his voice.

'Keep an eye on them,' Drimys replied, not taking his own eyes off Lycaste. 'And what in the world have you been eating? You've hardly changed.'

Lycaste reached instinctively to his face, touching his rough beard. 'That woman in my house said it's been *twelve years*. I've only been gone—'

'It has been twelve years! It's six fifty-nine! Have you been asleep all this time? And who are those people with you?'

Lycaste looked into the blue sky, as if it somehow contained the answer. 'Percy!' he shouted, waiting. 'Percy will know,' he muttered, nodding and scrubbing a hand through his short hair and sitting down on the bench.

Drimys was looking at him as if he'd lost his marbles. 'You left before the Plenipotentiary died. I remember the night you disappeared. Why did you leave? Was it Callistemon?'

Lycaste stopped smoothing his hair and glared at his old friend. Once again, he felt as if it was he that had died and was locked now in some strange, maddening afterlife where nothing was quite as it seemed.

'*Before* he died?'

Percy reached the first rise, scrambling on some loose earth as he realised he'd never climbed anything steep before. Below him, the cove had unfurled, a great glittering bite in the rocky coast, the sun on the green water dazzling his eyes. He sat, breathing hard, still getting used to the mingled pleasure and torture of exertion.

At once, he became very still. There was someone, some-*thing*, behind him. He remembered Lycaste's stories of home, some mention that the young man had felt watched.

Percy turned.

Deep in the shadows of the trees, a presence regarded him cautiously.

What are you? it asked, slinking closer, dappled with shade.

Something must have changed since Percy had last encountered Aaron's Spirit. He could see so much more now than he ever could before.

It was a deeper shade of darkness, something that disappeared when the light touched it. He extended his finger and felt the weight of something touch him in return.

You aren't a man, the shadow said suspiciously, in Percy's head. He comprehended with a smile that this was how he himself must once have sounded. It was unsettling, to say the least.

'No,' he said, 'I'm not.'

The weight on his finger and hand increased as something, invisible now in the light, slithered across his body. Immediately Percy sensed their souls reaching out to one another, trying to merge and blend.

Lycaste walked slowly into the surf, watching the water run between his toes and drag the fine sand away with it. Never in his life had he been told so much in so short a space of time. By rights he should now be sixty-three, for the Old World had somehow turned faster than all the others, speeding time along.

His life here had been taken from him, but from what they'd told him, he had not deserved that.

When he left here, Callistemon had still been alive.

Instead of relief, he felt sharp-edged fury, bitter tears stinging his eyes, an ache rising in his throat. Lycaste looked into the water, spotting the same garishly patterned fish investigating his toes, and splashed his foot, shooing them away. He remembered all the women, and men, who had arrived at his door with proposals of marriage, wondering what might have come of his life had he accepted just one of them, where he'd be right now. A dream of another world filled his mind, a dimension where he lived happily, unaware of how close he'd come to ruin. But it was not this life. *This* life had been taken from him for *nothing*. Now his friend Impatiens was gone, his house sold, his name all but forgotten. He might as well have died—

But then he saw Huerepo and the Oxel watching him, concern rumpling their little faces, and his rage flowed away with the tide between his toes.

'All right?' Huerepo asked awkwardly as Lycaste walked up to them. He patted the Vulgar on the head, smiling at the

Oxel, and sat with them on the pebbles. Poltor offered him the bottle – another fine, sweet Amaranthine wine liberated from Maneker's cellar – and he took it with a smile.

'We can buy this place back for you, if you want,' said Huerepo, flicking stones at Poltor's plackart. Together they had amassed enough Amaranthine sapphires to clog up the *Epsilon*'s hold, weighting it so awkwardly that it leaned at a visible, drunken slant on the beach.

Lycaste thought for a moment, surprising himself. 'I don't know if I really want it any more.'

Percy trudged back along the stones, walking parallel with the incoming surf and wetting his dust-caked feet. He saw Lycaste and the Prism sitting together a little up the beach, noticing how the sun had almost sunk below the rocks of the distant caves.

He looked at Lycaste with solemn interest, trying to see the resemblance.

You don't believe me, the Epir presence – a female – said at his side. *But you will.*

'Percy,' Lycaste said when he saw him coming, 'everyone's saying—'

'I know,' he interjected, picking up a pebble and looking apologetically at it. 'I appear to have buggered up my Bilocation. It's clearly more difficult than I thought.'

The two Vulgar chuckled. They didn't seem to care. Percy wouldn't have been surprised if they both had numerous debts out in the Investiture that would now be forgotten. The sunburned Oxel, dozing off the heat beside them, had very little comprehension of time as it was. Only Lycaste was looking at him sternly.

You see it now, don't you?

Perception swallowed, choosing his words carefully. The resemblance was clear.

'I *did* warn you that it was an experiment, Lycaste. I'm

sorry.' He thought for a moment, his human brain sluggish. 'You know, I'm quite relieved, actually. It could have been a lot worse.'

Are they one and the same? he asked her as he spoke. *Are you sure?*

I've watched him since he was a boy. There is no doubt.

'And Pentas's child is queen now,' Lycaste said suddenly, mystified, taking a large swig of the bottle. 'Can you believe it?'

Percy, who had never met the girl, could very well believe it. He could believe a great deal these days.

KIPRIS

They took the *Epsilon*, soaring high above the moonlit Nostrum Sea and landing in the rocky fields on the outskirts of Alvege, his parents' estate, on the lonely Eleventhling Protectorate of Kipris Isle.

Lights shone from the towers of the house, bathing the dry grass with glowing stripes. As the cool salt wind ruffled his hair, Lycaste was suddenly very glad he'd come under cover of darkness. He didn't want to be seen by old childhood acquaintances, didn't want to be recognised and questioned. They had done nothing but mock and torment him, these bored island folk, and he owed them nothing.

'Lycaste,' Percy said, obviously sensing his nerves. 'Sit for a moment. Breathe.'

They sat on a wall together, listening to thin music coming from the open windows. Lycaste couldn't believe they were just in there, on the other side of the wall; so close, so distant.

'They used to like to embarrass me,' he said, turning to Percy. 'Why? I've never felt the need to do that to someone.

374

Perhaps that makes *them* the strange ones…' He could feel his heart hammering, panic only a few breaths away.

'Remember the breathing I taught you,' Percy said, puffing out his naked brown belly as a demonstration. 'In through the stomach and hold.'

Lycaste did as he suggested, feeling calmer with each big breath. He looked at their feet as they dangled from the wall, clear in the green of the moonlight. 'What a silly story I'll have for them.'

He slid from the wall, moving to the window and pressing his eye to the thick, distorted glass.

There they were.

Lycaste's father was picking at something on the end of a fork, apparently ignoring his old wife as she spoke. Their Butler Birds hovered at the end of the table, in the process of conveying the remains of a large dinner back to the kitchens. Lycaste watched their distorted faces through the glass, calculating that they were both in their second century now, understanding that he was looking upon the calm lives of two people who thought him dead and gone. It wasn't often that you got to see the aftermath of your own life.

He chided himself, stepping away from the glass, remembering that it was supposed to have been more than a decade. Any grief could scar over in that time, he supposed.

Lycaste hesitated at the door, the sounds of their sharp, cultured voices coming through the carved holes in the wood. If they looked to their left, they would see his shadow through the lattice, but they did not. Lycaste remembered what a burden he once was to them, how very exasperating he must have been as a shy, dysfunctional young man, presented to expectant society only to disappoint. He pressed his ear to the door, closing his eyes, weeping softly as he made up his mind.

Lycaste stepped away from the door, their voices growing softer, taking another step, and another, until he could no

375

longer make out a word they said. He moved beyond the light of the windows and they disappeared from view. And then he was gone.

'Ready?' Maneker asked, lingering like a shadow in the hangar. Lycaste nodded, pushing past him and making his way to his chamber. He fell into his pile of clothing, nestling like a hibernating animal in the rumbling, insulating darkness of the *Epsilon*. He opened his eyes in the gloom and went to his slot of porthole, a wedge of reinforced, yellowed plastic, looking out into the darkness of the island. His parents would undoubtedly hear of something lifting from their gardens and disappearing into the sky. They'd never know how close he'd been.

Lycaste began to tremble, wondering if he'd done the right thing. He hurried to his door, shoving it into its slot and jogging down the passage. Maneker was already striding through the scullery towards him, the hiss of the closing hangar flanges following at his feet, the pitch of the motors changing. Lycaste moved aside to let him pass, sitting heavily at the table, and felt them lift away.

Percy sat in the flight deck, bathed in the green light of the moon. Maneker was trying to speak to him, but instead all Percy heard was *her*.

He came looking for me, the Epir Spirit said. Percy nodded. He knew. Their souls were so intertwined that all her knowledge, all her memories, were now his.

He saw the world as it had been, seventy-nine million years ago, and what had happened to cause all this.

And he saw the future.

MEETING

Lycaste took care to clasp his trembling hands together, trying with all his might to look interested in the chapel's astonishing ceiling.

Even someone like him, a simple coastal landowner born up in the outlying Provinces, had heard of this place, the chapel at the top of the Sarine City, the jewel in the First. His uncle Trollius had even been here, once, and brought back a tapestry copy of the ceiling that had long fallen prey to the moths by the time Lycaste came along. He saw now that it was no great loss; no tapestry could have come close. Percy, munching contentedly on something that dribbled down his chin, looked equally captivated, and they were both so engrossed that neither heard her enter.

'It's you,' came the voice he hadn't heard in twelve years. 'It's really you.'

Lycaste inhaled a deep breath, finally taking his eyes from the ceiling. An image of someone he might have known stood a little way off. At once he remembered why he'd fallen in love with her.

But it wasn't love, he told himself. *You know that now.*

Pentas was watching him gravely, unsure, and Lycaste suddenly understood that the clock was ticking. *Say something*, that interior voice continued. *Say something or she'll think you're the same awkward shutaway she was glad to leave behind.*

Percy nudged him sharply in the ribs and he burst into life.

'Sorry,' he gasped, 'your ceiling – it's … wonderful.'

Her eyes crinkled into a smile. 'I made some additions myself. Can you—'

'The household scenes,' he said instantly, pointing, and she laughed.

They stepped closer to one another, the last few moments before Lycaste's disappearance weighing heavily on the silence.

Lycaste felt Percy move away, no doubt genuinely distracted by the ceiling. He felt such love for his old friend the Spirit then, and all they had been through, that suddenly Pentas became just another person, standing before him as a thousand others had, waiting for him to speak.

Instead of speaking, he smiled and began to laugh. 'What a ridiculous story, eh?' he asked, tears in his eyes.

She grinned. 'What a *mess*.'

'I went away for twelve years,' he said, shaking his head in wonder. 'By accident.'

'You idiot.'

They were laughing now, looking into one another's eyes, the relief surging through them.

Pentas wanted to reach out, to hold him in some way, but could see that their closeness was too fragile to ruin with a touch. The twelve years that separated them seemed to have dissolved in an instant, and she was back meeting the shy, clumsy young man who owned a house by the sea. She remembered what had charmed her into telling him her deepest secrets, knowing that in doing so she had conferred too much upon him.

A muttering arose behind the bronze chapel doors and they swung open. Lycaste straightened, watching tear-blurred people come walking slowly in, eyeing him expectantly. He recognised the Amaranthine Jotroffe at once – he at least had not changed at all. Jotroffe nodded to him, a twinkle in his eyes, and Lycaste nodded back.

To the man's left was a Melius girl, not yet in her teens but easily the Immortal's height already. She wore the half-mask and facepaint of the West, the Shameclothes of the East, and was smiling broadly as she lifted the mask.

Instantly he recognised who her mother and father were,

seeing in her the man Lycaste thought he'd pushed to his death.

Callistemon's daughter.

'Come, Babbo, meet Lycaste.'

He bowed awkwardly as she came before him, noticing how the Shameplague had lightly scarred her features, and remembering the red welts that had covered Callistemon's face at the end.

'That's not necessary,' she said in Tenth, grinning a gap-toothed smile. Lycaste straightened, some instinctive part of him liking her immediately. 'Babbo?' he asked clumsily. 'That's your name?'

'No.' She giggled. 'It was my first word, and it must have stuck.'

'May I present Arabis the First, Queen of the Fifteen Provinces, Empress of Sligos and Mansour, Custodian of the Isles of Storn and Ion, Protector of the West and Friend to the East,' Jotroffe said grandly, clearly delighted by all her titles, as if he'd made them up himself.

Lycaste smiled back, still somewhat baffled by the quirks of fate that had led them, all of them, *here*, to the grandest room in all the Provinces.

An Amaranthine with a soft, kind face appeared at Jotroffe's side, perhaps the one they called Holtby, and further back he spied another seated, dark-skinned Immortal, smiling from one of the wooden chairs that lined the wall.

Holtby appeared suddenly shocked, even angry, and Lycaste followed his gaze to see that he was glaring at Percy.

'What's *he* doing here?' asked Holtby with barely concealed disgust. '*Trang Hui Neng* was one of them! He cannot be trusted. You should not have confided in him.' He paused, retreating to safety behind Jotroffe, and all eyes turned curiously on Percy.

'It is a long tale to tell,' said Maneker. 'Suffice it to say that this is *not* Hui Neng, only his corporeal form. I shall introduce you all properly soon.'

Holtby was about to interject when a limping Firstling joined Pentas. She looked at him sharply, and Lycaste had the sudden premonition that the man had not been supposed to come. 'And this is my husband,' Pentas said, softly. 'Filago.'

Lycaste nodded, catching Percy's eye.

'And Eranthis?' he asked. Pentas shook her head.

'She left, some time ago. The last letter we had, she was in the Threheng Counties, out east, wandering.' Pentas looked sadly at Filago. 'She is happy, though.'

'Now then, where is Sotiris?' Maneker asked, suddenly businesslike, raising his voice above the introductions. 'If he sleeps' – he ventured a nervous look at Percy – 'perhaps we can wake him?'

'I'll try,' said Percy, following on the heels of a nervous-looking Holtby. They came into a long, gilded hallway, the floors worn down into soft valleys by hundreds of years of Melius feet. More paintings gambolled across the ceilings, details of the formation of the First.

'That room,' Holtby said, pointing to a tall blue door, 'cannot be opened by any tool or blade. Some Incantation protects the material of every stone in the walls.'

Lycaste darted a look at Percy, who was already moving towards it, arm outstretched. The Spirit, taking sanctuary in the Amaranthine's body, could apparently now recall some of the deepest secrets of the Firmament, including the fabled spells of antiquity, like the one that had set it free.

Percy touched the varnished wood of the door with his palm, eyes rolled upwards into his skull, apparently accessing the memories of his borrowed corpse. His lips began to move.

'Aedile ... thirty-one blackbirds baked in a pie ... No, that's not it.' He frowned and looked critically at the door, some-thing dawning in his eyes. 'It is like the seal that locked *me* away. Abigail's Incantation. Not the same, but similar.'

Maneker was wringing his hands. 'Can you ... can *he* remember?'

Percy raised his eyebrows. 'Just a minute, have patience. The motes here are lightly distributed, but they will answer my call.' He closed his eyes, muttering under his breath, then opened them with surprise. 'This was chosen specially, by Aaron.'

He placed his hand upon the door.

> *'Long, long have I bewailed the severance of our loves,*
> *With tears that from my lids streamed down like burning*
> *   rain,*
> *And vowed that, if the days deign reunite us two,*
> *My lips should never speak of severance again.*
> *Joy hath o'erwhelmed me, so that for the very stress*
> *Of that which gladdens me to weeping I am fain.*
> *Tears are become to you a habit, O my eyes,*
> *So that ye weep as well for gladness as for pain.'*

His voice died away.

Nothing outward happened. Percy indicated to Maneker that he should try, and the Immortal pushed at the door.

It swung slowly open with the groan of old hinges, and there, crumpled and dangling half-out of the bed, his head bloodied against the tiles, lay Sotiris.

Maneker darted forward, kneeling and cradling his old friend's head in his hands. From the look of the dust, which lay thickly all around, even on the man's head and shoulders, he had lain like that for some time. The blood on the tiles, though light, was brown and old.

Maneker began to weep, a tearless heaving of breath that they all felt unable to turn away from.

'I knew in the dream,' he sobbed, 'I knew I'd lose you. Damn him – *damn him!*'

*

Percy watched from the wings as Lycaste went and knelt at Maneker's side, helping him lift the body of their friend back into the bed. He had never seen this man, Sotiris, before.

'You know,' he said, clearing his throat, 'he is not gone for ever. You can still find him.'

Maneker looked balefully up from the bed, Lycaste standing red-eyed beside him. The whole royal court seemed packed into the corridor behind them.

'He's out there, somewhere,' Percy said, noticing and licking a dab of jamfruit from his index finger. 'And I suspect I know where.'

Lycaste stood. 'You mean that?'

'Of course. It would have been much easier if I hadn't lost the Collection, but—'

'The *Collection*?' asked Holtby, looking between them. 'The pieces of Perception?'

'That's right,' Percy said guardedly.

Holtby shrugged. 'There's a second set down in the vaults, I forgot to mention it. Perception's twin. Would that be of any use?'

Lycaste and Percy looked at each other.

JOURNEYS

Jatropha, Maneker and Percy sat around the bed, looking at the still form of Sotiris, now propped up against the cushions, a peaceful expression on his tanned, sombre face. Arabis came to join them, bringing a chair with her, followed by the Amaranthine Percy had noticed sitting at the back of the chapel, Harald-something.

Percy spotted that Arabis held in her hands a pale cloth cap. Maneker took it reverently from her and presented it to Percy.

'The office of Firmamental Emperor is somewhat redundant these days,' he said. 'But, as the true and worthy inheritor of everything we see around us, *Perception* here ought to take it.'

Percy looked at the cap, understanding that it was a very simple crown, and glanced among the others present. Jatropha and Arabis, who already knew what he was, were nodding and smiling. He took the crown gingerly, feeling in its weight many thousands of years of use, questioning how it had managed not to fall apart over the years.

Arabis gestured for its return. 'May I?'

He handed her the crown, and she stood, placing it slowly atop his head. 'There. Crowned by a Melius queen. Not very official, but it should do, yes?'

Jatropha patted her on the head. 'It will do.'

'I will take Sotiris back to Gliese,' Maneker said to them all, looking sadly upon the late Emperor with his single glass eye. 'Cancri, his home, is not safe any more.'

Percy nodded, attempting to look regal, knowing the decision had nothing to do with him. The Pifoon Satrap Berzelius had managed to close the seas of Cancri manually, no doubt having found and begun to test the weapons within. Thankfully the Parliaments of Gliese, in Maneker's perplexing absence, had formed their own standing armies, protecting the tiny corner of the Firmament they had left.

'And I'll go east,' Jatropha said, 'to the countries of the Oyal Threheng, to shore up our relations with the Jalan.'

Percy clasped his hands together, wondering earnestly what a *Jalan* was, but said nothing.

'While I shall make my way out to the Investiture,' Harald said, his eyes meeting Jatropha's. 'We have been in contact for some time with its de facto Lacaille king, Ghaldezuel the First, who wishes us to know that he respects our right to the Old World, knows we have a common enemy in Berzelius and would like to meet.'

Percy looked at Harald, liking him immediately. 'I'll go with you, if I may.'

Harald beamed. 'The more the merrier.'

'Doesn't a queen have any say in the matter?' asked Arabis.

Percy turned to her. 'The choice is yours,' he said with a smile, seeing from the corner of his eye as Jatropha began to protest. 'With whom will you travel?'

'I want to go with the Spirit Emperor,' she said, reaching out to hold his hand, 'to meet this *Ghaldezuel*.'

Percy shrugged. 'You heard him – the more the merrier.'

OYAL-THREHENG

Commodore Palustris's galleon rounded the crimson coast, battling its way up the Gulf of Ezrom and on into the wide, perpetually storm-whipped waters of the Indris Sea. The squalls of the east, a band of enigmatic storms that raged and blew from the southernmost Provinces all the way to the Jalan capitals of Karakol and Jalandhar, could not be traversed by land, the reason often cited for the failure of the First to retaliate after Elatine's scuppered invasion. Instead the seas allowed a moderately calmer passage, but this being the Old World, they were infested with the writhing shadows of giant octopuses and the burbling song of monsters in the deep, songs that vibrated through the hulls of ships and woke tired travellers in the night.

Jatropha took to the deck, savouring the rolling, chalk-pale waves that swept up against the railings and dashed themselves across the masts. Within a minute of ascending he was soaked through, cackling into the wind. Poor Holtby, a nervous sort at the best of times, had chosen wisely to stay below.

The tall, red-painted Jalan barque, on first inspection appearing a little top-heavy for these frisky waters, bobbed like a cork, perfectly suited to the voyage home. Jatropha observed the great triangular sail above him snapping in the gale, its protestations loud amid the shriek of wind, and reflected on what a strange year it had been. 14,659 AD, the princess growing into her third year of absolute rule, and who should return but the missing souls of Lycaste and Hugo Maneker, their machine Spirit at their side. He shook his head in wonder, delighted, and gazed back out at the sea. Across the heaving water, a storm of dark, sweeping rain lay heavy over the ocean, and beneath the waves, dark things – whether weed or creatures, he didn't know – stewed. Jatropha looked into the depths, trying to make them out, ruminating on how the world beneath the seas was more densely packed with life than any rainforest of the land, a living soup that so often appeared barren. Life and death, he considered, two realms separated by nothing but a change of state, the light passing beautiful and distorted between them.

They landed at the westernmost port of Janar-Savajh, the barque blowing sideways in the gale and thumping up against a huge semicircle of wool-packed bollards, catching neatly in their grasp. Across the storm-hazed port, Jatropha counted half a dozen more of the tall Jalan ships, their rounded hulls allowing them to bob almost horizontally in the squall without capsising.

They lugged their bags ashore, wobbling down a thrumming gangplank and reeling in the wet gusts that charged across the bay. The Commodore, a gigantic Jalan who never left his ship, waved a huge hand from the stern.

Jatropha waved back, seeing him lumber below deck, and looked into the windswept forests that lined the cove. The air was so loud it drowned out Holtby's words, thundering across the woods of Jamnagh before being muffled by the sea. Jatropha pointed into the darkness of the forest, a country of woodland unbroken for at least a thousand miles, and they clasped their hats and cloaks to themselves before wading in.

The forest was made up of squat, hard-wearing baobabs so ancient and densely packed that many had grown together into thick, near-impenetrable coppices. Jatropha had come this way once before and knew, though there was no path, to walk into the wind.

The gale softened as they entered the ancient woods, and within a few strides they felt nothing but the stirrings of a breeze against their cloaks, though looking up they could see the tops of the trees bent double with its force. Holtby unpacked his flask of Decadence brandy and offered some to Jatropha, the two stumbling over the man-thick roots of the baobabs, following the breeze. Occasionally, through the trees, they spied lumbering Jalan shepherds guiding their flocks down towards the port, the scream of their whistles breaking through the din.

The day grew dark quickly, the thundering sky packed with cloud, and they stopped in a propitious tangle of baobab sheltered from even the smallest of breezes to light their fire. But the sly wind had siphoned through the roots and flowed just a little above ground level, blowing out their fire each time they tried to light it, and so they had to lie content in the company of the Greenmoon, visible every now and then among the racing clouds.

Jatropha gazed up at it, deciding he'd sleep better floating just a little off the hard earth.

'That's a fine talent,' Holtby said over the distant roar of the gale, recovering from his shock. 'I don't think I've ever seen anyone do that.'

Jatropha, deep in thought, hardly heard him. He was thinking of Eranthis's most recent letter to her sister, describing her adventures in the Threheng Counties. The waxy piece of paper had been stamped with the green crescent moon of the Jalan Potentates and the word 'Surath', the name of a citadel further down the coast.

She'd been gone six years, almost to the day. After that

386

night in the guesthouse on the mount she hadn't hinted at her feelings again, and Jatropha heard sometime later that she and Xanthostemon had even been – briefly – married.

He had never told her how unlike other Amaranthine he was, that love had featured in his life, off and on, and that the pain of loss had tried, and failed, to inoculate him against all feeling. She thought that life had filed him smooth, but that was not quite true. Now that she was gone, he felt her absence more keenly than any other. He missed her every day.

When the time had come, at Queen Arabis's behest, to journey into the East, he hadn't needed to think twice.

Jatropha blinked away the suggestion of a tear, noticing that Holtby had fallen soundly asleep, his cloak pulled snugly over his head. He was a good man, loyal to the Devout only on principle (they'd helped him, once, and he had felt obliged to them), soon seeing the errors of his ways.

When Jatropha glanced back at the moon, it had broken, glowing, through the racing cloud once more. He hesitated. Something had moved incrementally in the green-tinged light.

He remained still, watchful, his eyes tracing the lines of the baobabs. He'd met a lot of strange things in his time, but there were still some out there that had eluded him.

His gaze rose, picking out the curve of bony knees pressed tightly together; a gently rising ribcage; a snub-nosed face, narrow as a branch. The creature's gimlet eyes, heavily lidded to avoid the glint of the moon, were locked on Holtby's sleeping form. In the time since they'd made camp, it had crept close enough to touch him.

Jatropha marvelled. A Glauk; legendary flesh-eating beast of the Threheng forest, said to stand so still and straight that its prey simply walked into its grasp.

He looked at it through narrowed eyes, pretending to be asleep. The Glauk was about Melius height, but it was no relation. Jatropha thought it had more in common with the

Marmomen of the South – fuzzy, twitchy creatures more closely related to the tiny monkeys of antiquity.

The Glauk lifted its spindly leg a step off the ground, pausing at the zenith of the move like a chameleon, apparently undecided on what to do next, and placed its foot down a little closer to the sleeping Holtby. Jatropha could see the avidity in its eyes, a suggestion of a flicker, visible only by the light of the moon. The Glauk's fingers uncurled and Jatropha realised with a start that it was beginning the slow process of reaching; he'd better get a move on.

'Hello there,' he said softly. The Glauk recoiled, turning its bright, moon-filled eyes on him. He saw how swiftly it could move, all that conserved energy springing into life, and wasn't surprised when the thing rushed at him. He stopped its breathing almost instantly, the creature's long, bamboo-like legs suddenly unable to move.

Jatropha got to his feet and wandered over, inspecting the thing as it stood before him. It was using all its will to force air into its lungs, and as he stepped up to it, the Glauk's panicked eyes met his.

'I'm going to leave you here for a day, Sir Glauk,' he said in Low Twentieth, the language of these forests, whispering so as not to wake Holtby. 'You won't try to follow, will you?' The thing managed a *no*, a sharp flick of its eyes. 'Please,' said Jatropha, indicating the ground. 'Sit.'

It collapsed to its knees, still struggling for breath, and manoeuvred itself until it was cross-legged. He left it there, not far from Holtby, and went back to his place in the moonlit spot, musing on how even murderous things crave comfort and will change their ways to get it. Jatropha had known enough unpleasant sorts in his time, people with no scruples about killing, and had seen in them the same love of warm food, soft beds, laughter and love, the same fears of heartbreak, embarrassment and loss. Nothing, and nobody, was beyond change. He thought of Eranthis for the thousandth time. Not even himself.

It was best to let poor Holtby sleep, unaware of the death that sat, shivering and gulping for air, only a few strides away. These were arduous forests and the fellow would need his strength for the long walk ahead.

THE EAST

Eranthis finished making the bed, folding the fine sheets and stowing them in a row of wooden cubbyholes with all the others. When she was done, she stood back, hands planted on her hips, surveying the neatness of her cell. It was a good, small place, possessed of an incongruously large Jalan bed, desk and chair, free on the condition that she sang with the children at last Quarter every evening. Its single round, glassless window looked out across the lime-green fields, their rows of brilliantly twinkling waterways blazing sunlight back into her eyes.

She unfolded and donned her Shameclothes: a black children's-size gown and hat, long around the legs for modesty. Only the child size would fit her; another gift from the moneyless country she found herself in, given out free upon arrival.

Eranthis had been here, in the Bhorish Singing Academy, for almost half a year, sweltering indolently in the heat until sundown, when she walked to the acoustic fields to sing with the children. Singing was the one thing she had always been able to do better than her sister – how she had envied Pentas's ability to paint and draw, furious at her wastefulness of the talent – and it pleased her now to use her own abilities as a way of living. The Jalan of these parts, a varied bunch of half-giants and ogres, appeared to care little for her quality just so long as their children practised, for it was apparently a great and admired skill further east, where things mattered.

She sat on the stoop for a while, ring book in hand, awaiting the breakfast bell. The pyramidal edifice of the school rose above her, a light structure of wooden verandas hung with curtains of patterned cloth. Some stooped Jalan greeted her on their way down to the fields. She enjoyed their company well enough, though there were one or two that still refused to speak to a Melius of the Provinces, some even making the sign of evil behind her back. Those she did speak to conversed with her in First, the language remaining useful enough to get along by even this far east. She'd tried her hand occasionally at Twenty-Second, but never got far before they reverted helpfully to the language they assumed was her mother tongue.

She leaned back in the doorway, the metal ring book warm in her fingers, considering how pleasant it was to do nothing, absolutely nothing, for most of the day. Much had once been expected of her as the elder and arguably brighter sister, but unlike Pentas, she'd never been all that bothered about doing anything special with her life. It had become almost a pleasure to disappoint people; when she'd left the First, bidding her niece the queen goodbye and never looking back, it was with a sense of satisfaction; she had defied their expectations, confounded them, shown those that would, given half a chance, have tried to order her life for her that she was not the predictable sort. Leaving Xanthostemon had not been hard; the two realised soon enough that they weren't at all suited, saying no more of the matter. He was the quiet, troubled sort and possessed not a playful bone in his body. She supposed, on reflection, that those were just the kind of men she liked, then shooed the thought away with practised efficiency. You could love someone with the energy to melt iron, but let it grow cold enough and that power died away.

Eranthis thought about that, wondering how long it had been since she'd touched someone. They weren't the tactile sort out here, in the East. She remembered for the hundredth time how her hand had been drawn to Jatropha's across the blanket of her bed that night. Love, it seemed, *true* love, was to try to merge in the grasp of an embrace – to press, desperate, into another person's flesh and become one conjoined creature. And yet this could never happen. Love remained something always unsatisfied, an embrace repeated again and again, tighter and tighter, ever yearning.

Unfair, she thought. *And to what end?*

She looked out at the sweeping horizon of fields, their crop of nightfruit just starting to bud, hoping that young Arabis didn't chose her husbands the same way her aunt did. She received news from Pentas every couple of months, battered letters brought by the same Imperial bird each time. They were contemplating marrying Arabis to a young Jalan Potentate, to cement the union of East and West: a terrible idea, she thought. Probably *his* idea. Eranthis could think of better marriages; the young King Lyonothamnus, happily supplanted by all accounts and unaware of the atrocities committed in his name, was still unwed. He and Arabis were already firm friends, her sister reported, though the young man was in his twenties, assuredly much too old for her by now. Eranthis lifted her face to the sun, glad she was no longer a part of it.

'*Eranthis.*'

Her eyes flew open.

She searched the fields, heart thumping, feeling suddenly sick to her stomach.

There, beneath the shade of a Copperwhill tree, a familiar figure was making his way up the slope, followed by another she didn't recognise.

'No,' she breathed, fury rising within her. She stood, watching him climbing the hill.

He arrived at the school gate, pausing to let the hunched Jalan through. He waved, tentatively.

She shook her head. *No. Not here. This is my place.*

Jatropha looked up at her, apparently oblivious to the last. Eranthis clasped the book tightly in her fingers.

He came to the edge of the school's tiled courtyard, the cool Eyrall blowing past him from the west.

'Think of a demon and it shall appear,' Eranthis hissed, hoping against hope that he would think better of crossing the tiles and just turn around, back into the wind; turn around and leave.

He still hadn't said a word. In his hand he held a coloured piece of something. She gazed at the thing, not recognising it at first. A blue ribbon, punctured with a series of small holes.

Jatropha brought it to her, his palms open to show the letters of his name cut neatly into the silk.

'Where did you find that?' she whispered, folding his small hands into hers. The silk fluttered in the wind, and she closed their fingers over it.

'It doesn't matter,' he said, and a lump rose in her throat. 'It is yours, from me.'

MERIDIAN

Out beyond the moons of Indak-Australis, past the bustle of a hundred and eighty billion souls to the Whoop and the Never-Never and out to the very limits of the Prism Investiture, the worlds fell quiet. Beyond lay a desert of self-sustaining, oxygen-rich planets left over by the Epir expansion, their surfaces scoured and empty and swaddled in impenetrable cloud, and beyond *that* an icy vastness, each sun as lifeless as the last, a fallow wasteland of stars.

Berzelius's Optic, turned now on this no-man's-land at the

edge of its own galaxy, looked in silent awe at the lights in the darkness. The Luminary himself was half-asleep, slumped against the lens, descending into a nightmare of being pulled deep underwater. He twitched, eyelids fluttering, and scrabbled for the eyepiece, his ragged thumbnail catching on an unnoticed dial set behind the lens.

In that moment, one hundred and twenty-six decrepit listening stations emplaced throughout the Firmament opened their ears, and Berzelius sat rod-straight, his eyes bulging, eardrums squirting blood and rupturing across the ottoman.

Noise. Such noise as he had never heard before, and would never hear again; crashing waves of unending chaos and activity, the booming of industry, fired on a stellar scale, and the jostling voices of octillions.

Across the gulf of intergalactic space, the Thunderclouds were *alive*.

The Murmurian Domain floated in the Void like a glittering deepwater fish, its drifting school of neighbouring galaxies spread like lamps in the darkness. From a distance, the Thunderclouds' interior resembled a forest of glowering trees, the blushed, rosy glow of twenty billion stars peeping between their branches.

Drifting closer, there came the suggestion that the stars themselves were shrouded in a milky light; a landscape of softly lit cloud like a pale, cataract-blinded eye. Closer still and the distorted screams of the galaxy were like a nocturnal jungle, warbling and whistling across the depths.

A glint, a burnished sickle gleam of light sliding from curved glass, and it became apparent that the many thousands of stars and their atmosphere of cloud were *contained*. And indeed they were: encapsulated within the Ornaments, ancient crystal baubles teased finely as if between two great fingers, blown by the first generation of life.

The bauble's surface resolved; a colossal scratched wall of

crystal, pitted and gnarled as if secreted over time, its peaks capped with silver spires that branched at their tips, aglow with light. Inside, following the trail of a minuscule nautiloid ship as it made its spinning journey into one of the great silver veins of the Ornament's tip and through thick, milky atmosphere, it was possible to see that the glowing chandelier of stars were themselves linked, caught as if in a colossal spider's web. The very air glittered green and pink and blue, microscopic lights of ships flaring in the mist, and a slender, light-year-long form of a Sun Swallower was visible for a moment, only to be lost again amid the murk.

The shadowed forests at the Thundercloud's centre were each a thousand light-years broad, a hundred million stars drifting among their branches like fireflies. Their bowers and viaducts were home to processions of trillions, all making their way in towards a hanging crescent of gnarled plaque, darkly dappled in the shade of the forest and swarming with its own little clusters of decorative suns. The house of the Sarsappus, eternal ruler of the Murmuris.

The Wizard had, according to the tradition of aeons, decided to leave her filament ship, spending the last hundredth of her life on the great road. Her time was all but spent now, and a wonderful peace had descended over her. The viaduct up to the Sarsappus's house was so jammed with creatures great and small that she had to stand to sleep, but it was worth it; the promised secret would soon be hers.

Inside the house, whole weather systems lifted, curled and sank, dark clouds of warm, slanting rain sweeping in across the depths.

A sea of jostling peoples, of every structure and colour conceivable, from the leviathan to the inchlings, swarmed inside the space. The object of their desires was clear at one end – not because it was visible, it was far too far away for that, but because that was where the suns and crescent worlds had chosen to hover.

The Chair of Wishes was a coiled piece of furniture two hundred miles from end to end, upon which lounged the fifty-six promagistrates and the Sarsappus himself. To her great disappointment, the Wizard had never seen him and wouldn't have time to now, the wait lasting a century at best.

She swam high above the throng, past the decorative hanging macro-galaxy of moon-sized stars and Crescent homes – a honeycomb of interconnected worlds given the honour of inhabiting the Sarsappus's house for a season before they were moved on – bobbing in the currents, and into the deeper weather that separated the cloisters from the vault. Below, the giant inhabitants of the gone-before court now moved in the past, set aside from reality by their distance, but the Wizard gave them barely a second glance. Pets of all kinds were perched in the cloisters, or free and swimming, nipping playfully at the bright, twinkling dust motes of ascending craft.

She was the last of the fifty-six to arrive. For ten thousand years they had travelled, collectors of wonderment and knowledge, summoned from the highest echelons of their respective segments to the haunt of the Astrologer, high in the rafters of the court.

The Wizard ascended, the gleam of the water gardens dazzling her crystal eyes, seeing that they were all there, waiting for her.

The Astrologer, lurking at the bottom of a steaming pool, was asleep.

'Wake him,' she said sharply in Reflective. 'We're all here. Let us see what he has to tell us.'

But he must have heard, for a darkness rose within the pool, glimmering with colour as it ascended.

The long-armed figure, painted with a craquelure of varnish, stepped mightily out of the pool. The Wizard could see that at its heart was a scraped and dented diamond shape, once probably magenta or some such colour but now faded pink by an aeon of sun exposure. The core, said rather exotically to have been forged in the depths of another Thundercloud many millions of years ago, glinted in the light, winking at them. The Wizard had laughed with all the rest at this spooky, unhinged character, until the Sarsappus had chosen the Astrologer as his favourite.

'I was dreaming of my brother,' he said without preamble, glancing first at the newest arrival. 'Strange. I haven't thought of him in ... in an age.'

She heard him out, thoughts slowing, awaiting an end to opening talk.

'And what became of him, Astrologer? Your brother?'

'He was alive, in another *where and when*.' He hesitated, lost in thought.

'We were summoned, Astrologer, if you recall,' the Wizard said. 'I have travelled to the end of my life for the secret of your clairvoyance.'

'I warned you,' the Astrologer said, raising his mighty dripping head. 'It is a most unusual method.'

They looked at him, their shadows stretched long across the pool.

'Tell me, are you all sure?' the Astrologer asked. 'Do you want this? More than anything?'

'Yes!' they shouted, a scream to wake the dead in the heavens of all the galaxies, laughing together. 'Of course we do!'

He was laughing with them, the universal jabber of safety and friendship. 'Good!'

Excitement, as scarce as astatine, overcame the Wizard, and for an instant she felt as if she herself were drowning in the great pool before them.

*

The Astrologer watched them all die, one by one, poisoned by a substance so rare and valuable that it was now, after being administered fifty-six ways ten thousand years ago and travelling all this way with them, extinct. He swept back into his pool and dived.

At the bottom, he felt their souls pooling around him, drawn to the depths, heavier than the water, heavy as a star.

When they had joined with him, consumed, he looked down into the darkness, falling asleep once more.

And he dreamed of the future.

He dreamed that his brother was –

– that he was –

– *alive*.

In the darkness at the bottom of the pool, his seventy-four fingers fluttered, clenching into fists.

His brother was coming, now, this very moment, on his way across the gulf between the Thunderclouds. On his way and looking for him. On his way to find him.

He dreamed of some small creatures, like the Oseers of his youth, but changed, mostly hairless. They had followed his brother over, and now they were everywhere.

He dreamed of a battle waged across the viaducts, a battle of trillions. Sun Swallowers flitting between the plaqued lands, feeding in a frenzy. It was all as murky and patchwork as a memory, reflected, like something that must have happened to him a long, long time ago.

And there was more, so very much more.

This time he could see so much further.

EPILOGUE

MIRROR

He is home – his *real* home, on the cove. Lycaste looks up from his clasped fingers; he is sitting at his wobbly kitchen table, its one leg standing just a little too high off the ground, as if all the years have simply melted away. He listens: the sound of his breath, the distant exhalation of breaking surf. He opens his nostrils, drawing in the scent of varnish from the table's surface, watching dust motes hang still in the whitewashed vaults of the ceiling. Through an open window he can see the orchard and its groves of sculpted trees. Lycaste stares out across his land, listening hard, for the knowledge comes to him as clear as day: he has been brought here in his sleep.

An unseen hand, felt as a gentle pressure, clasps his shoulder.

'We need to talk,' whispers Aaron the Long-Life into his ear.

They walk together down on the wet sand, the surf sweeping regularly over their feet. Lycaste has already noticed, though he towers over the man, how their footfalls mirror one another precisely. He looks at Aaron, who is wearing an outfit he has never seen before, not even among the Amaranthine. A linen collared ... *shirt*, he supposed it was called, paired with mustard-yellow trews. He walks barefoot, and his dainty feet look even smaller beside Lycaste's great crimson toes, and yet for all the world it feels as if they are mirror images of one another, reflected by some medium other than glass, or water, and for the first time in his life, Lycaste does not feel the usual tingling butterflies in the presence of a stranger.

Because this man is *not* a stranger; that has long since become clear. He hadn't even needed to ask where anything was when he'd made the tea.

'What should we do?' Aaron asks. The question is spoken in the unaffected way someone talks to their reflection, when they know they are alone.

Lycaste doesn't know the answer. He can feel, in just the few inches of air that separate them, a vast celestial distance.

He turns his head to look down at the man; a long, lingering glance that takes in as much as it can, and wonders which of them is the future self, which the past.

'How is this possible?' he asks, still watching those colourless eyes. 'Maneker told me that you were—'

Aaron is already nodding. 'I asked myself the same question.' He glances up to meet Lycaste's eye. 'But we are both of us machine, from a certain perspective. We died so long ago that our soul has split in two.'

Lycaste glances out to the green sea feeling Aaron's renewed attention on him.

'Tell me more about your friend... Percy, is it? I'd like very much to know more about *him*.'

GLOSSARY

Cast of Characters

Aaron the Long-Life	Machine soul, now inhabiting the corpse of a long-dead Epir pilot
Ajowan	Jalan Melius, bounty hunter
Alfieri, Fridrik	Amaranthine, Satrap of Virginis
Amure	Melius, Westerling prince
Andolp, Count Murim	Vulgar, Drolgins landowner
Arabis/the Babbo	Melius, daughter of Pentas and Callistemon, future queen of the Firstling Hegemony
Berphio	Vulgar, mayor of Gulpmouth
Biancardi	Amaranthine Emperor of Decadence, ruled from 10,214 AD (deceased)
Billyup	Awger, opportunistic creature who happens upon Arabis and steals her
Borlo	Vulgar, one of the four kings of Filgurbirund
Calamus	Jalan Melius, bounty hunter
Callistemon	Melius, Secondling Plenipotentiary and Arabis's father (deceased)
Calvine	Amaranthine, whisperer of the seas of Cancri

Champion Tomothus	Vulgar, knight of Drolgins
Charoen	Amaranthine, assistant to Nathaniel of the Eye
Corphuso Trohilat	Vulgar, Inventor of the Shell
Cunctus	Melius, infamous Firstling king of the Old World and prisoner in the Thrasm, head of the Investiture-renowned Cunctite gang
Daniell Bulstrode	Human, retainer to Aaron the Long-Life during the English Civil War of the seventeenth century (deceased)
Drazlo	Lacaille, crewman of the *Wilemo Maril*
Elise	Amaranthine, Satrap of Port Elsbet, member of the Devout
Eoziel XI	Lacaille, king
Eranthis	Melius, of the Seventh Province, Pentas's sister
Euryboas	Vulgar, maker of Andolp's sauces, often known as the Lunatic
Fiernel	Lacaille, Knight of the Stars
Filago	Melius, Firstling general
Furto	Vulgar, crewman of the *Wilemo Maril*
Garew	Demian magician, traveller in the Westerly Provinces
Gargant	The Empress of the Gargantine Sovereignty, a mile long from nose to tail. Alien

Ghalangle	Jalan Melius, bounty hunter
Ghaldezuel	Lacaille, Knight of the Stars
Gramps	Leader of the *Bie*
Guirm	Vulgar, crewman of the *Wilemo Maril*
Harald Hundred	Amaranthine, banned from the Firmament
Holtby	Amaranthine, junior honorific in the Devout
Huerepo Morimiel Vuisse	Vulgar soldier
Hugo Hassan Maneker	Amaranthine
Ignioz	Lacaille, ancient hero of the Prism Campaigns (deceased)
Impatiens	Melius, one of Lycaste's old friends in the Tenth Province (deceased)
Ingo	Pifoon, division general to Luminary Berzelius
Iro	Amaranthine, sister of Sotiris (deceased)
Jacob the Bold	Amaranthine, Emperor of Decadence and creator of Perception (deceased)
Jaczlam	Lacaille, guest at the Fortress of the Small Hours
James Fitzroy Sabran	Amaranthine, penultimate Emperor (deceased)
Jatropha	Naturally immortal Amaranthine, born in 300 BC
Jhozua	Lacaille, Knight of the Stars
Jospor	Vulgar, second in command aboard the *Wilemo Maril*

Jumjagh	Cethegrande, father of Scallywag (deceased)
Kippo	Vulgar, mayor Berphio's brother-in-law
Kippus	Vulgar, one of the four kings of Filgurbirund
Lazan	Lacaille, chamberlain
Levisticum	Melius, Westerling king
Liatris of Albina	Melius, Westerling socialite and authoress
Luminary Berzelius	Pifoon, general and ex-butler, taker of the Vaulted Land of Cancri
Lycaste	Melius, shy landowner from the Tenth Province, Old World
Lyonothamnus II	Melius, Firstling king, deposed
Mawlbert of Cancri	Pifoon, general, one of the first to rise up against the Amaranthine masters of Vaulted Cancri (deceased)
Mumpher	Wulm, Cunctus's chief lieutenant
Nathaniel of the Eye	Amaranthine, keeper of the Cancrous Optic
Nazithra	Threen, witch and Spirit Oracle, friend of Cunctus
Nerephanie	Cethegrande, mother of Scallywag
Nerida	Perennial Amaranthine, Satrap of Alpho; member of the Devout
Old Mutte	Vulgar, innkeeper of the Fortress of the Small Hours

Osserine Sussh	Osseresis, bat-like wanderer of the Hedron Stars
Palustris	Jalan Melius, giant naval commander
Paryam	Vulgar, one of the four kings of Filgurbirund
Pentas	Melius, of the Seventh Province, Eranthis's sister and Arabis's mother
Perception	Machine soul of an Amaranthine-built AI
Poltor	Vulgar, cousin of Huerepo and crewman of the *Epsilon India*
Primaleon	Zelioceti, banker and Oracle
Sabran	Amaranthine Emperor (deceased)
Salpiglossis	Gheal, Grand Vizier of Levisticum's Westerling court
Samuel Downfield	Amaranthine, member of the Devout
Sarsappus	Emperor of the Murmunian Domain, Alien
Satrap Ilieva	Amaranthine, Satrap of Cancri (deceased)
Scallywag/Scaleag	Cethegrande of Drolgins, part-wolf, part-whale, friend of Cunctus and the Drolgins Spirits
Scarred Pitur	Lacaille, Knight of the Stars
Seerapt-Zaor	Epir machine Spirit, one of many trapped upon the moon of Drolgins for seventy-nine million years
Slupe	Vulgar, crewman of the *Wilemo Maril*

Sotiris Gianakos	Amaranthine, 118th Emperor of the Firmament
Steward Lofer	Vulgar, son of King Wilemo, steward of Hauberth Under Shiel
The Astrologer	Machine Spirit, Aaron's brother and favourite of the Sarsappus. Clairvoyant-in-residence to the Murmurian Domain for the last sixty-eight million years
The Formidable Marjumo	Cethegrande, grandfather of Scallywag
Tragopogon	Melius, cousin of Xanthostemon and Callistemon
Trang Hui Neng	Amaranthine, member of the Devout
Tzolz	Bult, mercenary and cannibal
Veril	Vulgar, crewman of the *Wilemo Maril*
Vibor	Lacaille, old friend of Ghaldezuel's
Virens	Melius, Lycaste's father
Vyazemsky	Amaranthine, member of the Devout
Wilemo II	Vulgar, one of the four kings of Filgurbirund
Wilemo Maril	Vulgar, Privateer captain
Wylde	Amaranthine, one of the first to take the Immortal Communion
Xanthostemon	Melius, brother of Callistemon
Zedory	Jalan Melius, bounty hunter

Species/Breeds

Amaranthine	Immortal humans, many thousands of years old
Awger	Melius/animal crossbreed reviled in the Provinces
Bie	Remnants of the Epir, evolved beyond all recognition
Bult	Cannibalistic Prism breed feared throughout the Investiture
Crone	Bird native to the Westerly woods, Old World
Cursed People	Speaking animals, often of lowly status and – unlike the Melius – often subject to disease
Demian Man	Cursed Person of a higher social standing, usually of independent means
Epir	Ancient Dinosaur inhabitants of the Old World
Epir Spirits	Indelible machine souls left over from the age of the Epir, bound to the iron cores of unhollowed planets and moons
Filth	One of the five original breeds of Prism, active during the Age of Decadence, frequently at war with the Amaranthine
Firstlings	Melius people of the First Province

Flotsam	The curious range of creatures that make up the great swarms that migrate across the faces of the Snowflakes. Alien/machine
Gheal	Breed of Prism native to the Old World
Glauk	Branch-thin primate predator, native to the forests of the Oyal-Threheng, Old World
Honoured Prism	Wealthy Prism who live on the surfaces of Vaulted Lands
Jalan	Giant breeds of Melius, from the Eastern Counties of the Oyal-Threheng
Jurlumticular Throng	Large Prism breed responsible for the Volirian Conflict, considered by most to be extinct
Lacaille	Impoverished Prism breed at war with the Vulgar
Lingatra	Excommunicated breed of Prism living on the planets and moons around the Indak Star, perpetually at war with itself
Lummey	Phantom of the Provincial Woods, Old World
Melius	Giant person of the Old World
Mempeople	Ancient Murmurian word for the mammalian remnants of the Osseresis
Monkbat	Old World bat

Murmuris	The mysterious ruling species of the Murmurian Domain. Responsible for the Sterilisation of the Mighty Shadow during Epir times. Alien
Ordure	One of the five original breeds of Prism, active during the Age of Decadence, frequently at war with the Amaranthine
Osseresis	Mammalian inhabitants of the Snowflakes
Oxel	Tiny Prism breed
Perennials	Amaranthine of advanced age
Pifoon	Wealthy Prism breed favoured by the Amaranthine
Pre-Perennial	Junior Amaranthine
Prism	Cluster of hominid breeds descended from *Homo sapiens*
Quetterel	Secretive, antisocial Prism breed
Ringum	Prism cross-breed
Sapiens	The last kingdoms of humanity, long gone by the Age of Decadence
Secondling	Melius people of the Second Province
Skinch	Bird native to the Westerly woods, Old World
Skyling	Melius name for the Prism
Sluppock	Biting mollusc native to Drolgins and its neighbouring moon, Nirlume

Tenthling	Melius people of the Tenth Province
Threen	Nocturnal Prism breed
Tup Tup	Bird native to the Westerly woods, Old World
Vulgar	Prism breed at war with the Lacaille
Whippertail	Bird native to the Westerly woods, Old World
Wulm	Long-eared, stocky Prism breed
Zelioceti	Secretive Prism breed

Places

Alchazar Mount, the	Castle in the Westerly Province of Pan, Old World
Amaranthine Utopia	Gardens on the Old World dedicated to the preservation of the Insane
AntiZelio-Coriopil	Water moon of Zeliolopos, Prism Investiture
AntiZelio-Formis	Largest moon of Zeliomoltus, Prism Investiture
AntiZelio-Glumatis	Volcanic moon of Zeliolopos, Prism Investiture
AntiZelio-Slaathis	Wooded moon of Zeliolopos, Prism Investiture
Aquarii	Satrapy nearest to Virginis, Amaranthine Firmament
Atlas Sea	The great ocean beyond the Westerly Province of Pan, Old World

Baln	Lacaille city, Harp-Zalnir, Prism Investiture
Blessing	Planet mostly inhabited by the Vulgar, Prism Investiture
Burrow-Lumm	Pifoon-owned parent planet of Port Halstrom and Pruth-Zalnir, Prism Investiture
Cancri	Sotiris's home Satrapy, at the edge of the Amaranthine Firmament
Desiduum	Free moon of Gliese, Amaranthine Firmament
Dozo	Township of Harp-Zalnir, Prism Investiture
Draalie	Township of Upper Milkland, Drolgins, Prism Investiture
Drolgins	Filgurbirund's largest moon, Prism Investiture
Epsilon Eridani	Vaulted Land, parent world of Port Maelstrom, Amaranthine Firmament
Epsilon India	Vaulted Land, Amaranthine Firmament
Eriemouth	Moon at the edge of the Prism Investiture
Etzel	Country on Harp-Zalnir, Prism Investiture
Ezrom	Easterly sea, Old World
Filgurbirund	Only planet belonging to the Vulgar, Prism Investiture

Firmament	The Amaranthine realm, 11 light-years wide, comprised of 23 Solar Satrapies
Firmament's End	Realm at the edge of the Firmament, ringed by the Gulf of Cancri
First Province	Ruling Province, Old World
Fizesh	Lacaille prison, Dozo, Prism Investiture
Foundries of the Interior	Enormous Foundries on the inner surface of Gliese, Amaranthine Firmament
Gimble	Free moon of Port Elsbet, Amaranthine Firmament
Gliese	Vaulted Land, capital of the Firmament
Glost	Vulgar moon, Prism Investiture
Great Solob	Free moon of Gliese, Amaranthine Firmament
Greenmoon/Yanenko's Land	The Old World's single moon
Gulf of Cancri	Border between the Firmament and the Prism Investiture
Gulpmouth	Capital of Milkland, site of the Lagoon of Impio, Drolgins, Prism Investiture
Hag Bay	Township on the coast of the Lagoon of Impio, Drolgins, Prism Investiture
Harp-Zalnir	Lacaille moon, Prism Investiture
Hauberth Under Shiel	City on Filgurbirund, Prism Investiture
Humaling	Star in the outer reaches of the Prism Investiture

Indak-Australis	Star in the outer reaches of the Prism Investiture, seldom visited
Indris Sea	Easterly sea, Old World
Ingolland	Island in the Westerly Provinces, Old World
Inner Second	Affluent lands in the Second Province, Amaranthine Firmament
Investiture	Large volume of wild space beyond the Firmament, given to the Prism by the Amaranthine on the condition of loyalty
Jalandhar	County of the Oyal-Threheng, Old World
Janar-Savajh	County of the Oyal-Threheng, Old World
Kalinor	Star in the outer reaches of the Prism Investiture
Karakol	County of the Oyal-Threheng, Old World
Kapteyn's Star	Star in the Prism Investiture, orbited by the Three worlds of Port Cys and its moons, Obviado and Obscura
Kipris Isle	Island in the Nostrum Sea, Lycaste's birthplace, Old World
Lorena, Fortress of the Small Hours	Inn at the bottom of the Lorena Well, Humaling, Prism Investiture
Messelemie	Moon at Firmament's End
Mersin	Port in the Tenth Province, Old World

Milkland	Country of Drolgins, Prism Investiture
Moso	Equatorial capital of Drolgins, Prism Investiture
Napp	Capital city of Milkland, also known as the Eternal/Silent/ Slow City, Drolgins, Prism Investiture
Never-Never	Realm at the end of the Prism Investiture
Nilmuth	Citadel in the country of Vracht-munt, Drolgins, Prism Investiture
Nirlume	Vulgar moon orbiting Filgur-birund, Prism Investiture
Old Satrapy/Satrapy of Sol	Satrapy containing the Old World and its accompanying planets
Old World	Lycaste's ancient home, chief planet in the Satrapy of Sol and sacred centre of the Firmament
Osserine Hedron Star	Snowflake-shaped world at the very edge of the galaxy
Out Whoop	The edge of known space, Prism Investiture
Pan	Land in the Westerly Provinces, Old World
Pandemonium	Planet of Indak-Australis, perpetually at war with its sisters, Prism Investiture
Pandemonium's Daughter	Planet of Indak-Australis, perpetually at war with its sisters, Prism Investiture

Pearn	Moon of Humaling, Prism Investiture
Piris-Perzumin	Country of the Murmurian Domain, Thunderclouds
Port Bonifacio	Honey/fuel moon, Amaranthine Firmament
Port Halstrom	Moon of the Prism Investiture, where the inhabitants are said to bleed from their mouths
Port Maelstrom	Tethered moon of Vaulted Epsilon Eridani, Amaranthine Firmament
Port Rubante	Tethered moon of Vaulted Sirius, Amaranthine Firmament
Proximo Carolus	Vaulted Land closest to the Old World, Amaranthine Firmament
Pruth-Zalnir	Lacaille moon, Prism Investiture
Sarine City	Capital city of the First Province, Old World
Sea Hall of Gliese	Palace in the Firmamental capital, Gliese, Amaranthine Firmament
Sepulchre	Ancient Amaranthine treasure hoard beneath the Girdis Mountains of Port Maelstrom
Silakbo	Star in the outer reaches of the Prism Investiture
Stole-Havish	Vulgar moon, Prism Investiture
Surath	County of the Oyal-Threheng, Old World
Tail	Land in the Westerly Provinces, Old World

Tau-Ceti; the Last Harbour	Formerly the twenty-fourth Solar Satrapy; fourteen planets, Prism Investiture
Tenth Province	Southern Province of the Old World, bordering the Nostrum Sea
Thornhill	Town in Milkland, Drolgins, Prism Investiture
Thrasm	Ancient Amaranthine prison on the Tethered moon of Port Maelstrom
Unzat City	Funnel-city in Dozo, Harp-Zalnir, Prism Investiture
Vaulted Alpho	Vaulted Land, Amaranthine Firmament
Vaulted Ectries	Vaulted Land, Amaranthine Firmament
Vaulted Sirius	Vaulted Land, Amaranthine Firmament
Vaulted Tamilo	Vaulted Land, Amaranthine Firmament
Vaulted Wise	Vaulted Land, Amaranthine Firmament
Virginis	Vaulted Land ruined by a large skycharge, Amaranthine Firmament
Voliria	Star in the outer reaches of the Prism Investiture, said to be the home of the Jurlumticular
Vrachtmunt	Vulgar country in the southern hemisphere of Drolgins, Prism Investiture

Westerly Provinces	Wild, internally governed Provinces west of the First and Second, Old World
Wherla	Moon of Humaling, Prism Investiture
Woenmouth	Moon at the edge of the Prism Investiture
Yire	Island in the Westerly Provinces, Old World
Zeliolopos	Largest of Tau Ceti's gas giant planets, Prism Investiture
Zeliovastus	Gas giant planet of Tau Ceti, Prism Investiture
Zuo	City on Pruth-Zalnir, Prism Investiture

Vehicles

Coilship	Pre-Decadence Voidship of the Immortal kingdoms
Corbita	Wheelhouse owned by Jatropha
Epsilon India	Pifoon-made Voidship, now owned by the Oxel. Lycaste and Perception's home
Gorgonn	Lacaille Colossus battleship
Grand-Tile	Lacaille Colossus flagship
Hasziom	Lacaille-made Voidship, captured by the crew of the Epsilon India above Port Rubante

Push-gig	Bicycle-like contraption stolen by the Awger Billyup
Vastuz	Lacaille Poacher class Voidship
Wilhelmina	Amaranthine ship of Decadence, liberated from the Sepulchre of Port Maelstrom and commandeered by Cunctus and his gang
Yustafan	Lacaille Colossus battleship

Miscellaneous

Age of Decadence	(AD 9000 – AD 10,550) Period of Amaranthine prosperity and technological innovation
Artery	Melius causeways through the Provinces
Bilocation	The ability – unique among the Amaranthine – to telegraph oneself magnetically between the poles of planets, made possible through the alignment of iron particles in their blood
Bloodfruit	Meaty foodstuff, grown
Crule	Melius unit of measurement, roughly equivalent to a mile
Diaphene	Amaranthine skycharge bomb, stolen long ago

Ducats	Currency of the Firmament
Fizzbomb	Lacaille bomb
Hollowing Lathe	Colossal machine used to scoop planets and turn them into Vaulted Lands
Leperi	The ancient language of the Epir, still spoken by the Spirits of their machines
Lumen rifle/pistol	Expensive and relatively rare Prism weapon, fires lasers
Middle Ingwese	Drolgins dialect
Modan	Westerling language, Old World
Orifice sea	Thin area of the crust of a Vaulted Land, bored for structural support and to allow access; often filled with water
Overlight	An effect of superluminal travel, whereby the light of every star blends together
Quarter	Basic Melius unit of time, equivalent to three hours
Reflective	The onomatopoeic, aeons-old language of the Thunderclouds, spoken all across the galaxy clusters
Ring book	Book of metal plates popular in the Provinces

Saint Anthony's Mouth	Hole at the bottom of the lagoon of Impio, Drolgins, Prism Investiture
Shameplague of the Old World	Sexually transmitted disease
Skycharge	Amaranthine bomb, capable of turning the air to boiling steam
Sparker	Prism weapon, fires explosive rounds like fireworks
Spring rifle/pistol	Crude Prism weapon, fires bolts with a loaded spring
Stickmen	Ancient but frequently defective Amaranthine army of Decadence, built from a special fabric
Superluminal	Faster than light-speed
Tetraluminal	Speeds above superluminal
The Magic Mirror	Ancient Amaranthine invention, capable of viewing the events of the past
The Shell	Contraption capable of preserving and transmitting a soul
Thresholds	Enormous and exceedingly ancient hollow-chambered bulbs; a method of travelling across galaxies in times long past
Unified	The language of the Amaranthine
Uyua	The sensation of fear, but experienced from a place of safety
Vaulted Land	Hollowed planet in the Firmament, containing an artificial sun and interior continents

Wheelhouse	Large rolling wheel, often made of wood, girdled with a ring of balconies and living spaces; used as transport and dwelling on the Old World
Zest	Westerling alcohol

ABOUT GOLLANCZ

Gollancz is the oldest SF publishing imprint in the world. Since being founded in 1927 Gollancz has continued to publish a focused selection of bestselling and award-winning authors. The front-list includes **Ben Aaronovitch**, **Joe Abercrombie**, **Charlaine Harris**, **Joanne Harris**, **Joe Hill**, **Alastair Reynolds**, **Patrick Rothfuss**, **Nalini Singh** and **Brandon Sanderson**.

As one of the largest Science Fiction and Fantasy imprints in the UK it is no surprise we have one of the most extensive backlists in the world. Find high-quality SF on Gateway written by such authors as **Philip K. Dick**, **Ursula Le Guin**, **Connie Willis**, **Sir Arthur C. Clarke**, **Pat Cadigan**, **Michael Moorcock** and **George R.R. Martin**.

We also have a strand of publishing in translation, which includes French, Polish and Russian authors. Gollancz is home to more award-winning authors than any other imprint, with names including **Aliette de Bodard**, **M. John Harrison**, **Paul McAuley**, **Sarah Pinborough**, **Pierre Pevel**, **Justina Robson** and many more.

✦

The SF Gateway
More than 3,000 classic, rare and previously out-of-print SF novels at your fingertips.
www.sfgateway.com

✦

The Gollancz Blog
Bringing you news from our worlds to yours. Stories, interviews, articles and exclusive extracts just for you!
www.gollancz.co.uk

GOLLANCZ
LONDON

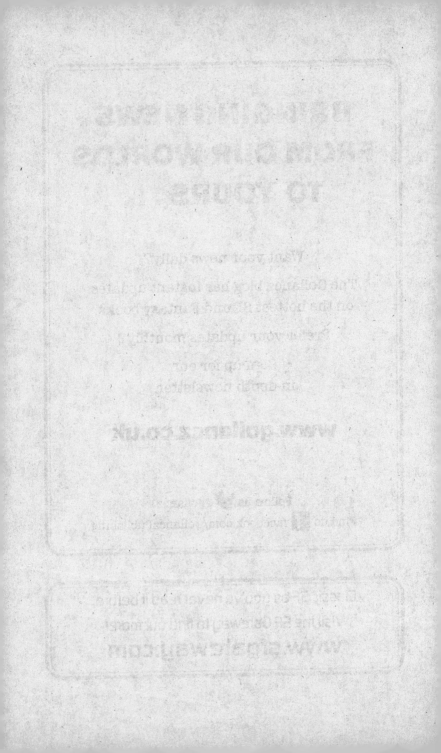